SOMETHING OLDE

THE DIVEL CHRONICLES: BOOK 1

DENIS JAY KLEIN

First Paperback Printing, 2017 Kwill Books

ISBN 978-84-946149-6-5

www.kwillbooks.com

For Mom: Series I, Book I, Page I: whose love
for reading remains contagious and inspiring—
4 score plus 12 and counting...
Sorry I can't crank them out as quickly as you read
them!
With love....

Something olde, something new,
Something borrowed, something blue,
And a silver sixpence in a shoe.

> TRADITIONAL,
> ENGLAND, *pre-1800s*

Hell is empty
And all the devils are here.

> WILLIAM SHAKESPEARE,
> THE TEMPEST, *1611*

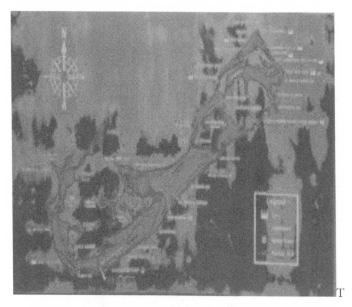

T

Tiny MAP OF Tiny BERMUDA

PART I

BAD THINGS COME IN SMALL PACKAGES

CHAPTER 1

SOMETHING NEW: BERMUDA

SATURDAY

The common brown sack sat on Clarke's sunny nook table as if it had just arrived from outer space.

It had, in a way.

Benny just dropped it off. Squat, squirrel-faced Benny. The dark-skinned man more familiarly known as Benny-the-fence. Come to think of it, Clarke couldn't remember Benny ever setting foot in his home before.

Weirded out by this realization, Clarke heard Benny's Jag receding down his street that no longer seemed so innocent. And the plain sack responsible for this wasn't nearly as impressive as he'd expected it to be.

Months and months of agitated normal-sounds waiting had just come to an end, and within seconds, been replaced by unsettled quiet.

He'd said to Benny that he couldn't look at the thing until he was alone. Instead of getting upset, which Clarke expected, Benny had turned and left. The pro hadn't even flinched. And Benny was definitely the pro here.

With the big wedding only a Saturday away, the package had arrived none too soon. They'd come close to missing the show, even though Benny had arranged for it a good six months ago.

Clarke had fantasized about pulling this off far longer than that and could peg it to the time immediately following his ridiculous retirement account fiasco. His stock broker, who just happened to be a Waters, had absconded with all his clients' funds. Absconded. He'd been better off when that word had remained beyond his crossword puzzle vocabulary.

The fantasy of righting this scale against the Waters was one thing. But to actually pull off this switch, to actually make away with a price- less heirloom, lay outside the realm of comprehension for an amateur like him. Hence the pro.

The replica's abrupt arrival was particularly jarring because Clarke had recently accepted the fact, with some relief, mind you, that they were going to miss the wedding. So, when Benny had appeared with it not ten minutes ago, the handoff of the sack had felt surreal.

And it still felt that way.

Benny had explained that it was worth waiting for quality; Benny knew such things because a lifetime ago— 1975 to be exact—Benny had indeed orchestrated the theft of the Tucker Cross. That crime had had the highest visibility imaginable. Queen Elizabeth II had been on her way from England to view the priceless artifact at the Maritime Museum. Only a precious few knew—and most of them were dead now—that Benny had been responsible for the largest gem theft in Bermuda's history.

And here he was at it again! With Clarke.

Standing stone still in his skinny kitchen nook, barely breathing, Clarke flicked a glance through his tiny window toward his patch of backyard. Stalling. As usual the sun's light slanted across his small patio, but his bicycle wasn't out there succumbing to his latest tinkering.

Clarke took a breath. Benny had reminded him that once he unwrapped it, things would proceed quickly. Benny had meant that there was only a week left before the wedding. But Clarke was interpreting his statement in a different light. That once he ventured to the "other side," his honest life was gone. Forever. The finality of this giving him pause. Of course, the act itself could always be undone by returning the necklace. But the intention was a different matter. The fact that he was supposed to be guarding the thing was only making matters worse.

Clarke's arms weren't making any hasty movements toward the sack. As the head of security of the five-star Princess Hotel where the real Divel Necklace was kept high and dry in-between weddings, his arms normally moved. He remembered that from just yesterday, as he stood at this precipice.

He replayed Benny's words in his head: How he'd been impressed with its workmanship. How this switch would be so much easier than the Tucker because it wouldn't come under immediate scrutiny. The Queen isn't even coming to view it, Benny had joked. Clarke liked the sound of that. Liked that per the Waters tradition, no one would see the necklace until the next generation got married off. It was the perfect timeline for the perfect crime, if the frozen amateur did say so himself.

Because of that, the replica's quality didn't need to be nearly as good as the Tucker's, Benny had mentioned. But it was, Benny had admitted. It was. And that had pleased him.

While Clarke's arms stayed out of this, Clarke's mind connected Benny's perfect crime comparison with all the true-crime novels he'd taken to reading. Time well spent, like training manuals.

Clarke could back out right now, if his legs decided to work before his arms. Laura would've known what to do. His deceased wife. A tough time had been made tougher when the loss of his retirement account had piled on top of Laura's death, three years back now. He'd been lost until this past year. Once he began to date Dee, and Morgan, soon after, on the other side of the island, he'd begun to live again. Begun to dig himself out of his hole.

Clarke prided himself on being a great swimmer. Making it easy for him to recognize the deep end of a pool in front of him. His arms worked just fine when he swam.

That did it. Ego moved his arms, allowing his fingers to approach that course brown paper.

Like a warming-up save-cracker in one of those books, he brushed the tips of his fingers together. This seemed too easy—which worried him when he recalled those crime novels by the likes of Ann Rule. Could they track him down based upon the recent change in his reading habits? Wouldn't that be something?

The hands that looked like his hands opened the sack, separated the loosely folded red wrapping paper, and removed the snapped-closed black case. Prying the case open with his thumbs, he discovered the regal, triangular, white-gold necklace resting in a form-fitting indentation lined with red satin. He placed it on his left palm as if weighing its purity. Wow. His teeth expressing admiration by biting down on his lower lip, which helped, actually, because it kept him from shouting out anything the neighbors really didn't need to know. That didn't stop his right palm from voting for Benny's perfect caper by slapping the table. Seconding the vote.

The sharp sound sent Hard and Easy leaping off the living room sofa in a pulse of dust. From the corner of his eye, he saw two dark flashes dart past the doorway. The living room was Laura's space. A place where she'd knit and read with the cats. After her terrible accident, he'd stayed clear of that room, but they still spent time there—habit, or remaining close to her. Neither had worked for him, to his dismay.

Freeing his lip, Clarke heard in front of the jury of his peers, his helpful neighbor, Mrs. Shorte:

Yes, I did hear Mr. Dearborne scream out that Saturday morning about 9:30 in the morning. I remember because I was giving a treat to my dog, Woolie. Anyway, I ran over as fast as my old legs could go to make sure he was all right. You all know Clark, (pointing), and you can imagine my surprise when I saw him with the famous triangular necklace in his hands that now rests on that table right there (more pointing)....

Back in his nook, Clarke most definitely appreciated the three large diamonds, the array of smaller diamonds all around, and the exquisite filigree. Such minute detailing reminded him of the rare metal workmanship he admired in many of Bermuda's historic buildings.

Trying to drag this strangeness into his normal world, the crossword doer wondered what the word would be for a replica of a replica—a copy of a copy?

He didn't know. But whatever the term for it, this copy was sure something.

Now that it was out, he didn't want to put it back. Its

picture hadn't done it justice. No wonder so many had chased it over the generations. What could have compelled the Waters to leave the thing locked up between brides like they had? Though, to be honest, it was a bit old-fashioned for either of his girlfriends.

He chanced touching it the way one tests wet paint. The large gems held fast, while the liquid color was indeed dry.

He'd never tell Benny how relieved he'd felt when he gave up on its arrival last week. Never. In for a penny, in for a pound, Mum had always said.

He looked at his Tour De France calendar magnetically pinned to his pale-yellow fridge. The count-down could now resume. It had been one year away, then six months, and now here it was October, t-minus one week and counting. He had all those blue, X'ed-out, day-of-the-week boxes to prove it. The sight of all those X's made this fantastic plot no longer deniable to the amateur true-crime-trained future thief. Any pirate knew that X's marked the spot. And Bermuda was well-known for its pirates, and its moon that was usually able to watch unimpeded from above all this water so deep.

There were no springs or wells here in Northwest Africa. Mma Kukuluel knew this was a dry place.

A poor place. It had always been. She believed waiting to be easier when you were poor, though being thirsty made such a thing harder. Things opposed other things here.

In a place where material possessions held less value, one learned that nature often filled in, compensated, maybe even led the way, like the Chieftain or shaman. And that was the way of existence, here, in Africa, where longstanding circles were strung together to continue a tribe's many stories during the sun's day and the moon's night.

With the rainy season taking its time, with Mma Kukuluel patiently and earnestly waiting on its arrival, she remained accepting of being poor and thirsty. Her storm would come. Soon, she knew, because her long life had filled her with wisdom that had settled in the spaces where money or water might have gathered, if she had lived her life elsewhere.

Here in Florida, Diane Waters hated waiting.

Or could the boys already be inside? Only that injured BMW sat in the lot and Diane had never seen their car. Diane had stayed in her big SUV with the AC blowing up her dress. It had seemed the thing to do being on the side of town she never visited. Hemmed in by all that litter out there, she was no longer so sure this was a good idea. The filth, the harebrained scheme, the boys she hardly knew— it was all enough to make her turn and get the hell out of here. Out there, cigarette butts covered the dried-up grass and bright sidewalk. And with her hands idle, she felt the urge to light up. Maybe just to have something to do, maybe because they'd help her fit in on this side of town, or maybe even because Mike hated them. She hadn't smoked in years. With wedding details consuming everything lately, she'd reconsider this after, if she survived the coming weekend.

Opening her heavy SUV door, she stepped down to

7

the course cement sidewalk that made her worry about scraping up the soles of her new cute flats. It figured that even the sidewalks were in bad shape over here. She loved her shoes—lots and lots of them. If she climbed right back into the cocoon of her still-innocent SUV, cigarette-less, she could be right back in her yuppie world before anyone was the wiser. And that wasn't such a bad idea.

If she entered that ratty looking diner, different things were going to happen. Bad different things. She knew this because she was going to make them happen. She thought, *fish out of water,* because there definitely wasn't water out here as dry as it had been, and, she'd never stolen anything before. Ever. Except for Millie's shoelaces in third grade.

Her dad called this being at a crossroads. And that was exactly what it was. An "f'ing crossroads." She took in the dirty vista, the one real crossroad coming in from her right, then toward the unpolished chrome gem that looked like oversized jewelry box.

I need to do this for my little girl. With Sandy's wedding only a week away, it was now or never. Fueled by years of dodging something invisible, with maternal determination compressed between her lips, she strode those tasteful yellow flats over that course surface like it was made of hot coals—well, hot anyway. Then her smart yellow and white sundress breezed through that chrome door with a confidence in her step that she wasn't really feeling. Shoes could do that for you. She couldn't remember the last time she'd stepped into a greasy diner. College. It had been two a.m. on a Saturday night, which had really been Sunday morning. Back in college. Surrounded by cigarette smoke.

The much younger and thinner hostess approached

Diane from a distance carrying hopeful menus in the crook of her arm. But the old-style cash register with its tarnished brass levers and those cute ceramic tops managed to greet her first, if one was into that sort of thing. Her sister, Donna, loved old things like that. But that tall floor sign with those plastic white letters was just dreadful: "Please wait to be seated." She was done waiting.

"Welcome to *Toni's Diner*. One for lunch?"

"Actually, the two gentlemen I'm meeting are already here." One of the boys had leaned out to eye the hostess as she went by. "My daughter's getting married next week in Bermuda. And they're the best men in her wedding." She wasn't sure why she was justifying her presence to this young girl wearing all that makeup. If she wanted to meet two strange boys half her age, in the wrong part of town, not at two a.m., that was her business. Cigarettes or not.

"Oh, how exciting," the girl gushed, crushing the menus with a hug. "Go right back."

Diane had met the boys at the engagement party months ago. Yes, it was a little strange to have two best men, but the Waters always had two best men in order to complete one triangle on each side of the wedding party.

Tradition. Tradition and the Divel necklace. It was Diane's albatross for one more week before she was supposed to unload it on her daughter, like all the other mothers and mothers-in-law of the Waters line had down through the centuries. Before her own wedding, emotional Diane remembered being skeptical of all the doomsday rumors that swirled around the triangular heirloom. But after she'd been filled in about its history on her own wedding day, she'd decided to take a no-lose approach:

translation—she'd avoided open water. How strange!?

Years later, it remained unclear why she'd taken her mother-in-law's warning to heart. But what *had* become clear, was that her no-lose strategy had somehow lost. It had affected her marriage in the worst way. With Mike being a climatologist, her husband was always around, in, or above water. As a result, a schism had formed between them that had only widened over the years. Because of all of that, the time had arrived to stop any and all real or fantasied curses from overtaking her only daughter. After hundreds of years of this nonsense, it was time for a Waters woman to fight back and break this chain. Even if she had to come to the wrong side of town to do it. Her only daughter was worth it.

Diane walked down this dingy aisle past the cheap high-backed booths and their silent silver music boxes. She tried to recall the boys' names. She had trouble with names in general. But their nicknames were strange to begin with. Cartoon names, or something—Ying and Yang, maybe? "Hi, boys."

"Hi, Mrs. Waters," they answered over one another.

They were dressed in similar shorts and t-shirts. Good. She needed a coordinated team—like the cast in one of her old college plays.

"Tell me your names again?"

"I'm Frick; that's Frack," said Frick, seemingly the leader of the two.

"Oh, that's right," Diane remembered now. Names from their college days with Sandy and Greg.

With them seated on both sides of the table, Frack—who seemed to be the sweeter one, she remembered now—scooted in to make room.

They already had milkshakes. One chocolate. One strawberry. Thick straws. The waitress came over and Diane ordered black coffee with cream.

Diane was aware she could still change her mind, realizing this mainly because of how stupid it was to not have had a drink or two before coming over here. What had she been thinking? Wanting to do something with her hands, she unrolled the paper napkin and freed the silverware. The three pieces were spotted on this side of town. This was the perfect time for a cigarette. Then her fingers could do something besides handling this filthy silverware. Neither boy smoked, though.

"Do you remember the talk we had at the engagement party? How you told me the financial business is a hard road these days?" She began cleaning her spoon with her napkin. "How most never make it to partnership status, where the real money is?"

They agreed heartily about their grunt-work status while sipping their milkshakes through those wide, striped straws. Their days of pouring over charts and small-font numbers were famously mind numbing, if not eyesight ruining.

"What if I had a way of making a whole lot of money real fast? What would you say to that?"

"We'd be interested," the Frick one said. What exactly did you have in mind?" They were aware, of course, that Mrs. Waters was in possession of a priceless necklace. If she was talking money, there was a decent chance there was something to it.

Whispering toward Mrs. Waters, with his leg next to

hers, Frack joked, "I'd buy a bridge from you if I could."
There were a lot of bridges in Miami. Diane could tell he
liked the way she looked in this cute dress, money or no
money. Her dutiful workouts for the wedding were paying
off.

Her steaming coffee arrived in its chipped mug, with
three little creamers encircling it. She tore one open with
her clear-coated nails—wishing for a shot of gin—then
cleaned the spoon once more before stirring.

She noticed the triangle formed by their two drinks and
her steaming mug. Three people, three drinks, three
creamers. Triangles. Triangles were always connecting her
to that damned Divel. She hated triangles. She had hated
them ever since they'd ganged up on her in geometry class
like an incomprehensible group of pack animals.

She tried a sip. It was strong and bitter and hot,
nothing like gin. Dumping another creamer in, stirring
with her cleaned spoon, the idea of trying to steal her own
necklace caused her to smirk. How on God's green earth
had she gotten here? Making another triangle with two
young men with strange cartoon names.

She tried another careful sip through her receptive lips.
The boys were being polite. That was good.

Diane had grown up on a working farm in central
Virginia with corn, the movement of horses, and the
sounds and smells of cows. One of her mom's favorite
sayings had been, if you plow a field, do it all the way. She
and her older sister, Donna, had heard it a million times if
they'd heard it once. And today it would be her off-her-
rocker sister that surely would believe Diane had lost her
mind.

It was Donna who could be counted on to find the colorful, eccentric way to do something. Not her. She should be the one here, not Diane, especially since Donna was refusing to come to the wedding. That was a whole other chapter to all of this. How had everything gotten so strange? She knew the answer to that question, actually.

The young waitress appeared, and no one wanted anything except more details from Diane—though Diane wanted to ask the wafer-thin waitress for a smoke. While Frick watched the waitress leave, Diane continued. "I have nothing planned out, really. It's more like intent." She started to say "You'll," but instead said, "We'll have time to work out the details on the fly." That last word connected her to her husband, who was always flying into his storms like a maniac. "I mean adlib, which I'm used to doing with my lines."

The boys looked at her like what was she jabbering about. Good question.

Clutching the cup two-handed because the loop looked dark and dirty, she said, "Well, I promised you this rendezvous would change your lives momentarily." She warmed with that word "rendezvous," though her tan always did a decent job when she colored out of embarrassment. She corrected, "I mean monetarily," as her hands trembled. "And I wasn't just talking hay." Farms again.

The sound of glasses from the kitchen reminded her they weren't alone. She sped up, as if the kitchen staff would pop out and witness that she really was over on this side of town. "I really do have a proposition for you." She was sorry as soon as that word left her mouth. God, she

13

was nervous. She couldn't even speak straight over here, even though, usually, that occurred because she'd been drinking. *Isn't this ironic?*

The Frick one, the more confident one, said, "That's kinda funny. What did you have in mind, exactly?"

"I'm being serious." Losing her composure for a moment—if she'd ever had it on this side of town—she crossed her legs away from the boys.

Frack frowned when her leg moved away. "Don't let him irritate you, Mrs. Waters. With his arm still resting next to hers, he said, "What were you saying?"

"You're very sweet," she said toward Frack. Collecting herself.

She crossed her leg back his way, and quickly laid out how they would try and take the insured Divel sometime during Sandy's wedding day. Without any of the details worked out, it sounded fantastic even to Diane—not fantastic in the "great" sense, fantastic in the Twilight Zone sense. This was the stuff that film noir movies were made of—the black and whites she usually watched alone— while Dr. Waters of climatology fame chased his storms. Storms that were named like they were his children. His family. While he flew into the eye of the things. A practice she thought was kind of crazy. Around all that water, no less. The whole thing was tragically comical, if you thought about it too much while drinking. Like a Shakespearean play.

She finished selling with an upbeat, "We all on-board? Because it ought to be a very interesting ride." Sorry about that word, too. Who'd written this script?

Calling the waitress over, the ringleader sprung for the

check. When she stood to leave, she read hesitancy on Frick's face. She couldn't have that. The stakes were far too high. And adding more weirdness in—if that was even possible—as she began to speak, she felt a cigarette in the corner of mouth. Her right hand almost started to retrieve it, but her practice with props helped her roll with it.

Like any good actress, using what she felt, this other woman inhabiting her body, who might've been smoking after sex, said boldly, "Do you think it's true what they say about cougars?" Frack looked at her like she was asking about large cats, but Frick got it and smiled.

Desperate, this other woman had brought this up because maybe all the money they'd split from taking the necklace wasn't enough of a lure. Seriously, did she really have to sweeten the pot? Whether she really could get frisky with them remained to be seen—right along with the rest of this coming weekend's mystery agenda. She envisioned how plenty of gin and plenty of smokes were certainly part of this scene, if she was indeed writing this play.

Regardless, her maternal instinct was urging her to decisively snuff out any resistance.

After reading Frick's eyes, Frack manage with boyish enthusiasm, "Uh, huh."

Diane answered with a smoker's poise, "If you succeed in ridding Sandy of the Divel, who knows what's possible." She smiled toward Frack, which lit up more than eagerness on his young face. Her wagging index finger immediately slowed his obvious interest in bedding her. "But," and she looked at both of them, "first things first."

As her nicely tanned legs escorted her out past that antique cash register and cheap sign, she felt soap opera sleazy. But the Divel was playing for keeps, so she had to be willing to do what was necessary. With business concluded on the wrong side of the tracks, literally, she climbed into her SUV, locked the doors, started it up, turned the A/C on high to blow up her dress, pulled away, and almost cried. This was crazy.

Wasn't it crazy how family tradition would restrict next weekend's itinerary, while this weekend traditions had been loosened. More than loosened. More like unhinged, as she played back the words that had come from her own nicely shaped lips. Without a cigarette and definitely without any gin. Then she began to sob.

About a mile down the road, the smell of her tidy white leather interior brought the old Diane back to planet Earth. She dabbed herself with Kleenex, confident that her SUV knew the way home. As she put the Kleenex in the little trash baggie, she wondered if she really could have done nothing—like her own mother-in-law had. That, seemed a little crazy to her. Three decades was a long time to wait. But to hell with the Waters legacy, the heirloom, and its hold on the Waters women. And to hell with Mike. She needed a drink. She swerved to avoid a bothersome small car making a right with its blinker on. She admitted, "You went a little crazy in there, didn't you?" That topic made her think of Donna again, who also went a little crazy at times, and who also liked her gin and tonics. Maybe that was genetic, too? But even if it was, at least it didn't come in triangular bottles. She felt better when her solid car crossed those tracks back to the cleaner

16

side of town. There was too much crime and way too much litter over there. How did people live like that?

CHAPTER 2

AN ODD SHADE OF SOMETHING BLUE

SATURDAY EVENING

Standing in the doorway of his tiny apartment, Greg placed his arm around Sandy's back.

Sweet, affectionate Sandy stiffened.

Nonplussed, he delivered his goodbye kiss anyway. Then he gave her a look that said, "What gives?" When she continued to give him a look back, he offered into their ongoing conversation, "You have your traditions. We have ours." The "you" meaning the Waters. But the "traditions" meant not only her bachelorette party—though that had been tame by today's standards—but more to the point, whatever was up with all this necklace stuff. He'd listened to it for months.

What was he going to do about it? Nothing. He was marrying Sandy because he loved her. All this ceremony stuff was, quite simply, unimportant. If they asked him to hang from a tree and screech like a monkey, who cared? Whatever it was, he'd do it—although jokingly, he'd drawn the line at wearing a medieval cape, dancing around an open-pit fire, and drinking chicken blood. At which point, animal-conscious Sandy had pointed out what an

18

absurd picture that made because chickens were protected in Bermuda.

Sandy responded, "That's not exactly my fault, is it?" She'd had to deal with way more than he had, because she'd had to navigate all the strange planning with Mom.

When he didn't answer, she got to the point. "Well, you better not have too much fun, fella."

"Look. We'll get drunk. Somebody will bring a lady. A dancer," he threw in as an acceptable descriptor. "Don't worry. I'll be in bed by midnight."

She smiled. "That's what I'm afraid of. Especially with Frick and Frack there. I found them in my illustrated crossword dictionary, you know?"

"Are they really?" he played along. Something new.

"Under the word 'numskull'."

"Would you quit that," he said half-heartedly, unsure what she had against them. As far as he knew, neither one had ever done anything to her, or any other Waters of her famous Bermudian heritage.

She leaned her upper body away, giving her words a chance to gain momentum. "Idiots. Dimwits. Villains. You choose."

"You have a matching illustrated thesaurus, too?"

"Don't change the subject."

"They're harmless. More talk than action."

"Promise?" Her tone conveying that she wasn't all that serious about this.

"Promise." He leaned in to get a real kiss this time.

Their pose apropos to all the dancing he was doing in this doorway. His lips did manage to touch hers a little longer this time.

19

He walked out. Just because her party was tame, did that mean his had to be?

She said through the screen, "See you tomorrow, if they don't land you in jail."

He indicated goodbye by wiggling his fingers up in the air.

Two hours later the cake arrived, the woman popped out, and all the men recognized her as one of the local Hooters girls.

Frick and Frack did encouraged Greg to do more than drink. When it came time for Greg to follow the young woman's tight figure into the side room, he recalled Sandy's send off. Maybe she was clairvoyant or something.

Sandy was quick; he liked that about her. She had only two years remaining of vet school. When they'd met in college, she'd made it clear she wanted no part of the Waters obsession with climatology. Her interests had always revolved around animals.

Clearly the best men and Greg were different than her, interested as they were in a big score, no matter how it happened.

With him thinking score, Greg followed the Hooters colors and shut the door to all of that, still unsure which voice would win out.

Worried about scoring a hurricane before the season ended, Dr. Mike Waters grumbled, "The damn season's almost over." He knew it, they knew it, everyone knew it. It's all he'd thought about for the past month. He opened the door with that cheap cardboard clock facing outward. According to Diane, he was returning to the scene of the crime. This large square room was Hurricane Central—his second home. Though Diane kept reminding him he had his order reversed.

On the other side of the room, Dr. Carla Banks turned to say hi, before returning her focus quickly to the boring monitors in front of her—mimicking that there was something emergent happening, which they both knew wasn't true. One of their running jokes.

With essentially two years gone and only one hurricane season coming next year to complete the timeline on his funded project, Mike was feeling some pressure. On having this room. On keeping his team together. On keeping the oasis trailer outside. On being able to conduct their SimTank trials. For the past two long data-collecting years, these resources had been put to use with one goal in mind: for man to be able to finally stop a hurricane in its tracks.

This home away from home was dominated by high-def displays, which were themselves generally dominated with clockwise and counterclockwise swirls, arrows, numbers, and colliding fronts. At the moment, nothing exciting was happening, and nothing exciting of the stormy-counterclockwise-variety had occurred ever since they'd become fully ready one month back.

"All quiet on the eastern front?" he quipped, as he dumped himself familiarly into a rolling chair that happened to have one of its four casters stuck.

"There's no fooling you, is there?" came over her shoulder.

He was tired of waiting. The frequency of hurricanes was a tale of two realities. The rarity was good, he knew, if you were a normal person. But not so good, if you were faced with the tight parameters set forth in his grant awarded to the National Hurricane Center's (NHC) Tropical Analysis and Forecast Branch.

Like his father before him, Mike had grown up wanting to be a climatologist. And just in one generation of computers, the profession had moved beyond just tracking and predicting storm paths, to the growing anticipation that man might actually be able to do something about them. In this regard, he was dutifully doing his part as the lead of his four-member R & D team dubbed *The Hurricane Busters*. The moniker not wholly original, but who cared? Ghosts, hurricanes or their intersection—possessed hurricanes—would no longer be allowed to spin around the world unmolested, if they had something to say about it.

The very single, much younger Carla, said, "Why is it when we need one, nothing happens?"

"I don't know." He rolled toward her by crab-walking with his long legs. The path less direct than one of their skittish hurricanes, due to that worn out, low-bid caster.

Carla concurred with Mike that they were ready for the next phase of their project. While their two other team members had expressed they were fine with the team spending the winter replicating and deepening their understanding of their successful SimTank trials. No one else was working with their secret anti-evaporative chemical formula—the key to their progress—so what was the rush? Better to be safe. Better to have a more intimate knowledge of the many different variables involved before they consumed their two-storm-max budget.

Carla's smoothly rolling chair approached him. "Well, didn't your mother ever tell you not to sneak up on people?" Actually, Mike knew she liked it whenever he snuck into the kitchen to eye the non-boiling pots with her.

"Since when did you become a people? You're a robot, keeping track of all those mind-numbing screens." This, the mundane aspect of their chosen profession, though computers easily kept track of the basics. Given the precursors for a hurricane, they then had to evaluate it for suitability given their grant stipulations.

"Don't let my shiny skin fool you."

They had spent so many nights poring over charts and formulas and these flat boring screens that he wondered whether his attraction to her was born of boredom, or stress, or that lovely skin that was so rich compared to his pale whiteness. "Okay. Then don't let my fantasies get in the way of science."

"Didn't your mother tell you not to give up on your dreams so easily?"

Mike liked the way she looked at him when she said things like that. It warmed the cold science they were embroiled in. It was predictable that the two of them were primed for action, given all this hurry-up-and-waiting. They had wondered together, half-jokingly, whether a more personal goal could temporarily substitute for another. None-the-less, it didn't seem to matter to her he was twenty years her senior, or that he was married.

"Yep, she did actually." Mike grabbed the arm of her chair, pulled their chairs together, which pivoted him around his one fixed wheel. After he finished stretching out his lanky frame, he continued, "Regardless of all my dreams, if nothing happens in this next month, we're stuck waiting till June. That's a long time away." He shook his head, wearily.

"Is that being positive? You're supposed to be the fearless leader. Encouraging and all."

He looked at her physique that got too little exercise because of this room. Just like his. Why hadn't he put a treadmill in here? That young, pretty face. Those vigilant dark eyes that didn't miss much and were presently drilling into him. "Hard to be encouraging after I've just paid for a wedding. You know what they cost these days?" As Mike said this, he pictured Carla's ailing battle-trap of a car outside. The public sector wasn't known for its bonuses.

"You could have funded an extra trip in our hurricane hunter. Three would be better than two."

"You got that right," raising his thick eyebrows.

"Okay. Didn't your mother ever tell you to stop watching pots?"

"I don't see any stoves."

"Well, when you stop watching, maybe something will happen? Until then, try planning an outdoor activity that can't be cancelled. That usually works."

"That's included in the wedding, too."

Carla didn't know that a significant part of every Waters wedding took place outdoors. "Then you've done your part."

"Yeah, but we're already in October. You and I both know it isn't the most fruitful of months. Plus, Bermuda only averages one every seven years anyway. So, I'm not likely to encourage much of anything, regardless of your hometown remedies."

"Believe me, Sandy will appreciate not having her wedding ruined. Anyway, we could still get lucky?"

"Maybe. Always maybe. Always a bridesmaid, never a bride."

"You won't be able to say that much longer," Carla chimed.

"Worse comes to worst, we wait. That's not the end of the world according to the better half of the team."

"That makes me think of that Nostradamus character. He became famous for predictions too, but did they help any? "

"You know my luck," Waters concurred. He waved a hand over his shoulder to signify that his bad luck reached far beyond this room.

"Take a vacation, then. It'll happen when you're gone. I'll call you. Let you know how we made out."

A Freudian slip?

"I am taking a vacation this weekend."

"Perfect. Don't forget to send a postcard."

He caught the twist in her tone. "Sorry you all can't come. Someone's got to man the store. Just in case." Quite typically, the crew would be twice the Buster's size inside one of those hurricane hunting planes. But regardless of size, it was always preferable to have no fewer than two pilots. Presently, only the Colonel and Waters could pilot, though Carla and Stacy were planning to study this off-season. So, worse-case-scenario, if they got lucky this weekend, Colonel Klink would pilot solo.

Carla said, "I'd rather come to the wedding and have

some fun. Get to wear something besides jeans." She smiled at him. "Realistically, what would be the odds of it happening while you're gone?"

"With my luck?" His hand went up again. "One hundred percent. Missing my own show."

Mike knew they were going in circles in more ways than one. Watching, flirting, and Carla hoping, while Mike kept her at a married distance. Minding the software and screens all day made one lonely for human contact, and tonight it was only getting later. Mike felt like putting his arm around her, but Carla would then want to drag him to their oasis trailer just down the path.

Things had not been going well with Diane ever since the wedding plans had begun, Mike felt. The process had put her in a foul mood, when Mike had expected the opposite. Mutual funds and women. He couldn't predict either.

Carla was looking at him with those eyes. Mike knew what that look meant but was afraid of what it predicted. Maybe he could predict coffee instead.

"You want some coffee? You look like you could use some coffee."

"You buyin'?"

"Sure."

They walked all the way to the back of the room. He did the honors and poured two cups of coffee from the well-used, eight-cup GE coffee maker that was more popular than the last-named storm in September: Francis. Unfortunately, they hadn't been ready for her. The chipped Formica table wobbled when he set the pot down. Nothing but the best in the public sector.

"Gee, you're swell," she smiled, holding the thick mug two-handed because half the handle was missing. She blew the steam away.

"Don't mention it."

"Where's my bonus," she asked with a twinkle in her eyes.

He thought of something, but said instead, "In the mail, with mine."

Mugs in hand, they ambled the twenty-foot by twenty-foot perimeter like a couple checking the fence around the yard. With the yard too quiet, Mike said good-bye to those sipping lips and long stares and that available trailer. As he climbed into his beat-up Honda Accord with the ceiling headliner hanging down in the back, it was really looking like Sandy's wedding would prove to be the last hoorah of this season.

CHAPTER 3

THE IMPORTANT THINGS IN LIFE ARE FREE

SUNDAY MORNING

Marcia handed Sandy a small present, supposedly, the best kind. Sandy peeled back the beige-colored gift paper infused with the fragrance of lilac; making her picture the purple flowers Marcia knew she so enjoyed. Opening the thin case, she recognized the charm bracelet she'd been eyeing for months from the local shop. From the silver bracelet hung an assortment of animal charms that Marcia had picked out for her. In particular, the two dogs gave it a personal significance. At this very moment, Sandy's two dachshunds were barking, downstairs. They loved to bark, as if the more they barked, the larger they seemed.

"This is very sweet of you." Sandy secured the precious old-style clasp around her left wrist.

"Don't be so quick to thank me. I'm told on good authority you're going to need every one of those. Rumor has it the necklace you're getting is armed with its own mysterious charms."

"That's not funny," Sandy responded, as she twisted up her mouth in a half-grin. She rotated the bracelet slowly to admire the different animals. "All this mumbo jumbo

28

necklace stuff is going to turn into nothing. You'll see," she beamed.

Sandy stood from her single bed. Though it would be more fun to just gab, they could do that while Sandy finished up her packing for her big weekend. With her wedding and honeymoon both taking place in Bermuda, she needed clothes for a week.

Her maid of honor said, "And if you really don't want a priceless necklace in the family, you know I'll take it. What's the problem?" While she remained seated on the bed, Marcia returned to folding and placing things in the small suitcase near her feet.

"Yeah, I know."

"I'll even take tall, dark, and handsome Greg off your hands, just to get it."

"Very funny." Sandy stopped folding a blouse. "Seriously, though, Mom's been so stressed out, when it's supposed to be me." Marcia's expression made it clear she wasn't surprised by that. Everyone knew Sandy was pretty easy going; willing to roll with the punches, as opposed to her mom, or even Greg.

In addition to the unmentionable mysterious wedding day ritual, Sandy knew her mother's sister in northern Virginia, Aunt Donna, was also adding to the intrigue. Even though Sandy had always gotten along with her, her aunt was giving a very generous gift in lieu of travelling to Bermuda for the ceremony. Neither Mom nor Aunt Donna had spoken of what had spooked her at Mom's wedding thirty years ago. But whatever it was, clearly, it had been quite dramatic. Sandy was doing her best not to take it personally. Mom had explained more than once

29

how her sister was quite superstitious, being as she was into Tarot Cards, horoscopes, séances, and those sorts of things. Well, she'd always been sweet and kind to Sandy, so it was just another mystery being added on top of all the other mysterious activities that were apparently a part of the Waters wedding tradition.

Sandy plopped down on the bed, sinking it like her softly sprung old Ford. "The whole thing is pretty strange, if you ask me. Getting married the same weekend, the same place, like my mother did, like all the other Waters women did. Who thinks this stuff up, that's what I want to know?"

Marcia agreed with half a smile and half a nod, the way she'd agreed all the other times Sandy complained about this.

Grabbing a pair of pants to refold, Sandy continued. "Family tradition is one thing, but weirdness is something different." They looked at one another sitting inside her neat-as-a-pin periwinkle bedroom. After pondering the once-and-it's-all-over aspect of it, Sandy added, "But if this is the worst of it, it'll be fine. If it makes Mom happy for me to continue our tradition, it's not so bad." She had already made up her mind to try to ignore how her wedding day wouldn't exactly be the day she'd envisioned. Partly because Greg became upset whenever she'd become upset. So, she was cooling it of late. Such was their little circle of things at the moment. *No, a triangle,* Sandy thought: Sandy-Divel-Greg. Yes, the Divel seemed to be in the middle of everything. She was so ready, really ready, to put all this hocus pocus stuff behind them.

Marcia grabbed a blouse and folded it in her lap, before

placing it on the "undecided" pile next to Sandy. Done, she grabbed the next random item near her. A belt.

"At this point, I'd just as soon let Greg throw it in the ocean, if that would make him happy," Sandy admitted.

"Or even sell it. Then I'd be able to care for one hundred animals for one hundred years at the shelter. Now that would be a wonderful Waters tradition."

Marcia looked up. "How many girls get to wear actual royal jewelry around their necks? That's kinda cool."

They both laughed, legs kicking, which sent the mattress-boat bobbing.

"You have to admit," Marcia continued, "it's kinda cool your wedding takes place in an exotic location like Bermuda. That starts the honeymoon right away." Seeing the positive.

Sandy found nothing to disagree with there. Over the past six months, she'd tried to disagree with her mom over this Bermuda business. Her innocent blue eyes were blinking away with the realization that this time next week, regardless of all the things she couldn't control, she'd be married.

With her head down, Marcia looked through the tops of her contacts.

Sandy asked, "What?"

"I have a confession to make. I got curious."

"Okay."

"After all your talks with your mom, I Googled it."

Sandy stopped packing. "I told you I wasn't going to feed into any of it since it was already way too much." When Sandy's challenging look didn't elicit any more information, she said to Marci, "So tell me, already."

31

"The short or long version?" They both knew how Marcia excelled at remembering facts, which helped her immensely as an English Lit major.

"We have time." There was plenty of deciding still left to do in this room.

"Well, it all started in 1609 when the *Sea Venture* was leading a large group of ships to resupply Jamestown. Maybe because there were already a lot of influential people on that ship, some royal managed to smuggle your necklace aboard. Apparently, it cost a pretty sum, which was the reason the Virginia Company was willing to take the risk of transporting it over open water the way they did. Anyway, the flotilla ran smack into a hurricane, which separated that ship from everyone else."

With Marcie pausing, Sandy asked, "That can't be all of it."

"No, no. The captain apparently spied land in the middle of the ocean, so he grounded the ship to keep it from sinking. It's rather an incredible, fact-is-weirder-than-fiction thing. Think of all the ways explorers have discovered countries; that one might just take the cake."

Sandy said, "Water?"

It took Marcie a moment to realize she was talking about regular water and not her relatives.

"Sure."

Sandy got up and grabbed two bottles of spring water from her pack, then handed one to Marcia. They both opened them and took sips. Then they leaned against the headboard to relax, eyeing all the clothes lying everywhere. Sandy kept changing her mind, as she considered colors and variety, not to mention, how pieces worked together.

This would have been so much simpler if pre-wedding, wedding, and honeymoon were all kept separate, like most weddings. But no, Mom had made it clear their weddings were decidedly unique. Sandy was already agreeing with that descriptor, and she knew she didn't know the half of it yet.

Just because Mom's wedding hadn't gone smoothly, that didn't mean hers was going to go down the same path. Why should it. They were different. Plus, that had been thirty years ago. Things changed— except maybe in this family.

Marcia twisted the cap back on her bottle. "The captain or admiral—whatever he was—guessed he had discovered La Bermuda, otherwise known as the Ile of Divels. So clearly your necklace is connected with the region in some way, though they never did spell that part out."

"Who knows?" A week away, and Sandy was already tired of talking about the thing most people had never seen because it remained locked up all the time. Two of the living people who had seen it, Mom and Dad, were downplaying the whole thing. Neither one of them had explained any of the hoopla that seemed to follow it, like the train off the back of a long wedding dress. She wouldn't' have one of those, either. Mom had explained that her dress should be short for the wedding. Something having to do with the temperature, Sandy figured. Yet another decision taken out of her hands.

Sandy fiddled with her new bracelet to take in the detailing of the individual charms, as Marcia began to fiddle with this tale again. Marci grabbed an opportunistic off-white blouse and began folding it like the perfectionist that she was.

"Well, he knew his history, because both names had been coined by the Spanish explorers almost a century before. That scrawny piece of land surrounded by all that water in the middle of nowhere had gone unclaimed all that time. With land being claimed wherever it lay, this land was the opposite because of the hostile weather, unseen reefs, and the lack of obvious natural resources that made it not worth the risk to get in there. Apparently, the Spanish were smart."

They both chuckled over that, then took more sips.

The distant barking coming from downstairs finally petered out.

"The next day they off-loaded the ship. The admiral renamed the place *Barmudas,* and planned to claim it for the Virginia Company, if there was anything worth claiming. They ended up building two smaller ships from the wood of the *Sea Venture,* and eventually reached Jamestown—too late to save it though. So, Bermuda's gain turned out to be Jamestown's loss. When they returned to Barmudas on their way back to England, they apparently dropped off your relative, leaving three to secure their claim." They both took sips.

"Did you know that by the next year, Shakespeare penned *The Tempest.* Isn't that cool? Hurricanes. *The Tempest.*"

Sandy tilted her head, this way and that. Four hundred years ago. Who cared?

"When a ship returned Bermuda in 1612, they officially began what was to become the oldest surviving English-speaking city in the western hemisphere. St.

George. And one of your relatives apparently held the very first official wedding there. No mention of the Divel, though. Almost as if it was already a family secret even way back then."

"I'll drink to that," and the water bottles got sipped again. The ladies were diligent about drinking their water.

They heard scratching nails at the bottom of the closed door. When the door was nudged open, one black and one rich-brown low-slung dog nosed themselves into the room like U-boats. They placed their paws up on the side of the bed, their way of asking to be picked up. Each girl helped one to the top of the bed. Sandy knew she'd miss Bran and Muffin while in Bermuda. But after the honeymoon, they'd all be moving into a new apartment closer to the dog park.

Marcia finished with, "Well, mystery or not, you're lucky your mom didn't get married in Nome. It's kinda cold up there right now." They chuckled.

The dogs set themselves down atop the bed to receive their normal dose of steady petting. Any folding or packing or drinking now placed on hold.

Due to the distance, everything about the ceremony felt condensed to Sandy, though it was still only one weekend. Everyone attending would stay in the same fancy five-star hotel, but given the distance, the number of attendees was kept small by the tradition.

That all her friends couldn't go felt barbaric to Sandy, but she eventually planned her way around it by announcing a post-wedding bash. So basically, only the wedding party was going: Marcia and Tillie, the dual maids-of-honor, and Frick and Frack, the dual best men.

Three boys. Three girls. Two triangles per the Waters custom. And strangely enough this time around, only three adults.

Sandy said to her brunette maid-of-honor, possibly as a way of summing up Google and non-Google, "As long as the wedding is official, I don't care about the rest. I'd walk through fire for Greg." Sandy had asked about that too, jokingly, with the possibility of a Caribbean air to the festivities. Though, really, the island wasn't that far south. Sandy remembered how her mom's face had turned serious. How that ever-present gin glass had rattled with ice. How her mom had taken a long time to think back before promising, that as far as her bad memory could remember, there was no fire. Only water in the form of rain.

Sandy wanted to pack Bran and Muffin. Actually, she'd planned for them to be her ring bearers. But that had been nixed, too. Sandy closed one of her small suitcases and recalled how she'd been prepared to adopt another doggie—with her mom's weird fixation on threes—if that would get her loved ones to Bermuda. It was easy to remember the day she'd asked, because she'd helped clean up the glass Mom dropped on the kitchen floor

Like daughter, like mother, Mrs. Waters was packing good and early so she could worry about more important things, like how she was going to steal her own necklace. Desperation had made her intent clear enough, but when she was left alone with it, nothing seemed clear. Or easy.

She wanted all of it finished as soon as possible. What *was* almost finished, was her companion, as she reached for it and pulled more of the refreshing elixir down her throat. She counted on her gin. And it was good that she could, because once Sandy was married off, it would just be the two of them.

As she thought back about family, Diane fiddled with her careless packing. It was still amazing how convoluted this situation was, and how it had managed to remain hidden from outsiders for so long. She wondered if researchers might untangle it all someday. But then Mike was a researcher, so she decided they wouldn't, since his research never seemed to go anywhere except around in circles with his storms. It was enough to make her head spin, which helped to explain why sometimes hers did.

Nothing else was going to fit in this suitcase, that much was clear. With her luck, her suitcases would get lost anyway. She wished the Divel could be in one of them when they did. That would solve her problems in one fell swoop. She didn't know what a "fell swoop" was and didn't care. As far as she was concerned, that old saying could go and take a swoop right along with the old Divel. No, not a swoop, a swim, she corrected, to be consistent with its storied past. Her history-teacher sister was always reminding her to be historically accurate. It still irked Diane that Donna was refusing to attend Sandy's wedding. But she knew why. She was afraid of that blasted Divel after what Diane had gone through at her own wedding. Diane didn't want to think about it anymore. It made her head ache.

While balancing her jewelry case in one hand and a drink in the other, Diane settled down gracefully on her comfy king bed. It remained an unappetizing task to try and pick out jewelry for the weekend. Nothing she owned could compete with the Divel. Love it. Hate it. It might be many things—possibly even cursed—but it was certainly exquisite with its detailing and all those diamonds.

Swirling the drink, she worried how the big talk would go Saturday morning with Sandy. She didn't want it to affect Sandy the way it had affected her. She sipped, comforting herself with the expectation that Sandy would handle it better than she had, because Sandy let things slide off of her more easily.

CHAPTER 4

THIRSTY BLOOD

NORTHWEST AFRICA

Mma Kukuluel had returned today. It was going to be some storm. Her storm.

Sitting near the cliff again, her mind peaceably skipped from different subjects the chieftain had emphasized over the years. How being miserly for so long had made it a part of the tribe's blood. A natural thing—like how tall you were. Miserly with possessions. Miserly with water. Miserly with time. How every animal dealt with thirst, miserly or not, while being poor was a human condition. He had told of how being miserly and being poor could course through one's veins like blood. But not wisdom. Wisdom accumulated over the generations, and then was passed down by story, their picture, and ceremony.

A cooler gust of air nudged her from behind, before swarming past and over the cliff. She turned her face upward, as if she'd been spoken to. She had. The dry blue was being chased away by pushy dark clouds right about now.

Accepting her fate in this place, this special place, certainly eased her sense of waiting. The inevitability of it had pulled the years along, until this month settled on this day. Now she sensed the hours were trying to corral the minutes, like when she'd called the children to eat.

She was a part of this cliff. Had been ever since her parents had brought her here over a hundred years ago. A long time for humans, not cliffs, she knew. She thought back to how often she'd been
transported here with the help of one of her thin, slightly dressed grandchildren or great-grandchildren or great-great-grandchildren. Sometimes they would stay to chatter. Not today.

Her riding cart was always pulled by that thirsty horse. Sometimes the horse would keep her company. Sometimes she would be unhitched and ridden back, if the child felt like riding. Like today. Though riding was optimistic for the slow gait of the curved horse.

The horse fit in, Mma Kukuluel knew, because Africa was not known for its straight lines. Either way, the wooden cart with a throw of thin cushion was left so Mma wouldn't be on the ground. The ground meant ants. Always ants. And they carried anything away and often did—even possibly Mma now, given how light she'd become.

One moment, the blind, one hundred nine-year-old Mukuroo woman was sitting in her wooden pull-cart in utter calm, and the next, the building maelstrom approached from behind. From the east. The winds swirled high, even as they swept dust along the cracked path near her.

Within the oven's heat and her patch of hat-shade, yes, the wind had turned its color of cool nearing the sea.

This was Mma Kukuluel's spiritual home;

The place where she'd been born;

The place where she had blossomed from an innocent girl to a childbearing woman;

The place where the grand circle completed itself in her family;

The place where she could feel the weather.

This dry Saharan Low was sweeping over the parched white soil, the cracked red soil, and those persistent ants. It sniffed at the moisture, its own sustenance, as it clawed its way toward that coast. To complete its own nature, suddenly the heavens opened up and the rain came down.

Mma clucked greeting to her storm in her native tongue: You have come. She felt the vibration but couldn't hear the sounds, but her storm could, like a mother sensitive to her child's voice.

Looking at the small telly on his kitchen counter, the green radar made it clear it was raining everywhere in Bermuda. This of course wasn't that unusual with Bermuda so small. When Clarke couldn't get on his bike, he'd enjoy a quiet morning and tackle the paper's crossword. What was different this morning was that he wasn't alone—and that didn't mean Dee or Morgan, or even Hard and Easy somewhere close or hiding in the living room. He glanced at the stranger over his mug. Clarke was trying to come to grips with the legal/illegal crosscurrents facing him as the clocked ticked down toward this weekend. Clarke tried the direct approach by addressing the intruder. "This is still my home," he said, as he looked from a safe distance from behind his mug at the red satin box on the table. Inside was his ticket to his future. But the ticket's destination needed to be filled in: outside biking in the fresh air, or on a fixed bike inside a prison—if they even had bikes in prisons. He hadn't done his homework, making him feel unprepared.

His skin goose-bumped. He wasn't this uncertain about things usually. Ha, he released some tension by joking the standoff away. This wasn't even the real necklace!? How was he ever going to deal with the real one, if he couldn't get a grip around the fake one?

He left the imposter alone, grabbed the normal newspaper, and stepped out his normal front door to sit in his normal, well-grounded porch chair while it drizzled out there. It was actually cleaner out here than his living room, though Dee said the whole house could use a maid. He loved coming out here Sunday's to enjoy the sun and breeze and the paper, but often it was after the bike ride rather than instead of. As he sat and opened sections, his mind wasn't on the articles, ads, or the puzzle before him. Closing the paper, he peered out into the gloom that looked like he was feeling. He wanted to get away from the fake necklace for a day. His two girlfriends certainly weren't helping him in this regard. Dee had gone with a girlfriend to the shoppes in St. George, while Morgan was pulling weekend duty at her resort.

According to Benny's ground rules, Clarke wasn't supposed to share their plan with anyone. Sharing would put their perfect crime at risk. But as antsy as Clarke felt, he sure felt like talking to someone. Unfortunately, talking to the necklace itself hadn't helped any.

Clarke was the security supervisor for the very prim

and proper five-star Princess Hotel, while Benny ran a pawn/jewelry shoppe in the notorious French Quarter section of Hamilton. Even though they'd known each other forever, they'd lived their lives in different circles. Oh, they'd run into each other while fishing, like everyone did on the island, but it would look suspicious if they started spending time together the very week a priceless necklace happened to go missing from Clarke's vault. Tomorrow, Clarke would return to work and follow his normal routine, though of course, the hotel would be in wedding-preparation mode. Then on Sunday, the day after the wedding, he'd take his planned days off, heading with Benny to the Caymans to close their deal.

This morning's real dilemma rested on when to bring his replica to the hotel. Benny had left that little detail up to him. With Clarke presently coming out of his skin, nothing felt right. Whether he brought it tomorrow or waited until Thursday, when the real one would be cleaned and appraised, both plans felt risky. He didn't want it home, either. It seemed out of place, when compared to his everyday things. Fake or not.

He rustled his last section of the paper, as if flapping away invisible spirits. Time to give his crossword another shot, which normally did work to entertain his mind. He filled in a couple of answers. Then the clue "Villain" jumped out. The answer was a five-letter word beginning with "K." The answer wasn't obvious. Today's puzzle would be challenging, like always, even if he got lucky early on like this. With his momentum stopped, he considered whether it would be easier to bring the Divel copy to the hotel immediately?

As soon as he took his mind off the puzzle, the old-style word popped into his head: knave.

Someone in the universe has a sense of humor, he thought, though he wasn't laughing.

"Yes. I knew you would come," Mma Kukuluel clucked in her native tongue. Her tone serious, but serious toward something expected rather than unexpected.

Her shaking forearms and weak legs propped her up from the drenched wooden cart. Her legs tingling from all the flat-dusty and windy-waiting she'd endured. With her waiting over, stumbling, she remembered how she had loved to run, just run, when her youth had propelled her. This life-memory filled her spirit and moistened her eyes with happiness, though the rain claimed it as its own.

Once Mma perched herself upon quivering legs, the wind nudged her forward. Helping her, as expected. Everywhere, large raindrops were plopping upon the cracked earth, filling ears with its vibrant song. Mma joined that song when she went over the edge toward her waiting family: Joining her mother. Now she would await her children.

The circle of things.

After their long trip across dry land, those thirsty winds began to rejuvenate themselves with the energy from that sea. In the process, they accepted their nature just as Mma Kukuluel was accepting hers according to the beliefs of the Mukuroo. This natural process, this destiny, had been fulfilled by these winds every year since the Saharan Sea had been choked from the ocean so many uncountable moons ago.

44

By Sunday afternoon, the previous non-boiling pots in Florida displayed the satellite images of Mma Kukuluel's high spirit amongst the low-pressure system pushing off the West African coast. Consistent with her beliefs, the Mukuroo viewed the physical body as a temporary vehicle for one's enduring spirit. Two hundred and fifty miles north of the equator, Mma Kukuluel's imbued winds began their westerly trek toward the modern thinking Busters.

Drinking in the moist sea as if those winds remembered Mma Kukuluel's thirsty-waiting, the infant storm-front meandered as infants do. Headed in the general direction of the Caribbean basin, the Busters would feed the storm's data into their supercomputer for modeling purposes. By varying assumptions concerning the key variables, different probability cones could be generated. Each representing science's best guess concerning the general direction of the storm, given its internal qualities and any external fronts or landmasses. As more data became available, and as the system matured, more specific individual storm paths could be generated that were referred to as "spaghetti models" because of their shapes.

For intervention purposes, the modern Busters looked upon a hurricane as nothing more than a huge steam engine. In the case of storms, the potential energy of heat was being converted into wind velocity high above the eye-wall, rather than driving the pistons and wheels of a man-made machine. It was this modern viewpoint, an engine, that the Busters were seeking to throw a wrench into, regardless of any ancient Mukuroo-inhabited storms or African non-straight lines.

One such non-straight line was intersecting Florida at this moment. There, Dr. Klink announced with his tepid October-watch enthusiasm, "Well, I'll be a monkey's uncle," randomly bringing into the mix another ancient African, non-straight line.

On the screen before him, prevailing wind direction, pressure gradient drop, humidity content, and cloud formation had all changed remarkably quickly off the African coast. Might this candidate storm mature into a Category I hurricane, as measured by the modern Saffir-Simpson Hurricane Scale? This latter condition was critical to the NHC's scientific quartet, since minimum eyewall winds of seventy-five mph were required before they'd be able to exit this square room, climb into a large, chemically-laden plane, and fly into the storm's eye for their first trial-at-scale.

This storm probably represented last-chance-motel for the season, Klink knew. But it was way too early to consider bothering Mike and Carla over this—they were down in the team's sun-faded blue trailer. The way station that had proven quite valuable to the Busters, given that Mother Nature ran twenty-four/seven, unlike humans. It saved them from the countless times they might have felt the need to run home for clothes or sleep or a wakeup shower.

Klink's remark did bring Dr. Stacy McDonald rolling toward him in her chair. Like the other pair, they had grown closer during the project. Affectionately, they were responsible for their new nicknames: "Colonel" Klink and

"Old" McDonald. His, because he was half German, while hers, due to her thick mane of grey hair she'd had for a good decade.

The Colonel was pudgy, but not huge, with a clipped graying mustache and tanned skin. He hailed originally from the quaint city of St. George, Bermuda, was divorced, and had two teen-age sons still living in Bermuda with his ex-wife.

In contrast, maybe because opposites really do attract, Stacy McDonald had never been married and was fit. She was childless, though in some manner she had adopted every storm she'd lived through. Plus, she had three stray cats by way of the local Humane Society. Named Her, Ri, and Cane, it was easy to call them to dinner, but not so easy to adopt another, unless she named the next one after a storm.

CHAPTER 5

STROLLING IS UNDERRATED

MONDAY

Clarke was carrying his next crime read to lunch. Still crimes, still detectives, but this was the first fiction in a while. This change was officially ending his three month True-Crime training wave. Half- jokingly, half, he wondered if his obsession with the genre might have left a trail of bread crumbs that some smart detective would uncover. Just like in the books. Like, for real. The smallest clue—for dramatic license, or because that's how life really did turn sometimes—often proved to be the difference between freedom and capture. He had always been a man of habits, so this new skin—this week, felt weird. To see if he could go with this new flow, if anything was really flowing, he was changing up his lunch spot today.

Downtown Hamilton's view of the Harbour always made these power walks easy on the eyes. But today, even the pleasing pastel-colored storefronts weren't registering. He was too busy anticipating more perfect crime details. Three-necklace-week details. The original. The original replica. And now his replica of the replica, that still lacked a good word for. Right at this moment, seeing that "Patience is a Virtue" sign in Mr. Jacobs' storefront window, he decided he'd wait till Thursday to bring his. That seemed best, even given last night's dream of someone breaking into his house to steal it. Out here in the light of day, this was clearly odd because who in their right mind would steal a fake, right? Man, was he twitchy.

And something about the walk seemed strange. Oh, the sidewalk was empty. As in, clear of the "cruising" crowd. There was definitely a cruise ship looming above the right side of the street, which meant they were probably preparing to leave port. No matter how many of these ships he'd seen over the years—and this one was only mid-sized—they towered over the harbor-side line of parked cars and scooters like they were toys.

The air was seasonally temperate in the 70s, and the slight breeze coming off the water usually made these walks quite pleasant. Having spent his life on this twenty-mile-long rock, he'd learned many life lessons that island-dwellers knew all too well:

The ocean was going nowhere.

The hard rock was going nowhere.

The hot sun was going nowhere.

And patience.

Sure enough, the ship began to separate itself from shore. It would head west behind his hotel and into the Great Sound, where it would escape past the Royal Naval Dockyard into the open Atlantic.

He ducked inside the Docksider Pub. He hadn't been here in a while. If he got lucky, a sports match from America or England would be on the tube, and if not, he had his genre-busting book. He hated going anywhere without a book.

49

Coming into a place like this reminded him of the jobs he'd taken as a boy. Wanting more for himself when he was sixteen, he had started at the stately Princess as a gopher. From there he'd made his way through Housekeeping and Security until, following the path of least resistance, he'd become the head of the Security team after senior people retired.

This placed him directly under the indomitable Hotel Administrator, Mr. Tuttleberry himself. Tuttleberry was famous for his hands-off style of management. And as such, was the breed of administrator that was as consistent and unflappable as the bedrock beneath them. Through the hotel's ups and downs, Tuttleberry remained Tuttleberry. Still short, still straight, still a stickler for going by the book. And, of course, still obsessed with his prized butterfly collection. Seated at a table in the near-empty restaurant, Clarke flipped back to being predictable by ordering a chicken-salad sandwich on whole wheat with pickle and iced tea. He wasn't a risk-taker by nature, and so if a detective tracked him down due to his predictable lunch order, so be it.

With no games on the telly, he cracked open his book and began Martha Grime's mystery, *The Black Cat*. Quickly it sucked him away from this weekend's caper and Tuttleberry's pomposity.

He hoped and expected this fiction read would not fill his head with more bad ideas, like from those true crime books. But if he was honest with himself, Clarke would have had to admit to having his fair share of bad ideas all on his own after Laura's death. A thirty-one-year marriage was something that someone didn't just shake off from and move on. She had kept him on an even keel, maybe more than he'd realized. His son and daughter had helped from time to time, but with them married and off the island, family loneliness had thickened about him until he'd starting seeing Dee and Morgan. He'd gone a couple of years without any relationships, and now he had two—when it rained it poured.

His sandwich arrived and he found himself unusually hungry, almost like he'd forgotten he was hungry. He considered whether moving closer to one of his children might be a good idea. That made him smirk. He was located in the middle of the two of them right now, which argued for staying put.

He acknowledged tall Jim at the bar and returned to his familiar sandwich. Long ago, he'd decided that predictable food was preferable to experimenting and being disappointed. The story of his life, until this week.

He focused back on the book and finished off a chapter—he had lately, without realizing it, begun to root for the criminal.

Paying his check, he headed outside to that empty sidewalk and back toward work. The breeze was now in his face. Before he knew it, the solid pink of the hotel appeared ahead. He took in its blocky silhouette. The few members of the younger generation that could afford to stay at this fancy place often boasted how they'd retire at some fantastically early age. Their plans often resting on get-rich-quick scheme or family money. Was he any different now from this group of youngsters that he'd felt disdain for because of their different work ethic? He decided a shortcut was a shortcut, even though the entitlement piece didn't fit. He was angry. Angry about a lot of things.

It was time for something completely different, like that Monty Python theme. Well he'd certainly seen to that. A win/win opportunity with the Divel insured. The newlyweds would make out like bandits, too. He needed to believe that, to square any of this with his refusing-to-be-quieted conscience.

He said hello to Mr. Barnsby as they passed one another. Yes, it was a splendid day with the clouds high and sparse. Just before the waterview was blocked by the hotel, he made out the stern of the retreating cruise ship in the low haze near the water.

Coming up on the hotel's short front drive, he smiled as he considered the familiarity of the hotel, and of both Dee and Morgan. How he had played with the fantasy of retiring with the both of them, because, well because, how could he choose between them?

He nodded to the gaggle of taxi drivers out front. The cabbies were as much Bermudian fixtures as the Princess's perennial guests. The whole perspective of fishing and freedom that these men jovially cackled about was pleasant to join when Clarke had the time or the inclination. Today he had neither, so he said hi and pushed on, like he did on those days when something emergent was occurring inside.

He walked through the front door and entered the establishment like he was just another guest. Sometimes he did that just for the hell of it. With Ami at the front desk flashing him her all-clear smile, Clarke headed straight to the manicured rear lawn of the hotel. Somewhat amazingly, there were no guests tucked back here, taking in the panoramic view. Even the breeze and smell felt wide. With those flags playing with the wind and those sailboats playing in the Great Sound, this was the perfect place to let your imagination run free. Far out to the right, only misty fragments remained of that large ship.

Clarke let his imagination play with other things that were barely visible, or he hoped would remain barely visible. On such a small island, where everyone knew everyone else's business, the opportunity to change one's life was as difficult to achieve as remaining incognito. And here he was attempting both. Was he a betting man? No.

Clarke made his way toward the water's edge and that erosion wall.

Historically, the most dramatic path for Bermudians to increase their standard of living was by pirating out there on the open water. This was an easy career choice to imagine for Bermudians given the area's unpredictable weather, all those reefs, the crisscrossing international shipping routes, and the lore of the Triangle that kept people talking whenever something sank in the unforgiving ocean.

He looked at the expanse of water before him. It was true that if someone ran into sudden wealth here, it often came from discovering what a storm or pirate had driven to the bottom. Of course, the most famous and most extreme case remained the Tucker Cross. Discovered just north of the island by Teddy Tucker in 1955, it had been on the ocean floor since 1594. And along some untraceable path through all that history, the invisible Tucker had led Clarke to Benny.

Clarke turned from the water. He was not in a hurry to run into Tuttleberry, though Tuttleberry was no doubt in his office admiring or reading about his petrified little creatures. Collectors and fortune hunters seemed to be everywhere on this island. Now look at him.

Reluctantly, he used his mike to check in with his man in the control room. Sometimes they all walked; sometimes one person stayed in the control room. Their three-member team generally remained fluid in order to respond to the daily dramas that unfolded on a regular basis inside this conservative institution. Some days such drama easily masqueraded as one of those high-end soap operas on the BBC. Or for that matter, *Faulty Towers,* he thought more amusingly.

After getting the "all clear" from Thompson, who was the only one who enjoyed eyeing all those screens because it allowed him to sit and eat—if he hadn't been napping—Clarke said, "Thompson. Why don't you walk some? Get some air. Okay?"

"Roger that."

Clarke said goodbye to those turquoise waters and hoped that history really did repeat itself. He was banking on it—pun intended— after Benny's successful waylaying of the Cross.

CHAPTER 6

NEW THEORY MEETS OLD HISTORY

The veteran tour guide, Mr. Heathcott, was known for prancing on his toes like a posturing rooster whenever he led his little "chicks" around the grounds for their tour. The beneficiary of his proud chest this late morning were the volunteers and interns being prepped to cycle through the NHC's Math and Science Center stations. Dressed in his pastel blue and yellow uniform, this front-man was busily sharing his most current and canned information before they were cut loose for tomorrow's assignments.

"As you're all aware, there have been six named hurricanes this season. All Cat I's, except for the third, which happened to be a Cat II. The next of this season will begin with 'G'—George, I believe."

His spiel had already run its full half hour. Winding down, he pointed toward the interactive touch-screens as they passed them in the large hall. "Presently, whenever the next storm comes along, modern man is still left at the mercy of Mother Nature. We, the NHC, along with climatologists all over the world, continue to be woefully unsuccessful in being able to intervene against these massive storms." Now the hook.

"Maybe it will be one of you?" as he connected with the eyes of each of the ten students, "that cracks this age-old problem for mankind." Heathcott was unaware of the Busters' cutting-edge research not four hundred yards away, but everyone knew where that eye-sore trailer sat.

Dr. Waters would have offered an addendum to Heathcott's rote presentation: that his team hadn't yet uncovered the precise percentage of chemicals needed to successfully intervene before the first six storms of the year, but now they were ready. Ready to inhibit the sea water's ability to condense in the atmosphere, which was according to current wisdom one of the key components of the engine that allowed these storms to sustain themselves over water.

Waters would have also offered the hopeful backdrop that nature interrupted itself all the time. Water temperatures were often too high or too low. Wind conditions too strong or too weak. The problem in a nutshell was that nature could make one or stop one, but as of yet, humans hadn't had the energy-of-scale to make a dent. The forces necessary to create the huge storms were too great compared to what man could bring to bear in the middle of the ocean. Tropical storms often covered hundreds of square miles and were part of an organized system making use of mega-kilowatts of energy. This made Waters' current strategy to intervene small particularly attractive and particularly smart—if it worked.

The four Busters were chattering at this very moment over that new Low to the east—this, possibly, Heathcott's chance to update his presentation. They all knew—even Heathcott would have known— that it was way too early to get excited.

Regardless, a little excitement out in the real world was

contagious after so much research time had been spent in their lab.

Ready or not, Frick and Frack were shooting hoops terribly down at the public recreation area. With the sun retreating beyond the concrete buildings and their busy, sun-bleached, graffiti murals, it was bearable to be outside, but not necessarily advisable. This explained the lack of competition for the other half-court that normally would be overrun with teenagers. One determined teen happened to be holding down the fort, hoping others might show up despite the heat. His dribbling and shooting were far beyond the two older college grads, who alternated taking, hence missing, shots.

For a change, the boys weren't complaining about their jobs as low-level business analysts in competing investment firms. Such firms were always controlled by a few senior partners, a status that took years and a string of lucrative clients to obtain. Unfortunately for them, most never made it that high up, and possibly worse, they both knew it. It took ambition and smarts and connections and luck, qualities that were sadly lacking from their resumes.

Given enough disappointments, the enthusiasm to reach such a lofty status was usually eroded away several years of reality. For Frack, the less ambitious one, his weaker prospects had already settled around him like Miami's humidity. While for the more energetic Frick, his work horizon still hung out there like a hot blonde on the beach shimmering in the distance. But would he ever be able to get her attention, no less, reach her?

Because of the numbers, because of the reality they

represented, the boys had been primed to listen to Mrs. Waters' scheme.

"Come on, Frick, you're either in or you're out." Standing in one spot, Frack was dribbling the ball like a novice. "What's it gonna be?" Frack was normally the follower of the two, so it was unusual that he was the one lobbying for Mrs. Waters' thread-bare scheme.

As Frack missed his shot, he considered that Frick might be toying with him. That maybe he'd already made up his mind to go along with the caper. What did they have to lose? Frack liked that the necklace was worth a ton, but he liked Mrs. Waters just as much. She'd been sexy as hell in that thin dress. He recalled her words, *You're sweet*. That would make a good tattoo. Maybe he'd get his second one at the parlor right around the corner.

Shaking his head to clear either the oppressive humidity or the impressive trance, it sounded to him like they had a real opportunity to snatch a valuable necklace. He had a head for numbers, not names, but he thought she'd called it the Devil's Necklace. That sounded right. She'd said it was famous for something or other. Frack wondered if having a name like that had made it famous, or whether it had become famous first? That confused him. The bounced ball hit him in the stomach, producing an airless grunt.

He grabbed the ball, dribbled, and trying to change his luck on the next shot, relaxed too much and missed the hoop, the backboard, everything. The wayward ball making that tired, rusty fence feel useful. Well, everything needed a purpose, Frack believed. His new purpose was to make Mrs. Diane happy. Happier. Happiest. That's how he saw it, and no one was going to tell him any different. Certainly, not Frick, who'd had plenty of women.

Frack believed this was the lucky break they'd been waiting for. "It's almost too good to be true." With Frick not making a move for the ball, Frack retrieved it. He pictured the way Mrs. Waters' tan skin looked so alive and healthy. It energized him, made his skin tingle. Dribbling back, stopping, jumping, he made a shot. This was a sign. His luck was changing. Frick bounced the ball back to Frack. Frack dribbled to his right, pulled up, and banked another one in.

"You're hot," Frick laughed.

And Frack thought, *so is Mrs. Waters,* but didn't share it. He didn't want any competition from the more experienced Frick.

In a delayed response to the prior question, Frick said, "It is almost too good to be true. There aren't any details, though. Think what would happen at work if we operated that way."

Frack thought, *I work without details all the time,* but didn't share that either.

"And the scale of it. It's far bigger than any of the stuff we pulled in college."

"It's not like you're the one getting married or nothing," Frack continued, as if ruining the wedding was a consideration. "And we're gonna be there already. So, we don't even have to make a special trip." Meaning, pay for the fare or take all that extra time to travel out there. Convenient. A convenient crime.

"It just doesn't seem right, that's all." Frick's sleeveless shirt was stuck to him. "A marriage and all. That's all I'm saying."

"Greg said they don't want the thing. How Sandy is pissed off and all. And it's insured, don't forget that part."

"I know. I know. I wonder if Mrs. Waters could really be doing it to protect Sandy, like she said. That it's bad luck." He watched Frack shoot. "I guess someone else's bad luck could be our good."

"And it's in a foreign country," Frack offered, as he retrieved his own missed shot. He'd forgotten to picture Diane's long legs before releasing the ball. He offered this last commentary casually, as if it was obvious that the distance, this selling point, made sense. A foreign prison somehow better than one back here in the States. Because here, people they knew could visit and embarrass them.

After his best day of shooting ever, Frack hated leaving on such a note—missing the last one. But if they stayed until he made another, they might miss the wedding. They grabbed the ball, grabbed their towels, leaned against the fence where there was shade, and drank their blue PowerAde. The rusty chain-link fence imprinted its pattern onto the back of their soaked shirts like tattoo templates.

Frick mopped his face with a rag of a towel. "If it's insured, the money would make a hell of a wedding gift." Both of them knew that any insurance claim would make a far better wedding present than the feminine china place-settings they'd been talked into purchasing.

This could work out to be an 'advantageous exchange,' just like what Dr. Whipple described in Econ." They watched the young kid make shots at the other end of the court. "Let me state for the record, her thin plan has holes in it the size of the Titanic. But if it offers us a chance to pad our sorry bank accounts, it's probably worth the risk." Frack nodded away while toweling off.

Frick continued, "Hell, I take risks all the time for nothing." A new clarity pierced his eyes. "Frack, can you spell no-brainer?"

Frack started to spell, "N-O-"

Frick interrupted him. "Can you say, off-shore account?"

Frack started to say, "Off-sh-"

"Look, I've done my research. I'm not going into this all starry eyed and unprepared, just to chase a piece of ass. The Caribbean is full of off-shore accounts. Did you know Bermuda is often mistaken for being in the Caribbean because of its coral reefs...?"

Frack didn't answer in time because he wasn't sure the question was finished.

"In fact, though it has the northern-most coral reefs in the world, it actually lies hundreds of miles north of that region. Forming in the process one of the three vertices of the Bermuda Triangle—the other two being the real Caribbean and Florida."

Yes, Frick had done his homework—only the wrong assignment for the wrong class. He wasn't about to commit a national crime without being familiar with the irrelevant history of that nation. Some called him a lot of things—like those hoods down on the corner of Semester Ave—but they could never mock him for being uninformed.

With emptied drinks and those towels, they climbed into Frick's leased BMW as Frack worked out what those three vertices meant based on high school geometry. "Are we really sure Sandy doesn't want it?" Frick asked.

"Why don't we just get it from the horse's mouth, huh?" As Frick pulled into the empty street, Frack speed-dialed Greg. "Hey. You guys still don't want that necklace, right?" Then Frack listened and kept saying, "Yep" When he disconnected, he pumped both fists. "We're good to go." A man on a mission. Missions.

"Then there's no earthly reason why the lucky son-of-a-bitch can't get married and get rich in the same day," Frick said. "Any ignoramus can see that."

"Who ever heard of anyone going all the way to Bermuda for a wedding anyway?"

Frick didn't answer, because he'd heard of couples who'd done just that.

"It probably won't even be legal in the states," Frack continued.

That brought a shared belly laugh in the sweaty car.

After draining the last drops from his colored drink, Frick added, "Devil's Necklace." He guided the car into traffic. "She was probably pulling our leg."

Frack wanted to pull her legs.

Six miles later they went up and over the high sidewalk marking the entrance to the off-street duplex they rented. As they climbed out of the BMW, they had unwittingly signed their wedding-gift secret-pack by leaving rust stains on Frick's cracked white leather.

Maybe their ship had come in. But Dr. Whipple had warned his looking-to-take-the-easy-way students from taking the easy way, once they entered the business world. However, the tenor of his decidedly distant, droll voice had most certainly been drowned out by Mrs. Waters' more recent, most energetic, postgraduate recruitment drive.

CHAPTER 7

TUESDAY TUESDAY

Clarke woke late, and was late, until he remembered this was one of the days he'd taken off because of the coming high-profile weekend. Time off was normally good in Bermuda because it allowed him to bike, read, and see his girlfriends. Wearing indoor flimsy sweats and a wrinkled t-shirt, he glanced outside. More overnight showers told him biking was out for now. Without riding somewhere to read outside, without using up some hours of the day, there would be too many hours left to think about Thursday. Well, at least he had a date tonight with Dee. Dee would want him to clean, but that wasn't happening. He'd just stay here and get lost in his book. He hadn't seen much of Easy and Hard lately, anyway.

Greg stirred late this sunny Florida morning. The fringes of a dream were still there: something about tossing a shiny metallic lure into the Atlantic to catch fish. He wasn't much of a fisherman, so he hadn't a clue what the dream meant. Sandy would know, but she wasn't here. He went through his morning routine on automatic pilot: shaving, showering, before he wedged out an involuntarily pressed shirt and pants from his over-stuffed closet. After the weekend's party, he wasn't particularly happy about having to work all the way till Thursday. But lacking enough time off, it was what it was, as his father liked to say.

Dressed in khaki business casual, he headed to the tiny L-shaped space that his landlord had advertised as a kitchen. This morning, his "home-cooked" meal consisted of the chocolate Cheerios, and the chocolate milk it produced from his 2% milk. If he rushed, he had a chance of being on time.

Greg Bliley had grown up on neither the wrong nor the right side of the tracks. There hadn't been any tracks in small town Freehold, NJ. Its claim to fame was the trotter track he'd spent a few summers working as a groom. Occasionally, he'd even wagered when he was fortunate to come across a reliable tip. The problem was, something that sounded good didn't always turn out that way. Besides that life lesson, his small-town upbringing had taught him humility, the meaning of hard work, the value of knowing your neighbors, and that your reputation counted for something.

Now look at him. He was marrying someone who was receiving a priceless royal necklace. In Bermuda, no less. Stuff like this didn't happen in Freehold, NJ, unless you hit the Trifecta.

Would this sudden wealth change Sandy?

He finished crunching his Cheerios and slurping his chocolate milk.

After graduation, he had taken an entry level computer analyst position with a local credit card company. He's needed something in the area with Sandy entering Miami Dade College's veterinary school. His job was okay, nothing more, nothing less.

Now closer to the wedding, Greg's mind considered options, especially with Sandy continuing to express her displeasure with the Devil thing-a-ma-jigger. As Sandy had put it, *I don't know one, not one vet who owns royal jewelry. My mom might have been into this sort of thing….*Truer words had never been spoken.

He eyed the few boxes he'd packed. Except for those and his clothes, the rest of this junk was being trashed by his father while they honeymooned.

He dropped the scratched plastic bowl into the sink and fled the studio for his seventeen-mile trip.

As he drove the boring drive into work, while hunting for a good song, he remained irritated over how the necklace stuff was affecting Sandy. She had said just yesterday with her unhappy voice, *Specifics from Mom yet to be determined.* Sandy's first impulse had been to sell the thing, which naturally was prohibited by the Waters Trust. Or throw it into the sea, where it supposedly had come from, which was certainly prohibited by common sense.

While getting stopped at the long light at the intersection that annoyed him, Greg remembered Sandy saying that it was insured for "a ton." Like she was dropping a hint. All he knew was he was being forced to take their last name in order to keep the thing in the family. That had taken some getting used to. But it was what it was, and certainly not the most important thing going on here.

By the time Greg reached work—hardly remembering the trip—his mind had decided something. As he exited his ancient Honda Civic with its tinted windows that he would risk leaving cracked without the call for a p.m. thunderstorm, his hazy mind cast its vote for tossing the Devil-thing into the ocean if given the chance—if things got really bad. Crazy thinking, he knew. But he was getting married in a week, so maybe guys became crazy right before. He'd even shared such sentiment last night with Frack. His grandfather would have put it: *A storm is abrewing, all right,* given the way he enjoyed being prepared for things.

SOMETHING OLDE

PART II

THE STORM

CHAPTER 8

CHILDREN AND STORMS

<hr>

TUESDAY PM

<hr>

"I don't care where it goes as long as it reaches seventy-five mph," Stacy "Old" McDonald said, responding to "Colonel" Klink's prior comment. Seated, rolling her chair to view another monitor, she looked back at him atop his favorite stationary stool. He was tired of trying to find the one chair with the four good casters. McDonald had it, anyway.

"Well, the odds are it won't ruin the weekend for Mike," Klink answered. "Look at the path it would have to take to reach Bermuda from there." Klink wasn't going to say what he and Stacy suspected, that Mike would choose the last hurricane of the season over his own daughter's wedding. Professional to the end. And knowing his wife, Diane, such a decision would be the bitter end, at that.

Admiring her ankles, Klink said, "But you're right. We could get lucky here." He was hoping she'd pick up on this theme, that was never really hidden very well between them. He hadn't seen those little white pom-pom socks for ages. He liked that she was old-fashioned, that she was perfectly at ease in her old throwaway clothes from the trailer. Her blue running top and white sports bra were sitting above those shiny blue athletic bottoms with that white line running down each leg—making her long legs look even longer. The shower in the team's trailer made running doable either just before or just after their shifts. Klink never ran, though. Fancying himself more of a watcher. It figured she didn't watch him the way he watched her, making her less superficial. He liked that about her. He began to imagine what she was wearing, or not wearing under those sweats.

She responded to his "lucky" comment with a flirty, "And we might not," as she sipped her black coffee contained by that no-spill lid.

With that little devilish smile of hers disappearing behind that cup, Klink was definitely worried she meant sexually. He knew she knew that he loved those old sweats. They allowed, "the little pillager," as she sometimes called him, to discover whether she was au naturel or not. His little treasure hunt, they liked to call it.

Stacy turned in her seat, looked him straight on and clarified, "With the hurricane."

Klink said "Oh," while he decoded her clarification.

Stacy continued, "I hope he's not faced with that call. We'd be lucky to get a storm this late, but it would give Mike an impossible problem." She took in Klink's mismatched trailer clothes.

"You think he'd really leave the wedding?"

"I don't think he'd dare. She'd kill him with the gun he taught her how to shoot. Wouldn't that be ironic?"

"Yes, ironic all right," he agreed, as his voice trailed off. The same thing was about to happen to him, if he didn't get to discover whether she was wearing anything underneath.

Stacy continued in her perky voice, "Then his daughter

72

would kill him a second time. What good is a wedding if Dad gets offed twice?" she offered with a naked palm twisted upward in support.

"That's why the groom's dad is there. He can step right in and do whatever needs doing without missing a beat." Exactly what he wanted to do right this instant in that trailer.

"You're making that up."

"Who's the one making stuff up? Killing someone twice."

"If you make us angry enough."

Klink didn't care for the direction this battle of the sexes was heading. He was a lover and a watcher, not a fighter. "Well, let's hope the storm isn't wicked enough to place him in a Hobson's choice." The very thing he was hoping to avoid—no storm *and* no sex.

She turned and smiled. "Well, maybe we could still get lucky?" she delivered with a left eyebrow heading upward.

He liked it when her eyebrows became optimistic. He knew darn well she'd worn those sweats because his reaction was predictable. They both appreciated this characteristic about one another because these huge storms they were grappling with were anything but.

Predictable Klinky asked, "How bout we—?" The phone rang, cutting him off. The landline. Their cells were actually their backup system. She pushed her chair over to grab it. "McDonald."

Stacy mouthed, *Carla.* Then he watched her listen and nod. She locked eyes with him and said to Carla and him, "The pot definitely seems to be heating up in the right direction. And at this early stage, it—"

Klinky stood up to place his hands on her shoulders.

"It certainly is moving toward me in the right

73

direction."

While Stacy listened, he massaged in the hopeful way he did. When she hung up, she closed her eyes to the storm out in the Atlantic that wasn't close enough or strong enough yet.

"What do you think?" Klink persevered. Rubbing away, also unconcerned with the faraway infant storm barreling westward at an unusually high speed. He wanted to go south, toward the trailer. It never ceased to amaze him how thick her hair was— opposites attracting again.

"She said to keep my fingers crossed." Stacy made a show of crossing her fingers on both hands. "I'm on watch. Can't you see?"

He could see. He knew she was trying to confuse him with facts. "Right here, then," cutting right through the two or three conversations they were having at once.

"Klinky." She put her hands on his hands and smiled. "You're getting a little kinky in your old age."

Someone could walk right in on them. But, in reality Carla was the only one coming, and that was later, though Mike popped in to sample their strong coffee from time to time. Regardless, this stark room was no place for romance.

"Then the trailer."

"What if Waters calls?"

"He'll try our cells when we don't pick up."

"We never leave our posts except for bathroom breaks," she said in a half-serious tone.

"Then imagine it as a potty break with a much higher upside. The storm's not going anywhere."

"It better."

"I haven't been with you since Friday. It's been torture." He made a hound-dog face that she found endearing.

"You gonna to be nice to me this time?"

"Ouch."

"That's all you have to say?" Her voice and posture displaying her best femme fatale, that both of them knew was amateur hour at best.

When she was sure he was looking, she peeked the back of her sweats down.

"I knew it." He squeezed her shoulders without realizing it.

"You're such a romantic, it kills me." She grabbed his hand, grabbed her cell, and decided to make an exception in the face of what could be the last of the season.

How could it hurt?

"Twice?"

"Listen you," as they headed toward the door. "Storms are like children; did you know that?" She stopped at the door.

"Keep going." He meant with both her legs, as he passed her to lead the way.

Klink moved the hand on the cardboard clock hanging inside the door. Now it read "Back in 15."

She pushed it to "30," then looked up at him. "A girl has to have her standards."

He couldn't think of a good come-back, so he silently pulled her down the foot-bare path toward the trailer.

She continued her previous thought. "Think about it. Storms are like children because storm-time like children-time either goes too quickly, if it's precious, or too slowly, if it's a nightmare." She had never had children and didn't care to, but she had friends who shared their stories. "There doesn't seem to be anything in-between. And the only thing that has as much relentless energy as kids, is

75

Mother Nature."

They approached the trailer with their hands linked to each other, but their bodies closer than when they'd started out. "What about adult children?" Klink chided her. As usual, they were on the same wavelength, even if they managed to be on different parts of the wave.

Always the gentleman, Klinky opened and held the flimsy aluminum door for her.

In the name of thirty minutes, she ordered, "Get in there. The answers better get easier fella, or you're going to be on double-secret probation."

Klink didn't know what that was, but it didn't sound good. "Is that the way they teach you to talk in Jersey?"

She slapped his bottom, propelling him into the confined space where time was altered one way or another. The light door slapped shut behind them. He watched her turn the flimsy lock and close the inner door.

He doubted the spanking-thing had anything to do with the probation-thing. But, lo and behold, time suddenly sped up when McDonald's sweats piled on the floor right along with those showing-the-way white lines.

Sam Bliley sat in his cozy den sucking on a longneck Miller Lite. He paused for a moment before calling Greg. Normally it would have been Marge explaining the facts of life to her son about marriage. But cancer had removed her from the playing field four years ago, so it was up to him now.

At least it was long-distance. "Hello, down there. How're things?"

"Just fine, Dad. Don't forget you're getting rid of all my junk while we're in Bermuda. The couple of boxes and the clothes I'm keeping are in the closet. Everything else goes to the dump."

"Gotcha. Won't be long now. Go grab yourself a beer."

Talking into his cell, Greg peered in the short, rounded fridge and said, "Looks like Corona for me. No limes, though. What can't wait until the end of the week?" He opened the Corona and settled into the dilapidated armchair next to the spindly table cluttered with keys and unopened junk mail. After taking a hit, settling down, grabbing the remote and turning on the game, the table wobbled when he placed the bottle and remote down.

"I guess it's about time for our little man-to-man talk."

"Theme of the week. Everyone is having "wedding" talks, so why not the men, right? You watching the game?"

"Yep." Mr. Bliley had the sound muted on his old RCA—the most advanced button on the remote. So he could think straight.

In the silence, Greg eyed all the mismatched furniture leftover from college that was destined for the dump. Then he returned his attention to the Miami Heat game.

Mr. Bliley said, "You know your mom was better at this stuff. But she would have wanted you to appreciate that the love you have for each other will surely be tested over the years. One way or another. Even when you love each other a lot."

The window-unit air conditioner turned itself on behind the elder Bliley. A woman's touch had all but receded from his home these past few years. Presently, his empty beer bottles littered the square coffee table like tall chess pieces.

Greg answered, "I think that's already happening with this necklace thing."

77

"Maybe the two of you are making more out of it than you should?"

"I don't think so, Dad."

"Your mother would have wanted you to understand the importance of patience and tolerance. This apparently is the Waters way."

"We're trying to respect her parents' legacy, but it hasn't been easy with how it's changed all of Sandy's plans."

"Son, what difference does it make, really, in the long haul?"

"What's more important to Sandy right now than her wedding day? Some ritual-thing has to take place. Her mom won't even share the details until the morning of." He took a hit of beer. "With all these secrets, it sounds like a cult or something. You know, like the stuff that happens in those New Orleans' movies with chickens and dancing and chanting."

"According to Mrs. Waters, chickens are protected in Bermuda the way cows are in India."

"Maybe that's why that law had to be passed? Sandy said the Waters held the first wedding in Bermuda?" His dad didn't say anything. "And if that's not enough, I had to agree to keep the Waters name without any hyphens, per their Trust agreement. That's what it took to keep the priceless heirloom in her family, even though she doesn't really want it. The point being, if I didn't agree, the Waters may have nixed the wedding. Sounds kind of medieval to me."

The A/C cut off behind Mr. Bliley. "Well, remember it's only one day. Then you get to spend your honeymoon in Bermuda. Your mother and I eloped to Atlantic City."

"I hear you. I just hope this family isn't off its rocker."

"Me too, because the acorn doesn't fall far from the tree."

"Sandy is normal as the day is long."

"She picked you, right?" They both chuckled. "That reminds me," his dad continued, "So, wedding traditions aren't all bad, right?"

"What?"

"Your party."

"Oh, yeah. That was fun."

"So, I don't want to hear anymore whining about all this stuff. Agreed?"

"Gotcha."

With that storm strengthening out in the Atlantic, Dr. Waters knew it was time to get permission to spend the team's money. He rang Dr. Braxton's secretary. "Hey Margo. It's Dr. Waters. Is Braxton tied up the rest of the day?" It was already five.

"She's in there doing paperwork. I'm sure she'd push it all in the trash for you. I would."

"I can wait till morning, if that's any better."

After a moments silence, he heard. "No can do, sweetie pie. As much as I like you, I couldn't shoehorn you into that lineup."

"Sweet-talk her now. I'll be right over."

"Hold on."

He disliked the political side of his profession, so he was quite happy that Braxton was such a capable administrator.

The next thing he heard was, "Commme onnnnn down." Margo recorded the daytime *Price is Right* episodes to watch at night. Her fantasy was to be one of the models up on the stage. Leggy looks were not a problem for her.

79

As he headed to the other side of the complex, Mike realized he'd been correct not to put this off until tomorrow. This meeting had to happen before they could fly. And there was no telling when "go" conditions might materialize. Nature had its own timekeeper for such things, which usually turned man into either a spectator or victim— the crux of the problem to begin with.

Before their funds could be released, Braxton had to give her okay that the storm fit their grant's stipulations: the storm had to be an official hurricane; the hurricane had to be out at sea and not an immediate danger of striking land; it had to be within range of their aircraft, and the eye had to be wide enough and/or the storm moving slow enough to provide the team enough time to deliver a sufficient amount of their secret chemical.

As he walked, Mike's thoughts turned to how the warm sidewalk was emitting the sun's stored heat. Mimicking the very process they were seeking to interrupt out over the ocean's surface. And like many cutting-edge scientists, he wondered why someone hadn't thought of it sooner.

He walked up the few steps, opened the right side of the heavy glass door, and stepped to the elevator bank. Three flights up, he found himself in Margo's nicely appointed domain. The room was plush by public building standards, with several nice paintings, a leather sofa and chairs—actually matching and not taped together—and a cherry wood desk where Margo sat typing away in a chair with four good wheels.

Margo's fingers stopped typing when Mike exited the elevator. She'd always had excellent peripheral vision with those sensual dark eyes of hers. Even explaining once, how this would help her interact more successfully with the live contestants on the show. Sitting straighter, she began with, "Long time, no speak."

"Yeah, I missed you too." Margo was a sharp looking middle-aged woman with her button nose and those vigilant close-set eyes.

"You haven't been over in ages. A good thing?" Following up her words with that friendly sigh, letting him know that it might have been so from a professional getting-work-done perspective, but not on a personal level.

"Yes, except the part about missing out on your sister's brownies."

"That hurt. Why is everything always about my sister? The way you fawn over her, I wish I looked like her. Will anything ever change?" She delivered with another playful sigh. Margo actually got along quite well with her identical twin sister, who happened to be a chef.

"That's the question of the hour, actually."

Dodging the climatology question for the moment, she said, "Me and Money-Penny. Pining away." She'd been single since her divorce two years ago, and made sure everyone knew her troublesome youngest was leaving for college this fall. "Go ahead in if you really came to talk to her rather than me." Whereby, she feigned disinterest by beginning to type again, at half-speed, mind you.

As he headed into Dr. Braxton's office, Mike heard Margo mumble,

"There's nothin' wrong with my brownies."

Whenever Mike walked into her bright office, he was reminded of its spaciousness. Those corner southwest windows, overlooking the small park and the harbor beyond, boasted quite a view compared to the Busters' stark ground-floor monitor room. He closed the door behind him.

Braxton sat behind her U-shaped desk, corralled as usually by all those short piles of papers and numerous small picture frames. As he approached her desk, she greeted him with, "Hi, Mike. I take it this means something's cooking."

With Braxton being a great cook, food often got dragged into their discussions.

"You could say that, Tammerie." He sat in one of the thick armchairs, rather than the matching tessellating tan, white, and black leave-patterned sofa. There were no rollers to break on these, though if she had any, they'd be working just fine.

Dr. Tammerie Braxton held a dual doctorate in applied mathematics and climatology. With current climatology centered on the mixing of air currents and related fluid dynamics, calculus was necessary to make sense of what was happening inside such volatile systems. She was a decade younger than her hot-shot researcher. Originally, that had given Waters pause, but Braxton had quickly dispelled any concerns Mike had with her strong diplomatic and leadership skills.

Along one wall, several monitors displayed different quadrants of the Earth's surface, compliments of the ring of weather satellites orbiting the planet. There was nothing too fantastic happening around the globe, except for the Low pressure that had exited the West African coast and a young typhoon in the China Sea. Braxton always seemed to enjoy when her project leads brought her back to the real science end of things. She had already made it perfectly clear how the Busters' first field trial could not turn into another Project Stormfury—the infamous cloud seeding fiasco from three decades back. As old as that was, it still represented a PR headache for the NHC, and hence, still interfered with Braxton's funding efforts.

Jokingly, he knew she would suspect him of trying to escape from his own daughter's wedding.

She started their discussion downhill with, "When it rains it pours." "You can say that again."

"Maybe your project will help keep you sane this week?" She swiveled her chair sideways. Her off-white silk blouse and full navy skirt looked professional, though her clothes were complimented by a plain wedding ring and large earth-tone necklace, compliments of the interior of Africa where she had honeymooned.

"Okay, how's the wedding going?" she asked, putting his "business" before their weather "pleasure."

Waters steepled his fingers. "It's going to happen, whether I make it there or not."

"That's as true for the storm as the wedding. You like the young man?"

"Greg's a good fit with Sandy. There's just a lot going on. I'm excited for them. Excited about this new Low, too." He nodded toward the appropriate monitor.

"You realize the timing couldn't be worse." Time for pleasure.

She'd already encouraged him not to push, because the winter would give them time to deepen their understanding of all the variables involved.

He answered, "Since when do we get to pick? You know who's boss," answering in a tone that made it clear they'd had this conversation before.

"So, let's hear why with all of this going on, you need to do it this week, if you get the chance?" She put her feet up on a short wooden foot rest. "And thanks to the boring meetings I've had all day, give it to me straight on."

He took a deep breath. "You know I much prefer to

dispense our chemical by laying the biodegradable film on the ocean's surface. That method has the added benefit of introducing a physical barrier between ocean and atmosphere, and is the approach that most closely mimics our SimTank trials."

Tammerie decided she wanted coffee, rose, and crossed to the sideboard across the room. "You want some?"

"No thanks. My system's already running."

She poured herself a nearly overflowing cup, then sipped the rich brew. First sip done, she made her way over to those corner windows.

Waters continued, "But, as you know, the wave tectonic specialists talked us out of using my surface plan. Even though I still don't fully buy it, the belief is that any rogue waves would defeat such a plan, making it too risky for us to land on the ocean and too risky for my thin budget. Our thin budget. Bottom-line, pun intended, we as an agency required something more predictable."

Braxton had listened to his spiel while gazing out the windows at the sky. Their friend. Their enemy. Their world. She came over and sat down and put her feet back up. "Yes, I remember, because that very discussion came up at the international symposium in Beijing." That sat Mike up.

"No biggie. You remember. I attended it back in the spring."

Mike nodded recognition.

She continued, "And now that you bring it up, there was that critical issue of how to transport large enough rolls to cover the necessary square footage. A weight versus area problem, which engineering hadn't solved yet. So, it was more than just the safety issue."

Mike answered, "You do have a great memory for details." He relaxed back into his chair. The unsolved issue making Mike's preferred intervention method a moot point for this season.

She asked, "Are you telling me we are ready to take the ocean out of its comfort zone?"

"Yes. Our chemical mixture is ready, and we have access to the newest hurricane-hunter Orion. Being able to fly above the water's surface while in the eye at least has the advantage that we can consider a much higher percentage of storms." Then he paused and looked toward those freeing corner windows.

"But?"

"But, possibly not as effective," he answered quickly, while nodding agreement to his own thought. "Time will tell," as he motioned back toward her monitors. "Either way, a delivery system has to prove itself at scale."

"Yes. The key point now, isn't it? That Low you're referring to could turn out to be a beaut. Perfect conditions. Nothing interfering with it for miles."

"That's what we're hoping for."

"What about the wedding?"

He chuckled, "Screw the wedding." She gave him a I'm-not-buying-it look. "No really. I should be able to do both, if the show begins soon enough."

Silence.

He knew that she'd heard what she'd needed to hear— mainly that they weren't acting out of end-of-the-season desperation.

"The Busters have done nice work to get us this far. Now go finish this. The Agency can certainly use it."

"Thanks, Tammerie. We'll do our best."

"I know you will."

85

After setting out and closing the door, Dr. Waters stopped at the walk-up bakery outlet.

Margo stopped typing.

"Thanks for getting me in."

She persisted, "There ain't nothin' wrong with my brownies." She looked up with her brownie eyes. "When are you gonna try some?"

He scanned the entire length of her food-free desk, moving his head, with his peripheral vision apparently not nearly as good as hers.

"I don't have any with me. I didn't know you were coming." Good vision, but not psychic.

He didn't know what to say. At the moment, he couldn't deal with any more decisions, faced as he was with one potential hurricane and one definite wedding. "Listen. If this project succeeds, I'll buy a batch from you and we'll eat them together. How's that sound?" Given the work and family pressures piling up all around him, the opportunity to share optimism felt refreshing.

"How about I type out a brownie order and get you to sign it, then they'll be good and ready when you get back?"

He crossed his heart while he headed back to his already overly-complicated week.

CHAPTER 9

ON BORROWED TIME

The tropical Low's vital statistics continued to intensify unusually rapidly due to the recent global warming trends: providing the southern Atlantic waters a great deal of potential energy (warmth) compared to prior years. Given the wind speed trend, the real possibility existed that hurricane force winds could be reached by next morning. This propelled the Busters into prep mode. As planned long ago, Stacy and Carla took first watch while the pilots would grab as much sleep as they could. This pre-launch schedule was set to maximize pilot rest time, as hurricane-hunting flights often turned arduous for the pilots, whether the trip to reach the hurricane was brief or not.

Before hitting the hay, the Colonel called Mike around ten. Sustained winds had crept up to fifty. When Mike handed off to Stacy at midnight, the winds had climbed to fifty-six. Stacy and Carla would cut the night's duty in half, Stacy taking the twelve to four shift, and Carla the four to eight.

Stacy watched the storm parameters grow stronger, as the young storm's direction continued to squiggle toward them in a basically westerly direction.

Carla received an optimistic update when she replaced Stacy. Wind speeds were up, pressure gradients down, and the eyewall formation was holding more definition than earlier in the evening. At six, Carla documented in the log that sustained winds had reached sixty-three mph.

She did the math compared to ten o'clock last night. They no longer required a fifty percent increase. Only a twenty percent increment would do it now, an occurrence that was statistically quite likely given the absence of land masses or competing fronts.

Carla prayed their luck would hold, now that they were really ready for their first trial-at-scale. They deserved this chance after all their lab work. But she knew their circumstance had the potential to turn bittersweet, if a Cat I materialized only to compete with the wedding in the worst way. Amidst the quiet of the morning, she wanted the storm, but remained worried for Mike if he was forced to choose. Was it so wrong for the scientist in her to want one thing and the humanitarian another? Regardless, she was loyal to Mike because he'd stuck his neck out when he'd given her this chance on his new team. And she'd be the first to admit that she now hoped to thank him personally. Around six, she received calls from both Waters and Klink, and the excitement of sharing the encouraging data woke her up from any pre-dawn grogginess.

At six fifty-five, the Colonel and Mike both pulled into the nearly empty parking lot.

The Low's winds were now touching sixty-nine mph, flirting repeatedly with seventy. Now only a seven percent increase would get them home. Or out.

Mike texted Braxton with a quick update. Everything was a go for the next five stages:

1. Reconnaissance;
2. Deployment of Measuring Devices;
3. Interdiction;

4.   Longitudinal Measurement;

5.   Analysis.

Which lay in writing amongst the short piles on Braxton's desk. And per that protocol, if the winds sustained themselves above the Cat I limit for one-half hour, then Stage 3 could proceed with the release of their secret chemical mixture within the eye-wall's perimeter.

Mike hung up the landline and began his anxious waiting alongside everyone else. While eyeing the monitor over Carla's shoulder, with nervous energy filling the room, Stacy and the Colonel opted for the calmer and more private air outside.

Twenty-five minutes later, the two outside cloud watchers waltzed back in. Stacy's t-shirt was now inside-out, suggesting they'd traded in calm air for frisky air. She asked, "Well?"

Mike offered, "Now we get to wait some more."

"What else is new?" Stacy agreed.

The Colonel shared, "We're not Climatologists. We're professional waiters. Where's my tip?"

Stacy grabbed his bottom.

That prompted laughter born from different types of nerves: preflight nerves, pre-Nobel Prize nerves, end of season nerves, wedding nerves, and post-sex nerve.

After the laughter died away, Carla swiveled around to face Mike. "Shouldn't you call the missus? Just in case?"

With all this attention on the storm's parameters, he'd forgotten. Last night, Mike hadn't bothered mentioning the latest storm to Diane because he hadn't wanted to stir up the hornet's nest. Or more accurately, the hornet herself. The storm might peter out for all they knew.

Sitting in her bright kitchen, Diane opened her cell

ringing out Under the Boardwalk. She was still in her sexy armless grey t-shirt and her white short-shorts with those blue hearts all over them. Mike hadn't noticed any of it last night. After checking the caller-ID, answering, and then listening, she heard her high-pitched voice finally share, "You're kidding, right?"

She stood up without realizing it, so she could pace barefoot through the house without realizing it.

Over the years, each storm had seemingly pulled him further and further into another life. Into another marriage. One millibar at a time. A life she no longer shared with him. This was wedding week, t-minus four days and counting.

She heard as she entered the long hallway, "Look, the thing is intensifying so quickly, we'll have plenty of time to do what we need to do. I'll be able to get to Friday night's rehearsal dinner, no sweat."

"Well, why should this week be any different just because your daughter's getting married?"

"All right. All right. This is not the time. There are bigger fish to fry."

"Yeah. Like your ass." She turned to avoid getting trapped in the spare bedroom.

"I'll make Friday. I promise. Just bring the formal clothes I need to wear. They'd get creased in the car, or wet, if I have to wear them into the hurricane."

"Wet, all right." She was not the mood to end their argument by cooperating with his attempted humor. Still moving at a good pace, she continued their jousting. "You best be telling me the truth, or Sandy will kill you herself." She disconnected the call at the end of that sentence with a press of her thumb, before dropping the blamed messenger into the depths of her purse near the front door. Out of sight, supposedly, out of mind. Would she be mature about this and only cut small holes in his clothes? No, that would just embarrass Sandy. He might not even notice. Men.

Marching back into the kitchen, she poured herself coffee. Her blood was up. Then the opportunity appeared. When one door closes, another one opens, her mom had said a thousand times, if she'd said it once. It would be a long day for him. The wings of opportunity would have plenty of time to transport her over those rough railroad tracks back to the wrong side of town. It took a long time to get over there for some reason, but not nearly as much get back. Mike probably had an explanation for that—westerly winds or something—screw that science-talk, too.

She dug into her purse to free her new friend—funny how an instrument traveled from scapegoat to opportunity bearer so quickly—and found Frick's cell number. She heard his self-indulgent voicemail message: "I'm busy with important business, but I'll call you right back. Go!"

The sound of the young man's voice gave her pause. He was the less gung-ho one. Then she said, "Hi. Remember me? Call me when you get this." She clicked off, her mood already improved. Opportunity, all right. The watchword of the day. It couldn't hurt to reconnect with the boys, just in case any of those nasty second thoughts were lurking about. No harm at all.

For the first time that she could remember, she was praying for a hurricane. Her world had been turned upside down again by all this Divel nonsense. Leave it to that necklace of hers. It had a knack for stirring things up but good, even if it was only every 30 years.

91

She finished her coffee, headed toward the shower, stripped in front of the full-length mirror, eyed herself critically, and pranced toward the square glass shower humming Under the Boardwalk. The question of the hour remained: Would she or would she not need to share herself with the boys to close this deal? She had needs. A chill shot through her, so it was fortunate the hot water tap was close. There was nothing like a warm shower to take the morning's nip away. And if that didn't work, there was always her gin. She'd be smarter before she left this time for the diner.

Clarke tried to sleep in with another day off. But with so much running through his mind, how much sleep he'd actually gotten was debatable. After piddling with odds and ends that had nothing to do with cleaning—even though Dee had mentioned how the level of dust in some of the rooms seemed to be layered like sedimentary rock— with the weather so nice, Clarke donned his helmet, mounted his grimy road bike, and pedaled west toward Hamilton.

He lived off of Middle Road in the interior of the island, though interior was a slight misnomer with everyone within a mile of major water. His was an easy commute whether he biked, rode his moped, or drove his sun-faded maroon Peugeot during the worst of the weather. Since it never snowed, the worst meant heavy rain. Heavy or not, showers tended to blow through quickly, so islanders learned to outwait them if need be. With his car's A/C permanently off, the Peugeot often went unused during the summer months. He kept reminding himself to get it fixed, but since he really enjoyed using either bike, and gas was expensive, the car never seemed to escape his stuffed one-car garage for *Jone's* white-washed repair shop.

Short of downtown, he headed left up the hill into Fort Hamilton. Its expanse of grass was a favorite place to read. Traveling over the deep, dry, overgrown moat, he set his bike and helmet down, pulled the small paperback from his knapsack, and headed for a slice of shade. Deserted and quiet as usual, the next novel was: A is for Alibi by Sue Grafton. Settling his back against the thick limestone wall near that old canon above him, it would keep its faithful watch to the south while he got lost in this latest crime novel.

When he looked up again, the shadows had lengthened, but the temperature was still holding in the seventies. He'd lost track of time. Standing and turning around, there were high wispy clouds stretching to the southwest. He guessed it was windy up there.

Bermudian culture was known for encouraging its workers to leave work promptly—five o'clock for most. Dee would leave school earlier than that if she could, so he mounted his bike to head home. He needed to get the simple fish dish started in the oven, before he'd get to shower this ride off himself. Pedaling home, he was looking forward to seeing her tonight. The ride went incredibly quickly, almost as if the closer he got to his date, the faster he pedaled.

The Busters had more prep work to complete before take-off could occur.

Off the phone, Waters directed Klink to head toward the airfield. Preflight details needed to be arranged. The National Oceanic and Atmospheric Administration (NOAA) was in possession of three Orion WP-3D

93

hurricane hunters that were familiarly named after Muppet characters: Kermit, Miss Piggy, and the newest— the latest and greatest—Fozzie.

Klink knew Fozzie was their plane because it was the only one outfitted with the new aerosol nozzles. The question was, if someone else wanted it for hurricane research, the Busters would need to lease it in order to make sure that had it, even if they ended up standing down. Otherwise, they could find themselves with a hurricane, but without a plane to deliver their chemical— one of the downsides to this airborne plan: expense.

Klink drove his green minivan to the airport, double-checked the available supplies against their manifest, and arranged with hangar support to have the chemical drums loaded on his call. Because of the unique mix of chemicals involved, those yellow drums would remain under lock and key until the team was ready to leave. Their secret chemical wasn't poisonous—it was in fact biodegradable—but they had painted on those scary crossbones decals to keep curious hands from becoming too curious.

As Klink completed his checklist, he was overcome by a premonition that the storm would weaken now that they were ready. When he checked in with Waters, he discovered that his fear was unfounded—some clairvoyant he turned out to be. Klink heard, "Two steps forward, one step back. Patience my friend. Stay put. We're sooo close!"

Klink went to get a tiny bite of something. With the rough ride ahead—if their luck continued to run— experience warned him not to eat too much.

With Stacy and Mike transfixed on the monitors, Carla

walked out as her Timex crawled past three. It was decision time. If they were going to leave soon, she should get coffee. But if not, a nap was in order. She followed the footpath toward the trailer, thinking about— hoping— how if the storm was named soon enough, how they'd be able to squeeze in most everything before the weekend. Assuming no complications. A big assumption knowing Mother Nature's capriciousness. Carla pulled open the weightless aluminum door. The cramped space greeted her with a musty smell. Someone had forgotten to leave the A/C running. Switching it on, pulling back the light military-grade blanket, pulling back the tattered but clean sheet, she slipped off her sneakers. The rest of her clothes would stay on. Closing her eyes to the shaded windows, she played in her mind how if the pre-hurricane Low developed into George, they'd soon be on their way to the airport. Predictably, they would don their uniforms— which consisted of pastel blue "BUSTERS" t-shirts with the team's picture on the front surrounded by a red circle with its requisite yellow slash— because Mike would want to snap a team picture. Her thoughts slowed, as predictable seemed sometimes good, *and...sometimes... not...when it involved storms...or Mike.*

She pictured the hurricane hunter aircraft Orion-something that was eating up a good portion of their budget. They would board the propeller plane with its four strong engines—she remembered that part for some reason—and then get down to business. The business that before the week was out could have them making history.

Back in the "waiting" room, the storm was flirting with the seventy-five-mph threshold. With those winds feeding their hope, Mike and Stacy awaited the big moment from one good and one bad rolling seats.

At three-sixteen, George was announced to the world by NHC's media arm. Effortlessly, the news-worthy event spilt across the wire services, teletype, internet, and TV weather channels. Waters had high hopes for this moment, already envisioning it as the watershed moment of his career.

At three-twenty, Mike dutifully called Diane. When she refused to pick up, he left her a subdued message: "We have a live one on our hands…see you in Bermuda, Friday."

Meanwhile, Stacy interfered with Carla's snippet of sleep. Carla splashed water on her face from the midget sink, slipped her sneakers on, and up the hill they hustled. It was executive decision time. Mike conferenced-in Klink at the airport. He heard himself say, "We've got our storm, folks. But here's the kicker. We're running out of daylight. There's not enough time to get out there, spread the chemical, and get out with our necks. I want to be able to see everything while it's happening."

Their chemical had been dyed red just so they could see it in the air and see it actually making contact with the ocean's surface.

Mike hoped he wouldn't regret this decision for the rest of his life, because anything could happen after the sun went down. Not to mention that he was about to shrink his timeline for getting to the wedding by a full day. "So, I'm proposing we meet at the airport, first-light. Oh-six-hundred. Well rested and raring to go. Keep all your fingers crossed that he stays above seventy-five. And if not, I guess you can remove me from the front of your shirts." He looked at the women. "Everyone good with that?"

With the news, Carla's posture sagged, like the air had

been let out of her.

"Get ready. Get set. Then we wait some more," Stacy said dryly.

The comment jarred Klink's memory. Klink said, "The Orion rep is waiting on an answer from us. She has a request for our plane."

Our plane. Waters made a snap decision. "Lock it up for today and tomorrow, will you?" He had been hoping to save on today's money. But his snap decision came when he realized they couldn't afford to have another team fly it today and have it come back in disrepair. An occurrence that was certainly not unknown after a plane danced with a hurricane. There went the budget.

With no place better, dressed in tight white capri pants and a yellow sleeveless top, Diane plowed back toward the same crummy diner on the same crummy side of town— she'd just take another hot shower later. At least she'd learned her lesson. Two drinks had started this hazardous trip out, and as soon as she lurched to a stop, a booster nip was snuck from the center console. Flinging open her door, she was accosted by the humid air. This time, her throw-away flats handled the coarse cement walk with little drama, thank-you-very-much.

Inside, she chose an empty booth away from the few customers.

When the boys arrived, Frack slipped in next to Diane. Both boys had their ties loosened at the top, a common sight given the humidity.

A little hungry after the drinks, Diane made it three shakes this time, making them a team. When the skinny waitress left, Diane leaned down and softened her tone, even though the place was all but deserted again. "Okay.

I'm not even supposed to share this. Not even Greg and Sandy know these details yet—" Her eyes flitted between them. The boys looked at one another, and then Frack leaned in especially close.

"By the instructions of the Waters Trust, the newlyweds must take part in a charm hunt—without any outside help or interference. What that means is that you will not be able to get at the Divel until after the hunt, which happens right after the ceremony. Once they finish gathering their charms that—" She almost said "guard," but stopped short of that. She didn't want to frighten them. "That adorn the necklace in the vault, they will probably stop at their hotel to change clothes before returning for the reception dinner. That's when you'll have your best chance to get it."

Then she went on to explain how they just couldn't make off with the Divel, because if they did, everyone would know who took it. That they'd have to be smart about it. Otherwise, there'd be no insurance money for anyone.

Over the grinding noise of their shakes being made in the kitchen, Diane said, "I will prevent the necklace from being returned to the vault. Normally, it gets switched out for its replica just before the charm hunt begins. Boy, oh, boy, I can just see the expressions on their faces when they find out the real McCoy has left the church—"

Their shakes arrived—two strawberry, one chocolate. They sealed the deal with a hearty toast. All for one and one for all. A team.

Frick said, "This is like having inside information concerning an IPO. But it's still going to take good timing and some finesse to pull this off, isn't it?"

Frack put his hand on Diane's forearm. Sounding very

sincere, he said, "If this is worth doing," as he got lost in her blue eyes, "then we should enjoy it." Mixing up his sayings. Rubbing her smooth, nice smelling skin, like she was a genie who had just popped out of a gin bottle. His face promptly colored the same color as Mrs. Diane's shake.

Trying to cover his embarrassment over the botched sexual innuendo, he used his free hand to take a manly pull from his drink. His throat froze, making his eyes squeeze shut from the pain.

Lubricated by the alcohol, Diane squeezed him back. But with his arm gone, his thigh was the closest body part.

Frack did a little hop.

When he settled back on the bench seat, Frack placed his hand atop hers. Pleased. Pain replaced by pleasure.

Frick asked, "You all right?"

Frack nodded, but he wasn't all right. He was lost in her blue eyes, his throat was frozen, and the touch of her hand was sending growth-inducing electricity to his groin. Like a witch character on TV who had electrified fingers. A good witch. A good-looking witch.

Diane said suggestively, "You are fine, aren't you?" Squeezing his thigh again. No surprise hop this time.

Frack nodded while squeezing that magic hand of hers. Like it shouldn't be going somewhere else right now, or maybe, that it should.

Ready to go, for several reasons, Diane withdrew her hand by sliding her nails up his leg toward his crotch. Before she got there, she scooted into Frack so he'd let her out. "I'm looking forward to being most appreciative when you succeed." That was enough. That was plenty. He was ready. She used that magic hand to retrieve an easy twenty from her purse and place it on the table. Standing,

99

she said, "See you both Friday." Then she took her smile, those nails, and her long legs past the antique cash register, back into the humidity, and over that rough sidewalk.

Back in her insulated car-world, the drive home gave Diane too much time to think about how the damn royal triangle was somehow dominating the triangle between her legs. She was lonely and had gone too long without a man in her bed. A man interested in her. The drama major came up with a name for this supposed TV sitcom of hers: *The Haunting of Diane Waters*. It seemed about right.

She'd lobby to get a handsome actor to play the lead. She'd play herself. And fuck Mike. He'd force him to watch take after take of her love scenes. She'd make a good actress, too. She had natural talent and plenty of old training, rusty or not. And if the director ordered her to practice to save time on the set, Frack would be more than happy to help her learn her lines. The wrong side of town sure had a way of offering new options.

The non-acting Dr. Waters had headed home to get a good night sleep, and to explain tomorrow's schedule to his disgruntled wife. He ended up sorting clothes for the weekend in a very empty house. Finished, he called Sandy. "Hi, honey."

"Hi, Daddy. What's up?"

"I'm home packing for your big day. How's everything?"

"Great. Everything's a go. I'm hanging out with Marcia and Tilley at the mall."

"Say hello for me. And look, I wanted to let you know that I'll probably be flying out early in the morning."

"One of your storms?"

"Of course. You know the deal. This could be the big

test we've been waiting for. I just wanted to let you know I'll make Friday evening, no sweat. Okay?"

"That's a lot to pack into one week."

"Believe me, I know. Your mother's already made that clear."

"Good luck, Daddy."

"Love you, honey. See you Friday."

"Love you, too."

After hanging up, Mike tried Diane, only to get her voicemail. He chose not to leave her another message—and now for the first time, understood the root of that word. Mess.

After a hectic day with the kids at school, Dee moseyed up to Clarke's pleasant blue home dressed in a coral sundress that showed some cleavage and some leg depending upon the breeze. His hot-date opened the screen door, entered, and the door announced her arrival with a slap. Easy and Hard were startled off the living room couch resulting in that characteristic puff of dust.

"I'm in the back," he announced from the backyard. Dee ignored looking left at the mess in the living room and made her way deeper toward the kitchen. She placed her sack on the light-yellow counter near the sink, before helping herself to some ice and some gin. The aroma wafting from the oven was wonderful and quickly displaced any surface irritation over that living room that was being treated like a shrine—albeit a dirty one. Her eyes swept over the calendar with all those X'ed-out days and the blue circle around Saturday—his big day.

Clarke heard the backdoor swing open and slap shut—closer but softer than the front's. With his sand-colored rattan chair angled toward the door, he admired her form

101

as she stepped across his weathered-white limestone block patio.

Kissing him on the back of the neck, she sat atop the matching chair with its faded red cloth seat insert. Designed to resist the humidity and the salt air, the material was doing a so-so job of it, like everything else on the island. Placing her drink on the circular glass rattan table between the seats, she slipped out of her sandals, folded her legs beneath her, melted back into the chair, and shared a happy-to-be-here-after-a-tiring-day smile.

Clarke admired Dee's foldable curves, thinking of her as a feminine version of a Swiss army knife. It would have been so easy to have included such a flexible tool in the caper, since her family was traceable to Jamaican pirates— he could use all the help he could get with this ambitious weekend plan. This, maybe a sign to include her, if he believed in signs. But he didn't.

"How was your day?" he asked.

"Long. It's always so lovely chasing those rascals," she delivered with whimsical sarcasm. "Yours?"

"Same old, same old. Reading at the fort." They chuckled over their well-patterned day.

His Bermuda shorts were presently hidden under his familiar-date apron that was covered by lots of black and white cats. "You hungry?" he ventured.

"I'm all yours."

"First things first." Tonight, he figured they'd enjoy a light supper and then spend some time pirating each other. It was in her blood, after all. Clarke took another sip and went to check the oven. After hearing the door slap shut, the cats followed him toward the fish. He noticed the sack on the counter, but since she hadn't mentioned it, he'd leave the mystery contents for later. "Dinner's ready."

102

"It smells good. What is it?"

"Sea bass and rice." Both loved fish and any kind of rice, as long as one or both were spicy. He spooned two portions onto plates with his oversized wooden spoon and fork set, grabbed two smaller dishes and a water bowl for his cats, and brought everything outside. Holding the door with his elbow, both cats followed the fish. The refreshing drinks would chase but never quite catch up to the spices, if he'd gotten the balance right. When they brought their dishes inside to soak in the stainless-steel sink, the cats remained outside to finish off their plates.

Done, turning his back to the counter, Clarke asked. "Okay, what's in the sack? I'll bite."

"That's the plan."

He said nothing.

With a mischievous smile, she delivered, "It's just a little present," in the same manner that the three stooges were famous for whenever they knew they'd be caught at something.

He knew that smile.

She snagged the sack, hugged him, and led him down the narrow hallway to the small front porch.

She shook the bag like it contained cat treats for humans.

"For me?" Maybe she was getting into the Halloween spirit early.

"Do you remember that show we watched last week on Egypt?"

"Of course." The show he knew he should have recorded. "Is this the DVD?"

"No, but I'm gonna let you pretend you're a man of prominence." She unfolded the top of the sack and pulled out a replica leafy crown befitting an ancient noble.

Replica in this case meant plastic from a costume shop.

Clarke accepted the crown and thought, *theme of the week*. It had a familiar smell he couldn't place.

"Grapes, just like the program," she added.

That was the smell. Clarke said, "If we take the sea route home from Egypt tonight, you'll get a chance to steal my treasure." Making good on her heritage.

Making good on spicing this not-so-innocent-any-longer street right up. Making good on this not-so-innocent-theme that was making Clarke feel that Dee would be able to see right through him—replicas and multiple women. Transparent. Transparent with his duplicities. Plural.

Dee moistened her lips and upped the ante with a soft, "You can start right now by fantasizing what a good servant girl I'd make. Then get lucky by having your way with me." She squeezed him with her arm around his waist.

"You've been drinking all day, haven't you?" he teased back. "You broke into the principal's locked liquor stash and been drinking while you graded all those papers."

"How'd you know? Were you the one hiding in the supply closet?" Her dark eyes were alive as they took in the man she loved.

They kissed, happy to have eaten the same spices for dinner.

"You found me out." The theme he was afraid of. How many others were going to find him out?

They hugged one-armed; the moment made more intimate when, in silence, they admired the vivid coral sky to the southwest. Bag in hand, Dee led him inside toward his crowning moment.

Clarke wondered whether she was going to put on last year's Halloween costume still hanging in the closet: that little maid thing with those black stockings and that white hand duster.

After the fun, spooning, Clarke realized Thursday was tomorrow. His demons had let him be during their fun, but now they returned. To get to sleep, he decided to count what was already pictured in his mind—priceless necklaces, rather than sheep.

CHAPTER 10

THE BIG DAY

THURSDAY AM

After seeing hurricanes travel unmolested in his dreams, Waters gave up on sleep around four. Grabbing his ready tablet on the bedside table, it awakened to show George still above seventy-five mph. Yes! Stronger, actually. Diane was turned the other way, breathing steadily. Maybe he could make it out without waking the sleeping lioness. When his feet met the floor, Diane said with an awake-voice, "You're really leaving, huh?"

"We've been around and around about this already. This is so predictable."

"I'll predictable you."

With her steaming, he retreated to the bathroom, shut the door, and ran water for his shave. This typical exchange brought into contrast that predictable was one thing, while being able to stop something from happening was entirely different. The very challenge, of course, he was facing with George.

As he nicked himself, he hazarded a guess that it could prove easier to alter George's course before ever making any progress with Diane. He sure hoped so.

As the Busters made their separate ways toward the

106

airfield over deserted roads, the sun peaked above the clear horizon. At the airport, their four cars found each other easily with the parking area all but empty. Clearing the commercial checkpoint with their NHC credentials, it was a good walk from there to the dusty-white, sheet-metal supply hangar. As it came into view, so did the long white plane sitting just beyond. The air was comfortably warm and the sky was cloudless, except for that thin line just above the horizon.

Stacy said, "This is such a beautiful morning; it's a good omen."

Klink responded, "You should know, you're the team's designated omen specialist." Then he turned toward Mike.

"You ready boss?"

"Yep," Mike responded. "There's plenty of daylight ahead. A perfect day for a perfect plan." He held his gaze east, as if he could see the massive thing.

Carla had her second cup of coffee in hand. "Yeah, what's not to like?"

Stacy cheered the team on. "Then let's do it, lady and gentlemen, seeing as we have a favorable wind at our backs."

"Time to make some history, I hope, at the risk of jinxing ourselves," Klink added. They walked toward the plane that looked so much longer than its pictures, and definitely bigger than the stubby-looking seaplane they would have used for the original surface-based plan. The large external radar pods in the rear, on the bottom and sticking out the front via that long nose, only exaggerated the size of it.

Carla said, "I sure hope we make good use of all of those."

Mike knew Carla was referring to the radars she'd be

controlling. But for him, it was that long needle-nose that was key. It was the plane's lightning rod. When it came down to it, that was the most important part of Fozzie, notwithstanding the engines and wings, of course. Lightning occurred frequently inside hurricanes. And more to the point, what most people were not aware of, planes were often struck by lightning inside hurricanes.

As they neared the steps, Mike checked for the characteristic burn marks on the nose. Either they'd been cleaned off, or this was Fozzie's maiden voyage for flying into a hurricane rather than around one.

Inside, Klink headed to the cockpit to begin his pre-flight check. Though both Mike and Klink were experienced pilots, they didn't get to practice in these huge planes as often as they would have liked. Mike's first task was to reacquaint himself with the locations of the controls. After a good look around, Fozzie's set up was identical to the other two Muppet hurricane hunters, as hoped.

McDonald and Banks headed astern, past their stations behind the cockpit, to double-check that all thirty bright yellow drums were aboard. When their count matched, they hooked them to the intricate hose system that would access them sequentially, making any unhooking unnecessary. Job done, they sat down at their own floor-to-ceiling control stations located on opposite sides of the center walkway. Small square windows on either side were letting light in. Sitting back to back, it was time to work the actual controls they'd learned from the training films they'd suffered through.

Faced with familiar controls, a new plane, plenty of chemical, his tight team, and a great candidate hurricane within reach, Mike was in his element. The lift in his mood rested kindly on his face, and was demonstrated by his sure, efficient movements. "I have a good feeling about today," he said to Klink, as he continued to test the expanse of controls surrounding him.

"Me, too," Klink answered. He was done with his pre-flight check. He looked at Waters. "This air-protocol will be safer, but I hope it doesn't turn out to be impossible for us to determine how much chemical is actually reaching the surface."

Mike, along with everyone else, was hoping they wouldn't have to fly too close to the ocean's surface to make sure their chemical wasn't just flying away in the wind. Waters adjusted himself in the co-pilot's seat. "You ready for this, Gustave?" using Klink's first name familiarly. If they were risking your lives together, it was time as any to be familiar.

Klink blinked his eyes and turned a smile toward his boss who had somehow learned his name. "Yep. Let's hope all our surprises are good ones today."

After Mike checked that the team was ready at their individual stations, he got everyone to exit the plane. The long white bird with the blue stripe running down its length sat imposingly behind them. The ends of each propeller were striped in red and blue, just like their t-shirts, thanks to Waters. Waters surprised everyone with their new red, white, and blue team caps. No expense was too great for the little-team-that-was-gonna. Waters was of the mindset that a team that dressed together, sank, swam or reached the Nobel podium together.

Moments later, someone from the hangar agreed to snap their pic using Mike's phone. The employee asked, "Where is everyone else?" He saw these hurricane hunters off all the time, and normally they carried a much larger crew.

"This is all we could scrounge up given those dangerous chemicals we're working with," Mike offered.

Beginning to lean away from the plane, the man said, "Well, this must mean you have a live one out there. Good luck with whatever's in those drums." He straight-armed the phone back to Waters, happy to leave.

Cleared by the tower, taxiing, and then rolling, the liftoff of the pregnant plane was incredibly gradual. In a wide, graceless bank, Klink guided the shaking Orion over the coast where that endless ocean was presently calm and inviting. The very opposite of what they would find once they reached George. The plane was anything but a fighter. Strength and carrying capacity were its strong points, not agility. Continuing to gain altitude and speed slowly, the ride smoothed out once they entered calmer air at altitude.

Stacy was waiting to test the chemical dispensing system, which would begin only after they'd passed the one-hundred-mile coastal limit. It would be bad PR for NHC, if they managed to sicken people along their own coast, bio-degradable or not.

The skeleton team of four hummed along in the plane in their matching t-shirts and caps. The men had short hair, or no hair in Klink's case. But the women boasted shoulder length hair. So, one brunette and one thick, grey ponytail had sprouted out the backs. After the initial system tests were completed, Mike reminded everyone to take something for motion sickness, if they hadn't already—everyone would be at-risk today. The two Busters who hadn't taken anything yet—Klink and Stacy—took meds with a swig from the bottled water they'd brought aboard.

110

Stacy was located on the starboard side behind Mike, while Carla was positioned on the port side behind Klink. Mike got everyone's attention by raising his voice. "I just wanted to say if I didn't say it back there, just how momentous this occasion is, regardless of how few know what we're up to."

Carla raised her voice to answer. "We're not carrying an atomic device, are we?"

Klink said, "That's what those two Orion decoy planes were doing back there, right? But our real atomic device, ladies, is Mike's brain."

"Damn, I would've picked a different part of my anatomy." As Waters said it, he turned and tried to spy Carla through the cockpit door. On the same wavelength, Carla leaned back and smiled at him. Klink was flying this leg.

Carla was responsible for operating the three different radars, and for deploying at different times, the Global Positioning System (GPS) dropwindsondes that would transmit back to them pressure, humidity, temperature, and wind data.

Stacy would dispense the anti-evaporative mix. When they crossed the one-hundred-mile limit, Waters announced, "Okay back there, you're a go to test the nozzles." Stacy crossed two fingers on her left hand, threw two switches in succession with her right, watched the green lights come on as they had earlier, and then opened the airflow control to #1 through #4, one at a time. All four nozzles measured unimpeded airflow compared to their known capacities.

Stacy announced, "Here goes nozzle #1." Flipping another switch on her console, everyone watched as red chemical was ejected by the nozzle located behind the port outside engine. Klink announced, "I see it!"

One at a time, Stacy proceeded through the other three, each of which was located behind a turboprop. The system was good to go; another hurdle passed.

WP-3Ds had flown countless hurricane hunting flights. So much so, that the plane's well-known specifications made it easy to plan out the logistical portion of a flight. The plane had an approximate flight limit of ten hours, give or take, depending upon altitude and wind conditions. How much time spent coming and going determined how much time they could spend in the eye. With eyewall heights capable of reaching ten miles, compared to the Orion's ceiling of five, they would be flying through rather than over George.

Stacy turned to eye the field of yellow, poison-labeled drums weighing down the tail-section. She didn't care for all those black and white skull-and-crossbones symbols one bit. Even though she knew the chemical was safe for them to touch and breathe, the sheer number of drums packed into that tight space, so close to her, was freaking her out a bit. She thought in terms of water. Water was safe, but it could drown you. She reminded herself not to look back that way. At least she was working near Klinky, which was the only place she really wanted to be. But with him up in the cockpit, he didn't have to look at that field of yellow metal. They were vibrating and humming back there like bees. And everyone knew bees stung. And she was allergic to bees. She hoped the color wasn't a sign, but literally in her bones, she knew it was.

When the plane finally stopped gaining altitude—which had kept everyone swallowing to clear their ears—at least the flight was nice and smooth up here. Klink knew they had now entered the autopilot, monotonous part of the trip. The amateur ornithologist began thinking, *More like a Meleagris Gallopavo (Florida's large wild turkey), than a Cathartes Aura (Florida's turkey vulture).* He had turkeys, food, on his mind, given the small breakfast he'd grabbed. He would have preferred the latter bird that could fly well, because he believed before the day was through, they'd need it. He knew this plane was solid, but only the floor had been reinforced to handle the additional weight of equipment and supplies—nothing had been done to strengthen it for hurricane force winds. Sometimes too much information wasn't good.

Plus, he was aware of the basic physics here. He hoped the additional ballast of those drums would help them slice through George's winds. Yes, it was harder to change the direction of a dumbbell than a piece of paper. But, once changed, the heavier item was more difficult to stop.

CHAPTER 11

KISSING THE OLD DIRECTION GOODBYE

Thursday! Dee had awakened early also to get herself to work, and was already in the shower when Clarke rolled out of bed. Needing a mirror that wasn't fogged up to shave, Clarke headed to the smaller half bath down the hall. Finishing quickly, he'd bike to the hotel and just shower there. Getting on his biking gear, he made sure he extracted the important sack from the linen closet before Dee exited from the bathroom.

The amateur thief brought the sack to the kitchen, stuffed a camouflaging apple and a granola bar into it as lunch props, then set the lunch sack in the pantry ready to go. Business taken care of, it was now time for water for coffee, though he could have used something stronger now that things were beginning. Three cups of coffee were what the doctor ordered when Dee was over, and his tried and true dirty-white coffee maker would crank those out. By the time Dee walked into the kitchen, Clarke was sipping his black coffee while hers waited on the counter. Together they downed some OJ and yogurt, before she grabbed her to-go mug of coffee and he his lunch. Heading to his skinny garage where he kept his old sun-faded maroon Peugeot, his black moped, and his blue bike, they both ignored all the boxes he no longer knew the contents of. When he hefted the wide door upwards, its three rectangular windows rattled in protest.

He turned back toward her and said, "Wish me luck," before pecking her on the lips.

"Good luck, love. I'll take some too." She headed toward her little Nissan Versa in the driveway, while he followed rolling his bike onehanded. The driveway was made of two rows of cement blocks embedded in the dense soil. Balancing her way down the right path, she hopped into her car, backed up and headed to work with her usual wave out the window. She stopped at the end of his not-so-innocent street, turned right, east, toward school, and just like that, Clarke had the distinct sense he had just kissed goodbye his old life. It felt a little dramatic, but it also felt true. Like true-crime.

He placed the sack and his book inside the saddlebags that rested on either side of the bike's rear tire, and off he went into the early morning chill with the distant sun low to his back.

The ride into downtown Hamilton would take fifteen to twenty minutes. Normally the trip would refresh him, but with all his nervous energy, he seemed to be only breaking even in that regard. As his legs peddled away, so did his thoughts. Bridging him all the way back to when he'd first started at the hotel, when he'd been looking for a job, no less a toe-hold for a career. And now look at him. He was smack in the middle of the biggest wedding the island had witnessed in years. The Princess had certainly hosted its fair share of big weddings. But for this one in particular, the vault would be opened later this morning. He would be one of two extracting the Divel from its precious charms. If he could have worked out some way to switch it this morning, this perfect crime could have taken place much earlier. But alas, that would raise too many issues with him never being alone with the thing.

Instead, the necklace would receive its usual cleaning and appraisal in preparation for its viewing tomorrow night at the rehearsal dinner. Everyone at the hotel wanted to see it. The history buffs of the group realized that in years gone by, ownership of such ostentatious jewelry told the tale of who really was of noble blood. If Clarke remembered correctly, the Divel had been traced back to King Charles III's possession before its trail was washed away by unsubstantiated rumors.

Present day, Benny had estimated the Divel to be worth well above ten million dollars US. This didn't seem much of a stretch, given that at its last official appraisal back when Dr. and Mrs. Waters were married, its value was half that.

Pedaling along the clean streets with the small cars and scooters whizzing by, he pondered how such an heirloom should have more likely proved to be a positive force in its owners' lives—providing them with monetary security, for instance. But instead, the review of the Waters heritage through the newspaper archives and word of mouth suggested just the opposite. Whether this was fact or a product of some reporter's drummed up sensationalism, who knew?

Regardless of any of this hocus pocus, Clarke remembered how the articles had raved about how ornate the necklace looked. Plus, legend maintained that no matter how good it looked on land, it was basically all but invisible in water. Something about the color of the diamonds and the way the light reflected off the filigreed white gold when in water.

After making his way passed the pastel-colored shops on his right and the variegated colors of the Harbour and all those small white boats on his left, the pink of the hotel became visible. Around to the service entrance, dismounting, he locked up his getaway bike. Done, he extracted the sack containing his all-important lunch and made his way under the camera that was suddenly annoying given his defection to the illegal team.

Feeling exposed with the incriminating evidence in his hand, he hustled up to the third floor where there was a room available to employees for changing and showering. Along the way, his eyes did an amateur's job of avoiding looking at every security camera. This was what it felt like to be behind enemy lines. He didn't like it and hustled toward the room that most others never bothered with— this, another key component of their perfect plan.

It wasn't helping that Thompson was probably watching his every step from the control room. Though it did help that he could be asleep. After making his way down the regal-colored hallway that felt tighter and less level somehow, he stood rigid in front of that spare room.

For a jury of his peers, Clarke rehearsed how he was just carrying his lunch into work. That's all.

So far, not so good.

He was sweating in more ways than one. As he fumbled his master keycard out, Benny's thick voice reminded him, unhelpfully, *In for a penny, in for a pound*.

He held the plastic card over the slot. He could still take the fake home. The prop. The worthless piece of junk jewelry. That's all it was. A prank.

Abruptly, the card slid through the strip, as if mother nature—gravity—was weighing in on this momentous decision. That small full-steam-ahead green light appeared. He slipped in, heard the door click shut, and took advantage of the moment to slump against the solid

117

door. His heart wanting out of his chest.

There were no cameras in here. He pushed off the door, opened the small closet, and stashed his lunch up top amongst all those extra blankets and pillows.

There wasn't much in this room. Two double beds, a TV, a desk with paper supplies, a coat closet where he was able to keep extra clothes for himself, and the fully stocked bathroom.

Shower time.

When Clarke stepped out, he dressed in his blue slacks, white shirt and blue blazer uniform and exited the room with a stride that was far more composed than when he'd snuck in. Just another day. Except today. When Tuttleberry gave the word, he would play host to the genuine article.

Clarke did a so-so job of trying to distract himself with the daily humdrum security issues. After repeatedly checking his watch, after late-morning came and went, Tuttleberry finally summoned him and Thompson to his office.

His heartbeat reminded him this was it.

Together, they received the keys from Tuttleberry to the safety deposit boxes inside the vault.

Before he knew it, they were standing inside the vault and Clarke was fiddling with all those keys. They had to try combinations by trial-and-error before both boxes were unlocked. This was an integral part of the double-tier unlocking process that protected the Divel, since no one knew the exact keys beforehand.

Thompson was excited as Clarke to see the real thing. Under the auspices of the vault cameras, Clarke hinged up the rectangular metal lid, took out the tousled red velvet pouch that reportedly contained the charm hunt instructions, and spied the other red velvet pouch resting underneath.

Around the bottom pouch that was supposed to be holding the Divel inside, there were four items situated at the four compass headings: a large rusty nail, a rounded piece of smoothed wood— maybe part of an oar, a map, and a long-legged plastic bird. These had to be the protective charms, though they looked rather ordinary to Clarke. They were so unremarkable, his dad came to mind. He'd been a collector of junk.

Clarke reached out to touch the rusty nail that might have been from some famous shipwreck, he guessed, before snapping back his hand as if shocked.

Thompson flinched backwards and lost his balance against the wall of lockboxes. Here were the two security professionals caught on tape for a jury of Clarke's peers, apparently repelled by the famed necklace's defensive charm system.

"Just kidding, Thompson. Just kidding. Divel humor, my good man."

"You got me there. They say those things are cursed."

Clarke knew they said the Divel was cursed, not the charms. The charms were supposed to be good. But it was no matter. Anything that encouraged people to stay away from this box could only help at this point.

Clarke opened the second pouch, reached in, slid out a hinged box, and opened the lid upwards. There it was!

The triangular necklace was dominated by ornate white gold and all those diamonds, just like his replica. As they both gawked at its magnificence, Clarke thought again about how it was too bad the switch couldn't be made right here right now. But Thompson hadn't been brought in for a third, because Benny had feared that too many people meant too many lips. And loose lips sank perfect crimes just like ships, apparently.

Clarke pointed out to Thompson which box the replica was in as compared to the one they'd unlocked for the real McCoy—just in case Thompson needed to know.

With fingers thick with too many issues, Clarke inched out the Divel from its indentation and away from those charms. Yes, the workmanship was magnificent. His arms, his fingers, something, was charged, but regardless, he was pleased with its resemblance to his replica.

Far away in Florida, the small vector arrows on the NHC screens displayed George's abrupt course shift. It had been meandering on a westerly course forever, but those arrows had just reoriented themselves to a west by northwest direction.

Tucking the Divel back in, Clarke and Thompson escorted the entire lockbox to a secure room for the necklace's cleaning and appraisal. Along the way, cameras tracked the trio's progress.

While they waited for the appraiser to arrive, while they guarded the thing, Clarke unfolded the thick paper of the wedding day instructions to peek at the itinerary. As the thick paper that had been creased for three decades resisted his efforts, his amateur criminal's mind turned to cats and curiosity. He chuckled, laughing away his own clumsiness. Would Hard and Easy have had enough sense to steer clear of all this? Yes.

Thompson looked at him funny.

Clarke covered with, "Don't you think it's a little funny that people actually say this thing is cursed. I haven't been for-real shocked yet — OW!" He snatched his hand back again.

"That's not funny."

"You want to touch it? Here."

"No."

CHAPTER 12

WE'RE GOING IN!

Mike closed his tablet, placed it on the floor beside him, and announced to Klink after hundreds of miles of flat ocean had slipped beneath them, "George's vectors just shifted to the northwest." He mumbled to himself under the wash of vibration all around them, "The damn thing'll probably keep turning in that direction," bringing to mind Carla's joke about planning an outdoor activity.

"You say something?" Klink asked.

"Just that I'm a lousy forecaster, which is why I'm doing this for a living."

Ahead on the left, Mike took in the tall cloud formation. He announced through the headsets, "Let's look alive back there. We'll be introduced to George, shortly." Carla and Stacy's eyes popped open from their naps. Their odometers read: 1187 miles. So, it would be approximately twelve hundred miles back. Leaving them six hundred miles to play chicken with George.

Or in terms of hours: three hours out, three back, so three to do what they needed to do within the eye. Approaching the mammoth storm from the southwest, the plane's radars were now faithfully capturing reams of atmospheric data.

Klink angled the plane eight degrees north of east to intersect the towering portside wall of clouds. Ahead, multiple cloud banks were being lit up from within like neon lights by streaks of lightning.

Mike's alert mind fiddled with how the frequency of the flashes could almost be made to fit with Morse code— Keep Away, in hurricane-speak.

Mike clicked his harnesses closed, Klink followed suit, and Mike announced, "Okay, ladies, time to tighten your belts back there." Stacy and Carla swiveled around to face their consoles, locked their seats in place, before cinching their harnesses tighter.

Faced with his informal readiness checklist, Mike now remembered
to turn the lights on in the cockpit as high as they would go. One of the lessons he'd learned the hard way, and yet another example of the difference between book knowledge and practical experience. When, not if, Fozzie was struck by lightning on the needle-nose, the flash would blind the pilots if the lights were low. That said, with it being dark to the portside and brighter to the starboard, any normal pilot would be heading right. Mike knew neither he nor Klink qualified on that score at the moment.

With the rain bands tracking around the eye in their characteristic counter-clockwise direction, Klink directed the Orion to penetrate those clouds by coming in from the same direction, lessening the wind speed relative to the plane. Unfortunately, this practical strategy could not protect them from the ever-present and ever-dangerous wind shear, the abrupt updrafts and downdrafts inside those flickering rain bands.

Klink tracked along the outer band now clocked at eighty-nine mph. The cloud system was impressive, but by using radar, Carla was able to direct Klink toward the thinnest section of clouds. At precisely four thousand feet,

Klink sliced into the southern wall. Not too high, but equally important, not too low. The toy plane with the toy name immediately received a noticeable boost from George's winds.

With the increase in both the number and pitch of Fozzie's creaking metal joints, Stacy stole a peek at all those large, brightly colored, chemical-filled metal bees she'd been doing a great job of ignoring. Something induced her to say a prayer, because quite frankly, the public sector wasn't known for the best workman or workmanship when it came to accepting low-bid contracts.

"Hang on!" Klink shared through Stacy's headset.

Lightning slashed the sky to their left. Then those lashing elements and the constant shaking made the small team in a small plane realize just how vulnerable they were, if they hadn't realized it already.

Forewarned, the plane that used to be able to fly dropped big-time, leaving their stomachs near the ceiling.

Then Act II commenced when rained pelted the windshield, forcing Mike to switch the wipers on high. Really high. If they'd been driving in a Florida hurricane, they'd be sitting on the side of the road to wait the storm out.

Cutting the jostled plane more and more to port, Klink finished slicing through the first of the three large rain bands. The pressing grays and white flashes of lighting were constants now, as was the shaking yoke in Klink's hands.

A brilliant flash at the nose of the plane sent hands up reactively. But it was too little and definitely too late, though the bright cockpit lights had actually made it better than it would have been.

Mike reacted, Wow!?" as he sightlessly grabbed onto the second yoke to steady himself.

Klink shouted, "We're going in!"

Stacy clenched the side of her seat with her hands. Back in tranquil Florida, no one had said anything about screaming pilots.

Hail piled on.

Then like a switch, it all stopped.

Stacy breathed to Carla in a high voice, "I hope this means we reached the eye."

Carla looked at the green-tinted radar screen and said optimistically, "Here comes number two."

While George shook the plane and the plane shook everything including speech, Stacy managed, "I'd rather be in a solid pew than a thin tube of metal."

Carla leaned back in the aisle and shared, "I'm happy and scared at the same time. Weird, right?"

Stacy's "yep" came back broken up with multiple syllables.

"We're being shaken, not stirred, like my favorite martini," Carla said. Neither one laughed at the good joke.

Stacy answered, "Next trip I'm bringing earplugs and gas masks. Live and learn. I hope."

Huge raindrops pelted the plane. Everyone's stomach was left near the floor when an updraft jerked the plane to forty-eight hundred feet.

Stacy swallowed air to clear her ears, then turned a dial to increase the cool air blowing on her head.

Carla said, "Here goes nothing," as she twisted a dial, pressed a button four times, deploying more dropwindsondes to go forth to collect more data for later analysis. Shoulder straps snapped taut when the plane

125

dropped five hundred feet. Then it leveled off just long enough for the crew to get their hopes up, before plummeting again. Both rear passengers snatched at the stash of plastic bags under their desks. Hearing them crinkle open, before using them to lose their breakfast.

After the rain let up, Klink glanced out his window toward the props. Doing a double-take. *That's not possible.* His right arm pointed to where it was most needed, across his body. The words, "We've lost an engine," were shaken out of him.

The closest propeller was sure as hell stopped, because those red and blue stripes on the prop were clear as a dark day. Given the press of the discovery, Klink ground his molars together until there was the tiniest crunch in his mouth. *This is how it ends,* he admitted. We're going to die because we had to take the new plane. The untested plane. The plane they were forced into using after being forced into this airborne plan. He wanted to see Stacy, unforced. He wanted to say goodbye to his kids. *Climatologist abandons post, crew lost at sea: Story at 6.* That's all he needed.

They could survive with three props. Two even, in calm air. One, if empty or close to the coast. But they didn't qualify on any of those accounts. He spit out a tiny piece of grit from the tip of his tongue, as good an expression as any about of all of this, never mind the broken tooth.

Partly due to the loss of one engine, the next change of wind caused the plane to lose its mind and snap downward. Klink and Waters pulled on their yokes, fighting against the death spiral. Sound and unsound molars clenching tight, as both pilots threw their weight and muscle behind truth, justice, and the American way. When the plummeting ceased, Klink increased the lateral turn rate to finish cutting through the second band. When he feared a glance, the altimeter read a low three thousand feet.

The rain stopped, but soon returned when they entered the third band. There was less lightning here—which should have been good— but that made it darker.

Klink's tongue fiddled with the tooth that felt different, that felt wrong, like this flight. They had volunteered for this, when the weather had been pristine back in Florida. Idiots, or Nobel prize winners? *Do you have to be alive at the time of winning?* the crazy question came to him out of the shaking greyness.

In back, both women were retching into their plastic baggies.

As if George was convinced they had passed their eye entrance exam, or maybe more to the point, he'd played enough with his newest toy plane, Fozzie broke through the thinnest rain band into a shockingly serene, blue sky. Everyone seemed to have forgotten about the eye. Thank God for the eye.

The relief was measurable, as four bodies relaxed back into their seats.

Mike turned his head to peer over his left shoulder. "You girls all right back there?"

Both were wiping their mouths. Carla sputtered first, "That was bad."

Stacy shared, "We both lost our lunch. And we didn't eat lunch."

"Too much info ladies," Klink said, since he had no intention of sharing anything about the tooth his tongue kept fiddling with.

Klink looked out to check the inoperable engine, before guiding the heavy plane upward away from all that water. Not only were they heavier than a normal hurricane hunter, they now had less power. Releasing their chemical would improve that balance, as would restarting that engine within the eye's more normal atmospheric conditions. He was hoping that both would take place before they risked the trip back out.

Carla announced, "I might need another bag."

Stacy answered, "How 'bout new pilots."

Klink looked at the altimeter: thirty-four hundred feet, as the cumbersome plane leveled off above the choppy water below.

Carla unlocked her chair and swiveled to look at Stacy. Stacy put words to the sentiment that seemed to be vibrating between them. "Who said these big hurricane hunter flights are a piece of cake?"

Carla leaned her head sideways toward the cockpit, "Stupid smart people, that's who."

With the plane clear of the inner eyewall, Stacy began another test of her connections by throwing four toggle switches. Only three pulses responded. The nozzle behind the interior port engine that was no longer working, was no longer working.

"Nozzle 2 isn't functional," she announced to everyone. I'm turning it off in case of blow-back." All she needed was to fill the plane with red chemical, rather than George's eye, after leaving those needed-or-not gas masks back in Florida.

"I second that!" Klink yelled too loudly.

Everyone heard Mike respond, "Okay. If three is what we've got, three'll have to do. Three nozzles then." The new team mantra. "It'll take us longer to empty the drums, if we have enough time to empty the drums…" After the anxious moment's pause, Mike chattered on, "I hope there isn't a pattern here. Three engines. Three nozzles. Scientists love patterns, you know. They make things predictable. Even unwanted things, like having four crew, not three."

Waters then turned the cockpit lights off. Saving them for the optimistic trip out. Then he offered, "I've got the problem, I mean the plane. Take a breather."

Klink let his arms go limp. With them numb-tired from fighting the yoke all the way through, he said, "I wish my mouth was this numb." Waters asked, "What?" unsure what he meant.

"Nothing, Chief."

Waters decreased engine speed, lowering the pitch of those three engines, as he guided Fozzie closer to the water's dark surface they had so desperately needed to reach today. Less distance to their target meant less chemical would be lost to the wind. But the release wouldn't begin until they put a little more distance between themselves and that trailing eye-wall. Too close to that edge, and George's winds might suck the chemical away. Waters altered the plane's path to run SW to NE, essentially perpendicular to George's present course. He would sweep back and forth, getting ever closer to the NW quadrant, until the drums were empty, or they caught up to the far eye-wall.

Leveling off, Waters said, "The wave heights are substantial here. Probably twenty- to thirty-footers. Too high for the original surface-roll protocol."

Stacy shared, "I thought you'd like to know that our chemical deployment time has been extended by eight percent. The remaining three nozzles have to divide the fourth's original twenty-five percent between them." It didn't sound like much, but with one engine down, who knew what would turn out to be the limiting factor for their first field-trial. Now far enough into the eye, Banks turned back to her controls to release several more probes for the pre- versus post-chemical comparisons.

Waters steadied the plane. "Okay, McDonald, let 'em rip." Everyone watched the red streams spread out behind the plane from those three working nozzles.

The white caps below began absorbing the red mist like cherry juice atop ice. The further they flew from the trailing eyewall, the smaller the wave tops became. In this section, it would have been possible to deploy their rolls on the surface. Challenging, but possible.

Stacy monitored the three nozzles that seemed to be working perfectly. But even with this going well, she said to Carla, "I could use a stiff drink."

Up front, in the relative calmness, Klink stood up to straighten his cramped legs. "I'm going aft to stretch." Hand-grasping his way down the aisle to Stacy's station, he leaned against her chair and shared some bottled water. Putting his hands on her tense shoulders, he began to rub. "How you doing, kid?"

From behind them, Carla said, "Klink, look at this, will you?"

He stepped over and steadied himself against the back of her chair.

She offered, "This might be storm-related, or there really could be something else out here. What do you make of it?"

"Can't tell for sure. Has it moved?"

"No."

"Just keep your eye on it, okay?"

130

Meanwhile, Mike was sweeping the plane back and forth so their red chemical could do its thing with gravity.

Klink shared water with Carla, then turned back toward Stacy.

She smiled back at Klinky.

He slid a sneaky hand down her side to grab an opportunistic body part.

A little late, she pushed his hand away. "Distracting me like that." She rechecked the readouts for the expected flow rates. "Everything looks good here, Mike. How's it looking from there?"

"I see lots of red. Red is good," Mike answered back.

Quiet Carla was busy twisting a knob and pressing a button, twice, as she deployed two more dropwindsondes.

Klink started in on Stacy's shoulders again. Under the influence of his fingers, under the wash and vibration of the three props, Stacy emitted, "Mmmmmm," letting her brown eyes melt closed for a moment.

"Klink. Take another look, would'ja?" Carla said.

He turned, bent over and gazed at the nearly empty screen. "If I had to guess, I'd say an unknown weather aberration or, another plane is sizing up George. I hope Fozzie's new radar is working." He straightened up. "Time to relieve Waters."

Just inside another hour, Carla said to everyone, "We're past the midpoint of the eye. Meaning that approximately half the square footage of the eye's surface had been covered." From their research data, that was the minimum percentage necessary to have an effect on the storm. "The rest is gravy."

Stacy chimed in so everyone could hear. "The drums are three-quarters empty. At this rate, we'll be done inside half an hour, leaving us an extra half hour to get out of here."

The waves near the center of the eye looked to be less than ten feet. Mike said to Klink, "Our surface protocol was doable here. I sure hope this air protocol proves effective." It sounded like he was going to say more, but didn't.

After a brief delay, Klink answered, "I hope you're right. Either way, we both know the data won't lie. I'll be right back. Potty break time." He stood, stretched, and headed aft again.

As Klink cleared the window, Mike looked out that side and noticed a sharp reflection above the port wing-of-bad-luck. Klink heard him say something about a reflection, but wasn't sure. Reflections at sea were fairly common and were often due to wave tops or schools of fish.

Klink stopped behind Stacy, squeezed the back of her neck, then whispered, "We've never done it in a plane before. There's plenty of room back there behind all those drums." He pointed, just in case she'd forgotten where the field of yellow metal lay.

"Some women get turned on by chem—"

"Klink, get up here!" he heard Mike shout. "Carla, you got anything on those radars of yours?"

With a little shove, Stacy helped Klink toward the cockpit, and away from all that unfriendly chemical.

Carla answered Mike, "I've had a blip. It's come and gone. And now it's back." She turned toward Mike but couldn't see him with Klink in the way. "If I had to guess, I'd say it's another hurricane admirer."

Klink reached the cockpit, then looked where Mike was pointing out Klink's window. Klink's tone was serious when he decided, "It doesn't look to be in the air, does it. But you know how crazy perspective can look from a plane."

Mike moaned, "That stupid-wing-of-bad-luck."

Klink heard Stacy ask, "What's happened to the wing? First an engine, now a wing."

Mike spat out, "Impossible! It can't be."

Carla answered, "There's something there all right. The signal's clean." Mike brought the plane around. As he did so, both pilots saw the glint appear above the good wing.

With all the supplies they'd brought, Waters hoped out loud, "Did anyone bring binoculars?"

Stacy answered, "We have some in the back." When she unclipped herself, and faced all those drums, this was not her field of dreams. She scurried back there, grabbed the binoculars from their cubby, and made it back through the obstacle course without being stung.

Mike focused the field-glasses, then commanded, "Klink, take us down, close and personal."

Klink asked, "Closer than this?" They were flying fairly low.

"Yep. Down, boy." While bracing himself with one hand out, still looking through the glasses, Mike said, "Stacy, do me a favor and cut the chemical. Most of it's out, anyway."

Maybe they didn't need more. Maybe Mike wanted to see more clearly. Or, maybe they shouldn't be testing whether their chemical was actually safe on innocent bystanders. This was too many maybes over an open sea, in the middle of a hurricane, where no one needed anyone maybes, Klink believed with his bad tooth weighing in.

Klink angled them toward all those reaching waves,

as the chemical ceased flowing behind them.

The pilots peered at the reflection just above the wing, watched it disappear behind it, before reappearing under the wing.

Closer, the pieces of this most unwanted jigsaw puzzle were now surreally displayed to Mike.

A plane?!

A boat.

Correction, boats.

Rolls of something.

Then it hit Mike like a ton of water.

"Oh-my-god!"

He was watching someone carry out his protocol. Shivers shot through him. Shifting his right hand to the yoke—maybe to steer, or more likely, to steady himself—he foisted the glasses toward Klink. "Tell me you're seeing what I'm seeing?"

Klink took a look two-handed. "I can't believe it."

Both ladies appeared in the cockpit, grabbing for those glasses.

Mike thought, *security breach.* Someone had gotten hold of his plan.

But how had they beaten them out here?

Stacy counted out loud. "One, two, three boats." One plane. Chemical rolls, stretched out beyond the plane. The waves were giving the boats some difficulty in this section. She lowered the binoculars and said with measure in her voice, "Fact is stranger than fiction."

Carla took the glasses, before producing a subdued, "It's our twins down there."

Stacy said to everyone, "This is definitely not a good

134

sign."

Carla asked, "Bermuda Triangle anyone?" Though she didn't sound too positive about it.

Mike recognized the one plane in the world that could have pulled this off. The same plane they would have used. A turboprop Shinmaya US-2—the only commercial plane in the world designed to land upon open ocean.

The lettering on its side looked Chinese to him. Literally.

Mike felt like a man who had dated a woman, broken up, only to find her dating a friend the very next day. Violated. He had put a lot of sweat and time into developing that plan from scratch. Someone, somehow, had gotten hold of it. Then the science part produced admiration in his voice. "They solved the microfilm weight problem."

In a clear, calm voice, Mike heard close to his ear, "If they're intervening, and we're intervening, who knows what will happen, or why?" Stacy couldn't have said it any more succinctly.

Klink muttered, "Stacy's right. Who knows how much chemical has actually been delivered?"

Carla said too loudly, "Overkill."

Klink kept the yoke turned in, continuing the slow circle above their twins.

Carla said, "I feel like waving, but I'm not sure why."

Mike knew of many examples in the literature where competitive research had produced situations like this. Sometimes you knew about the other team, and sometimes you didn't. And all too often, circumstances turned nasty.

Then it dawned on Mike how they'd been beaten to the show. He'd waited overnight—though the stolen plan was a different matter. Had someone at NHC sold them out? Had one of the Busters sold him out?

As they circled, as that trailing eyewall drew closer, the waves grew in height.

Klink said, "The waves are getting larger."

"Get them on the radio," Mike said. "They've got to get out of there."

Klink fiddled with the radio and hailed them on an international SOS frequency. No answer. He tried other frequencies. "Their entire crew might be in those boats, just like we were going to do to keep the weight down given those heavy rolls."

Yes, all those shiny sheets were running toward the horizon, but there were plenty of gaps because of all that wave action. The undulations were also rocking the white plane, and as if to emphasize the point, one boat left the surface and came down with a light-flickering splash.

Mike considered whether releasing more chemical might drive their alter-egos back into the plane. But with his luck, tomorrow's headline would read: *Sore-Loser Climatologist Poisons International Competitors!?*

If the eyewall came much closer, Mike knew the squat plane would have difficulty getting airborne.

Carla said, "It looks like they're turning back."

Mike believed in the international community of scientists. So even though they were thieves down there, they were brother thieves, and soon to be in trouble.

The Busters watched those small boats and that fat plane grow seemingly smaller, as the big ocean became more active around them. Rushing back, two of the small boats careened off of one another before bumping into the mothership.

Once the Busters came back around, they surmised that two ant-people must have made it inside. At least they hoped they were inside, with only one boat left with someone in it. Klink tried the radio again.

A voice responded. Not an English voice.

"Is that Chinese?" Klink asked.

Stacy said, "Yes." Her cat Ri responded to Chinese from the TV. She didn't know why.

Then they heard, "SOs. SOs. SOs." Though the accent was strange, the distress in that male voice was clear.

Mike's stomach was curling with the possible human tragedy unfolding right below them. Close but far away. More dispassionate, the scientific portion of Mike's brain had to give them credit for solving the engineering problem the Americans hadn't solved yet. He figured it would be the cutting-edge Chinese if anyone, because of the resources they were committing to mitigate the effects of the typhoons in the Pacific. And now look, this might be there reward.

They all peered out a starboard side window as an orange dot jumped into the large waves toward the plane.

Klink repeated the obvious, "They've got to get out of there." As team-lead, Mike thought, *What about us?*

A wave carried the dot-person into the bobbing plane.

Minutes passed, as they all watched that final crew member struggle to get aboard.

Then those four strong Mercedes engines kicked on. The sight of the plane beginning to move filled Mike with hope. He was very familiar with that plane. If four engines could get them out of there, those four were it. Amazingly quickly, the plane pulled away from that sea of chemical rolls and those small boats.

Waters looked on with his grim mouth and bunched eyebrows.

Klink cheered them on. "Go, go, go." Emphasizing each word with his upper body.

As the seaplane neared liftoff, a taller wave smacked its bottom from the side. Fortunately, this was a flying boat, so there weren't any flimsy pontoons to get knocked off. The design of the plane handled the crest of the twenty-footer easily. But when the trough of the wave appeared, the plane went airborne. And with it not up to minimum airspeed yet, the nose dove into the next crest like a swimmer diving under. A huge splash of sun-splintering spray created a rainbow. When it cleared, the plane had come to an abrupt halt back on the surface. All four props chopping and slicing water to a halt.

The next crest caught the plane the wrong way, turned it sideways, and tipped one wing into the water. Carla brought her hands to her face. The plane was now leaning to port.

Everyone remained stone still and stone quiet.

When Klink moved again, he sent out a Mayday Mayday Mayday triple.

It made Mike think of their new mantra. Three rain bands. Three nozzles. Three Chinese boats. Three letters in SOS. And now Mayday triplets.

The problem was only an identical airboat could get in there to rescue the trapped plane. And if one tried, it could easily suffer the same fate.

Except for the wash and vibration of their three engines, it was ghostly quiet inside Fozzie.

Klink said quietly toward Mike, "It feels like we're leaving comrades on the battlefield, something you never do." He swallowed and kept swallowing, seemingly to control his emotions. When he next looked over at Mike, he offered, "*We* need to get out of here."

The ladies reluctantly left the cockpit to return to their stations. When they got there, Stacy mentioned, "If we manage to get out of here with only three engines, I'm going to adopt a cat endemic to China and name him George."

Mike tried to restart that motionless prop. No dice— not a good day to be in a plane inside of George. He glanced downward at the defenseless plane floating on the surface, before forcing himself to look away. "I've got the plane, Klink." His voice was sick with grief. As he steered the Orion away, the sluggishness of the big plane suggested it too preferred not to leave any comrades behind. Never mind, one engine down, it might be reluctant to take on George, period.

Everyone strapped in.

Mike remembered to turn the cockpit lights back up.

Carla began to sniffle.

Stacy heard Carla sniffling, which induced her to say another prayer for their trapped comrades.

Saying goodbye to this seductively serene blue sky, they sliced into the innermost band. The ride instantly became rougher and much darker. Vicious rain and lashing wind soon opposed Fozzie's escape back toward truth, justice and the American way. The storm might not have been any worse, but the ride was thrown this way and that with less ballast and one engine down.

Minutes before, Mike had been rooting for the Chinese. Now he was rooting for their rattling plane to hold it together. Rain, wind, and lightning became everything, until their stomachs reminded them that the elements were not everything. When the plane settled in-between an updraft and downdraft, Carla released two more GPS probes.

Fozzie finally punched through this band that seemed wider than before. The rain and shaking stopped, the altitude stabilized, and Klink took over for Mike. Klink brought the plane higher before puncturing the next wall of lightning and rain on their starboard side.

With the chemical part of the trial done—or overdone—Stacy had nothing to do but hold onto her seat. When her belt worked itself loose from the constant jarring, she cinched it tighter.

Encircling the plane, bright flashes blinked all around them before there was a brilliant flash outside the cockpit.

When a downdraft ripped at the planes' starboard side, it twisted Fozzie toward the ocean's surface. The Orion's massive wings were seemed defenseless against the shifting air currents, even as both pilots worked on over-correcting the twist. Losing altitude too quickly, Fozzie finally eased back toward the horizontal, as rain slacked off in this section. Ten long minutes later, Fozzie abruptly punched through to serene blue sky. Both men whooped. Mike cheered, "We're through!" as if the women couldn't see the sunshine out their small windows.

With the ocean's surface only twenty-two-hundred feet below, both pilots coaxed the underpowered plane up to a safer altitude.

Altitude improved, Mike took over and turned Fozzie for home.

The plane remained incredible quiet, though it was filled with a white noise hum, just like the trip out. Mike lowered the cockpit lights. He knew they'd been lucky not to have used Plan A. With the long uneventful trip ahead, he remembered the conference in China last year, so maybe that was the connection. Attempting to make himself feel better, he considered whether they might have developed the plan independently. But in the end, it was too much of a stretch. Given the likely connection, he was left feeling responsible, like when he'd watched new-driver Sandy drive the car out of the driveway right into her first accident.

Sandy.

He had a wedding to get to.

Tonight through tomorrow, data collection would continue. And at some point, analysis would begin. But he had Sandy's wedding to get to. He'd completely forgotten.

One hour after the Busters survived their escape, the incoming data suggested George had strengthened by five miles per hour and turned three degrees farther north.

At two hours, those figures were seven mph, and another degree north.

At three hours, by the time battle-tested Fozzie approached the Florida coast, another four mph and another click north.

When they landed, Waters contacted the NHC to double-check their data.

"The damn thing is strengthening and swinging north," he shared with Klink, who was too tired or too depressed to move from his seat.

Waters was betting sure as heck—refusing to say right as rain—that when he checked the latest multi-colored, triangular probability cones, Bermuda would be in the bounds of one of them. Maybe even centered.

Klink looked over. "You sure?" he managed, after a tired delay.

"Yep."

Waters heard a new rattle and looked behind them.

The women were holding up the cockpit door. Carla offered, "Let's all get some sleep, then the three of us can dive into the data tomorrow morning. While you," as she looked at Mike, "need to vamoose to a wedding."

"Vamoose is right. George might close Bermuda's airport."

Waters took notice of the needle nose on the way out. Sure enough, the characteristic burn marks were there. Fozzie had been initiated.

Overnight, all four Busters slept fitfully. Waters woke early, and just before he walked out his door, he'd had the strange compulsion to move the guns in the house.

Predictably, he detoured his Jeep toward the NHC first, trying, but failing to surprise the other Busters who were already there.

The pattern of the data was consistent. George had strengthened, quickened, and stayed on its North-Northwest swing.

What had gone wrong?

Waters cursed that the other team had added all that unknown chemical. They had a confounded trial. What a waste.

Aiming his workhorse vehicle toward the airport, the sense permeated him that during this time when he had had the most to gain, he'd managed to lose the most instead.

And making this all worse, was that they might have even entered Project Storm Fury territory. Despite this, he needed to enjoy Sandy's big day if he could.

CHAPTER 13

DINNER RESERVATIONS

Occupying Thompson's favorite seat in the warm monitor room, Clarke's hands and feet were tapping away. He never liked being cooped up in here, and today, his skin was crawling with nerves. His eyes swept over the row of HD monitors giving different views of the hotel, but his mind wasn't paying any attention. He was going over the details of their plan.

The timetable for this weekend was flowing like molasses, and even that didn't feel at home here anymore the way it had to be imported onto this island like so many other things. He was getting ready to export something, including probably, eventually himself. Of course, those imported true-crime books had more than warned him that it was the criminals who took the shortcuts that got caught. He turned the A/C two degrees colder. When that wasn't enough, he lowered it another notch. Now he could see why Thompson fell asleep in here—that is, if he needed to find another reason.

The Divel had been cleaned and appraised, confirming what Benny had maintained all along. It was worth a cool ten mil US at this point. Soon to be a hot ten. Though with anything this unique, the appraisal really functioned as an estimate. Ultimately, the worth of any rare gem was determined by the discerning eye and the depth of the pocketbook of the buyer.

Clarke was more than ready for tonight's dog-and-pony show, when the real thing would make its first public appearance in decades. The rehearsal dinner was set for seven. Yes, again he replayed how it was just too damn bad that he hadn't been able to make the switch, as close as he'd been to it. And it was going to be too bad again tonight. But, if he tried to make it happen, it would likely come back to bite him in front of that jury of his peers:

Yes, I wasn't sure why Clarke asked me to go do that just as the Divel was on its way to the dining room—you all know Clarke (pointing), but now it seems clear....

No, he had identified the time immediately after the wedding as the weak link. The stretch of time when the newlyweds and the limelight were going one way, and he and the Divel would go another. Perfect.

He'd add a tie to his uniform tonight so he looked spiffy. Unfortunately, it was all too easy to see that nice-looking picture, hanging thirty years hence in the post office. A good-looking WANTED poster because of that tie.

Tuttleberry had already confided to Clarke that he might be too nervous to handle tonight's little ceremony—that Clarke might have to do it. So, the amateur fox might actually find himself carrying the chicken to its owners. More temptation.

Regardless, Saturday's agenda was more important than tonight's.

Sunday's too, of course, when he and Benny and the Divel would be leaving on their brief "fishing excursion" to the Caymans in Benny's private plane. There, they would split any fish they'd caught, 50/50.

PART III

THE WEDDING

CHAPTER 14

STORM WARNING

FRIDAY

Everyone involved with Sandy's wedding left Miami on the nine-twenty flight out. Everyone except Dr. Waters, who missed it. He'd be on the twelve-twenty, arriving at Bermuda International at three thirty-five. Since it was a short cab ride to the hotel, the six o'clock rehearsal was still easily makeable.

As Waters boarded his commercial flight, he knew it was too bad the Busters couldn't have just dropped him off in Bermuda. They'd been in the vicinity. At two fifty-five Bermuda time, Waters heard the pilot of the Air Tran jet announce, "We will be experiencing some turbulence as we enter Bermuda airspace."

Waters chuckled out loud, "Turbulence, all right."

The prim woman on the other side of the aisle looked at him like he was crazy. Maybe he had gone a little crazy in the last twenty-four hours. Who could blame him? *Tammerie, that's who,* he thought.

With him entering Sandy's wedding-space, it was time to put all this out of his mind. All those coral shallows surrounding the island sure looked beautiful, just like they had thirty years ago.

147

Dr. Waters managed to meet up with his family at the pastel pink, five-star Princess Hotel just after four o'clock. Conveniently, it was the location of the rehearsal, the rehearsal dinner, and where everyone would be staying the next two nights—except for the newlyweds after the wedding, of course. The guests of honor would head ten miles east, where they would stay at the Grotto Bay Resort. The beautiful bride had made it generally known that any mysterious necklaces, curses, or Bermuda's infamous triangle were in no way going to fiddle with her wonderful amorous honeymoon.

After a perfunctory greeting from Diane, Mike parked himself on the bed. He was exhausted from two long days of bad news; predictably, he fell asleep. Meanwhile, Diane fiddled with her clothes, her makeup, her hair, checked on the girls, and then just before they were to meet up with everyone to go downstairs, she roused Mike so he could shower and dress.

Because of another wedding, they were unable to rehearse tonight at the ornate Anglican church where tomorrow's eleven a.m. ceremony would be held. So instead, a side room at the Princess would fill in prior to tonight's dinner.

With tomorrow's ceremony slated to be quite brief, the rehearsal followed in-kind. Afterward, everyone was directed toward the formal dining room. Hungry, they were looking forward to the festive dinner promised by the renowned Princess chef. Reaching the spacious room, the hostess, dressed in a formal blue uniform, directed them to a long table-clothed table with "Waters" scripted on a tented card. This table was set off from the rest of the room by a line of waist-high plants atop a half-wall, ensuring some minor privacy during this rare viewing of their heirloom.

Having decided that he could handle the moment—that he could deliver the Divel—Mr. Tuttleberry waddled down the hall away from the echoing vault that always gave the outdoorsman a fear of being buried alive. Following close behind him were Clarke and Tammy Vee, doing their job, but by doing so, making Tuttleberry's fear of being closed in, worse.

Of course, Tuttleberry had taken extra precautions for this walk. Four extra guards had been strategically placed inside the hotel. This was the watershed weekend for him. After the Divel was secured back in his vault Saturday noon, and the charms joined it Saturday evening, and everything was buttoned up nice and tight, he fully planned to return his attention to where it belonged. His butterflies. In his twenty-one years here, he had never faced so much history, and he hoped to never have to do it again. History was anxious and heavy; thicker somehow in real life than all those pictures and words in the books. Plus, if this wedding somehow went south, his hoped for tranquil retirement filled with his butterfly collecting could be jeopardized. And that was simply unacceptable, after so many years of planning to take up his near full-time hobby, full full-time.

He stepped onto the empty elevator with the ornate red velvet case under his arms and those gold braids swishing back and forth. Stopping smack in the middle of the elevator, not even attempting the maneuver of turning around, Clarke and Tanya Vee followed him on. Riding the shined elevator down, the doors opened, and Clarke stepped out to check the hallway. With the "all clear," Tammy Vee guided Tuttleberry around so he could make his way to the dining room and those waiting guests of honor.

As the security team passed a group of outside windows, the wind howled between the buildings. Not a minute later, as Tuttleberry made his way past the bar area, a local forecast coming from the wall-mounted TV announced an official hurricane warning for the low-lying island.

Just as the wedding party's drink orders arrived at their table, Tuttleberry arrived at the entrance to the dining room. Halting his careful progress, he came up on his toes to spot where the mother of the bride was seated on the other side of that row of plants. This was habit. This is what he did before he closed in on his target butterfly.

With his forearms becoming numb because he never went after butterflies with his arms held straight out like this, Tuttleberry made his way stiffly toward the head of the long table. He hadn't a clue what type of plants they were, but butterflies didn't care for them, so he didn't either.

Tuttleberry was now having to concentrate hard on not dropping the case with his arms growing tingly. Walking cautiously, he was dressed in his dark blue Princess blazer, pink lapel pin, white button-down shirt, and one of his famed custom bowties. The staff, dressed in the same colors but without the bowtie, knew he preferred them because they looked like one of his prized little creatures.

Tuttleberry swayed to an unsteady stop at the head of that long table, before inquiring solicitously, "Mrs. Diane Waters, I presume? I am Mr. Tuttleberry."

The din around the formal table ceased.

"Yes." The incredible familiarity of that case—as if it had been just yesterday rather than decades—lit up Diane's eyes. Then next, what spread across the rest of her face was the oh so innocent memory of her mother and herself; how she had looked and felt that day. So naïve. So young. So hopeful and bright, with her future sprawled out ahead of her like that endless water surrounding Bermuda.

Amidst Diane's emotional swirl, Mr. Tuttleberry pressed forward by reciting per the Divel's tradition: "May I present this heirloom to your daughter?"

"Yes-of-course," Diane sputtered out against the weight of all that history and tradition. Her voice flat. Her throat tightening up, as if it meant to choke off those words from escaping. She thought how simple this could be if she knocked the thing toward the boys. Let their young legs make a run for it. But of course, things were never slated to be that simple. Instead, in reality-land, she was trapped by the weight of it, just like her naïve, all-eyes daughter.

Under the press of Tuttleberry standing there expectantly, Diane squeaked out, "Sandy-is-right-there," though she wished she could have sent him toward another innocent young woman. A decoy bride. Unfortunately, she gave the ghost away by indicating the real bride with an abbreviated flick of her multi-braceleted wrist. To her credit, and somewhat impressively, she retrieved that wayward hand faster than any known drinking reflex.

With everyone focused on the ornate case, Diane looked pointedly toward Frick and Frack. Expressing with her eyes and head, something like: *Look how valuable it is. Velvet case. Gold braiding. Guards. Look! Just look! I told you so, didn't I?!*

151

Next, Tuttleberry came up on the bride, stumbled to a stop, and almost dropped the case in her lap. Righting himself by making it look like his stumble was an intended ceremonious pause—like maybe before the Queen—Tuttleberry fumbled the hinged velvet lid upward.

Sandy had done nothing but complain about the heirloom. But here, next to it, this close, she was awed by its ornate detailing and how the light was dancing within those large diamonds. Her mother had described it, but words hadn't done it justice. After taking a needed breath, she said, "It's beautiful."

Tuttleberry managed, "You will honor us, honor the Divel, by wearing it at your ceremony tomorrow. This is why you have made such a long trip. God bless you." Then he nodded, before performing another respectful half nod, half bow, like he might have practiced for the Queen.

Mom had mentioned to Sandy that she would hear the specifics of how the Divel would affect the wedding day schedule during the traditional wedding-morning talk.

Sandy heard herself say toward her mom, "I can't wait till our talk tomorrow."

Diane's tight lips released, "Nor can I." Then quieter, she spit out, "Where is a decoy bride when you need one?"

Sandy answered, "What?" but was already hypnotically focused back on the heirloom. The angle of light from the ceiling was making the necklace seemingly pulse with an uncanny iridescence. In response, Sandy's left hand rose toward it, like the time she'd been hypnotized in college.

Tuttleberry snapped the lid closed far harder than he intended, sending color to his face. He stiffly turned, and briskly waddled toward the entrance. He was leaning

152

forward the whole time, as if he needed to counteract some magnetic pull between the heirloom and Sandy.

Stiffly, Tuttleberry dumped the case into Clarke's waiting hands as soon as he reached the doorway. Arms dead.

Shaking his arms out, he required no more convincing that he'd let Clarke do the delivering of the thing tomorrow. It gave him the heebie-jeebies, as if it was vibrating or he was vibrating. Something was vibrating. Tuttleberry was sweating but good under his jacket. He'd never held anything that valuable before. And didn't care for the feeling one bit. It was as if someone had tensed up all his muscles until he walked and talked like a little robot man. He was going to be quite relieved when the bright, heavy thing was locked back up in the dark along with its new swarm of fresh charms.

Once Tuttleberry reached the control room, he watched Clarke and Tanya Vee finish securing the red satin, tasseled escapee back into its long safety deposit box. Pleased that this stage was behind him, Tuttleberry headed to his office for a shot of fortitude. He'd earned it; it was stupid of him not to have had one before he'd gone near the thing.

When he opened his draw, and unscrewed the top of his burnished metal flask, he was reminded of Shakespeare's quote from *The Tempest*. As the warming shot spread down his throat, he thought, *Hell* is *empty*, but finished the famous quote by substituting "Divels" for "Devils."

Of course, he had no way of knowing that all of the Divels were most definitely not here.

CHAPTER 15

THE MIS(S)DIRECTION

PAST-PRESENT-FUTURE

The strange thing that only the security staff, the family, and the insurance company knew, was that the real Divel no longer stayed in the vault during the wedding. Long ago, the Waters had eventually come to the realization, given the Divel's notoriety, that they would never be able to have enough security, never have a normal wedding, if the bride wore the real thing to the ceremony. Eventually, someone would steal it, and that would be the end of that. Hence, the need for a substitute, which was now referred to as Replica Era I, in the Trust.

Then after generations, with the heat off, an enterprising couple took the ritual full circle. What was the point of having such a peerless jewel if it never touched a princess's skin? So, in the early eighteen-hundreds, a bride who loved being the center of attention, royal jewelry or not, chanced wearing the real McCoy again: Replica Era II was born.

Naturally, everyone went on believing it was the replica, so subsequent brides followed suit. But for this ruse to work, for this show to be financially feasible, a compromise had to be brokered between the Waters' Trust and the insurance carrier. Otherwise, the insurance premium would have become astronomical. From the subsequent negotiations, based upon the premium cut, it was decided that the Divel would be worn to the wedding proper, but not participate in the much riskier afternoon island-wide charm hunt. Once that agreement was inked, a system was needed to guard the supposed replica that was now genuine again, just in case. Some amount of security, but not too much that might alert people like Benny that the real thing was out and about again. Over the past hundred years, this system had been distilled down to the point where only the head of security participated in the wedding. Outwardly, this could be sold to the press that the prestigious hotel was paying its respects to its oldest, most consistent, and most distinguished guest. In reality the head of security swapped out the real McCoy for its stand-in, so the former could high-tail it back to the vault, while the latter went in search of those coveted charms.

Clarke was counting on all this as part of his perfect plan, and what Mrs. Waters was planning on as far as her imperfect one.

Everything else was expected to follow the normal routine for a Waters wedding. If, that is, you called carrying out a most serious Halloween-weekend charm hunt immediately following a wedding, normal or routine, in order to counteract a water-cursed necklace.

CHAPTER 16

HALLOWEEN CELEBRATION

The next item on the itinerary was the Halloween celebration that took place at Fort Hamilton, located on just the other side of capital. Making their way to the front of the hotel, the guests commented upon the attentive staff, the tastefully decorated interior, and the full-sized metal sculpture of Mark Twain seated to greet arriving guests.

Frick said to Frack, "Maybe there's a reading promotion going on?"

Frack nodded knowingly, and whispered back, "Pretty impressive place if Mark Twain came here."

The wedding party congregated, while Dr. Waters saw to their cabs. It was by all accounts a beautiful evening. The temperature was holding in the upper-60s, and the steady wind from earlier had subsided to occasional breezes.

Given the expanse of dark clouds to the south, Mike was doing his best to deny that George was interested in their little party. But barely three miles to the southwest, near where Bermuda's protected white-tailed tropicbirds swooped from the South Shore cliffs, the outermost spiral of George licked high above Gibbs Hill Lighthouse. This historic lighthouse had become famous for saving countless ships from beaching themselves in the shallows approaching the southern shore's famous pink beaches.

With it still being light out, those who had ventured up those endless spiraling stairs could see the darkness spreading out over the water. On the narrow catwalk ringing the top, gusts of wind convinced any straggling sightseers that it was prudent to come down. And just as the last of the climbers exited to the small parking area, a light sun shower teased them.

The southern-most stretch of island.

George's northern-most clouds.

Back at the Princess, Mike took one last look before ducking into the cab. He hadn't mentioned to Diane how George appeared to be following him. If Diane knew how poorly the trial had unfolded, she would just lay into him again. As he sat next to her and that sleek black dress of hers, he considered whether hurricanes could be Bermuda's seven-year itch; would George be the storm to scratch it? He cringed with the growing possibility that George might ruin Sandy's wedding. Murphy's Law revisited: Waters' Postulate.

The ride to Fort Hamilton was incredibly brief. Turning right up a semi-circle entranceway surrounded by trees, they traversed a large, overgrown ravine, that was playing host to costumed ghosts. Up top, the small festival was decked out with lights, music, and costumed partiers. The large flat grassy area was bordered by low buildings to the west, while to the south and east, the fort's large-block limestone wall stretched around the perimeter. Atop that thick wall ran a thin metal fence, as if extra security was needed to keep someone out, or everyone in, given the steep drop-off. To the southeast, the view had grown noticeably darker.

The sunset below the high clouds was deceptive in its brilliance. As the sky darkened in all directions, Mike

157

couldn't help but notice how the high clouds began to occlude the initial stars like spilt paint. When he spotted dry lightning to the southeast, their tragic flight to stop George flashed in his head. Half-an-hour later, with the Waters group running out of steam, with talk that someone felt a drop, Mike used his cell to call the cabs.

CHAPTER 17

MOTHER-DAUGHTER TALKS

THE BIG DAY

Overnight, the island's weather worsened with more wind and more rain. As people woke up amidst the white-noise rain, and they hazarded a look through the wet windows, Hamilton Harbour was littered with white caps. The really early-risers, those whose rooms favored the south or east, were able to snatch a glimpse of the just-above-the-ocean orange globe before it was snuffed out by that blanket of clouds.

Unable to stay asleep with the commotion atop the bed, Diane rolled awake. She should have known. Mike was gawking and making twisting motions with his hands towards his laptop. With no "good morning" between them, she padded her manicured toes toward the small bathroom filled with cosmetics. Nostalgia greeted her from her own big day so many years ago, and, how it had ended. Badly, that's how, after the tiring quest in bad weather. The sound of the slapping rain against their east-facing window only brought those feelings closer. She amused herself with the possible improvements in the charm hunt instructions, if they ever allowed her to amend them: that future newlyweds should be so instructed to keep rubber boots in the vault, along with the Divel. That

159

would be more useful to each couple, she knew, than receiving a royal necklace that the bride would get to wear one whole time before it became just a bragging right at the gym during massages.

She eyed her short blond-hair in the mirror. It wasn't awful. Handwashing her face, running a brush through her hair, she came out and rang Sandy's room. Marcia answered, and after a party-line conversation through Marcia and Tillie's enthusiasm, mother and daughter arranged to head down for their private breakfast in fifteen plain-Jane minutes.

Diane climbed into jeans and threw on a casual short-sleeved blouse. No make-up expected.

Like mother, like daughter, Sandy showed up at her mom's door dressed in jeans, a wrinkled top, no makeup, and her easy-care, short blond-hair cupped around her face.

After the brief elevator ride, Diane led her daughter toward the small café that was always clean and nearly empty this early.

With no need for menus, Diane ordered coffee, juice, and croissants for the both of them. As the older waitress headed toward the kitchen, the wet footprints on the floor reminded Diane of the wet footprints from thirty years before. It felt a little eerie being in this seat rather than Sandy's.

Not a moment later, another staff person appeared and mopped away the water with a tiny implement that looked like a circular head of curly, white hair. Diane guessed it was some fancy European tool. Wherever it was from, it was decidedly different from the old-fashioned mop they'd used on her wedding day. The continuing parallels to her own wedding were creeping her out. She needed a drink; she was looking forward to getting her coffee so her hands would have something to do. A cigarette would be nice, but she hadn't smoked in years. Mike hated them.

When the coffee arrived, they both began with cream but no sugar. Unfurling their folded cloth napkins, Sandy looked nervous to Diane. Then the orange juice came in short, wide glasses, along with the croissants on fine china, an assortment of jams, and fancy dollops of butter in the shape of shells.

While they buttered, and Diane finally had something to do with her trembling hands, she broke the ice with, "Well, here we are. Your day has finally arrived, sweetie."

Sandy sipped her strong coffee, blinked her blue eyes, and answered, "At least it's not an outdoor wedding. That's something."

This moment had been a long time coming, but with Diane not being an over-thinker, she just leaped. "So here it is. You deserve the full treatment, I guess, like I got from my mother-in-law." On some level, Diane wanted Sandy not to underestimate the thing, to take the Divel seriously, no matter how fantastic all this was going to sound.

She believed the safest course would be to stay as close to the true facts as possible—here, she happened to be in agreement with her sister and history teacher, Donna. Here went everything. "A long time ago our necklace was secretly banished from England. Apparently some noble with considerable influence arranged to have it taken to Jamestown. And this history, mind you, dear, is reliable because notables such as John…gosh, I'm terrible with names. Your aunt would kill me. I think it was John Cabot, of Pocahontas fame, who was aboard the Sea Venture. That ship became separated from the other seven or eight ships during a hurricane. And it ended up being grounded upon the La Isla de Los Diablos (The Isle of Devils) to the Spaniards."

Across the small nicely appointed breakfast table, Sandy nibbled and blinked away, as she waited to hear how Mom's history lesson would affect today. Her day. How the history part would affect the Divel part, because that part was still a mystery based upon the Google information.

Diane pulled a corner off a croissant, placed it in her mouth, and took her time chewing it before swallowing. So far so good—and one less triangle in the world. "The first European to discover Bermuda was a Spanish sea captain, Juan de Bermúdez, in 1503. But it was so hazardous to reach by boat, you see, that the island was never officially claimed by Spain."

After this bunch of facts, they both nibbled, whereby that triangular croissant was transformed into a pentagon. Donna like pentagons much more.

"Anyway, so everyone ended up stranded. After unloading the cargo, the ship was so busted up, that the only way they were going to escape was to build two smaller ships with the good wood. After finishing these, they finally pushed on to Jamestown, but not before they left two men behind to secure their claim to this unmanned place. Apparently, a command decision had been made not risk transporting the Divel over open water again, so it was left behind. When the ships returned from Jamestown, instead of picking up the two men, they left a third, a Waters. And the way the story goes, the three of them entered into riskier and riskier contests to win the unclaimed necklace. When one of them drowned, the necklace happened to be in possession of your ancestor.

No further contests took place after that. Anyway, that is the reason our family travels to Bermuda for its weddings—the necklace has not been moved off the island in four hundred years."

Sandy's big eyes remained on her mom, but when Mom didn't seem finished, Sandy kept chewing away.

Diane stopped to catch her breath. Stopped to take a pull of coffee, forgetting for just a moment that it was only coffee. Good coffee, but she was disappointed.

Sandy's big blue eyes continued to blink away, but she began multitasking by picking apart her croissant. Like mother, like daughter. That was what Diane was afraid of.

Edgy, feeling like she'd left her smokes in the room— even though she hadn't smoked in...decades—Diane pushed on toward the finish line. "Anyway, the long and short of it is, sweetie, the necklace has stayed on the island ever since. And has been passed to the first bride of each generation, like I shared with you at home. If it was a male Waters, the name carried on, like your father and me. While if it was a female Waters, the name was kept as a condition of the Waters Trust. like you're getting ready to do with Greg."

Diane paused to consider her creative sister's take on all this. "And your interesting Auntie Donna found this history a bit too weird, being a history teacher and all. After she dug around in the archives here and in England, she refused to come near the little triangular thing a second time around. As she put it, it would be coming out of the vault and away from its charms, nearer to water. Anyway, she's not really clairvoyant, like she tells everyone. The history is common knowledge in the family." Diane's hands flipped palm up to express this well-known fact. Then she whispered, "She even expressed her belief that there seemed to be a connection between it and the increase in plane and boat accidents in the area. Isn't that something?"

Sandy stopped chewing. Of course, she'd been hoping all the mystery swirling over the table would begin to clear up. But the expression on her face said otherwise.

"I tried to tell her that the number of boats and planes had increased during that same time period, so naturally accidents had gone up—at least that's what your scientific father had to say on the subject. But your aunt just looked at me and said something like she wasn't a math teacher, she was a history teacher. Anyway, you know how Aunt Donna can get with her séances and natural cures." Then leaning in closer, Diane whispered, "She has most definitely apologized for not coming with an extremely generous gift." Then Diane touched her lips with her napkin, as if covering her lips might help contain the secret she'd just shared. Too late.

Sandy put her polite hands in her lap. Leaning back from the table, the expression on her young face expressed that she was already good and ready to distance herself from this fantastic family tale; no time like the present to begin.

Diane took a breath. So far so good. She was a little embarrassed about this next part, but she had committed herself to doing right for Sandy. All in. "So, dearie, after my own wedding day, once I was involved with the Divel, I decided to follow suit."

Sandy took a sip of coffee. "What do you mean?"

"Well, I'm not going to tell you what my mother-in-law said to me," she said with a voice softened by emotion. "But, you should know that that was when…I made the decision to avoid water." Diane's eyes became moist.

"Shit."

Sandy's eyes flared wide.

"I told myself I wasn't going to cry." Her cloth napkin was brought delicately to one eye, then the other.

Sandy declared, "I never knew that was why you avoided water your whole life. That sounds rather fantastic, Mom. Not necessarily in a good way," suddenly in the mood for butter on her croissant.

"No kidding. So, like I did, you're probably asking yourself right about now, how does this affect my day? For starters, you'll be wearing the real one at your wedding and for the rest of the day—even though everyone will think you're wearing the fake." Diane whispered, "That's an honest-to-goodness Waters secret."

Before taking a bite from the now buttered pastry, Sandy leaned forward. "You mean, another one?"

"I guess. The public believes you'll be wearing a fake. The Waters have maintained that ruse to keep the thieves away." A wicked smile broke out on Diane's face. "Anyway, once I hand the necklace to you, you might just find your mother venturing out on one of those beautiful little boats we flew over." Diane's smile expressed just how much pleasure she was going to take breaking free, in the Divel's own backyard, no less.

Sandy asked, "Is there anything else I need to know about this afternoon?"

"Oh, sorry. I got lost thinking of Grandmamma for a moment." Diane took a deep breath, took a delicate bite, and washed it down with cold coffee. "All of this has—"

The prim waitress appeared out of nowhere and promptly refilled both cups of coffee and poured more water, unasked.

Mrs. Waters dabbed her mouth with her napkin,

though there was nothing detectable on her lips. "What was I saying? Oh, all of this has become part of our little wedding-day ritual."

Suddenly afraid to share more, Diane diverted into, "And let's not leave the men out of this." She placed the clean napkin back on her lap. "If you trace our recent family history, they have developed a keen interest in weather and hurricanes. Naturally your grandfather and father fit this pattern to a T."

Sandy was still awaiting those specifics, and the longer she waited, the more she was beginning to resemble a tight, polite ball.

Diane's eyes focused off into the distance for a moment. She was remembering the day Mike had shared that he was a climatologist. "And this damn priceless thing seems poised to exert considerable influence upon the Waters clan for some time to come, just like it did with the English royals."

"And today?" Sandy persevered, as she looked down at the croissant that had been reduced to whatever was smaller than crumbs.

"Well, today—"

The waitress revisited to offer a choice of fruit pastries, ice cream, or coffee cake with rum sauce. Sandy politely refused dessert, while Diane went for the cake because of the rum. Something was better than nothing in this life.

With the mention of rum, Diane had lost her place again. "Oh. After the ceremony, you will complete the treasure hunt that every couple has taken part in down through the generations. You and Greg will visit sites about the island to retrieve what the family has come to refer to as charms. No one knows if these charms really hold any power or not. Who knows?" Diane flicked away this difference of opinion with eyes that shot toward the ceiling. She knew darn well Donna believed they did—but Diane remain committed to not scaring Sandy the way she'd been scared.

When her eyes came down, she noticed the quick waitress returning with that rum sauce.

She took a bite and realized she should have asked for extra sauce, like an extra shot. Diane said, "So these charms will get locked up with the Divel at the end of the day." Diane paused to place another scrumptious bite in her mouth. The sauce was good. "Some people guess they actually counterbalance the spell of the little monster." And after that, another joyful, unburdening bite occurred. She was beginning to feel better, even smile. It was mostly out now. The richness of the cake, the rum, was blissful.

Scientific, modern-age Sandy looked at her mom as if she'd really gone off the deep end. "So, that's the big secret?"

"Honey, it is what it is. Welcome to our loony family," as her fork circled in the air. "I went along to get along. No biggie. After your father and I completed our little treasure hunt, the honeymoon helps make up for it. You forget about it." She left off the *for a little while part.* "It's only one day, so what's the big deal?" Minimizing now. Then she joked, "And we haven't lost anyone to the sea yet, right? So, it's entirely possible that my being careful around water was completely unnecessary." After she took another forkful, Diane added, "Though I like to look at it as a no-lose proposition."

In her own careful way, she had just warned Sandy en passant, while denying during this rummy moment how much it had cost her marriage. Never mind all those people who died on the Sea Venture, or that one of the

167

original three on the island, did as well.

Sandy's voice softened, "I gather. Sounds like a lot of hocus-pocus to me." Sandy looked at a young couple as they came in and sat across the aisle. "Honestly, if it's going to be this much trouble, I'd rather not wear the thing. You know how I feel about fancy jewelry. I've told Greg as much."

Diane felt trapped into reacting as a mother rather than a friend. "I know. He's told me. Told his friends. The whole world seems to know about our socked away royal necklace." Diane was laying groundwork here, just in case the necklace should go missing for some *known* reason.

Sandy sipped cold coffee.

Though their big-little talk really hadn't taken very long, it was time to get ready for the late-morning ceremony. A wedding this early in the day gave the newlyweds the entire afternoon to gather all those charms. This was a schedule that had proven very practical over the generations. Allowing ample time for everything collected during the long day to be tucked away nighty night before the evening's moon and its light and its tide could discover that the Divel might have been out naked gallivanting so near so much water.

Diane scraped the last of her delicious dessert up with her fork, then cleaned that off with her lips and then one tastefully-polished finger. When she pointed that sucked clean finger at her daughter, she remembered, "Oh, one more thing. You'll get the instructions for your treasure hunt right after the ceremony, because I don't get them from Mr. Tuttlebuttle until then." Her poor memory for names had somehow combined "Tuttle" with the "b" in Clarke's "Dearborne," coming up with an easier-to-remember rhyming name. "Then once you're finished with your hunt, you'll meet up with everyone for dinner around six.

"Mr. Tuttlebuttle? You mean the little, stiff man who almost snapped my fingers off?" She tried a weak smile in the face of it all, but it never blossomed.

"No, no. The nice looking tall one." Noticing Sandy's concerned expression, she offered, "It'll be fine, sweetie. You'll see. Just fine. Then you get to enjoy this romantic place while we all scat home."

"If it ever stops raining."

The wind howled outside.

"If it ever stops raining."

"I thought Dad was going to do something about that," Sandy joked brightly.

"Very funny. Let's get this show on the road."

Diane put the tab on her room, and just before she stood to leave, she noticed a thin smudge of rum sauce around the edge of her plate. She ran another hopeful finger over it. She was ready for more pleasure, pure and simple, with or without all this drama.

As they made their way back to the elevator for the short ride up, Diane realized she'd forgotten to mention the reason the wedding always took place during Halloween week. Contrary to rumors over ghoulish costumes, spirits, hauntings, or things masquerading as other things, the truth was it had to do with practical weather factors: The weather in October was still warm but not too warm for formal clothes; the seawater was warm enough for the full range of outdoor activities; and most relevant, the frequency of hurricanes was significantly lessened this late in the year.

Her professional husband could add that the monthly rainfall totals were also lower, compared to the summer

169

months. But George's rain-bands were telling anyone who was listening that they didn't give two Halloween tricks about any long-term data. Then was then, and now was now.

Diane believed the big talk had gone much better than expected. But it still hadn't been easy. In fact, it had proven to be much harder than learning her lines in one of those plays she'd starred in during college. But that cake and sauce had made up for it. Relieved, she strolled down the tasteful hallway, swiped her room card, and entered to find Mike glued to his laptop. Immediately she was confronted by the rude fact that her old life was predictable, even if she wasn't a so-called seer like her sister.

With lips pressed together, he was mumbling and cursing about the storm that apparently was called George. But she was in such a good mood, she asked, "George doesn't look good?" When he didn't answer right away, George seemed to confirm this by rattling something outside.

"It could ruin the whole weekend," he shared. Then he looked up. "We could even get stuck here."

Diane wondered if she'd rather have him inside, or, outside measuring the storm and its lightning wearing the damn metal Divel around his damn neck. She imagined it up on the roof. Up high, away from Sandy. The perfect metallic, triangular, lightning attractor—a completing two kinds of research with one bolt, type of thing.

While undressing for the shower and more water, Diane pictured getting on one of those cute little boats after all these years.

Stepping out, toweling off, wearing nothing, she pranced toward the kitchenette. Mike didn't even notice.

Apparently, she couldn't compete with George's measurements. A male, no less. It was definitely gin and tonic time.

The ice clinked lightly in the fat glass. Then she sipped. Sipping some more, she took her time heading back to the bathroom. And if you could drink nude, you could put on your makeup nude and continue to drink. All these changes were kind of exciting. Diane, the new Diane, was bone tired of having been told that it was unsafe to be near water. She was ready to get back in the shower and dance to prove it. She toasted this delicious idea while admiring her shape in the tall mirror on the closet doors. She was great shape for her age, and certainly good enough to attract a man. Just not Mike. After drying her hair with the blow dryer, she started in on her makeup.

She didn't read much, only magazines and such, so when she had taken the time to familiarize herself with the family history and how the Divel had come to the island, she had taken the subject seriously. It was the same with her brushing up on all this Bermuda Triangle stuff. Years ago, her insecurities compelled her to learn as much as possible about the history she, they, had unwittingly become such an unwilling part of. She finished off the drink that was getting diluted.

There is too much water here.

Finishing her makeup, she considered whether she ever really accepted doing less and less with Mike. She wasn't sure. She looked at her drink and was surprised to find it drained. No, she decided she hadn't accepted it. She'd done her best to live with it. Survive it. He'd had his work. She'd had Sandy. But now her little girl was moving on. Flitting through her mind was whether Mike had a mistress. Well, a mistress besides his work. She headed back to the closet to get dressed. "Shower's ready," she announced to the spider-legged scientist.

Mike grunted something and snapped his laptop shut. For a moment, Diane thought he might bring it into the shower with him. When he disappeared into the bathroom, she poured herself two more fingers with ice.

After looking in the mirror, she used the glass as a prop to practice what she was going to say to Mr. Tuttlebuttle when she failed to produce the Divel. It took a few takes, but when she was satisfied with her performance, she clicked on the TV for company. Turning the volume up to hear over the constant howling of the wind that sounded like an animal in distress, an ad for cemetery services scrolled across the bottom of the snowy picture.

The topic made her think of all her husband's relatives that must be under the island. As part of her quest for the Waters history, she considered whether it might be interesting to look up some of their gravesites while they were here. She pulled her sleek black dress from the hanger. Quickly, the thought of viewing wet tombstones turned unappealing. If she was going to do something controversial, that emotional space was reserved for her cathartic boat ride. The shower started. Yes, even in the rain, the scenic coast would be much lovelier than a muddy, dismal cemetery.

CHAPTER 18

THE CHURCH

The wedding was slated for 11 a.m. inside the gothic Holy Trinity Cathedral in downtown Hamilton. Being inside was good. At 10 a.m., with the coast clear inside but not out, Mr. Clarke Dearborne and this very tall man, Mr. Thompson, reported to the Waters suite to hand deliver the Divel to Diane. After she received the ornate pouch, Diane slid it into her over-sized handbag.

With the pre-wedding handoff accomplished, Diane walked the Divel to Sandy's room. Standing on the hall-side, Diane wished again that she had a twin available, just like the hotel.

One knock was all it took, as if there'd been a secret code agreed upon. Flip flops approached the door.

Sweet Tillie was all made up with her hair done, but wearing the sweats she'd slept in.

Diane offered lyrically, "I've got a surprise for you."

Making way, the three girls were all set to go except for their dresses, as they crowded around Diane when she placed her black purse on the bed. From it she extracted the necklace with the flourish usually associated with magicians. Marcia and Tillie's eyes lit up, while Sandy appeared to be trying to control herself after her first meeting when she'd been drawn to it.

It didn't take long before they were all chattering about its fine metal detailing, the exquisite swirl pattern repeating

173

in-between the smaller diamonds, and how such artistry was generally lacking from modern- day jewelry—never mind those obscenely large diamonds. Restraint over, just like the night before, Sandy's hand began to reach for the heirloom.

Expressive Marcia touched it first, only to snap her hand back from a tiny shock. "Ouch." All of them then play-acted like it was a scene, like the priceless thing wasn't defenseless just because it had sat in the dark for thirty years. It still had juice—static electricity juice.

Before Diane left the girls, she slid and fastened the white gold chain around her daughter's beautiful neck. Her mother had done the same. Diane's eyes moistened with the act. It looked beautiful on her daughter. There was no denying that fact, but still the same, she hated admitting it to herself—well, to it, really.

The idea popped into her mind how her sister had explained over cocktails that any such money collected— if it should ever go missing—would surely be cursed. "That's how curses work," Donna had said too-matter-of-factly for Diane's taste. How Donna had emphasized, "I don't even need my tarot cards to confirm something that obvious." To Diane, getting rid of a curse and getting paid millions of dollars to do it seemed a no-brainer—like staying on the right side of those tracks, or never living where it always rained— whether she was an historian or an accountant or just a cursed, lonely ex-actress housewife.

Diane told the trio it was time to get those dresses on—pink chiffon (matching the pastel color of the Princess Hotel) just-above-the-knee dresses for the bridesmaids, and the same length, but low-cut, white wedding dressing with its detailed stitching down the back,

back, for the bride.

Diane returned to her room, stuck the card in the door and entered. When the door closed, Mike said, "Maybe we should consider postponing the ceremony until things die down out there?"

Diane brushed his idea away with a snicker. "As far as I'm concerned, the Divel will be very comfortable outside. And your daughter will be just fine with a cabbie who knows the island. Mr. Tuttleborne made it clear he's chosen the absolute best cab driver to insure they complete the charm quest successfully. Plus, this Mr. Forequay will be driving a 4-wheel drive vehicle, making it that much safer—their cab thirty years ago hadn't been 4-wheel drive. Some little hurricane was not going to derail Diane from her own personal quest to be rid of the thing—in fact, the way she was figuring it, the bad weather would only help cover the boys' tracks during their escape.

Diane put her short black dress on with her black pumps, while Mike climbed into his dark blue suit. All the men were wearing dark blue suits.

Fifteen minutes later, Diane rounded up the female portion of the wedding party. Five minutes beyond that, the girls left for the church before the guys, who were following in ten minutes.

Outside, the rain had eased up. When they slipped out the entranceway to enter the two cabs, the whipping winds were the worst of it. Even with the pink complimentary umbrellas, the slanted rain got their shoes wet. When Sandy came last through the door, George swirled around the hotel and howled with intensity. If Tillie hadn't snatched Sandy's arm when she did, Sandy might have lost her balance and ruined her dress.

Out in the parking lot, Diane spotted Mr. Tuttlebuttle

sitting in his sun-faded, maroon Peugeot. Facing the front of the hotel, she knew he would wait for the men to leave before following everyone to the church.

Reaching the tall church, the ladies dashed under shelter with coats and umbrellas held over their heads. Inside, with its beautiful leaded- glass windows, dark stained wood, and one hundred-foot ceiling, the church felt and sounded secure to Diane—she'd forgotten just how big and solid this room was. Standing in the tall, dim room with all those candles running down both sides, there was a palpable sense of safety as compared to the small windblown cars.

After taking in the details of the cavernous room and all that stained wood up on the ceiling, the bride and her maids of honor were directed to their left-side room where they would wait to be summoned to the ceremony.

When the men arrived fifteen minutes later, they were ushered to the opposite side of the church where they were sequestered in a matching room.

The third triangle, the three adults, then made their way down the middle of all those countless wooden pews. Taking their time, they stopped when they reached the organ at the far end of the long room. If the small wedding party in a foreign land under a large hurricane hadn't realized how few they were, they really knew it after being divided into three smaller groups inside this huge refuge.

Clarke pulled up behind the church, came around the front, and slipped under the front entranceway that always amazed him. Knowing he had the time, playing it cool, he admired the arched ceiling, open wrought iron gates, tiled floor, and ornate double wooden doors with that matching black-iron detailing. What a fitting place to hold an historic wedding. He'd be pleased to be so lucky. Pulling the solid door open, he was greeted by the very dark, very tall, very long, candle-infested, flickering room whose sheer size reminded him of a football arena. It even smelled dark in here. With everyone at the far end, he knew they'd have to come back this way to leave. Meaning, all he had to do was wait. Easy.

Then once back in the car, the swap would be simple. Or, in case someone might be walking past, he could even do it inside, as dark and isolated as it was back here. The replica was right here in the inside pocket of his trench coat. Options were good to have. The perfect plan.

Alone with his best men, Greg heard Frick say, "That necklace is something, all right."

Greg attempted a smile, but his mouth wasn't working right. Anyway, he was unwilling to get into that right now. The pre-wedding willies had snuck into this dimly lit room, even after they'd closed the door really quickly. The tall leaded window was the only other way in, but only muted colors and the sound of pelting rain were getting through. In fact, the candles atop the two rectangular tables were producing more light. He began to walk around the two end-to-end tables, as if trying to outrun his invisible butterflies that so easily matched his speed. The special day had arrived in force.

Frick took several looks at the pacing Greg, before attempting to extract more information from the moving target. "Okay. If you feel like walking, keep walking. What happens this afternoon?"

"Don't know yet. Don't know yet."

Frick looked at Frack. "But it takes up the better part of the afternoon?"

"Apparently. Apparently."

"Sandy hasn't told you anything."

"Nope. Nope. She was to find out this morning. Go over to her side and ask." That was a good idea. Then he'd get to keep walking in circles, undisturbed, unblocked. Maybe the butterflies would follow them.

Greg had picked up on this pattern of threes, of triangles, with everyone split up like this. He was kind of surprised there were only two tables, and that they were rectangular. But his butterflies reminded him that each rectangular table could be cut into two equal triangles. They were everywhere—butterflies and triangles—and he was circling the darn things at the moment. He moved to the outer perimeter to get as far away from one, if not both.

The best men glanced at each other. Frick said, "Well I'm sure the girls wouldn't appreciate that. How 'bout telling me what happens after the mysterious afternoon happens." Speaking in the groom's new "repeater" language.

"Afterward. Afterward. We plan to stop at our resort. To change."

"But you don't know when, exactly?"

"No."

"Has she even told you where you're staying?"

"Grotto, man. Grotto something. Something to do with caves. All I know."

"Good. Good," Frack echoed, joining the pre-wedding dialect.

"Maybe Sandy plans to post pics about the caves."

Greg didn't answer. Silence repeated silently was even easier.

Frick tried again. "Okay then, since you're traveling

incognito this afternoon, why don't you call us when you get back to those caves? Okay?"

"Sure. Sure. Anything." Answering just to answer. At the moment, he felt lucky to know his name, which was soon to change. All this unknown ceremony stuff with the Divel was compounding all the unknown stuff looming over the rest of his life. Plus, he didn't feel so great after all this circling.

Frick added to the difficult discourse, "All I'm saying is, don't remind Sandy to take it off."

Greg was hardly listening to this drivel. "Sure. Sure," as his arms swatted away invisible somethings next to his body. "I'm getting married in half an hour." Another half, just like the tables.

Outside, with increasing fury, wind lashed the rain against that artistic window with its religious themes.

Frack tried, "Look at me for a sec. You'll be fine as long as you don't melt in the rain like that wicked witch person."

But that didn't help either. Not even Frack laughed at his own joke.

Frick snapped his fingers. "Almost forgot. Put this in your shoelaces." Frick produced a pence coin from his pocket. This was the task he'd been assigned at the rehearsal. As part of the Waters tradition, it needed to be placed somewhere in the groom's left shoe.

Something concrete to do was good, though Greg had to stop moving, giving the butterflies a chance to swarm all through him.

Out in the main room, the organ began to play. That was the signal for the boys to come to the middle of the large room to await the girls. Diane watched Mike turn, join the boys, from where he would soon be escorting Sandy at the back of the marriage train. Beyond the boys, in the dark near the middle aisle, Diane made out the outline of a man that had to be the seated Mr. Tuttlebuttle. She was counting on tradition here, like everyone was today. She knew he was under strict instructions not to interfere with the ceremony in any way; he carried himself with a no-nonsense air, like someone who could be depended upon to do what he was supposed to do. That was good, maybe even a little comforting in a strange land, in the dark, up against the Divel as she was.

After Mike said something to Greg, the groom began to stiffly make his way toward Diane, his dad, the minister dressed in his dark robe, and the old organ filling the hall with its almost lazy resonating tone that probably had some significance that was lost on Diane at that moment.

When the organ music changed again, the girls emerged from their side. Frick paired up with pink Marcia, Frack with pink Tillie, and Mike with white Sandy. Then down the center they came. Sandy looked beautiful with all those candles flickering off her naïve, eager face. Beaming.

Diane wouldn't have been surprised if there was one candle here for every year Bermuda had been a dry home to the wicked triangle—she hadn't noticed so many at her own wedding. Could there be thirty more in here? Anyway, Mike was the researcher, so let him count them. Or better yet, maybe she could get Mr. Tuttlebuttle to confirm that while Sandy slipped away. She liked that she was thinking clearly about how to make this all work.

Given the weather, unsure about the possibility of any outside shots, the lone photographer who had snuck in amongst all the subplots, began snapping interior shots. The flashes were consumed by the tall room instantly. But they irked Diane, like they had thirty years before. They were simply out of place in this room that echoed intimacy and a keeper of the Waters secrets, even if it was cavernous.

The brief vows were followed by specific instructions involving the necklace, and how the couple was to be its ward and protector for this

generation. Then the modern couple was duly pronounced man and wife, just as in days of olde, though it was promptly sealed by a heartfelt, modern day kiss. And as the Divel's own storied history foretold, the escapee charm-free necklace sat smack in the middle of the action, literally.

When their lips came to life, the organ came to life, adding a different kind of energy to the deep, flickering room surrounded by the storm that had been all but forgotten in this sanctuary.

With everyone congratulating the happy couple, the time had arrived for Diane to unload the scripted instructions upon her hapless daughter. The water-resistant parchment that was not known for its flame-retardant qualities, had been burning a hole in her dry pocketbook for the last hour.

Diane pried her daughter away from their small energetic group to complete this part of the wedding ceremony in private. Leading her beaming daughter back through the middle of those empty pews—as if Sandy's smile was lighting the way, and it was—Mr. Tuttlebuttle's shadowed profile loomed larger and larger ahead of them.

This was it.

He was it.

The last obstacle in the way of the Divel's escape. She had rehearsed this part in the mirror; if her short-lived acting career was worth a damn thing, she'd either remember her lines, or ad-lib coherently like the Vegas comedians she enjoyed.

Diane approached the security man sitting in the shadows of the last row like a B movie private dick in his trench coat. All these shadows compliments of the wedding, could only help with this, she rehearsed, but the closer they approached Mr. Tuttleborne, the thinner they became.

With stage nerves, which everyone said were normal and healthy because they shouted you cared about your performance—but she found only gin to be healthy for her—she projected, "Hi, Mr. Tuttleborne." "Would you mind if us girls speak back here in private?" She finished delivering the most important line in her life with a wink. But the shadows definitely hadn't helped with that. On stage that could be fixed. Not here. He had to know it was time to pass on the quest instructions.

She waited. No breathing, no organ, nothing but her baby, the heirloom, and this funny-named security man who was no joke.

"Not at all," he answered graciously. As he stood, he seemed to remember his manners when he said to the bride, who was literally beaming on two accounts—with her smile and that necklace, "Congratulations, Mrs. Waters."

"Thank you, Mr….Dearborne," Sandy paused, guessing, Diane figured. The dark was apparently making everyone unsure of people's names, not just her.

Clarke made his way to the other end of the football

field. As he went, the obligatory smile he'd thrown on his face faded. He'd been ready, and now was disappointed with the delay, and displeased he'd been unable to find a gracious way to remind Mrs. Waters of her responsibility.

Tuttleberry's warning remained fresh in his ears. He was too close to the end to risk misstepping. Okay. He'd waited months, so he could wait a few more minutes. To get his edginess under control, to demonstrate a calm exterior, he went to congratulate everyone down front.

It was a long trip with all those dark pews spanning out like ribs, and all those candles flickering away up there. Yes, he'd be pleased to get married in an historic church like this and believed both Dee and Morgan would feel the same, though his memories of Laura produced a curious longing in him.

It was surprising, really, how this huge, dark sanctuary loosened intimate moments whenever Clarke came here. For the first-time he considered whether Laura would be okay with him remarrying. Really okay with it. As he listened to the new hymn fill the room, he was of the opinion that she would be.

In their short dresses—one black and one white, which seemed fitting—Diane slid into the second to last row, Sandy following suit.

In silence, Diane dug out the hot-potato velvet pouch and shoveled it toward her daughter's innocent lap. She felt profoundly close to Sandy, and maybe because of that, noticed the exact moment that her hands lost contact with the charm hunt instructions. They were in Sandy's lap now, meaning, the weight of the quest now rested squarely on her daughter's pretty shoulders. Diane's tie with the Waters legacy was almost completely severed, in a direct sense, at least.

Sandy accepted the ornate bag in silence, just as Diane had so many years before. Just like it. Stitched into the front of the pouch was a blue and red design, like a family crest, which Sandy was now eyeing in the dim light.

At a time when Diane should have been focused and pressing to complete this exchange, she found herself dawdling. Daydreaming. Reminiscing. Stalling? *Snap out of it, before that Tuttle-person comes back.*

Diane's lips approached Sandy's long silver earring that looked antique but wasn't. With tenderness befitting the moment, Diane shared, "Honey, here is what you need to complete today, as I did before you. Follow the instructions faithfully. But as you read this, some of it will be outdated, so just improvise according to the spirit of the manuscript. By the end of the day, it will all be over with." She certainly hoped so.

Diane noticed that Mr. Tuttleborne had sat himself down near the organist. It was time to get Sandy out of here. She said more rapidly, "So we will see you for dinner around six. Until you're through with the quest, no one is allowed to call or help you from outside the cab, and you are to call no one else for help. It's up to the two of you, now." Getting it in again, wanting no one to interfere before the boys got their chance.

What had been lingering within Diane, now escaped into the shadowed silence between them. Regardless of everything she was saying to put Sandy at ease, there was fear here for her daughter. Plus, the fear she'd be found out for not switching the Divel was piling on.

Lightning flashed down the right side of the church, waking both women up, if they needed waking. The sooner Sandy got started, the sooner this would be over. God willing. "Okay, girl. Go get this done, then we can enjoy ourselves tonight. Good luck, dearest." She kissed her only daughter on the cheek, then removed the lipstick smudge with her thumb.

Literally, nudging Sandy on her way, once standing, Sandy motioned for Greg to join her. With Greg, ahead of the pack, the couple made a bee-line toward the front doors. The wedding party took notice and began to follow. Diane noticed that Mr. Tuttlebuttle was way down near the organist talking with the minister about something. Perfect.

When the front doors opened, as soon as Sandy went through under the arched overhang, the storm raged anew.

From behind everyone, Mr. Tuttlebuttle was coming up fast.

The wedding party began to encourage the newlyweds into the storm so they would reach the safety of their ride before they got too wet or blown away.

The watchers threw rice, but it didn't' stand a chance to reach the newlyweds or the cab with the sideways gusts.

Tuttlebuttle came through the door just as Greg slid in behind Sandy from the curbside and closed his door.

The huffing security man said, "I thought they—"

The cab pulled away smartly from the curb just as he had been instructed to do.

Whew!

As the newlyweds pulled away, as their own waiting began under the overhang for their own cabs to take them back to the large pink hotel, Frick knew they wouldn't get their chance until after Greg and Sandy finished whatever mysterious hunt they were on this afternoon. Then Greg would call—assuming Greg remembered to call. That's what he'd weaseled out of Greg, while Greg had practiced his prewedding circling, like a flight waiting to land. Yes, if they were going to get their shot at the necklace, it would be back at the caves. All they needed to do was make sure they got over there before Greg and Sandy returned to the Princess Hotel for their dinner. That is, if they returned. Frick knew what couples did during honeymoons. Plus, there was this storm that only seemed to be getting worse. Maybe the caves would fill up with water, making it impossible to reach them, or for them to get out tonight. He'd have to remember that, because Mrs. Waters said nothing about needing diving equipment.

After Mr. Tuttlebuttle stopped speaking, after those three words, Diane indicated for the two of them to step back inside to escape the unfriendly elements. To have more privacy. In the dim foyer, she offered how in the excitement, in the storm's lashing winds, "We had to hurry the couple into the cab before the wind blew them away." Then she paused for effect, as rehearsed.

Then her eyes went wide, like one of the parts she'd played back in college. "Oh-my-god," was the same line she'd spoken back then, too. Years of practice paying off.

She looked toward the front door as if she was planning to chase down Sandy, like she'd looked stage-right in *The Grinch that Stole Christmas*. Practice makes perfect. "They, they, can't be interrupted until they complete the hunt." That was the new line; a lot of *theys* in a storm, which succeeded in delaying any new pursuit.

Proud of herself for how authentic her delivery sounded, she knew in her heart that she would have made a talented full-time actress if she hadn't married Mike. The dim lighting and the sound effects of the storm were helping her performance, she believed, unlike the bright shadows near real stages that could trip you up. After those performances, she'd always celebrated with a drink; that still sounded like a great idea, if the non-4-wheel drive cabs could get them through to the hotel in this.

Mr. Tuttleborne's mouth had dropped open, keeping him silent. Diane didn't rush him. Then he asked, "But, what about the security of the Dive? It'll be running all across the island."

Diane had rehearsed for this, too. "Yes, but remember, Mr. Tuttleborne, you and I are the only ones who know the real one is out there. So, it will be just fine. Just fine, indeed. Until they return after their hunt. After their very safe cab ride that you arranged for them, I might add." She winked at him, as if the two of them were sitting in a bar having drinks. She was proud of herself for that last part, adlibbing. Sometimes the new material worked, sometimes it didn't.

Ships in the night, Diane hoped. Pirate ships.

Everyone was still outside, which was good.

Mr. Tuttleborne hesitated a moment. "Okay. Maybe you're right. So…it will be returned to me and only me, at the end of the hunt." Not a question. "Will you bring it to me, or will your daughter?"

"I will get it from her and return it to you, myself." After the slightest hitch, she added more of what was supposed to be part of this role, that she had first fleshed out on the wrong side of those tracks. "I could still be wearing this dress." Ad-libbing some more. In for a penny, in for a pound. If she was considering sleeping with the boys to grease the skids, why not this sexier, grown up real

187

man? He was definitely being too nosey and too conscientious for her liking.

On cue, the raincoat she'd been holding closed against the elements fell opened, displaying that long, tan leg inside that long slit in her black dress. "Will that be satisfactory?" Her rich red-lipstick smile piercing the shadows. Shadows that were now clearly supporting the greys and blacks of the Film Noir movie she had always wanted to star in: *The Isle of Divels,* or maybe more to the point, just: *The Divel* (Horror or Witchcraft)—unless, or when really, she received those good reviews, meaning there'd be more than one film with sequels coming. Her forwardness and the threat of a sequel colored her face, which was impossible to see in the dark, under her tan. Although the thought of success had momentarily gone right to her head and the rest of her sensually-charged body, the idea of the sequel had scared her like thunder. Clear thinking, she did not want any part of that sequel. She wanted this film finished, but good.

In the midst of this fantasy that had burst toward freedom after thirty years of tyranny, Mr. Tuttleborne offered, "I sure hope so, Mrs. Waters. For all our sakes." He swiped at his forehead, as if he was also hot in here the way they were both wearing outside clothing while her legs were speaking sex.

Diane watched him exit. He was cute, in a British stand-up-proper way. She would certainly have a drink with him, even more, if it would help keep the evil little Divel from latching onto her Sandy. She inhaled deeply, like she had discovered a cigarette in the dark—Film Noir, all right—her performance was deserving of a celebratory bottle of champagne.

Finally, everyone was on their way back to the hotel. Frack was thinking ahead, like a good partner-in-crime. Alone in this small cab with Frick, he said in code, "Maybe we should track down some caving helmets with those little light things on them. Just in case. To look the part."

Surely, the sun wasn't going to be coming out to help anyone see today. Any idiot could see that. Plus, they were talking a lot of money here. "I watch those adventure shows, you know. A little thing like that often makes the difference between success and failure in a cave." If he wanted to have Mrs. Waters, he was willing to become a caving expert real fast. His desire illuminated how a small, bright, strategically-placed light would come in real handy, in the dark, with a long, tan woman, wearing no clothes.

Frick just looked at him. "Don't you think they're going to have lights in those caves if people are paying good money to stay there?"

"I guess you're right."

The boys had understood from Mrs. Waters that the quest across the island would take the better part of the afternoon—even in good weather. To Frack, that seemed like a lot of wasted time, since Mrs. Waters was right here, so close, in the same swanky hotel with clean sheets and cold booze.

A hotel. Any idiot knew what hotels were used for. Especially a foreign hotel.

Frack's untethered fantasies began to include Mrs. Diane in this afternoon's extracurricular activities. She'd looked hot in that sleek black dress with that slit up the side. Feeling a little possessive, he was glad Frick wasn't interested in her. As the cab sliced through the rain, Frack pictured what she'd look like in a black caving helmet and that black dress. A new combination. Sexy. In the dark, with their two little lights on, helping them find the reflective zippers.

Clarke's perfect plan had been sunk even before he weighed anchor. What was he going to tell Tuttleberry? He needed to contact the couple, but he was prohibited from doing just that. And what about Benny? He'd leave him out of this mess for now—plain, pure survival. This was his part of the plan, not Benny's. The amateur hour part, that smelled like it was going to take far longer than its allotted hour.

Clarke's short drive to the hotel was a lonely, wet affair, made worse because it was distinctly different from what he'd expected. The two replicas were burning a hole in his jacket. He came quickly to the realization, the rationalization, that perfect plans by definition needed to contain their own contingency plans. Otherwise, he would soon be facing Benny empty-handed.

Feeling too warm, he replayed Tuttleberry's instructions: *This is very important. Remember how important this assignment is to me personally, the Princess Hotel, and the Waters. I cannot stress enough how important this is to all of us. And please remember, in addition to what I have just said, the treasure hunt after the ceremony is just as important as everything else. In this regard, remember, the bride will have detailed instructions. So, she is the boss. Got me?*

No, it's got me, he thought.

While water splashed under the car, Clarke second-guessed his decision not to chase down that hired cab right now. Before it was too late. Or, way too late.

Now his hands were tied but good. The charm hunt needed to be completed without any hitches, because if something happened out there, who had possession of the

Divel, when, would be called into question. Then either Tuttleberry or the insurance company would want it authenticated before its return to the vault. And that couldn't be allowed. Clarke cursed the endless gloom all around him. How the hell had this happened?

His thoughts turned frantic. His eyes darting this way and that, as if searching for the cab he needed to find but couldn't go near. What if he rammed it by mistake? Who could see out here in this?

For a moment, he'd gone a little crazy. He calmed himself. The rhythm of the wipers helping. Worst-come-to-worst, he'd have to wait to make the switch at the tail-end, when Mrs. Waters returned it. She'd been right, that dress was hot. He needed to keep his focus.

She was right. No one else knew. *Right as rain,* then he excused himself for the pun that was trying to lighten his mood a tad.

So what difference would waiting make?

That calmed him a little more.

The immediate problem remained: What to do about Tuttleberry?

And of course, Benny. His timeline was off with Benny.

Two things were off, and that was two too many out in a hurricane that was already scattering the pieces of his perfect plan.

PART IV

THE CHARM HUNT

CHAPTER 19

THE QUEST

After the rain, after the wind, after the rice that never reached them, and after the car door shut all that out, Sandy looked at Greg and took a breath. "The big mystery package has arrived." It was on her lap.

Glad to be alee of the storm, Greg said, "So open it already." His tone one of, let's get this over with, whatever it was.

With the quest slated to take the better part of the afternoon, the cabbie had pulled away from the church smartly. Though once away, he slowed, realizing none of them actually knew the first destination quite yet.

From the center of the backseat, Sandy asked the driver over his left shoulder, "Is there a light in here?" Still feeling odd that the driver should be on her side.

Aarone handed back a thin pink flashlight to his nicely dressed passenger. "Compliments of the Princess. I'm Aarone, by the way, your designated driver and tour guide."

Sandy undid the drawstring, opened the oversized red velvet pouch, and withdrew the folded-in-half, yellowed, thick paper. In very small print, instructions were laid out in a scripted hand. In the left margin, each paragraph was set off by a yellow triangle. The symbol appeared layered, as if woven by needle and thread. Under the circle of light, Sandy rubbed the first triangle with her finger. Surprised when it really was just ink.

Skimming the first paragraph because it only contained the general expectations for the quest, there was nothing new here. And the English was olde, dated, sort of what Mom was talking about. Her eyes gravitated to the second thread-gold triangle, and then followed the tiny circle of light along its first line.

Without his reading glasses, Greg was unable to see the letters. To include her new husband, she said upon finishing this section, "We're supposed to take a ferry someplace," as if this was a modern-day reality show. The pilot for the new *Hurricane Show.*

Greg reacted, "You must be kidding. In this? I don't think so." He swept his hand toward the maelstrom out there. Not ideal ferry weather. His first executive gesture as a husband.

"That's what it says here, honey," Sandy conveyed in a tone and with an expression that she was only reading what someone else had written hundreds of years ago.

Like any good Bermudian cab driver, Aarone knew how to be patient and friendly. Bermudians in general were friendlier than most, owing to the islands precarious existence literally in the middle of the ocean. Such a location, such a climate, such a soil, had convinced the natives long ago that they were dependent upon outsiders for their existence.

Aarone had prepped himself to talk up the island's many great points and its rich history to boost his tip, but they weren't going to transition to that part of the ride if his passengers drowned in the Harbour. Even if the ferries happened to be running, which he doubted.

Aarone pulled to the side of the road and stopped. That the newlyweds survive the quest was important enough for him to twist in his seat, rather than rely on that rearview mirror. Time to weigh in on whether or not he drowned today, especially with the leftover stew waiting in his frig. "Are you sure that's what it says, Mrs. Waters?"

Sandy returned to the first paragraph. "It says Ferry. I've been given strict instructions by my mother not to screw with this thing—excuse my French, Mr. Aarone. Barring…barring needed interpretation. So, I'm going to follow the letter of the law, as my ancestors have apparently done. If I don't, apparently, I'm, we're—" as she made a circular motion, sending the beam around and around, signifying that she and Greg were now a unit. "Cursed by this thing. And I'm not going to be the one in the family known at all future weddings as the bride who broke our chain." On that last word, she looked down at the heirloom. "Which actually feels warm at the moment. My blood must be up, as you say it."

The necklace's stones and white gold were reflecting light in a most fascinating way. Seemingly pulsating.

Lightning flared to the south, placing them all in an eerie silhouette befitting Halloween—never mind all the diamonds and the lightshow they seemed to share like a circuit. Storm against man. Light against dark. Electromagnetism and optics against heirloom.

In silence, Aarone turned forward to await instructions. Given the import of these instructions, Sandy added, "Nor as the Waters who reawakened the Curse of the Devil." She met Aarone's eyes in the rearview mirror.

In the popular guidebooks Aarone kept abreast of, he knew they mentioned how many of the islanders tended toward superstition. He wondered if this bright young visitor might be trying to scare him—for what purpose he wasn't sure.

"Yes, ma'am." Curse or not, there wasn't any reason

not to be agreeable to his special fare. And if it turned out there was, he'd have the right to ask for a larger fee at the end.

"Let me see if there's more info."

Greg remained silent. As far as he was concerned, this was her show. Her thing. She was wearing it. She'd had the talk with her mom. He was going along for the ride, literally. He was in a pretty decent mood about it, considering. He was pleased to be done with that small circling room and its pre-wedding willies, pleased to be out of the elements, and pleased to be sitting next to the woman he loved. It hadn't sunk in yet that they were married, probably because a cab was not how'd he'd pictured them starting out. And there was no good reason to share how he was still prepared to throw it right in the water, if her kvetching—a good Jersey word—started up again. Or for that matter, to let Frick and Frack have it. They seemed interested—more than interested.

Agreeable or not, wearing his baseball cap and rain gear, Aarone didn't particularly want to drown, even if they were supposed to walk onto a ferry in this. If ever there was weather for stew, this was it. Even his faithful dog, Sammie, knew better than to come out in weather like this. Besides, the tip wasn't big enough to suffer through a drowning. And the way he was figuring it, if he stayed clear of any boat rides, he'd have a good story to tell his grandchildren someday.

Having removed his eyes from her low-cut gown, facing forward so it would be easier to deliver the bad news, reacquiring her upper chest and by default the sparkling stones in the mirror, Aarone very politely offered the pièce de résistance. "The only reason I say this is because our ferries are probably not running today. Plus, they don't hold cars. Scooters, but not cars, you see. Does it mention where the ferry is supposed to take you? Is it the ferry where something awaits you?" He almost added "fair maiden" in some sort of quest-speak but stopped himself. "Or is it where you're headed that is important?" Anticipating the maiden's response, he turned on the chariot's wipers.

Greg looked over at Sandy, "What's it say, hon?" His voice all gung ho. After all, there was a honeymoon suite awaiting them somewhere out in this mess. Nothing was insurmountable here. How could a little college-like treasure hunt stand in the way of them reaching that room? True, this was a Category I hurricane, but they were safely inside a 4-wheel drive cab and the roads were passable.

The flashlight's beam stopped crossing the page. "Okay. The charm we need is located at the Maritime Museum. Maybe when they wrote this, the ferry was the best way to get there?"

Greg shrugged.

Aarone said, "You are correct, fair princess." And with a flourish, he turned the cab around and headed whence they came. "Without the storm, the direct route is the ferry across the Great Sound—about three miles that way." He pointed toward the tumultuous water out his side. "Instead, we have a trip of about ten miles along South Road, which will take us all the way to the far western tip of the island."

With the hunt formally begun, the couple settled back into their bench seat, leaning into each other to relax. Eventually, Sandy's head discovered Greg's right shoulder.

As they headed back the way they'd come, lightning streaked the sky to the south—the direction they were headed.

Clarke's mouth dropped open when a cab that looked just like Aarone's passed him going the other way. He was tempted to turn and cut them off. But in this weather, he wasn't sure it was them. And even if it was and he did, he'd probably get fired—not to mention draw attention to his secret perfect plan. He'd read the charm hunt instructions. He knew where they were headed. That meant they should have been on their way south, not here. He was seeing things. Actually, cracking up under the stress of his first crime. Some criminal he was!? Squinting, leaning-forward, he needed to get a grip.

Pulling a left and quick right into the hotel's small front lot, Clarke decided to leave the replicas inside the Peugeot's glove box. Hustling inside, dripping all over the lobby, he shed his raincoat to wait for the wedding guests to return. Wanting to mention one more thing to Mrs. Waters, as soon as she walked that dress back into his hotel.

It wasn't long before the Waters filed in. He congratulated everyone, intercepted the sleek looking Mrs. Waters, and wouldn't you know, that alluring slit under her raincoat reappeared like magic. Black magic.

She said to everyone, "I'll be right up." Her eyes seemed alive to Clarke. She was flirting with him again. Clarke smiled, "I hope you were pleased with how everything has gone so far."

"Wonderfully so, Mr. Tuttlebuttle. Wonderfully so."

He ignored his new name again and leaned in a little closer. "I wanted to mention that it would be best if we kept this little change with the Divels just between ourselves."

"I understand completely. My lips are sealed."

As Clarke walked away, he wondered could that really be true—lovely lips as they were. In all of one day, she had gained quite a reputation for drinking around the hotel. She was a pro.

Diane headed toward those elevators. What was up with the men involved with Sandy's wedding and their weird names? Frick and Frack. Tuttleborne and Tuttlebuttle. She found her dull reflection in the elevator door and congratulated herself on her subterfuge. She knew her name. Diane. A normal name. Unfortunately, Tuttlebuttle only seemed to be confirming how conscientious he was. She might have to divert him but good.

The door opened and she stepped inside the small room. As the quiet elevator rocked upward, she visualized the good-looking Mr. Tuttlebuttle. Older, but certainly not too old. If she was considering sleeping with the boys to protect Sandy, what was wrong with someone closer to her age?

She reached her room. Sure enough, her stick-in-the-mud husband was on that laptop. She silently turned toward their mini-bar. She wondered if all parents felt so liberated after their child's wedding, or did it just take one as strange Sandy's? Change was in the wind, and there was a lot of wind about.

Clarke made his way toward the rear glass doors. Toward his outside oasis in the back where he could think straight. His mind was already considering way too many unforeseen possibilities. Cutting to the chase, their plan had come apart. Looking at the wind-blown scene beyond the manicured courtyard, he was glad he'd peeked into the instruction pouch. Somehow, knowing where they were headed provided him with some small comfort, even if he wasn't sure how he could act on it. The idea of having options seemed to be a good thing to him—unless they were bad ones. Unfortunately, intercepting that cab and needing to deal with Benny, both fell in the wrong pile.

Looking across the Sound in the direction of the Royal Naval Dockyard, he knew it was the same location from where the Tucker Cross had been stolen. Was the location cursed or something? he laughed to himself. If that was the case, he should be driving there right now to make the switch. The problem was, without the ferries running, he couldn't get there in time.

Clarke steadied himself with a few deep breaths, considering what Mrs. Waters had said about being the only ones who knew. That was true, so there was really no reason to rush off to do something foolish. That calmed him.

A flash of lightning froze his countenance in the glass. Having his mug-shot up there like a criminal's, reminded him of Benny. He needed to call Benny.

The question remained: Should he wait for them to get back from crisscrossing the island, or try to pull off "accidentally" intercepting them somewhere? His boss would have to answer that question. He needed coffee, or something stronger. He walked into a small galley kitchen and grabbed a black coffee to-go.

He parked himself in a small sitting area with four cloth chairs, a matching couch, and three tables displaying magazines lying in neat rows. He took a sip. It was only lukewarm.

Yes, if he could get permission to contact them for security reasons, this might be easy to solve. The problem was the Divel's protocol superseded the hotel policy, because the hotel's policy was based on the Divel's protocol. It was all swimming in his head. He eyed the cover of an *Elle* magazine where a slender European model was wearing a necklace that looked cheap compared to the Divel.

He gulped more coffee. The good part was he had plenty of time. Worst case scenario, he'd wait for them to bring it back. He wasn't a weatherman, but it seemed to be getting worse out there.

Benny had explained to the neophyte criminal: Any schedule change is cause for concern. The last thing you want to do is make your partner anxious.

He finished off the coffee, crushed the cup before dropping it into the decorated trash can, and headed toward Tuttleberry's office. Along the way, he became concerned that by broaching the subject of the Divel's escape, he might induce Tuttleberry to ask for the Divel's authentication upon its return. Problems loomed everywhere, even from solutions. Maybe *he* was cursed.

The Waters wedding group was more than content to lounge inside until tonight's dinner. Everyone except the boys, that is. After getting a look at that necklace, Mrs. Waters hadn't exaggerated one bit.

Fearing she might be with her husband or Greg's dad, Frack's fantasies turned to hooking up with her and that sleek black dress. Money and sex were on his frisky mind, which was no different from back home. Except, conveniently, here, he and Mrs. Waters were already in the same hotel. He didn't have any mining helmets yet, but that slit was doing a great job of illuminating things all on its own.

With Frick entertaining himself with his phone, Frack considered, *location, location, location.* Emboldened by being in a foreign country, he speed-dialed Mrs. Waters. For his trouble and his fantasies, he got her voice-mail, so he hung up and texted instead:

> *Some unknown person would love to c*
> *u for unspecified reason :)*

He was hoping she'd be bored and drunk. Maybe she'd think he wanted to discuss the Devil Necklace. That would be okay. More than okay, either before, or, after ripping that expensive dress off her. It was already ripped, right?

When Frack stopped pecking on his phone, Frick said without looking up, "You are so full of it. I told you she'd be tied up."

"Very funny. And stop being so negative. She's in the hotel, so maybe she can break away. You owe me a six-pack if she does."

"Deal." He smiled. "There's nothin' like easy alcohol."

Diane was having a boring conversation with Sam about the strength of the hotel's construction materials—his specialty—when her phone vibrated in her purse. They were seated in the crowded upscale bar having a liquid lunch. Knowing from the sound of the alert that it wasn't Sandy, she ignored the call until Sam excused himself to the bathroom.

Diane peeked in her purse. The drink and the message warmed her up on this wet day, until it dawned on her it might mean the boys were getting cold feet. She rang him right back. "What's your room number again?"

When Sam returned, she excused herself, feigning tiredness, even if he was a nice man like his son. Crunch-time was crunch-time, and the boys needed to be all-in.

Sam was only too happy to see her back to her room. As they took the elevator up, Diane hoped the boys would yet prove how industrious they could be. She believed industriousness was worth a reward. The elevator dinged, and they made their way over the thick-carpeted hallway with its regal blues and reds.

Diane said, "See you later," and walked into her room seeing you know who, you know where. It was enough to make her drink—or keep drinking actually— though seriously, she wanted a cigarette at this point. She walked directly into the bathroom, took her dress off, freshened up, felt a little wobbly, walked out, shimmied into jeans, and made small-talk by asking how his storm was doing.

Mike stopped typing. Glanced up. "It's almost as if this thing followed me here," he admitted.

"I'm going to check on the girls and boys. I'll see you later." Five doors down, it was time for a booster session.

On the first knock, Frack opened the door.

She heard herself say, "Is this the gym with the liquor workout program?"

He smiled. "Why yes, madam. Actually, I can tailor a workout program specifically to your needs." That smile saying, he wished, as he closed the door quickly behind her.

When he caught back up, she noticed the smile still plastered on Frack's eager face. How absolutely young he was. But regardless of what a shit Mike was being and regardless of the stress of the weekend, the priority remained Sandy and the Divel. "You know the deal. The Divel, then me," she reminded him, saying it loud enough so Frick heard it too. As she came in, she wobbled a little bit, so Frack helped her to a seat with his arm. "One devil for another," she heard some new person say out of her mouth—trying on her new persona, like a new part in a play. If the boys delivered, she would be so relieved and grateful that maybe she could lose her head and reward them with a piece of nice little ass. Reward herself.

Frack asked solicitously, "Can I get you something from the minibar?" Seeing that she had had a few, he hoped one or two more might lubricate the works and loosen the hatch on ye older ship.

Frick stayed on the bed, on his phone, while Frack and Mrs. Waters sat in the two chairs next to the small round table in the corner. They lounged, making small-talk while sipping on those tiny bottles of spirits, until Mrs. Waters motioned toward the rain-drenched window. "At some point the two of you are going to have to get your asses out to Botto Bay in that." Then she stood, wobbled, and made her way toward the bathroom. "If, that is, you have any designs on getting this one." On the "this one," she supplied her own home-made exclamation point by wiggling her tush, just like she'd done when she made one of her dramatic stage exits.

In the tiny bathroom behind that thin door, it seemed self-evident to her that vacationers *did* act differently while on vacation, just like actors. And, how. Railroad tracks or not.

CHAPTER 20

DESTINATIONS

By now, the little-cab-that-could was well on its way to the Royal Naval Dockyard. With gale force winds delivering sheets of rain and lightning on the ocean-side, the storm was approaching from the south. When the coast turned slightly northwest, the winds began to boost the cab from behind. Once the cab became more controllable, Aarone offered, "So far so good. We're a little more than halfway now."

Greg chirped in. "From what I understand, this is not a race. We have all day, right?" The sound of deeper water being kicked up into the wheel wells interrupted him for a moment. "So, there's no problem with you taking your time."

Somewhere along here, Sandy's hand had found its way into Greg's. Now every sideways blow, sound of deep water, or flash of lightning was bringing an involuntary squeeze from her left to his right. Like a circuit being completed.

Entering the elevator, Clarke decided it was the lesser of two evils to inform Tuttleberry. That maybe Tuttleberry would give the okay to intercepting the newlyweds for the purpose of protecting the hotel's reputation. Still, there were too many unknowns here, and that wasn't even counting Benny's reaction. Benny's presence was lurking in the background, along with the storm's. If the storm hadn't already been named, he would have named it Benny, not George. Exiting the elevator, he looked out the window at the tempest and tried out, "Benny." It fit.

Clarke continued on toward Tuttleberry's secretary. All it took was one nod, and she buzzed him in given the weekend that it was. Clarke always took note of the smartly appointed office with its neat wood desk, neat chairs, small tables, and those closed and locked filing cabinets. Symmetrical. Everything was symmetrical, including the water colors. Even that long, low glass case containing his prized butterfly collection was in two equal sections. If someone forced Clarke to guess—like at carnival—he'd venture that Tuttleberry had the same number of specimens on each side.

Tuttleberry was sitting behind the middle of his desk, naturally, eyeing the centerfold of a butterfly magazine. At least that's what Clarke thought he was always doing. As the general manager of the hotel, Tuttleberry was fortunate to have direct reports that performed their jobs well, giving him loads of time to keep abreast of all the current butterfly news.

As Clarke approached the desk located in the butterfly capital of Bermuda, he wondered if he should stand in the middle of the rug to keep everything balanced. He half-joked that if he checked, there might even be a circle on the carpet—like those prompts used to tell actors where to stand. He aimed himself for one of the chairs, amused by the thought that the room might tilt. Of course, none of that mattered if you could fly.

"Hi, Winston. We've got a bit of a situation on our hands." Clarke preferred to call Tuttleberry, Tuttleberry. But in private, Tuttleberry preferred first names. Clarke remembered this had something to do with Tuttleberry's belief that no self-respecting butterfly would ever be named Tuttleberry. But Winston?

Winston folded the two halves of the magazine together, closed his laptop to the Butterfly Blog, and said, "Okay, Clarke. Fill me in. Coffee?"

"No thanks. But you might want something stiffer." Winston, never one to require much encouragement, deftly unlocked a drawer—even though his outer door was always locked—and withdrew a silver flask. "Go."

"It involves the Divel, sir."

Winston unscrewed the small cap with familiar dexterity and took a quick nip, wincing from the imported medicine. Immediately, he replaced the top with that tinny scraping sound. When Winston opened his eyes, it was Clarke's signal to continue.

"Unfortunately, the original didn't come back from the ceremony." Going straight to it like a shot at the doctor's office. "Neither the parents nor myself received the necklace back from the bride. So, it hasn't been switched out for the replica...yet." That "yet," a nice touch on the fly.

"That is not good." The top spun off and another shot went down.

Clarke watched the effect spread across Winston's face, which probably explained all those blood vessels in his nose. It would be quite understandable that Winston nipped a bit while waiting out in the bush to capture his next prize. This week's medicine, like every week's since he'd known him, was whatever liquor Winston's cousins bootlegged onto the island. He had a sufficient number of cousins, apparently.

Winston's eyes regained their balance. "That hasn't happened since, well, since the mid-1800s." That tinny scraping sound occurred again.

Clarke waited for Winston's eyes to reopen, but when

they did, Clarke was unsure what to say. He vaguely recalled that old story from the previous century, but the main point here was that authentication had been requested after that incident.

Winston grumbled, "That was a very long time ago."

"Yes, yes it was. We can handle this situation more easily than they were able to because everyone knows we have a replica now. All we have to do is regain our chain of evidence."

"Chain of what?"

He smugly thought, *Chain of fools,* but repeated, "Chain of evidence."

"So, we should call them?" Sounding like he was thinking out loud. Clarke hoped this was the beginning of his go-ahead.

But Winston followed it right up with, "I'm so flustered this has happened on our watch, I forgot we can't call them. Their Trust agreement forbids it."

"It's something having to do with the ritual that wards off its curse." Hoping of course the mentioning of that would have an impact on Winston, even though Clarke didn't believe in such mumbo-jumbo, any more than the man-in-the-moon.

"Oh. Yes, yes. Their curse. We can't have any of that, now can we?" The mention of that word caused Winston's fingertips to itch against that top with uneasy anticipation. Any fortification against curses was welcome on the eastern part of the island where he was from.

Clarke was fighting like hell against himself, as that metal-on-metal sound occurred again. Would Winston ask for it to be authenticated? If Winston said no, then the switch would be a piece of cake. And Clarke believed timid Winston would say no. Until Clarke brought it up. Then Winston would appreciate the opportunity to protect himself against any curses, new or old. Clarke sensed this was what people meant by vicious circles. And then it piled on, that it was often some innocent remark in the crime books that gave-the-ghost-away.

Winston pried the collar away from his neck with his index finger. The enormity of the situation had robbed his mouth of saliva. He unscrewed that top, took another hit, and wiped the distasteful situation from his mouth with the back of his hand. When he looked up at Clarke, he said, "Well, what are you still doing here, mate? Figure something out without bringing the curse down upon our necks. That's all I need at my age—close to retirement and all. A state-protected chicken hanging above my front door. Blood dripping all over the place. For all my neighbors to see. There'll be family shame in this if this Divel curse-thing goes bad." Winston's eyes looked far away again, like they probably did when he was searching the woods for his next catch.

After a pause, Winston focused back on Clark. "Can you imagine what God-awful thing happened to the executive of the Maritime Museum after the Tucker Cross crucifixion." Winston's fingertips itched against the top again. "In front of the Queen, no less." Winston then froze stiff, just like he had once described to Clarke how butterflies reacted when frightened.

Clarke had his mandate. Sort of. Do something without calling them.

Expecting the room to tilt as he exited, Clarke gave the secretary a smart nod before following it up with, "Good night," though he meant to say, Good day. It was anything but a good day, and it was dark like night out, and it already felt too long for it to have been just the day part of a day.

He headed to the third-floor room, grabbed his wrinkled London Fog raincoat and his mismatched taupe

211

drawstring hat, and hustled toward the elevator.

The elevator seemed hopelessly slow to arrive, and then the descending part took even longer. As soon as he exited the front door, he pulled up short. Looking out into the teeth of the storm, it was obvious this wasn't the smartest thing he'd ever done. Protected by the small overhang from the worst of it, George was spitting on him. With the wind whipping his coattails, he tied the blasted belt that he normally never used. Thank God for the drawstring, that just so happened to make him look like some new Australian actor. At least there was some solace to be had, that if he couldn't get to the newlyweds, no one else could either—Mrs. Waters' point. Given the Trust, given the storm, George could almost be viewed as an ally at this point. A blustery ally.

He returned to the foyer to call Mrs. Waters.

Mrs. Waters answered with, "Hello, who is calling?" as if she hadn't recognized his name when it popped up on her caller ID.

"Hi, Mrs. Waters. It's Clarke Dearborne, again."

She hitched for just a moment, then said as if a puzzled had been solved, "Oh, I recognize your nice voice. Have you come up with a Divel solution, my good man?" mimicking her best English accent.

The way she phrased this, caused him to ask, "So you think there is something to this Divel-thing, after all?"

"How is that?" she asked, as if she hadn't heard him very well.

"It has made you clairvoyant."

"Ha! You're a funny full-grown man, Mr. Tuttleborne." He didn't pause nearly as long on this name change as the last one. "Anyway, I've been thinking about it. What is Sandy and Greg's itinerary after they finish the hunt?"

"They will finish up on the east end of the island per protocol. Since that will put them over near their hotel, I suggested they change out of their formal clothes before coming back. Good thing, looking at this weather."

"Yes, a very good thing. Where will they stop?"

Diane was having a little difficulty pronouncing her words. "They will stop at… I remember something about caves: 'C.' Cotto Bay Resort, where they'll be spending their honeymoon."

"Okay then." Clarke's girlfriend, Morgan, managed Grotto Bay Resort. Very convenient indeed. Things were improving. "Is that all you wanted?" sounding disappointed.

"Yes, thank you. I'll call you when I know more."

"Yes, please do, Mr. Tuttlebuttle…And come by the reception tonight, if you can. All of us could use a little extra motivation in this storm."

"Thank you. I might just take you up on that. Bye, bye."

Clarke hadn't been out to that side of the island as much as he would have liked. Never mind that it was a whole twenty minutes to get there. Morgan always brought a smile to his face. Rain or shine, and this definitely qualified for the rain part.

Win/win.

Hands on the Divel.

Hands on Morgan. He'd surprise her and enjoy watching her face light up the way it did—he and everyone else could sure use more light on a day like today.

With the poor weather, he was glad to be driving his workhorse Peugeot. Heavy was good, though he wouldn't be winning any speed records getting over there. It was times like this that it was nice to have an old beat-up car so you didn't have to worry about it getting damaged.

Rushing to his left through the light rain and heavy wind, he unlocked the car, climbed in, and started up the tired engine. Wipers on. Lights on.

Before he pulled away, he checked the glove box. Just in case. The light hadn't worked for years, so he reached in blindly, feeling for the sack and its two replicas. Good to go.

He made a right toward downtown. With the car being rocked by the wind, with the old wipers swiping the best they could, Benny came to him. He was headed toward Benny's.

Clarke had no desire to stop and face Benny without the Divel, even though he'd be passing close to the French Quarter section of town where Benny's pawnshop was located. Benny's Shoppe, that was normally cramped, dingy and frankly, uninviting, would be even more so today. Plus, it was black as ink out, and everyone knew that people were burgled all the time in the French Quarter in the dark. Given the empty streets, Clarke wasn't being rational here. But the problem he faced wasn't exactly rational either.

Compounding his sense of unease was the stark contrast between Morgan and Benny. Simply put, it was the difference between pleasure versus pain. Her bright smile versus Benny's wrinkled animal-face. Positive versus negative karma. Honest forthrightness versus underworld seediness. And if he allowed himself the luxury of extremes, maybe even life versus death.

No, there'd be no detour to Benny's. And Benny had warned Clarke to stay off their cells. But that still left Clarke the option of calling from another phone. As soon as he considered this, he envisioned his trial where someone would no doubt assert:

Yes, I overheard Mr. Clarke Dearborne, the man sitting right over there (pointing)—you, all know Clarke—talking on the telephone to Benny-the-fence on that Saturday, around noon.

Slicing through deeper water, Clarke most definitely did not want to be either a dead-duck trapped in a courtroom, swinging upside down in this wind fouling up his front porch, or stuck in a ditch inside his workhorse Peugeot. That left one option that he could live with. Well, live with, as long as he didn't get struck by lightning or run off this road that looked thinner with water rushing down both sides. He'd find a payphone at a gas station on the way. And if he was struck—and for some weird reason that didn't seem to be as nearly threatening as facing Benny in person—then the Divel Necklace might really be cursed.

He slowed down as he made his way past downtown Hamilton. Front street was flooded; possibly his tires weren't as good as he remembered. The taller buildings on his left were deserted and quiet, while the Harbour on his right was anything but. The small white boats looked like those horses on a merry-go-round that went up and down with the music. But there wasn't any music, just a howling wind.

It had been so long since he'd used a payphone that he wasn't sure where to find one. Not to mention, one that worked. As he nosed the car into the constant gloom ahead, it occurred to him he'd been faced with way too many decisions today. And the day wasn't even half over. He wasn't cut out for this crime stuff. It aged you.

The first gas station wouldn't appear until he escaped downtown proper—that much he knew. The Harbour was beginning to burst over the erosion wall in fingers of white. When he passed the Underwater Institute at the far eastern edge of both the downtown and the water, his hands let go of their death-grip on the wheel. Whoever had named that place, knew what they were doing.

Why he had to look for an outdoor payphone today of all days, in a hurricane, killed him. Well, at least he hoped not. The tired wipers needed replacing. Maybe it was time for a whole new car. He pulled into the first station he came up on, saw a phone box, turned off the engine, and stuck his fingers in the tiny coin box in the dash looking for change. He got lucky. Lucky in the face of the lost Divel, Benny, and the raging storm.

Unlucky would have meant no change, forcing him into the little white store:

You all know Clarke Dearborne (pointing). Why he needed changed for a phone call in an electrical storm mystified me, sir, but now it seems clear enough, if you're asking me why….

Coins in hand, Clarke opened his door. The wind ricocheted it off its stop, sending it back into his shin. Rubbing the searing pain away, he held onto the door, forcing it closed. Fisting the coins while holding his hat down with his other hand, he tucked his chin in and leaned toward that wet metal box in the electrical storm.

Now, would the blasted thing work? Would he be able to hear Benny's unpleasant voice in this tempest? It didn't take a genius to realize he was crazy to be out here. Bermudian homes were famous for their functional shutters. And that's where he should be right now, hunkered down behind them, with either Dee or Morgan, or both. Another triangle. But that triangle was only a fantasy, as opposed to the Divel which was very, very real. Three times real, if he counted his prisoners in the glove box.

Leaning into the wind, he picked up the slick receiver, pulled it to his ear, and heard nothing. "Great," he spit at George. Was anything going to be easy today? He tapped the silver latch and got lucky. Dropping the coins in, he listened to them fall, dialed Benny, and pushed the small silver loudness button three times before ending up back where he started.

"Hello," Clarke heard Benny's low-key, animal-like voice through the wind.

Amateur Clarke almost mentioned his name. "Something's happened." A lightning flash produced static over the line. He was never going to see Morgan.

Clarke raised his voice to be heard over the thunder. "We're off timeline."

"I kinda figured that already. I thought you told me that never happens." He said this in the same tone as when he'd said to Clarke: *Change, any change, is unwelcome when dealing with millions of pounds.* Benny had been a short boy who'd grown taller to become the short man he was today. Seemingly never having enough to eat as a youngster, he ended up being slightly overweight his whole life. Suspicious and insecure by nature, he'd been raised by an alcoholic mother who often made excuses for why she couldn't keep the promises she made to her only and needy son. By the time Benny had grown to be a short, fully-grown animal, it was only natural he expected the world to operate by these age-old rules.

"I know. I know. It never has, except—"

"Except, when?"

More static.

Clarke paused to wipe water from his nose and mouth. It was difficult to hear every word, though Clarke knew full well what Benny was saying. However, through the static, George was letting Clarke know who the real boss was out here. Clarke was third on this totem pole. "Except the one other time in the 1800s."

"—pare me the history lesson…" He heard Benny say, before more static cut in. "You still there?"

"Yeah. The mother didn't return it to me. By the time I reached them, the bride and groom had left for their hunt."

"I thought you said she knew she had to exchange it. That the mother always knows it has to go back to the vault."

"I know, I know. Somehow the mom didn't remind her. She seemed drunk. And the newlyweds were anxious to get their quest underway with their honeymoon suite waiting."

"You said this couldn't happen."

"Well, it did Benny." He pulled his hat down before the wind took it away. "To the both of us, I might add."

Benny's voice capitulated they were still a team. "Okay. Where does that leave us?"

"I'm working on it. Shouldn't change anything, just delay things."

"Let's hope so, for both of our sakes. I've made promises."

"I'm working on it—".

Clarke heard a click.

"—I'll call you as soon as I know something." Finishing his thought, just in case Benny hadn't really hung up on him.

Benny had heard enough. There was always an excuse coming from the unreliable people he dealt with, though he had expected more from Clarke. It was times like this that made him feel more like a judge, or maybe a priest, than a fence.

He reached for the chocolate cookie he'd pilfered this morning from the local bakery that had closed before officially opening. Today was supposed to have been a good day. Rising from his too tight chair behind his tight desk, he hobbled stiff to the bright front room where his jewelry business was conducted. Humidity like this always made his joints stiff.

As he devoured the moist cookie, he hazarded a peek at the storm through the yellowed venetian blinds hanging in his thick rectangular window. He had ignored his arthritis today because today was supposed to have been a good day. No longer distracted by such promise, his old joints were letting him know it was business as usual. Swiping his fingers clean against his old pants, business as usual prompted him to make a phone call he didn't want to make—just in case this got worse rather than better.

He'd been successful in business because he kept his promises. And conducting business this way had helped keep him in safe(r) in some less obvious ways. Like, for one, not having to worry about being cursed by someone's relative. Every family on the island had at least one witch-talker available amongst their clan. As far as the locals were concerned, these were the secret weapons on the island. Benny didn't like weapons—human, supernatural, or otherwise. He preferred plain ol' uncursed money.

CHAPTER 21

THE CUR-*SED* TREASURE HUNT

Aarone announced to his quiet passengers, "We're coming up on the Museum." Given the heads-up, Sandy unclenched her hand from Greg's, unfolded the parchment, and aimed the circle of light at any last-minute, cowering-in-the-dark details:

*No outside contact or direct help, though modes of transportation are allowed.

Lightning flashed to her right. In the flash, Sandy spied something overwritten by the script. Down at the bottom. In the middle. There was a seal. It was so faded it was hard to tell whether it really spelled "St. George" or not.

Greg said, "That necklace sure lights up when the lightning flashes out there." He kept watching it until the sparkles petered out.

"It's amazing, isn't it?" Sandy answered, though she was trying to decipher all this old writing:

*The official quest must be completed in customary wedding apparel, no later than the first Fore-Night.

"Aarone, what's a Fore-Night?"

"That, my lady, is an old English term for the period of time between twilight and bedtime. It—"

"Thanks." Sandy's eyes reacquired where she left off:

Five destinations will be used to gather charms—that will enhance yours chances of reaping the benefits from the five marriage-related themes destined to improve your luck:

Something olde, something new
Something borrowed, something blue
And a silver sixpence in a shoe.

Sandy recalled this verse was credited to the Victorian age. But to be cited here, its origins could easily be older still. It was only now, reading through it the second time, that Sandy made the connection that the first charm and its location corresponded to: *Something olde.*

Now, at least, there was some rhyme and reason to this family ritual. The hunt, the quest for charms, was an extension, an expression, of the wives' tales that were focused on providing the marital couple with a favorable wind as they begin their life together. As opposed to the wind out there, that was most definitely not helping.

With the weight of this history in her lap and around her neck, Sandy came around to the same conclusion that most of the brides had before her. That it was easier just to go along to get along.

She read on:

4 acquisitions and 1 act are necessary to counteract The Curse of the Divel Necklace….Designated Charms must be stowed away with the Cur-sed Object to have the….full, beneficial, and desired effect.

Reading, Sandy missed that the cab was passing a huge stone wall on their left. After making it through the tight stone entranceway, Aarone announced, "We're here. Entering Royal Naval Dockyard proper. Maritime Museum straight ahead. By far the longest trip I've ever made to get here."

Sandy stopped reading. Did making the couple traverse one end of the island to the other in some way symbolize the new couple's commitment to each other—

rain or shine? They definitely had the rain part down. She hoped that one of them had mailman genes in the family. When the cab hit a small bump, it knocked her from her reverie. "You have any mailmen in your family?" she asked her new husband she suddenly didn't know enough about. "What?" Greg said.

"Nothing, honey."

When they finished passing the white-washed, large-stoned walls on both sides of the road, Aarone said, "We are now in is the largest and most visited attraction on the whole island—six acres worth. These large walls fortified the Dockyard against attack—from either land or sea, or even storm." That last part sounding like it was just added on. "This far-western location guards the entrance to the Great Sound on our right, though you can't exactly enjoy the view at the moment. The largest cruise ships dock here, while the smaller ones actually cross the Sound and dock in Hamilton Harbour. The place we just came from. Going that route, Hamilton is only three miles—"

Sandy wished they could have taken one of those to get over here, though Aarone's details were interesting, and would have been more interesting if it hadn't been her wedding day.

"In that direction," indicating it with a quick nod to his right. Aarone slowed the car to negotiate some tight curves, then pointed with his left hand. "That's the cavernous Queen's Exhibit Hall. They keep documents related to shipwrecks there. And it happens to be the location where the famed Tucker Cross was stolen from. And over there," pointing again, "is the Commissioner's House, which was the world's first cast-iron building. It's very old. Incredibly, it has three-foot thick limestone walls, and a circular veranda that boasts a three-hundred and sixty-degree view from up top.

Pulling up to a stone building, Aarone finally got to stop the cab with its two worn tires in the back. The wind and rain had slackened off, conveniently. "We're here. I told you we'd make it," he boasted, as he unclenched his hands from the wheel, flexing his fingers.

Greg chimed in. "Do you think their even open in this?"

Sandy squeezed his hand. "There's only one way to find out, honey. Let's go."

From the front seat, two windbreakers and two Bermuda caps were handed back. Maybe Aarone had been a boy scout. Both caps displayed: "Princess." One set was pastel blue and one was pastel pink. Out of habit, Aarone began to reach for his door to help his passengers exit, but caught himself after remembering his strict instructions.

Zipping up, Sandy stuffed the papers in her large rectangular outside pocket. Greg came around, opened her door, and they hustled through the light rain toward the dimly lit entrance.

When Greg grabbed the handle of the glass and wood door, and pulled, the door rattled but remained shut. Shut. Locked. "You shitting me?" That's all they needed— three-foot-thick walls, no less.

Sandy read the sign: *Please use other door.* She opened the left side and gave him a sideways glance. Words way unnecessary.

A fortyish woman with large brown rectangular glasses, a long sleeve green blouse, and matching olive and off-white checkerboard skirt was perched behind a glass-paneled counter stuffed with model relics. The part-time actress offered, "Well, hello you two. Are you…lost?" Like a repertory actor in *The Tempest*, she almost said "shipwrecked." But at the last moment she managed to improvise and not stay within her own storm-themed play. These two actors were dressed for a wedding scene.

The bride said, "Not exactly. Are you open?"

"That's an interesting question, since the show is always supposed to go on. Right? So technically, we are, though we're more like…prisoners today," she said, after rejecting *castaways* or *marooned*. "We can't leave to get home, so the doors stay open. It certainly doesn't hurt that we're inside a fort. And I can tell you, you should win the "Best Dressed" Oscar for today." She almost asked where they were able to get such authentic-looking costumes on a day like today. She knew all the shops.

The bride shook out her jacket, slipped her fingers into her pocket and produced some papers. "To tell you the truth, this location is part of a treasure hunt we're on—"

The woman thought, *Kids! They're not actors. Are they crazy or something?* "You kids. You're always looking for Adventure, Adventure, Adventure, with a capital "A.""

"This is the get the 'something olde' part," the bride shared. "I guess something old like the Sea Venture, if you have it? Do you have one of those?" Sandy looked at some of the built models inside the case. Her mother told her to interpret, so she was interpreting.

"Why, yes." The woman's nicely featured face brightened itself right into sales-mode. "The *Sea Venture* was the original ship that grounded on the island back in 1609 during a tempest. Probably just like the one out there." She came from behind the counter and walked over to another case where small boxes were neatly stacked. "Makes you glad you're on land right now, doesn't it?"

"Yes, it sure does," the groom agreed.

"Some minor assembly is required. Is that okay?"

The young man snickered. "Isn't that what everyone

224

wants to do on their honeymoon night?"

The woman looked back at the newlyweds, as if this groom actor had just misspoken his lines.

The young woman slapped the brand-new husband's arm, before saying to her, "No *problemo*. After the trip we went through to get here, I'd put it together, even if I had to lick it to make it stick." The woman thought that sounded strange, too.

The groom smiled at his bride. "I like the sound of that."

She play-slapped his arm again, then handed over her credit card to pay for the cheap model. The young woman sounded sincere when she delivered with a bright smile, "Thank you. You don't know how much this means to us."

The part-time actress clerk thought the girl was overacting.

The credit card took its time going through, which was often the case in bad storms. "You're not staying for anything else?" the clerk asked, as she handed over the grey plastic sack to the young overdressed woman.

"We'd like to, but we have other places we need to visit. Don't we, honey?"

The groom agreed, "Yes, we do." Whereby he steered his social, model-building wife toward the front door by placing his hand in the middle of her back.

"Well of all the strangest things," the part-time actress said. "Good luck," she shouted, as she heard that right-side door open then close. She was a little worried for them out there in this modern tempest, as opposed to the one in her scene. Trained to use whatever setting or prop was at hand, the storm helped her get right back into character.

Back at the ranch, which happened to be pink, something triggered worry in Diane. Despite this dismal weather, she was hoping the kids would have better luck on that ferry than she and Mike had. That had been the last time she'd been on open water. Sick on open water, actually. Somehow that topsy-turvy ride had made it that much easier for her to avoid water all these years. That's how it had begun, she recalled, way back at the very beginning. That stupid ferry ride. She comforted herself with the fact that Sandy wasn't prone to sea sickness like she was. Thank God for that.

After opening and closing Sandy's door, while making his way around the rear of the cab, Greg glanced at the tread on those rear tires.

When both passengers were in, Aarone said to the shoppers, "I hope that went well. Where to next?"

Sandy announced, "One down, four to go," in her optimistic voice. Retrieving the parchment, after a short delay, she relayed to the team, "It says here we're supposed to find the highest vantage point that affords us a panoramic view."

"We practically passed it on the way," Aarone answered without hesitation. "Gibbs Hill Lighthouse. It's back the way we came. Just off South Road. The road we spent all that time on where the pink beaches are located."

Greg piped up, "I didn't exactly see any pink out there."

Sandy gave him a pained look. "Well, then it's my turn not to see anything pink. I'll be on the beach-side now, spoil sport. Mr. Negative can just stay on his side of the car." Then she folded up the parchment and tucked it back into her pocket.

In the rearview mirror, the tour guide saw the bride

stick her tongue out at her new husband. Drama over, he navigated the car back through those tall stone walls.

Driving along, they crossed a tiny bridge where the name of the road changed from Somerset to Middle Road. Aarone's patriotic flare produced, "That's the smallest drawbridge in the world."

Sandy looked out the side. "Where?"

"I told you, you wouldn't see anything," Greg chided her, as he turned around and looked out the back. There was nothing there, except the road. "What's it for besides mystifying tourists?"

"It's not used much anymore. But it allows small boats to travel from the Great Sound on our left, to Ely's Harbor, on our right. Otherwise, boats have to travel all the way around the tip we just came from. And that's a long way around in a boat—"

Greg joked, "It's a long way around in a car." Sandy turned her head and just looked at him.

Aarone continued overtop the words that weren't being spoken in the back. "All the way up and all the way back. Half of it in the ocean that is usually rougher than the bay. The real curiosity of the thing is that the bridge opening is so narrow, that someone has to be topside to guide the mast through the opening in the road. Actually, the little thing is pretty famous. It's on one of our postcards; a banknote, too."

Since the start of their quest, either the wind, rain, or both had been making a commotion. On this side of the smallest drawbridge in the world, rain began to come down without much wind. The deserted road became even more difficult to see. Whenever Aarone flicked on his high-beams, they didn't help. At least his fog lights were making the edges of the road more visible, even if those edges were flowing.

With the storm approaching from the south, Aarone chose not to take the coastal road back to the lighthouse. Instead, staying on Middle Road, it brought him up to their destination from the rear. Now right behind it, they wound up a small hill into a semi-circle parking area. Aarone snugged the car near the squat shop's entrance. The gift shop on the right sat flush against the white lighthouse that shot upward into the gloom. Through the swiping windshield wipers, Aarone pointed while saying, "The door is right there."

The pair jumped out.

Greg said, "Only one door. Good."

Sandy opened it first try.

CHAPTER 22

ABLE TO LEAP TALL BUILDINGS IN A SINGLE BOUND

The bright little shop was over-grown with touristy nick-knacks. From behind a counter that was partially blocked by the gift-jungle, a middle-aged man looked up with surprise from the large, lie-flat, spiral-bound book titled *How to Build your own Sailboat.* The man picking up a new hobby said cheerfully, "Hello there. You're my first customers of the day. May I build you a boat?"

Greg said, "We could use one. How long will it take?"

Sandy cut through the pleasantries with, "My new husband is being funny. We actually need something from here—we're on a treasure hunt." Unfolding the parchment, trying to keep it dry, she finished reading the section to the right of the third yellow triangle.

The shopkeeper's eyebrows arched upward. It was possible he had a couple of lulus on his hands. But all types came through. Lulus were allowed. He noticed all the 'l's in those two words. Since childhood, he'd enjoyed using a concentration of letters. This, just one of the many lonely gift shop games he used to keep himself from going lulu. That, and being on the lookout for new hobbies that he might or might not actually take up after reading all about them.

Still reading, Sandy muttered to no one, "You're kidding me." The men didn't get it, but the knickknacks did. They'd heard this before.

Greg came up next to her. "Under 'Something New' we're supposed get to the high point and peer out in all four directions. Then provide some kind of drawing of each view…" She looked at Greg, "I guess as documentation." Then returning to her parchment, "After that, we have to purchase something that signifies the location."

Greg twisted his face up. "Drawings? I was hoping this would be easy like the last one."

Mr. Boat Builder remained quiet. Whatever they were up to, they'd done it at least once already.

"Me, too," Sandy agreed. Pointing her finger toward Greg, she offered, "We won't have to draw anything. We can snap pics with my phone."

"Great idea."

Lulus all right, Mr. Boat Builder thought.

Trying to get into the marital spirit of things, Greg said, "New views. Maybe it's metaphorical for new horizons?"

"I like that," Sandy smiled.

With a loud gust against the front of the building, the wind cast its own vote.

Yes. The shopkeeper was sure they had earned those "l's" already. *Maybe earned them like wings?* he thought, but wings didn't have any "l's." And wings would definitely not do them any good up there today.

Again, they all heard the wind beat against the front of the little shop that was smart to be cowering against the tall, vulnerable lighthouse.

Greg leaned into Sandy. "Who's to know whether we really go up there or not?" As he said it, he looked at the possible spoilsport on the other side of that counter. "We can buy one of these little lighthouse thingies and some postcards and split?"

"I won't tell," the concerned man said like he meant it. He wasn't even sure he could let them go up there on a day like today. "Plus, it would ruin my day if I lost someone up there."

Sandy chewed on her lip for a bit, before responding to her pragmatic new husband. "The Divel would know. My family would know. And I'm not going to be the Waters who breaks this chain." She stared down Mr. Boat Builder. "Where's the stairway to Heaven?" End of discussion.

Mr. Boat Builder didn't understand the comment about the devil, but he wanted no devil stuff in his shop. With his right arm going right, "Outside. To the right. I'm not even going to charge you. I have a longstanding policy of not charging tourists who come through here trying to set some record. I would caution you, though, about going outside when you reach the top. You can see to the north and east out the door from the inside. Maybe that will be enough for you to win your twenty-five-dollar gift certificate from the camera shop in Hamilton. They're always running these blasted promotions."

Greg said, "He's a comedian." Mr. Boat Builder chirped, "Someone dare you into this during a drinking game last night?"

"Something like that," Sandy answered. She pulled Greg toward the door.

As they went out, Mr. Boat Builder threw his voice. "You're paying for the souvenir, though. When you come back." He said this to guarantee they'd be coming back, because he wasn't a liar. After the door shut, he said, "Children." This was said in the same tone as "tourists," but it contained an "l."

231

Sandy took a little detour to the cab to fetch her phone with its decent camera, then scurried back through the light wind and rain to meet Greg at the entrance. The slender white cylinder appeared to shoot up impossibly straight before disappearing into the gloom.

Inside, the walls were lightly colored, the staircase was round and tight and steep, the stairs were clean, and the curved silver railing was easy to see.

Near the bottom, as if they had all the time in the world, they paused to read:

100 Years
Gibbs Hill
Lighthouse
Centenary
1ˢᵗ May 1846 to 1ˢᵗ MAY 1946

Sandy snapped a pic of those dates superimposed upon a beautiful landscape, then snapped another of a map of the island that indicated at the bottom:

YOU ARE HERE

Greg eyed the scene where the white lighthouse was portrayed against the backdrop of a tranquil blue-skied day. He pointed, "You see the sky in that picture? That's the way it's supposed to look when they let you go way up there."

Sandy didn't bother responding to the spoilsport. Staying down here was not an option. In silence, except for the wind that occasionally howled, Sandy pointed the way she wanted Greg to head. To lead. Up. Up those disappearing steps. To be the fearless leader.

Dutifully, Greg headed up.

Sandy followed, and as she began to silently count the

steps, she had the distinct impression that they'd become puppets in some fantastic game. The problem was, someone else was pulling the strings.

Occasionally, Greg grunted ahead of Sandy, as Sandy trudged and trudged and trudged up those endless stairs behind the grunter.

They continued upward by using their legs against those steps and by pulling on that railing with their arms. And up. And then up some more. Somewhere in the thirties, Sandy's cute, hopeful counting dropped away. It wasn't fun anymore. They'd passed through several landings already without stopping, each containing some interesting touristy history—if one felt like resting or learning. But Greg had refused to slow down for anything. She had created a monster.

With the elements quieted, with the structure feeling nice and solid, after going in circles over countless steps, Sandy said to his backside, out of breath, "I'm picking up a theme here…on this trek…of ours. Odyssey…I mean. Those who seek together…stay together."

Greg didn't answer because he was tired and wanted to get this over with, because he was out of breath, and because he was worried this wasn't the worst of it. It never seemed to help him when his hunches were proven correct, and this climb appeared to be shaping up exactly like that.

After an incredible number of pushes with knees and pulls with his right arm, he abruptly came upon the smallest, dimmest landing of all. The sounds of the gusting winds were close again, like they had been on the bottom landing. There was a short ladder attached to the left-side wall, and just above it, a small door. No more steps, just a few rungs. No more circles. They had reached the top. He pulled himself to the top of the ladder and craned his neck to look out. The slender door led out to a very narrow catwalk surrounded by another metal railing. Everything was wet out there.

Catching his breath, he asked, "Why not take the picture from in here? Look how much you can see that way." He pointed toward the sky that they could see a lot of because the lightning was piercing it like there was an electrical grid hidden in the clouds. After all that work to get this high, Mr. Boat Builder's advice sounded even saner from Greg's too-high vantage point.

"We're supposed to take all four directions," Sandy answered without hesitation.

Greg didn't have a response to that. At least not one with words.

With him looking down at her, with his mouth open, she pleaded, "Look, if my mom did this, I can do it."

"She didn't necessarily do it in a hurricane." At every turn, his best braking efforts were being summarily defeated by his gung-ho partner. He decided something. He came down, put his feet back on the landing, put his arms around her, and whispered, "Let's make love right here." Could he distract her with sex? Get her to come to her senses—well, appeal to her other senses, that is.

Tired, with her neck warm, surrounded by the dim light, a howling wind, and a family quest, speechless with being offered what she wanted but couldn't enjoy at the moment, Sandy squeaked, "Now? After one thousand steps?"

"Then we'll take all the pics your little heart desires, right through that window while wearing our birthday suits. Won't that be a great honeymoon memory? Much better than going out in all that electricity, nude. Who would do that?

234

"You've gone a little crazy, haven't you?" she said half-seriously. "I remember some old novels from college where characters went crazy during arduous quests like this." After smiling a sweet smile that was mostly hidden by the dusk of this small landing, she offered her amorous fearful leader, "Later, big boy, if one of us has the strength left to remove our clothes." Then she kissed him.

As soon their lips parted, Greg got in, "Only one?"

"It only takes one. Don't you remember *Arney's?*"

She knew darn well he remembered the club they'd gone to last New Year's Eve.

And with that fond memory neutralizing any objections, she turned him, and squeezed his butt toward that tiny door waiting so patiently but not quietly up there.

One or two irresistible forces were now compelling Greg toward the irresistible forces out there. This was absolutely crazy. Greg had never been afraid of heights, but this was the perfect time to start. Survival instinct kicked in, way before he actually squeezed out onto that wet, skinny landing with the wind howling. Keeping his back to the lighthouse, he straight-armed the slick railing with his left-arm, while his other hand tracked the center of the lighthouse. When Sandy popped out, she copied his form, until she decided to steady herself by keeping both hands on the railing. Her lips were pressed together, and they locked eyes for a moment, saying without speaking: *crazy, let's go, you go, take your pics.*

Ignoring the wind and the rain for the moment— which was next to impossible, it was impossible not to take in how endless the branches of lightning looked from up here. Greg wasn't moving. With Sandy stone-still right next to him, she removed the hand holding the railing and her phone at the same time to snap a pic.

One.

Putting her hand with the camera back against the wet railing, the two of them inched away from their escape hatch. On this side, the center structure was blocking most of the gusts. The light rain was annoying, but not nearly as worrisome as the wind, or those bolts that were warring between Heaven and Hell.

Sandy's legs were tired, and her arms were growing tired. She said to her grumpy wind-blocker, "This is crazy, let's hurry." She wasn't sure Greg heard her. The camera in her hand wasn't making it easy to keep a good grip on the railing.

After a slight delay, Greg responded, "I think 'hurry up' in these conditions is crazy. Anything is crazy." He was inching along as fast as someone should inch who was newly afraid of heights.

They had gotten lucky with the rain, but the wind was beginning to buffet them as they came around.

Greg stiffened against the stronger wind and clamped both hands firm to steady himself. But when he moved his body, the wind caught Sandy and snapped her against the railing where gravity took over.

CHAPTER 23

DIVORCE, ITALIAN STYLE

"No—" barked Sandy. Doubled over at the waist, the wind had been knocked out of her, which was obvious because it was all out there. Greg reached for the closest shoulder, the only one he had a chance of snagging in time before she went over. Yanking her away from the precipice, pressing her against the center structure with his arm straight across her chest, his heart was pounding; he hadn't been the one that had almost shown the phone the quick way down.

Sagging backward against the lighthouse, with her chest heaving, Sandy said, "I lost the phone. I think it went over." After looking at each other, speechless, breathing hard, she said dumbly like she was in shock, "You want to go get it, or should I?"

Greg didn't like the sound of any of that or what it implied. That they'd be continuing after just what happened. And, that to continue, he'd have to go down all those steps, which meant he'd be climbing all those steps to keep doing this. Way too much, already, and he hadn't even gotten far enough to realize he'd have to go back down yet again—if he wanted some nooky later.

With it raining harder, but the wind letting up, he looked down at their feet. Fully expecting it not to be all-hands-on-deck, miracle upon miracles, her phone was cowering in the shadows. Greg pointed, speechless, toward the newest definition of what a "smart phone" looked like. Smarter than them.

Sandy said into the wind, "Thank God. That saved you a trip."

Slowly, carefully, squatting, she reached to pick it up. It was scratched and the glass was cracked. Would it still work? She took a pic close to the floor and eyed the result. They'd gotten lucky. She leaned toward Greg's legs and said up to him, "Maybe you should come down here?"

He bent down next to her. "You okay?"

"No. Why don't we walk around on bent legs like this? It'll be safer. I'll try not to ruin my dress, but at least we'll live."

"Sounds good to me."

So, that's what they did. They made their way around the catwalk, crouched over, bodies close to the center, with right arms extended straight to the railing. Twice, Sandy stuck the camera above the railing and snapped pics. With their knees complaining and the elements complaining, Greg felt it was too dangerous to try and get that last pic directly into the wind.

Greg said, "We should go in."

"Okay."

They turned and made their way back. Sandy ducked through that small opening first. Down the short ladder, they plopped down, thankful to give their tired knees and legs a rest. On the tiny dim landing, Greg sat real close to his new bride in her smudged, wet wedding dress. Three shots. Done. Whatever they got, they got.

Greg said, "We may be cursed the rest of our lives, but at least we're alive."

"The Waters curse be damned. I've never been so scared in my life—what's left of it."

Leaning their shoulders into one another, Greg said, "This is crazy." His breathing and heart were beginning to calm down.

"Was. Was crazy," Sandy corrected.

Neither of them wanted to move; neither of them felt like going back into George, which at the moment had them surrounded.

Greg turned and put his cheek next to hers. When that went well, he turned his head and kissed her. If she could have a one-track mind on her wedding day, why not him?

Sandy pecked him back.

"Ready?" he asked.

"No. Wait a sec," as she held a vise-grip on her phone.

She meant "down," he meant "sex," as long as they weren't running right to the next crazy place. This was supposed to be a honeymoon, after all. Why not start right here? It was certainly a private place. His adrenaline was flowing. He unzipped her windbreaker, slipped his hand inside, and felt for an opportunistic body part. He rimmed her breast where the fabric met skin, just under the necklace. It felt nice and warm in there.

Exhausted, when she finally realized what he was up to, she pulled his hand out. "Are you kidding? I almost went over." So much for a little nooky.

With all hands back on deck where they belonged, tired by the climb, the near fall and all that crouching, if they didn't move soon they might not move for a long time.

Sandy pushed herself up on weak legs, hugged Greg after he stood, and then led him down the first step.

Greg wondered what was coming next on this trek of theirs. He hoped each charm wasn't going to be more difficult to get, or they were in real trouble. What could be more dangerous than being this high up in an electrical storm? This was only number two out of five. As he circled downward, he considered the possibility that

239

Aarone had given up on them and left; honestly, that possibility didn't feel half bad to the exhausted groom. His wedding day. If he'd had more energy, he would've laughed.

Sort of numb, Greg followed his better-half, though he wasn't so sure of that anymore. He chuckled out loud from the tension, from the absurdity of it all. Was anything safe? Could he count on the normal things, like whether he would get to ravish his pretty bride on their wedding night?

"What's so funny?" Sandy wanted to know. "No, don't tell me." She twisted around and snapped a picture of Mr. Funny Man. The flash blinded him, sending his hands up to his face. "Nooky? I'll nooky you, all right."

When Greg could see again, he worked on catching back up to his wise-ass wife. But as he accomplished this, he considered it one of the dumbest things he'd done all day. So far.

At the bottom, Sandy headed straight for the cab. Climbing in without saying a word. When Greg appeared outside the car, he leaned toward her window and gestured toward the gift shop.

"I'll go in and get our little lighthouse." He'd go get the charm— make amends—though he wasn't sure why she was so pissed at him for wanting her on their wedding day. Things had sure gotten twisted around.

To Aarone, the bride's mouth looked taut in the mirror. Serious. "How was it?" he asked.

Sandy blurted out, "It was crazy up there. Crazy, crazy…crazy." She slumped down nice and low in the seat. "How old is this place, again?"

"Gibbs Hill Lighthouse was first lit May 1, 1846. Its effect on maritime safety was remarkable. Before it went

240

active, there had been a long and consistent history of shipwrecks on the nearby dangerous necklace—"

Sandy flinched on that word.

"Of coral reefs just offshore. Something like thirty-nine vessels went down. It has one-hundred eighty-five steps—"

"I can tell you about every one of them. Twice."

"And a quaint gift shop."

That word "quaint" finished what "necklace" had started. There was nothing quaint about falling through space surrounded by lightning. Quaint was old women sitting still, enjoying tea. She was sitting still, but there surely weren't any teapots up there, only a tempest.

When Greg walked into the shop, he heard Mr. Boat Builder say, "I was hoping to see you again." His glasses were down on the end of his nose.

"Me, too."

After picking out his favorite tiny lighthouse from the assortment, paying for it, and wishing the man well with his boats and all of Bermuda's endless water, Greg headed out into heavy rain.

When Greg slid in, Sandy turned to him. "Got it?"

"Got it." He handed off number two. She peeked in the brown bag. "We're not even going to develop those pics. I'm putting the memory card in with everything else. Even your pic on the stairs will help. If someone wants to check, let them check. I'll pick up another card for the rest of our honeymoon."

That sounded just fine with Greg. It wasn't his show.

Aarone asked, "Where to?"

Greg said, "Some place real low. Really low." He wanted to rewrite the quest to better ensure the safety of the next crazy couple—if they survived, and maybe even if they didn't survive. Regardless, Sandy was acting kind of weird. He remembered Dad explaining that things changed after you got married. Greg hadn't figured it would happen quite this fast.

With shaking hands, Sandy dug out the paper from her jacket. "I have a brand-new appreciation for good and low. Maybe we'll use a sleeping bag on the floor tonight." Not a question.

"Whatever," Greg grumbled. If she could do it, he could. And if he wanted to get any action later, it would be smart of him to join her rather than argue. Though it was possible she meant that his big night wasn't looking so big all of a sudden.

Sandy turned on the flashlight, the light on the page quivering as she acquired the next triangle. "This parchment is doing a fantastic job with all this water."

Greg looked at Sandy but said nothing.

She noticed him looking at her. "What?"

"I wish we were so lucky."

CHAPTER 24

BORROWED CAPTIVES

Surrounded by tired, surrounded by wet, Sandy felt bone tired and bone wet. Alee of the wind and those railings and heights and steps and that second charm, Sandy read the next section while that small circle of shaking light reminded her of just how close she came to taking the quick way down. "We need something famous that's been borrowed." She looked toward Aarone. "Nothing specific this time. What do you think, Aarone? Some place nice and low. And I'm not kidding."

"That's easy. A Tucker Cross. They sell them at the Underwater Institute in Hamilton."

"Then the Underwater Institute it is," Sandy repeated. Relieved the decision had been so easy. Relieved that it sounded really low. Twice relieved, something that's not so bad when one is out in a hurricane.

Greg chimed in. "It's got the perfect name for today." Finding Sandy's cold hand, he gave it a little squeeze.

"It's back near where we started," Aarone sighed. They were going in circles. But wherever it led, it led. "This reminds me of the videogames I played as a kid, where you had to double back to win."

Greg said, "Right now, as long as we're not one-thousand feet up, I'm happy." He grabbed at Sandy's thigh in play.

His hand reminded Sandy of how sore her legs were after the lighthouse portion of the quest. As the car sloshed through the rain, her fatigue and the constant drone of water and the swish of those wipers put her in a restful trance. Sometimes it seemed those wipers were up to the task, and sometimes not, just like her. After her brief rest, returning to the sensations inside the cab, feeling Greg's hand again, which made it real that she was married rather than being on a game show, Sandy asked, "Okay, Mr. Historian. I hope this place is downriver."

"Downriver or not, the Institute has a long history of owning and displaying seafaring artifacts that have been borrowed from the sea."

Sandy repeated thoughtfully, "Borrowed? That's an interesting way to put it." She didn't fully understand his point, which made her wonder whether she was more exhausted than she realized. That maybe tomorrow, in the light of a day that actually had sunlight, it would make more sense. She needed to get her second wind, if she wasn't going to be the first Waters to break this family chain. Something about that didn't seem attractive either. She felt she was getting contrary, which happened when she was worn out, like when she pulled long hours at the animal shelter.

"Everything seems to find the sea here," Aarone shared.

The road, when they looked at where the road should be, was flowing now. Aarone headed back toward Middle Road, toward the interior of the island. There wasn't a soul out—apparently, most Bermudians had common sense.

Sandy realized that the safest place they'd visited so far was inside that lighthouse—just inches away from the most dangerous place. She was definitely tired. So tired, that maybe Greg's hand was helping to keep her upright in the seat.

With Aarone having to plow through more and more

water, the storm conditions sounded like they were worsening. As the heart of George approached the island, moving cars were now under threat of either being washed or blown from the road.

"We actually passed right by it on our way out of Hamilton," Aarone informed his quiet passengers.

Greg grumbled, "You're kidding."

After a delay, Sandy said, "It doesn't matter. We have to do these in order, anyway."

Greg ignored rational Sandy. "Is it really at ground-level?"

Aarone shared, "Besides that, it has interactive underwater exhibits, so you'll be able to pretend that you're actually underwater, if you want to. They've got a lot of historical pieces. Things for underwater exploration, and that fascinating Treasure Room, where they display recovered gold Spanish pieces and pirate booty." Aarone slowed down to negotiate a curve. "Remember the Tucker Cross I told you about? Well that diver, Teddy Tucker, used a lot of that equipment to haul up the Cross." Then after a pause, he widened his spiel. "And they have a wonderful five-star restaurant." After thinking for a moment, Harbourfront, I think it's called. In the back. Right on the water. If it ever stops raining, that is. It's very romantic."

Sandy said, "I like the romantic part." She squeezed her new husband's hand. "It almost sounds like the Tucker and the Devil are sisters," Sandy misspoke. "Crown jewels of Bermuda and all."

Then it became quiet, except for the car speaking in the language of water: wheel wells filling, wipers swiping, and thunder warning. After watching rain, rain, and more rain, Aarone turned onto Front Street. When he maneuvered into the empty parking area for the

Underwater Institute, only the section closest to the Harbour was underwater.

The newlyweds dashed under the covered front patio, after which they quickly met the friendly woman inside, behind the counter.

Sandy pointed to the glass case where an ornate imitation gold Tucker Cross sat front and center. "Number three's going to be easy, just like Aarone said." After she paid, she reiterated, "No sweat at ground-level, huh? What's next?" Energized, her step was a little livelier, and her neck felt a little warmer as they headed back to the waiting cab.

Back in the car, Greg sounded a little grouchy when he half-joked, "I'm sorry we didn't get to stay longer in that nice dry, low building."

Sandy unfolded the parchment, ignoring him with her intent to finish this hunt but good. "Let's see what's coming next."

CHAPTER 25

BEING IN THE MIDDLE OF THINGS ISN'T ALWAYS BAD

Like an actor considering the different ways to play a role, the more Clarke thought about the Divel amidst all this dismal gray, the more he realized he couldn't come off as too desperate to retrieve it. Just a little bit of patience here could go a long way to convincing others that he had just been doing his job, nothing more.

Things do come to those who wait, he reminded himself; there were different types of waiting. He was hoping for the sandy-beach open-air type, rather than the prison-bunk bed type. With the storm intensifying, his attraction to Morgan was also intensifying. Clarke's body began to foreshadow his heightened anticipation of seeing her after a long month, like a gambler whose body was primed for lady luck. Or were his heightened senses just remembering the last time Morgan kissed him and those dice during their Grand Bahamas vacation?

Women-memories were a hell of a thing.

The car had sped up on its own.

Shaking his head to clear it, he pulled his foot off the gas. Concentrating more intently on this section of Middle Road in the interior of the island, over the next hill, amongst the lonely gloom, it didn't take long before the constant drone of the trip, along with Morgan, drew him away from the sameness of the street all over again. When the car plowed through a sharp left, he yanked his foot off the gas. But this time he wasn't quick enough, as the car slid off the road jerking to a rude stop.

Unfortunately, he knew exactly where he was. The Edelson's front yard. The front yard that occasionally flooded, but never like this. And sure enough, he was up against Johnny H's dark blue Honda. And on the other side, it looked like Meyer's white Camry.

Everyone had probably waded across that lake where they'd be comfy cozy having hot tea with Mr. and Mrs. Edelson in their front sitting room. He considered backing up to escape, but he knew these people. Plus, driving away was inconsistent with his leaving-no-evidence-behind strategy. Marks on Johnny H's Honda would fit the ones on his old brute like a glove. Those true-crime reads were paying off. Because he was aware that before a jury of his peers, he'd have to try to explain why, why, did he try and hide something so inconsequential? And that would unravel everything right in front of some smart barrister.

Grudgingly, he pushed open the door and slogged across the front yard. His shoes were hopeless now. Tea time with his neighbors. It had been a while since he'd seen their pineapple doorknocker.

The boys were definitely not drinking tea at their private party. From Frack's standpoint, it was miserable out, so what could be better than having Mrs. Waters "paying it forward" by sharing the goods. In this regard, he kept filling her up with drink and small-talk, very small-talk, which he was a pro at. As time meandered on, as Frack finished off another little bottle of whatever-it-was, he wondered his most philosophical thought of the day. *Could I become addicted to Mrs. Waters, like Corona Light's with lime?* At least it was an optimistic bottle-half-full question, rather than his characteristic pessimistic type.

From Frick's point of view, there was nothing wrong with making money and getting laid. He understood Frack's position. But he was only interested in the money part, even though sex usually cost him dough. This opportunity had been handed to them because they were supposed to be in the right place at the right time. Lightning or no lightning. Rain or no rain. Wind or no wind. If Greg and Sandy could reach their resort in this storm, so could they. But with the weather this bad, he wasn't keen on moving any time soon. They still had hours before tonight's reception, so he was trying to stay relaxed and not drink too much, unlike ignoramus over there. Maintaining hope that the weather would begin to get better, because it didn't seem it could get any worse.

With worry and guilt percolating in the back of her mind, Mrs. Waters halted their small-talk session. What if someone came looking for her and she wasn't in her room or at the downstairs bar? Someone. Ha! She wanted to be looked for. That was the problem. Mike wouldn't miss her. It was Frack who was feeding her ego. And it was nice to be wanted for a change. With the boys' final pep-talk completed to her satisfaction—the alcohol certainly helping in this regard, she pointed her afloat ship back toward home port.

CHAPTER 26

BABY TALK

With Sandy reading the next section, Aarone let his hands and arms relax. To the front of him, he admired how those large drops were able to dance off the hood so high. When he shifted his eyes to the rearview mirror, he noticed the groom struggling to keep his eyes open.

Sandy announced, "This one's different. We have to find a fitting charm related to the sea, under the sea, in the blue sea, that was used to find or discover lost things…No location is given, but it states locations can't be duplicated. The five locations must make a pentagon, and I quote: "'Even of the most Irregular shape.' Irregular is capitalized…Aarone?"

Greg recalled with his eyes shut, "High school geometry with Mrs.
Stevenson. Five apexes. Five stops. Pentagon."

Aarone said, "The Bermuda Aquarium, Museum, and Zoo."

Greg said, "With all those names, can it qualify for our last two locations?" before he yawned.

"That's why I thought of it. It's got a little bit of everything. And— you'll like this part—it's not that far. Plus, it's headed east. Didn't you say you wanted to stop at Grotto Bay before heading back to your reception?" He was hoping that whatever strange pentagon they were in the process of completing, that it wouldn't be connected to the old practice of live sacrifices. He hated blood; hated dead chickens even more, like any pure-bred Bermudian.

"Sounds good to me," Sandy chirped in.

Before Aarone pulled away from the Underwater Institute, he wondered if witches used pentagons. Now he wasn't so sure he wanted to complete this pentagon— Halloween weekend, no less. Aarone very much wanted to live to see both Sammy and his stew. "You know," he said while gazing at that nice low building still conveniently located, "we could get that stuff right here."

"Aarone. I'm not taking any chances with this stuff. Got me?" "Yes ma'am. Got you."

"Let's finish this." Sandy looked over at Greg. His eyes were closed. When she gave his hand a little squeeze, his eyes popped open like a doll's. A worn-out doll.

Aarone guided the car upstream, then made a right onto Front Street, heading east. A ton of water was coming down the slight incline from downtown, so even though he was going with the flow, he took it slow. He had spooked himself a little with the pentagon and witch talk. He hadn't been caught in a hurricane since he'd been a tot. He remembered being scared. And he was experiencing a little bit of those nillies—as Mum had called them—right now. But he'd keep that part to himself. He was the captain of this ship, and captains were supposed to get their ships and his crews through anything.

It would be a short trip to the Flatts where the Aquarium was located. All Bermudians knew the Flatts. It was a village built around an inlet, that led north out to the Atlantic from the internal Harrington Sound. Recently, the area had been transformed from quaint fishing village and harbor choke-point to a concentration of upscale housing overlooking said harbor choke-point. It was in this very picturesque and quaint setting that the Aquarium had witnessed all that new construction out its front door.

Four or so miles east of Hamilton, about halfway between St George to the east and Hamilton to the west, it was not only a narrow water passage, but a limiting factor for east-west land travel. Drivers were forced to either head north around the Sound, linking up with North Shore Road along the ocean, or, taking Middle Road or South Road, both running close to the ocean to the south.

Aarone chose the northern route, rather than Middle Road, because the storm was coming from the south. As Aarone made a right on North Road to track along the ocean, Sandy felt her neck warm again. Curiously, it had happened on and off throughout the day.

As the tiny cab with its worn back tires approached the Flatts, Mr. Guide Book said softly to his one awake passenger, "You might find it interesting that the aquarium is the most popular attraction on the island. It was built around the turn of the century in a joint effort between Bermudian environmentalists and American academic scientists interested in biological research. They have a room-sized indoor water tank that was the first coral reef milieu of its size in the world. And it's known for biodiversity, interactive displays, and the many plants and animals that have been categorized for the interested. Also, a large flock of pink flamingos call it home. Monkeys, seals, you name it, they've got it. And what might be related to your quest specifically, there was a guy named Beebe who performed historic underwater research. He dove deep in some funny named thing."

"A funny-named thing?" Sandy repeated.

"I think it's pronounced, baby-o-sphere."

"We have to get something that goes underwater for finding things. A net, a spear, or maybe this baby-o-sphere thing," Sandy said. "I'm not sure whether it should be colored blue, or just that it was used to submerge people under the blue sea."

"Well, Beebe used that thing to dive to a record depth—a full half-mile under the ocean—and discovered marine life that had never been seen before."

Sandy started to say something, but when she noticed that Greg's eyes were still closed, she became quiet.

Five minutes later, Aarone pulled into the small semi-circle drive and snugged the cab close to the dark cedar wood making up the front entrance. "I'll stay right here," he admitted. Even if this was a no– parking zone, there was no reason on a day like today, out of habit, to move the car across the street into that sliver of a parking area right next to that leaping inlet.

When Sandy placed her hand on Greg's arm, his eyes opened slowly. "I'm awake. I'm awake."

Sandy wasn't happy about getting wet again. She'd been wet and dry so many times today, she wondered whether she might get sick from this—in her wedding dress, no less. Now that they had arrived at a zoo, with wildlife suddenly on her mind, her wedding-day problem-solving mind considered that her present discomfort might be the reason why fish chose not to jump out of the water.

The over-dressed treasure hunters hustled under a large overhang proudly held up by five thick cedar posts. Complements of a local tree. Those posts, along with the matching double front doors, were more suggestive to Sandy of a wilderness lodge rather than a zoo. Walking into the dimly lit entranceway, Sandy's eyes needed a moment to adjust. When they did, there was a woman sitting in a cage on the left side of an otherwise empty, dim hall. Strangely, the only light was coming from an open

253

door before her on the left, and a tiny circle of light in front of the woman inside the cage.

This was some zoo.

Sandy passed the brightly lit doorway on the left—the gift shop, maybe.

It appeared this zoo person was actually the admission person. Having the cashier in this cage-booth was strange. Funhouse-strange. Halloween-strange. In yet another wedding-day-creative-idea flash, Sandy considered that either the woman was on display, or maybe, that they let the animals roam the halls on slow days like this. Anyway, inside this cage the young woman was reading a magazine the way Sandy had been reading the instructions in the cab. In the brief amount of time it took to go from rain-dark to hall-darker, Sandy felt compassion toward this unknown woman and her like challenge.

Sandy looked at Greg, unsure whether they were supposed to pay her, even though the gift shop was behind them. Feeling magnanimous, feeling maybe the cashier was being forced to save on electricity while trying to be safe on this unsafe dim day, Sandy said, "Pay the lady, honey."

While he did, Sandy made a bee-line into the bright room.

The bright overhead lights ran the length of the front left side of the building and would have done an airport runway proud. Maybe this explained the lack of electricity for the rest of the building. Sandy walked straight toward the well-lit, matronly-looking woman behind the counter, who was being allowed to roam free in this brighter area.

The part-time worker seated behind the long glass counter watched the overdressed tourist come her way. This was practically her only customer of the day.

Certainly, of the afternoon. A motivated customer. She, on-the-other-hand, because it was just after her lunch and she'd been caught by surprise, didn't rise to greet her.

"Hi," offered the young woman wearing the white dress covered with a pink windbreaker and matching hat, gaudy jewelry and blue eyes.

"Hi. How can I help you?"

"We're looking for a...baby-o-sphere. I think," the bride said, trying to get it correct. A young man then walked into the room looking like he could use a bride.

The bored woman sought clarification, "Like, baby with the bath water?" Water was on everyone's mind.

"No, we've got plenty of water. Just the baby-thing." Of course, Aarone wasn't here to clarify any of this for the fish-out-of-water bride.

"Not a big one, a baby one," the young man offered, as he demonstrated by bringing his hands closer together.

"I see...baby, uhhhh." As she thought, her long fingernails roll-tapped the counter, as was her habit when she played *Twenty Questions*. "A...a bathysphere.," she delivered with a smile of recognition, as her fingernails assumed the down position—the found-answer position.

The young woman added, "A model of the kind that went under the water. Does that make any sense?"

"We just happen to have exactly what you're looking for, if it's what you're looking for." Walking toward the display case, she wondered who would go out in a storm dressed like this? She reached under and withdrew a model that was definitely not blue. "A baby bathysphere at your service."

The young woman hesitated. "Do you have any blue ones?"

"Hmm." Trying to remember, she had to go to the beginning of her sales spiel: "Specifications. The original

255

was made of one-and-a-half-foot-thick steel. Five thousand pounds. Windows clear three-inch quartz. Four-foot nine-inch diameter. Room for two. Beebe suggested they paint it white to attract fish, but I don't think they ever did. The interior was painted black."

"Oh." The bride making a small circle with her mouth.

The matronly lady with her khaki colored rain clothes, wearing nothing close to blue, understood there wouldn't be many customers today. This could be her first and last sale right here, a whole $8.95 without tax. She couldn't remember a day, not one day, when she had failed to sell one item while manning the gift shop. Her personal pride ventured, "No, but we have authentic blue decals, if that helps." Whatever authentic blue decals were? Make the customer happy, wacky and over-dressed or not.

"We'll take both. Pay the lady, honey," the bride offered in her best four-out-five voice.

Nothing in the old manuscript had banished decals from the charms. She'd been told to be flexible.

The little round non-blue replica in its rectangular white and black packaging was placed in the sack along with those authentic blue stick-ons. When the bride grasped the non-blue bag, she felt a draft on her neck, and commented as such. "I've lost count how many times I've been wet and dry today." Pulling up her slicker's collar, she shared with the groom, "I hope I don't get sick and ruin our honeymoon."

The groom concurred. "I want you good and healthy later for the honeymoon-phase proper, thank you very much." The frisky groom in the bright room squeezed her bottom, propelling the bride into the counter.

"That's more like it," the bride smiled, as the antique necklace on her chest flopped forward. She turned and hugged him one-armed while kissing him with both lips.

256

"There hasn't been enough of that today."

"You two just get married or something?"

The bride beamed, showing off her ring that was definitely playing second fiddle to her necklace.

The matronly woman watched as the frisky tourists exited right, toward the storm—not turning left to visit one single exhibit.

Back in the cab, second-wind Sandy said, "See how easy that was?" Lightning flashed over the inlet, tracing her profile with a brilliant white outline.

Greg asked the head cheerleader, "Don't you ever get tired?" in a way that made it clear her burst of energy was making him feel more tired.

Sandy checked her damaged phone for the time. "Unless something really bad happens, we'll have time to rest in the room before dinner— if that's really want you want to do?" She smiled in the dark at him.

"I could fall asleep right here," Greg admitted. "But I'll get my second wind, no pun intended."

"After I find the next location, you can nap awhile, honey. Store up your strength and all." She boosted this message by squeezing his crotch. Squeezing-her-tush payback.

Sandy placed the bag with the other bags on the floor, then dug out the document. When she acquired the last triangle, she read out loud, "Fort St. Catherine."

Aarone let out, "Oh, boy."

A languid, "Oh boy, what?" echoed from Greg.

Aarone reacted because this fort was where the original ship, the Sea Venture, had grounded itself in a terrible hurricane, just like this. Plus, it was located at the northeastern tip of the island—as far out as you could get without going into the sea. Even more famously, it was one of the three vertices of the Bermuda Triangle proper. Only hours before, they'd been at the northwestern tip of the island. Mr. Dearborne hadn't lied when he'd said they'd be travelling all over Bermuda. Some destinations had been unspecified, but the first and the last were as far apart as one could get and still avoid the sea.

Traveling along North Road next to the agitated ocean, Aarone heard his deceased father's voice say, *like a madman,* like he'd always said whenever Aarone did something stupid for no good reason.

The voice spooked him into almost missing the next curve. Dad had prided himself on always being prepared. In particular, he'd hated driving on bad tires like this. Earlier in the day, it was self-evident to Aarone why he'd taken on this day-long quest. He needed the money, plus he was going to prove to his father that he could do this, no sweat.

But now, out in this mess, his father wasn't helping, which was oh so typical.

The closeness of the couple in the back was making Aarone feel lonelier up here in the front seat all by himself. He was happy for them, but sadder for himself. Everything was in the backseat, unless you counted his father's ghost, who always seemed to be in the wrong place at the wrong time. Why was he risking all this when he didn't have anyone waiting for him back home? To his left, out amongst all that grey, the ocean was a vast landscape of whitecaps. Unfortunately, his frenzied wipers couldn't keep up this much rain, or his father's dismembered voice, causing him to slow down. *Better to be safe than sorry,* he next heard Dad pipe up with.

As if he was cold, his teeth began to chatter. But he wasn't cold, just jittery, the way he felt whenever his dad watched him too closely doing something. He clamped his mouth tight. He needed to get a grip. Everyone's safety depended on him getting a grip, never mind these nillies. At least he had Sammie at home. Sammie was home all alone, under the bed, probably. Smart Sammie.

It was raining harder over here, and how on God's Earth was that possible? Crossing over a large bay via a low bridge that had water leaping over the short cement sides, then rounding some dark curves, the headlights of the too-small cab with the too-empty front seat and the too freaked-out driver lit up the line of colored bottles along the top of that curved wall on the left. This was the unofficial entrance to St. George—very unofficial—but most Bermudians were unofficial.

Aarone made his way down St. George's main street. The quaint shops on his right always looked nice and did so even in all this rain with that spooky darkness behind them. When that ribbon of a road appeared on his left between those small nondescript homes, Aarone pointed the little-cab-that-he-sure-hoped-could against all that water coming down that long hill.

Heading straight north, he passed by lonely homes on his left and that field of sparse trees looking lonely on his right. Aarone was not thrilled about this part of the trip, and his father knew it, because they both knew what was coming.

When he reached the top, the thin road fell away sharply. At the bottom was that famous hairpin right leading to that steep drop-off into the lagoon—if you weren't careful. A beautiful lagoon, but a lagoon, nonetheless. *This is not a car-boat or a car-plane*, his father pointed out unhelpfully.

At the apex, Aarone braked the better-to-be-safe-than-sorry cab. To him, the wet road resembled a section of a roller coaster where riders would pick up tremendous speed. There he sat, resting himself and the car, testing those brakes and reassuring his father he'd be careful on the most dangerous roller coaster in Bermuda. It had won this dubious award three years running now. With the rain pummeling the still car, Aarone squeezed the brake pedal with both feet. If the drum brakes got soaked, hello lagoon. If there had been a car shop right here, he'd put this maneuver off a little longer by getting some new rear tires installed after they checked the brakes.

From the backseat, the princess said, "Are we here, Aarone?"

"No, fair maiden. I'm just making sure the brakes are dry before we head down this other side." His voice was good and steady, as if he were back in control of things.

He removed his left foot from the brake pedal first. Then his right. The car began to roll toward the thick gloom down there. At such a slow speed he could feel the brakes scratching, which he believed was good sign. The last thing he wanted to do was join Nicki Nelson down in that lagoon.

The thin road appeared to become even thinner as he approached the bottom. Aarone took that right turn carefully. Only that frail white fence separated them from that beautiful inlet that even Aarone couldn't see in these conditions. The inlet that was just west of the fort. To his front and to the right, east and south, lightning flashed in quick succession, maybe acknowledging he'd made it past the worst.

When he dared a little gas and a little look in the mirror, both passengers had their eyes closed. They were resting quietly. When the rain stopped, Aarone heard the wind howling. Out to sea, to his left, frequent lightning and thunder appeared closer and sounded louder than before. Then the sky lit up directly in front of them again.

Maintaining a slow speed on this short straight section, a large field opened up on Aarone's left. With some relief, Aarone knew the field meant they were really past the worst of it. His eyes found the reflection off the necklace in the rearview mirror. Distracted by the light, the cab lurched off the road. Aarone steered the car right back out of the shallow ditch. "Sorry," he whispered, as he looked in the mirror at Sandy's eyes that had popped open. The bride didn't say anything, possibly because the groom looked to still be sleeping.

A moment later, Aarone made the left and wound his way up the grassy hill dotted with all those low trees. At the top, Aarone pulled the soaked cab into the small rectangular parking area next to the fort. The fort that was perched on the very northeast corner of the island. Two coasts at once. The north and the east, though they could only see the north with the eastern view blocked by the fort's tall western brick wall.

Aarone nudged the car forward, careful to stay far away from another sheer drop-off. Ahead, a field of angry sea brewed out there. On his right, the lot was immediately bordered by a low, double-wide, stone wall that sloped toward that sea, as if it were sinking. Maybe it was.

The fort's taller, manicured brick wall lay just on the other side of the it; between the two was a thin, dark, no-man's-land space.

There's probably more inviting going on there, Aarone's father's deep voice added in, so Aarone would be warned, for anyone stupid enough to walk over there in the dark. *Don't go outside.*

I haven't all day, Aarone was quick to answer right back.

A large gun turret on the other side of that second wall sat guarding the north coast, as it had for centuries. At this point, Aarone was all too glad to stop the tiny cab and rest his aching shoulders and neck. Paint-stripping rain began pelting the cab. Lightning and thunder surrounded them to the north and east; almost territorial in their ferocity, if Aarone hadn't known any better. And he wasn't sure that he did, right at this moment.

Down at car-level, the dominant east winds were blocked by the fort's wall.

The groom's eyes were still closed, and the bride was digging out that trouble-making parchment.

Aarone turned off the windshield wipers. Everything could use a rest.

Everything can use a rest today, his father's voice guided him too little too late.

They weren't moving, but with the wipers off, Aarone felt cutoff because he couldn't see out the front—a feeling he'd never liked. With nothing to see or do for the moment, fatigue rushed him. The groom had a good idea back there. Aarone was ready to be back in his warm, rented, pastel yellow home with its solid limestone walls ditching Dad in the process.

CHAPTER 27

SIXPENCE IN MY SHOE

Remaining as still as she could so as not to disturb her resting husband, Sandy speared the parchment with her tiny light, while lightning was busy spearing everything else out there. The last paragraph said to enter the fort and place a sixpence atop the easternmost wall. This time they were leaving something behind. That was as good a way as any to end their afternoon, she believed. Maybe this taking-things-away and leaving-something-behind—a balancing of things—could even be a metaphor for marriage. Who knew?

She didn't want to ruin her love's rest, but it was time to get this over with. She nudged his eyes open. Thunder doing the rest.

"We home yet?" he said a little sleepy and a little grumpy.

Sandy wasn't sure what home he meant. "We're at our last stop, honey." Given his grumpiness, she had ruined his day again—the count lost at this point. Her jaded mother would have told her not to worry about this. That the quest was just the beginning. That this was what married people did in the Waters family. It all seemed to begin with this wet, charming charm hunt. And the real mystery was not whether the Divel was water-cursed or not, but how the parchment managed to survive so well after getting wet every thirty-odd years?

Greg was groggy, but rattled off at half-speed, "Charms. Storm. Bad tires."

"Wake up, sleepyhead. One of us has to go through the fort—only right over there." She indicated the large dark mass off to their right. "And place the coin that's in your shoe on the east-most wall." She was hoping Greg would do it, though she wasn't sure either one of them should get out of the cab. There was too much of everything out there—except for coins.

Greg took too long to respond.

She asked Aarone, "Which wall is that, Aarone?"

"The north shore is directly to the front. So, it's that side over there." He pointed out the driver's side of the car. With the windows fogged up again, he grabbed a small rag and started clearing them off.

Sitting here, Sandy sensed the thunder was reaching them more quickly after the flashes than it had back in the capital. Dad had taught her this weather lesson when she'd been little. And at this point in their stormy day, she was convinced that young children would have had more sense than the three of them put together. The storm was closing in on them.

She said again, though she wasn't sure if she'd said it the first time, "I'm not sure we should go out there." She grabbed his arm, though there was a small comfort, too small, that the coin was in his shoe and not hers. Regardless, Team Waters couldn't head for their honeymoon suite until this was done.

"I'm awake. I'm awake. I completely forgot about that little coin Frick slipped me." Saying this in a tone that conveyed: Didn't forgetting about this make it unnecessary? Wishing. "Look, it's your family thing." Greg wasn't disagreeing with her, exactly.

Sandy turned her head away from all that distracting

264

lightning, looked at him and said no more. What else had to be said?

"I'll do whatever you want me to." He placed his hand on her forearm, letting her know this was really true, despite his hesitancy.

"It says the sixpence is supposed to be placed on the farthest rampart overlooking St. Catherine beach and the water below. Maybe this is a way of paying tribute to the people who brought it here on the Sea Venture."

"I might get blown out to sea," he said, as the car was rocked by the wind. Wiping his left ear with his sleeve, he pointed, "Look at it out there." They couldn't see much with the windows fogged up again, but it wasn't exactly dark for long with the way the lightning was increasing in frequency.

"It's definitely gotten worse," Sandy agreed in a soft voice.

He whispered in her ear, "Who would know if we didn't do it?"

She whispered back, "Aarone, for one."

He brought his hand up to hide his mouth. "Let's get him to do it. Two birds, one storm."

"I heard that. Someone would have to go feed my dog."

"That's a deal worth making," Greg offered, suddenly more alert. He followed up with, "It doesn't say both of us have to do it as a team, does it?"

"No." She was being most understanding.

Greg straightened in his seat. "Then I'll go." Chivalry was not dead yet, though he might be all too soon. It was common knowledge that knights wore metal armor, even in electrical storms.

"Are you sure about this? Maybe we should let the storm pass?" Sandy expressed her concern once again.

"It might actually be safer in there than out here. Aarone, you want to change your mind?"

"I'm forbidden from helping you out there, remember?" That detail sounding very convenient at this moment.

"Oh, that's right."

Sandy patted his arm. She liked the sound of him getting inside. "Get inside quick, okay?"

Aarone said, "Maybe we should all get in the fort? Not to help, but because that's what forts are for."

Greg felt for the coin, loosened his shoelace, and placed it in his pocket. Better to do it here then out there. Better to do anything in here than out there. Coins were metal, though. He wished that rubber gloves had been included in the quest kit.

Greg wasn't one to drag out unpleasant tasks. Before he got all dramatic and told Sandy he loved her, he slipped out the door and stepped right into a deep puddle of water. Looking through the window as if this might be the last time he'd ever get to gaze into Sandy's big blues, instead of mouthing words he wanted to say, the necklace sparkled lightning back at him. That figured. He wasn't sure how it figured, but it did. Nothing's going to hap— which was when that huge flash near the fort bleached his thoughts white.

He wiped his eyes with the back of his hand. It wasn't even his damn necklace, and he was out in this. He looked down where his shoes were submerged. Then another flash, smaller, helped him to see. In the light's backdrop, like a photographic negative, the fort's raised western wall loomed just on the other side of the parking area.

The drops plopping down were huge. If he lived, he wanted to ask Dr. Waters how drops could get as big as grapes. He liked grapes, the seedless red ones. He was hungry, which seemed good to him, because he couldn't remember anyone ever dying in the movies wanting to eat grapes.

He wished he had remembered to tell Sandy he loved her. When he reacquired the entrance after more lightning, Greg pushed off from the car. Sloshing around the trunk, he headed toward the dark opening that was flanked by arching tight walls. Inside, he was protected from the grapes and the wind. Following the short walk, it curved back on itself to the right, where it abruptly stopped at a stout wooden door on his left. Locked.

"Locked." Another door locked. Then he worked it out.

"Closed." He retraced his steps, pausing at the edge of the overhead cover— which he now considered the edge of reason. The rain was pounding the tiny cab. To its front, fading out into nothingness, were those two weak headlights. His future was in that car. But before they could honeymoon, this had to be finished. He fingered the metal coin in his pocket, still wishing for those gloves.

He couldn't reach the eastern wall, and certainly didn't fancy telling Sandy he'd failed at finishing this crazy treasure hunt.

If he couldn't get to the far wall, never mind see the unseen ocean on the other side, what was he supposed to do? Show some initiative, that's what. Could the coin reach it, if he threw it really high and really far?

He made a sharp right into the rain, keeping as close to that sinking thick wall as he could. Being careful, he tested the ground first before continuing on. Three-quarters of the way toward the ocean where that thick wall disappeared into the ground, was far enough for him if it was for enough for that wall.

The time had come to satisfy the Charm God so they could end this madness.

He faced the tall wall, stepped back into the path of the right headlight of the little-cab-that-could to get a better angle, and then wound up his pitching arm.

Aarone announced, "I think your husband's out there," as he turned the wipers on and pointed. "It's either him or my father. But I'm betting on the groom."

Sandy leaned toward the center of the little cab and didn't see anything. "Where?"

"On my side, to the front."

Sandy leaned right. Sure enough, they watched the groom throw something toward the fort. "Why is he playing baseball at a time like this? His college days are over."

Greg threw his body into it—his wedding night depended on it, and on some level, their marriage. Threw that coin upwards and far, east, toward the fort, up toward the rampart he couldn't see, toward that beach on the other side of the fort, toward the water he knew was lurking ever so close, toward history and the end of their quest, toward the original wreck site of the Sea Venture, and unwittingly, toward one of the three corners of the Bermuda Triangle.

With her face right next to the window to see around Aarone, Sandy gawked at her husband's exaggerated follow-through. "It looks like he's thrown a ball, and I'll bet you anything the two best men are out there fighting over who's going to—"

A brilliant flash was followed by a loud, sharp crack, jerking both passengers away from their side of the cab.

When she noticed her spider-webbed window on the next flash, Sandy said, "Holy Jesus!" Her hands flew to her chest, which felt warm. "My windows cracked. Something hit my window."

Aarone twisted around. Sure enough, the back window had been struck.

Refocusing on her husband, Sandy watched Greg stagger backward into the headlights before stumbling down to hands and knees.

Greg was blinded by the close flash. Seeing stars, he rubbed his eyes with gloveless hands. Off-balance, crouched, the air felt strange. Tingly and sticky at the same time. And smelled burnt. Without his sense of sight, he leaned forward so as not to fall on his ass.

Taking a moment, moving in slow motion, he pushed himself up, wiped off his gritty hands, and then looked directly at those bright headlights. They looked just like lightning and not like lightning, all at the same time. That was weird.

He stumbled toward that light—hoping this was leading him away from the drop-off.

Two out of the three of them saw more lightning; all three heard the thunder.

This strike sounded closer to Greg than the last one, which didn't seem possible. He began to close and open his eyes like a robot, to see if that would help regain some vision.

That was when he realized it was still raining, or, that it had begun to rain again.

His clothes weren't smoking or on fire. That seemed good. Too wet to catch fire, he thought dumbly.

Not seconds later, there was another huge flash on Greg's left. The flash or the sound of the flash propelled

Greg into something hard. The front of the car, or, a wall with lights. He hugged the hard, wet, warm surface. He'd found the hood. Greg believed he couldn't do that again in a million years. That is, now that he was remembering what just happened, if it had really happened: the coin had been struck by lightning.

By feel, Greg began to slide himself around the passenger-side of the car.

Greg had not seen the burnt coin ricochet off the 17th century cannon, nor heard it when it was denied access by the twenty-first century safety glass.

He fumbled for the door handle, managed it open, plopped in backwards and banged into his bride. In the dark, Greg didn't notice the frightened goose-bumps that had hatched on Sandy's legs. In a flat, unenthusiastic, possibly even an electrically-shorted voice, the ballplayer said, "Don't send a boy to do a man's job." His door was still open.

"Are you all right?" Sandy implored. Wrapping her arms around the waterlogged animal. His legs still out in the rain. "It looks like you swam to the original wreck site to hand-deliver the coin. You're the man."

Greg stayed right there in her protective arms. After a while, he rubbed both eyes with closed fists. When he thought of it, he patted his clothes. Yes, his clothes weren't smoking. Too wet, just as he had thought. Only then did he raise his legs into the cab, that felt higher than before—like an SUV. Closing the door, he congratulated himself on making it back alive.

Reduced to its barest elements, their wedding day had transmuted into some kind of primitive survival test. They both enjoyed their reality shows, so this would have been perfect for Survivor, Bermuda Episode, except, could they film in all this rain and wind and electricity? Everyone knew cameras were made of metal.

Sandy said, "What happened out there? Are you all right?

"I like the second question, first." His voice a little stronger this time.

Aarone said, "Those lightning strikes were close."

"Locked. Locked up tight. I got rid of it. As far east as I could get it."

After a brief delay, Sandy asked with a high voice, "You threw it?"

He was most definitely not in the mood to play *Twenty Questions* or *Jeopardy*—though if this was *Jeopardy*, she'd left off the question part. He decided it was a good sign that he realized this. I was charged—he laughed/grunted when he thought this—with getting rid of that damn thing as far east as I could. The thought of all that light shivered him cold. The burnt air still smelling sharp like cheese. He mumbled, "I don't even like cheese."

"What, honey?" She rubbed his hands. They felt warm.

Aarone turned the heater on high.

"Didn't you see the lightning?" Greg asked thickly.

Unaware that he had actually been struck by a part of the bolt as it went to ground, she answered, "We saw the flashes. I wanted to drive away after the second one, but Aarone convinced me to wait for you. That you could still be alive—crawling out there on your hands and knees."

"At least the car didn't explode," Greg quipped half seriously.

Aarone reacted with, "No, but we got a cracked window out of it."

Greg felt lethargic and thick-tongued and didn't understand the crack about the car.

Sandy pulled his windbreaker around him. "Are you okay?" His cap was still stuck to his head.

271

He mumbled, "Can we go home now?"

Sandy said, "Grotto, Aarone, if you please."

Aarone mumbled, "Thank God. Let's get away from the lightning capital of the world."

Greg thought in slow motion, *Thank...Christ.* But he also remembered that they weren't going home home. They were still in Bermuda.

Careful of the drop-off, Aarone turned the tiny car around, followed the ribbon of road past the inadequate fence and back up the hill, before he allowed himself some good deep breaths. The farther they pushed through the rain away from the fort, the less lightning and thunder chased them. Aarone went right over the top of that long hill and kept right on going.

Eventually, Greg tested his peripheral vision by looking out the window. Unfortunately, another flash piled on. Just before it flared, he could have sworn he saw a witch pointing at him. Or maybe, pointing the way they should flee? But it was definitely a witch. Banishing him from the east, because that's what witches did. From the roadside, backlit, she was wearing a black hat, black gloves with long white fingers poking through, a black knitted dress longer in the back, with charms hanging from the front, and nothing, nothing else hanging in the front from the waist down. White legs. The whitest legs he'd ever seen. Barefoot, he thought, though that part he wasn't sure of. Signaling him? Offering herself to him? He'd heard island girls did that.

Moving shadows doused the dancing lights out there. Greg considered sluggishly whether he might be hallucinating. Exhausted and soaked, he was distantly aware that too much electricity was a bad combination with water and metal—a knight as he was and all. Then one of his scraped knees joined the conversation, reminding him that he had not been wearing metal on his knees.

Greg's eyes darted this way and that, trying to keep up with the lightshow and any dancing, pointing witches. During a moment of seeming darkness, he clawed at the window as if something were close.

Sandy asked, "You all right, honey?" She took his right hand. It still felt warm, like he was releasing excess heat, which fit somehow with the way her neck and chest felt.

Greg placed his hand in-between Sandy's thighs. Her legs felt cold. Nothing had been right since the Divel and George had double-teamed him. If he could get rid of just one of them, maybe it would help. He wanted the boys to have the damned thing. Yes, that seemed right. He didn't want it hanging around Sandy's neck any longer. And, backing up, if they had done it earlier, he and Sandy wouldn't be out here in this God-forsaken weather being enticed by semi-nude, frisky witches, risking life and limb. Good and fed up and definitely not thinking clearly, he was not sure that any of this was more than a bad Halloween dream.

If this quest was any indication of how things were going to go while they were on this island, he was ready to be driven right to the airport. He knew it was over here somewhere. If, that is, Aarone had told them the truth when they'd passed it coming this way to get to the fort with its locked door and extra walls. He hadn't thought this going out, hadn't thought about it clearly, but now coming back, he wasn't sure who was telling him the truth about anything. This pence business at the fort hadn't worked out so well. Locked. It wasn't his fault. Someone should have known it would be locked in this weather. Yes, he was good and tempted to ask Aarone to drop them off. Didn't they have lightning rods all over the airport?

His thoughts were jumbling all over themselves like tumbling lottery balls. And he'd come to another big decision. He wasn't going to share any of his Halloween candy with Sandy after she'd sent him into that fort—that would show her.

His electrically-altered mind kept his eyes peeled for more unclothed witches pointing the way. He needed to know the way. These exotic islands were something in the dark, a real challenge to his peripheral vision with all those shadows dancing this way and that.

Greg asked Aarone, "Are we protected from the lightning by the rubber tires?"

"Tonight, I think I'd feel better if we had a rubber boat inside a rubber room." The windshield wipers were flying again, but not fast enough. Aarone had taken it slowly going down that long hill back into St. George. "This is the worst storm I've seen in years. We all should be home by a warm fire. My dog tried to convince me to stay home this morning."

Then not a moment later, Aarone announced, "Grotto Bay, here we come. It isn't far. Just on the other side of that causeway we came over."

Greg kept rubbing the inside of Sandy's cold legs for luck. Exhausted, Greg's head found Sandy's shoulder. Sandy asked, "You rubbing me for luck?" He grunted.

"You were brave back there."

He grunted again. Brave-speak, like Vikings or Neanderthals or gloveless knights. Dumb metallic knights with metallic coinage and unprotected knees.

After some curvy roads, they crossed over that very long, low, thin causeway that was covered with water. Aarone stayed dead center with each side underwater.

Once the little-cab-that-could made it across that dark bay, it headed up another long hill against the current.

When the car turned into the resort, Sandy reached for the parchment. "I'm pretty sure the quest-proper is over, but I better double-check."

Aarone stopped the tired car at the entrance.

There was nothing else listed. At the bottom of the second page, she spied another faded seal that matched the one on the first page.

Sandy sighed. All those bags were on the floor around their feet. She said to her resting husband, "Going through all of this junk today has taught me things. About us. About people. I wonder if that's why they do all this, and not because of anything having to do with this necklace."

Greg was too tired to think or too shocked to think. He mumbled, "You learned I'm a witch, like in the Monty Python movie." He had witches on the brain.

"You bet, Wicked Witch of the East. Or should I call you Thor, The Thunderbolt King?" When he didn't answer, she said, "Honey, grab all the charms. After what we've been through, we're not letting any of them out of our sight."

Then she leaned forward to talk to Aarone who was slouched in his seat. "Aarone, we couldn't have done this without you. You've been great. I'm going to give you this now, even though I know you're waiting to take us back." She handed him an envelope. "You did a great job keeping us safe through it all." Leaning between the seats, with the Divel still in the middle of everything, the fair maiden kissed him on the left cheek.

After the couple walked in and a porter walked out to help with the luggage, Aarone pulled away from the semi-circle entrance and parked. He was most ready to lean his seat back and take a nap, but first, he ripped open the sealed envelope. Inside, fished out one six pence coin, unburned, and four folded bills. Four very large bills. What an incredible tip from an incredible lady. He smiled. Now, he could nap. He'd buy Sammie some big bones for being such a smart boy. And some retread tires for the rear. As soon as he closed his eyes, everything disappeared.

Meanwhile, Clarke had finally extricated himself from the Edelson's neighborhood Mad Hatter tea party. He'd had a cuppa with the tea drinkers, a cuppa with the coffee drinkers, and then a nip of scotch with Mr. Edelson. Covering all ports before pulling up anchor, being neighborly, with nothing to hide—nothing extra that is— everyone agreed that insurance could await fairer weather.

After backing his boat-car onto high-ground, he recommitted himself to reaching Grotto, Morgan, and the Divel. At least nothing from the accident could now come back to haunt him in front of a jury of his peers. All it had taken was a little bit of time, which he had plenty of given that the newlyweds were traipsing from one tip of the island to the other in this mess.

PART V

THE DIVEL

CHAPTER 28

GROTTO BAY

The ragged newlyweds checked in. When the porter reappeared from fetching their bags, he led them through the misty rain down to their bay-front room a million steps away. Instead of one main structure like the Princess, this honeymoon hotspot was populated with separate buildings spaced out over a grassy campus. The porter explained that the large gray bay out there that they really couldn't see was the one they must have just crossed, twice, if they'd really come and gone from Fort St. Catherine in this. He clearly didn't believe them, and his jovial tone conveyed they were crazy if they had. Greg said, "I agree with you there."

To the dazed Greg who was stumbling and leaning on Sandy heavily, he was tired of steps, but thankful that the pointing witches and the stabbing lightning were leaving him alone. *Maybe witches are afraid of caves* he kept to himself smartly. He'd never actually seen a witch in a cave before.

When they reached their room, Greg tipped the porter, believing that would have been a far better use for that pence coin than playing baseball at that fort—especially since a rain delay should have been called. When the substantial door closed with a thud, he locked it from the inside with that bar. They had made it.

When he turned around, his energizer bunny wife was in the process of peeling off her damp wedding dress. Dropping it to the floor next to all those bags, the rest of her clothes followed suit when they formed a pointing-the-way trail toward the shower. She looked back at him with a most bewitching smile that would have suited any honest-to-goodness witch. Another nude witch. Was she the good witch? He remembered they had those too, which produced a knowing smile.

He was feeling electrical again, guessing this was the good kind. His trail of clothes joined hers. Then Thor the Thunderbolt King joined her as they began to fool around literally underwater. As Sandy let her hands play, she admitted, "I'm not the least bit surprised at your resilience."

Both honeymooners were so preoccupied on beginning the honeymoon proper, that neither paid much attention to the albatross around her neck. Never mind her matching bangles and earrings.

First things first.

Afterward, toweling off, Sandy's fancy jewelry appeared out of place to Greg. It rubbed him the wrong way that the necklace had managed to stay right in the middle of their fun after what it had put them through. "You make a pretty good cheap-woman-of-the-evening with all that jewelry." His tone complimentary.

"Given the pedigree of this necklace, I take exception to the cheap part. Otherwise, thank you, Thor, your new nickname for several obvious reasons. Apparently, everything is working just fine after that lightning bolt, though you still look glassy-eyed to me. But I'll take credit for that part, too," she giggled.

As Sandy wrapped herself up in a thick towel, Greg's erratic mind considered some far-afield thoughts. Forgotten thoughts. Out of place thoughts. He wanted the gaudy thing off her, all right. Maybe so Frick and Frack could get it. Maybe to even separate them from this curse thing that had almost killed the both of them—if you believed in curses or bad luck or whatever. Never mind those nude unhelpful witches that were in the middle of all this somehow—with all their pointing either the way to go, or, not to go.

Greg's foul mood was of the opinion that he wouldn't give anyone two pence for the electrified thing, never mind six. Lying back on the bed, ominous feelings lay close to him. Feelings that were being aggravated somehow by the Divel's lurking proximity. He got under the covers and pulled the sheet to his chin, like he'd done as a kid. Common sense told him those nude, unhelpful, pointing witches were involved with the necklace somehow. Why else would they intercept them in the middle of the hunt? No one else had been able to find them all day. *They might still be hiding in-wait,* he thought accurately. He wondered why witches were always women and felt he should know the answer to that. Regardless, he felt a little better when he realized that the boys could fight the witches over the Divel. He'd stay out of it. He was a lover, not a fighter. He didn't want to have anything to do with any witches—they seemed way too confident, the way they stood out in the storm, semi-nude and unafraid, unlike him.

Sandy came over to the king bed with that over-sized white towel wrapped around her. She looked bone tired, and still hadn't made an effort to take the darn thing off. It was up to him to protect them. Like at the top of the lighthouse. Like at the fort.

With the covers cinched to his chin, he heard thin metal clanging, as if the hangars in the closet were being swayed by the wind, or even a witch. He was ready to act, partly because his peripheral vision was working again. If a Halloween witch poked herself out of the closet, naked

281

from the waist down, it would confirm everything. Whatever everything was.

His thoughts began to tumble again like they had after the pitch he'd thrown at the fort. Even though he was lying down, he tensed himself to act quickly if that door opened.

More hangars clanged softly. So softly, that if he hadn't been listening, he'd have missed it. That figured, if the network of witches—*a coven*, he thought—had time to prepare by knowing which room would be theirs.

His skin was crawling. Even though he was tired, or maybe because of it, he felt he should do something before it was too late. Yes, it was too coincidental to his discombobulated mind that they chose to show up today of all days. Which could mean that if the cur-*sed* thing was taken off, maybe the witches wouldn't attack. They'd be safer. He raised his voice, so that any witch in the closet would be able to hear him so they'd know that he wasn't going to be caught with his pants down and the sheet up. "Why don't you take that thing off? I think everyone is right. It's better off in a vault sitting next to all those charms." Maybe the witches could get to it only after it was separated from its charms. That made sense.

She saw him eyeing it with his intense stare, like he was being hypnotized by it. "We got so wrapped up in everything, I forgot to take it off," Sandy offered with a sheepish grin. Dropping her towel to the bed, she reached behind her neck. She couldn't manage the antique clasp. "I need help."

"Understatement of the day. But I love the pose." He admired the supple physique of her nice smooth shoulders and back.

"Down, boy."

He made a dog noise, badly. "I thought this was our

horneymoon?"

"I hear most marriages fail because they don't leave enough for the other 99 years."

"Ouch."

She stayed perched on the edge of the bed.

He fumbled with the clasp. "Looks like once it's on, it's on." Blackmailing her with his tone.

"No. The answer's no. You're cutoff until this thing is off. You're impossible. But cute." She twisted her head to try and look at him.

"Okay, okay."

He reached up and got a tiny shock for his effort. "Ow," snatching his hands away. "I've had enough electricity to last a lifetime." He shook his hands out. "And who came up with the term 'static electricity'? It doesn't seem very static to me." He was growling again, like that low wind running between the buildings. He was primed for something else to happen: for a witch to show him the way or show him too much or to trick him into the wrong way. He flicked a glance past her neck toward the closet door that was vibrating with that hanger noise again. Even in his haze, or maybe because of his haze, he knew enough not to share any of these peculiar sights and sounds with Sandy. It had been a strange day. *Only one day*, he reminded himself again. Then he wondered if Aarone might be a witch, because everything that had happened hadn't happened until they'd been near Aarone. But then astutely, he corrected his silly inaccuracy: a warlock. That was the name for a male witch.

After his unsuccessful first try, she encouraged him with, "It's your electric personality, my dear."

Timidly, his fingers approached the white metal. No shock this time, though his fingers tingled as the clasp came free. He had trouble with bras, too. Then he kissed

283

the back of her the neck, atoning for his grouchiness. "There, all better."

"That feels nice."

She took the metal triangle and its chain from him. "Where should I put it?"

"As far away from us as possible. How about the parapet at Fort St. Catherine? Lightning could find it there." Actually, he would have liked for her to leave it right there on that table, so the boys and the witches could fight over it.

Greg leaned back, pulling the sheet up so it was covering his mouth. From his count, each of them had almost lost their life today, and he hadn't really registered Sandy's cracked window. He had questions without answers. And pragmatic Greg believed there came a point when lacking good answers, things just needed to stop. He kept that sheet cinched tight against his nose, so only air could get in. *Better safe than sorry,* he thought, though he thought a witch should be saying this to him rather than the other way around, as his eyes darted toward that closet.

As Sandy got up to survey her options, she looked back at Greg and caught him staring. "You're looking at me the way that writer looked at his wife in *The Shining.* Remember how that movie scared the bejeebers out of me." As she headed toward the room safe, she heard herself ask, "You're not writing any books, are you?"

"First, you asked me about being a mailman. And now a writer. You're acting strange."

Based upon things not getting any better, he decided it was time to act. Removing his protective cover like a superhero removing their special cape, Greg swung his legs off the bed to get ready for what was coming next. He wasn't sure what that was, exactly, but it was coming. His legs wobbled as he stood and he made his way into the bathroom to splash water on his face. "Why don't you just leave it on the table? Maybe it will walk away," he said while toweling off. Way closer to the truth than he'd intended.

"You're a comedian now."

He didn't feel like a comedian. Or a mailman. Or a writer. Until this very moment, he had never understood what people meant when they said that one spouse often wanted to change the other as soon as the marriage license was dry. Though in a moment of clarity, Greg didn't believe anything was dry yet—except for that amazing parchment.

Before he headed out to check the closet doors, Sandy stepped in with a satisfied look on her face. Apparently, she was all done playing Hide-and-Seek.

"I hope you threw it out the door."

"I'm not saying."

"Oh, another trick or treat?"

"Something like that." She scratched his back with her fingernails.

"Ahhhh. You're not going to distract me; I'm not looking for anything else today."

"Oh, you spoil sport." She stuck her tongue at him, making sure he saw it this time. Then giggled, apparently in a good mood after surviving the afternoon.

She looked toward the front door. "It's in the little safe next to all its charms. They're getting a head-start on becoming acquainted."

"Hell, why'd you do that?" How were the boys or the tricky witches going to get at it in the safe?

"I figured it might as well get used to how it's going to be spending the rest of our marriage." She sidled up closer to him.

"No, I meant why'd you lock it up? We have to take it

back in a little bit."

"This way we can see the hotel. Get a snack or something, before heading out. We still have an hour before we need to leave." It was only 4:30. Given the day's ordeal, neither one of them was in a hurry to rejoin the others. If there had been a box to check for staying put and crashing, they would have checked it.

He turned toward her. "Okay, good thinking. Give me the little key while you get ready."

"Tell me a secret first," at which point her arm disappeared behind her back.

His electrified brain wanted to share there was a semi-nude witch in the closet—that they weren't really alone for any secret telling—but he continued to avoid the whole mess. "If you don't stop that, we're never going to make it to the reception."

"That's no secret," she fake-pouted.

He kissed his cute bride.

So much for fake resistance, as she handed over the key.

Key in-hand, Greg left her in the bathroom, turned on the TV, and pondered his options. The first option was to throw on normal jeans and a normal shirt.

He knew not much of this was simple, or, tangible. Eyeing the closet while its doors rattled, his mind flew to the term "Gordian knot" from his college days. This was certainly a complex situation that held no satisfactory solution in the ready. Having jumped all afternoon when the Devil said jump, a part of him didn't want to make such a momentous decision without her. But a paternal part, the part goading him toward action ever since that lighthouse mess, felt differently.

After giving the witch or witches ample time to come out whether improperly dressed or not—because he was not going into the shadows after them—the time to act had arrived. Without any definitive answer in words, but with his skin crawling, without any nude pointing witches trying to trick him so he'd know to do the opposite, he did the easy thing and called Frick. Then he whispered and turned his back to the closet so the witch, or witches, couldn't get inside information on their competitors. "Where are you two?" Greg asked.

Frick said, "We just arrived at Grotto Bay resort. A hell of a trip getting over here, buddy. Where are you guys?"

"We just got here, too. Perfect." It was as if they'd synchronized their watches, or some cosmic force was bringing them together. He was going to outsmart this coven yet. A little eerie, if Greg let himself think about it. Plus, what were the boys doing here at this exact moment? Trying to sneak up and surprise the newlyweds, newly-wedding? He guessed that might be something the two of them would do, rather than wait at the reception like normal best men.

Greg started to ask whether they'd been helped by a pointing nude witch. No, he wouldn't exaggerate. Sandy always gave him hell when he exaggerated. Semi-nude. But then he heard hangers clanking, so he turned back around so as not to be blindsided. If he was honest with himself, his peripheral vision was still compromised. But there was nothing wrong with his hearing.

He said, "If the timing of this hadn't been so coordinated, maybe we wouldn't be able to pull this off." Meaning that they might not have been able to get this past the hovering witches. "Anyway, I'm going to give you what you've been angling for, which will help the two of us out, believe me—" The witches would then follow the boys rather than them. Perfect.

Frick said, "Good."

"Okay, so don't stop at the main desk. Come through to the back of the first building, go to the right, and down a set of long steps. At the bottom, go left. Two buildings, I think. Room…" He looked on the outside of the door. "3801. I'm staying on the phone till you get here. Don't knock." He thought of both Sandy and the witches. "And definitely don't come in," again, thinking of everyone. It felt crowded in here, after being just the three of them in the cab all day.

"Okay, we're coming 'round…I see steps left and right. We're going right…"

"Coming down the hill now. A lot of steps here…to the left. See you in a sec."

Greg said to Sandy around the half-closed door, "You want a Coke from the machine?"

"Yeah, thanks honey."

As far as he was concerned, the witch could go thirsty. Drink rain water for all he cared, like the primitive, superstitious natives he'd heard that dotted the island. *If witches drink anything*, he thought, because he'd never seen a witch actually take a drink. Only point and stir.

While Greg placed the key in the safe, he thought about that witch's "tell" of pointing somewhere so you knew to do the opposite; how it might even hold some similarity with vampires and mirrors. But these confusing thoughts dropped away when he saw how much his hand was shaking trying to maneuver that key. He needed to concentrate. After opening the safe and removing the Devil from its charms, he relocked it. Outside, George's winds howled with intensity, along with the commotion coming from inside that closet. With everything getting agitated over the Divel's freedom, he thought, *Join the party*.

Not taking any chances with all the women inside the room, Greg went outside to hand the boys their future—

288

and theirs, given the insurance. Sandy would be able to open up her own clinic now. He wasn't sure she'd be okay with this when she found out. Because, of course, she would find out. But she was as tired of the thing as he was, reminding himself yet again how they'd almost been killed. And—as he looked for the boys—she loved him. That was important. He figured she might be angry at first, but if she could change him, he could change her right back. The balance of that seemed right for a marriage and all.

The boys appeared out of the dim mist wearing their hats and rain slickers.

Without saying a word, Frick accepted the necklace from Greg.

A big smile broke out on Frack's face. Greg looked at him as if he was the dopey one.

"Okay, see you in a little bit," Greg whispered, getting rid of them and it. The thought of it made his skin crawl again. Sort of like how electricity or those nude pointing witches were making him feel. Seminude. He wasn't sure why he kept exaggerating.

The boys disappeared back into the storm.

Greg closed the door as George howled anew. He'd forgotten the sodas. Comfort foods like Coke were supposed to make everything better. He turned around and got two. Yes, he could stand for things to be twice as good. That made perfect sense, and already he felt better. Amazing.

Drinking his Coke, Greg was psyched to face whatever was coming next. He said too loudly, "You ready in there? The rain has stopped."

"Sure am," she answered. Sandy came out wearing a nice pair of navy slacks and a cream-colored short-sleeved, fleecy sweater with a scoop neck. "I'm glad we're done." She ran her fingers through her short blonde hair.

He wanted to be away from this room, that safe, and that closet that apparently was a gathering place for agitated witches. "Let's walk up to the main building and check the place out. Maybe I'll get lucky and they'll have a game room or a gift shop," he added, smiling. Then he kissed her.

After the nice kiss, she leaned back. "No more gift shops, okay?

Maybe that was the wisest thing either one of them had said all day. He'd married a smart cookie, all right.

Holding hands, they headed up all those stairs, their legs reminding them that they were over their limit for steps today. At least it wasn't raining, but the wind was sure howling. He hoped it was too windy for any nude witches to skulk about. That they might be banished or kept away like an exorcism, though he believed it might be called a windism. He was sure cross-word Sandy would have known "warlock." At any rate, if any of this worked the way it was supposed to work, the witches would now follow the boys. It made him feel good that he'd outsmarted them. Mission accomplished. As he hummed the music to Mission Impossible, he realized this was the second thing that had gone right this afternoon—the first being how he'd earned his new name in the shower.

CHAPTER 29

MORGAN

With those windshield wipers swiping the pitted windshield for all they were worth, Clarke found it amusing that he might be the first person to buy a new car because it needed new wipers. Money gave you options.

Continuing to plow east toward Grotto, his mind couldn't stay away from calling Morgan before he got there, even though he really wanted to see the surprise on her eager face. The constant gloom was working him over, and the fender bender hadn't helped his mood. The sound of a friendly voice would be most appreciated right now. Driving one-handed, he dug out his cell that had been strangely quiet all day. Ringing her office number, there was no answer. She was probably busy with leaky roofs. With only three dark miles to go, he called the main number. Not recognizing the woman's voice, he asked for the General Manager, Ms. James.

Forty seconds later, Morgan's chipper voice came through like a transfusion to his psyche. "Hello, Grotto Bay Swimming Resort." His modern-day Doris Day.

She'd been tipped off.

"Very clever. Hedging your bets, I see." He was the one hedging his bets.

"Can you believe this weather?"

"It's something, isn't it?" Thinking she was too.

"A damsel could be in distress surrounded by this much water. Wind too. Don't forget the wind."

"Just what I was thinking," he agreed, as his car was buffeted by another gust.

"Bad night to sleep alone, you know?" It had been about a month since they'd been together.

"First things first."

"I agree." Her general temperament was agreeable, making her perfect for the hospitality industry and perfect for him. What she presently was agreeing to she hadn't a clue, but it never seemed to matter.

"Tell me, have the new honeymooners, Mr. and Mrs. Waters, arrived yet?"

"That's exactly what I'm talking about." Honeymooning was her favorite topic when it came to him.

"Stop it for a second." He chose not to add: "this is serious." The car hydroplaned through a deep spot, forcing him to jerk his foot off the gas. The car had sped up since he'd gotten on the phone.

"Oh, all right," her playful voice relented.

"Have they checked in?"

"Hold on to your boats." She checked the computer. "About an hour ago."

"They still there?"

"What do I look like, a one-armed roofer? I've been busy over here."

"No, you're too good with those hands to have only one."

"As far as my hands know, yes. Who would go out in weather like this?"

He said, "Hornymooners." Misspeaking.

"Well?"

In the dark, his cheeks colored. "I'll be there in five minutes." But as soon as he said it, he realized it hadn't been such a good day for keeping promises.

Clarke made the left up the long U-shaped drive and parked. Cinching tight his trusty hat and coat, he ran through the rain to reach cover. Inside, Morgan's young face greeted him like a beacon of goodwill.

Immediately, she pulled him into a backroom and locked it— making it difficult for him to kiss and run. After helping him to strip off his wet things, she kissed him again. When Morgan came up for air, she said, "I checked with Selahe at the front desk. She hasn't seen them leave."

"Did they place any valuables in the hotel safe?" Clarke was so far along with his perfect crime, he'd forgotten that only Benny knew what was going on.

"This sounds intriguing. What's going on, Perry Mason?"

Good question. His motor was running, for one thing.

"How should I explain all this?" he stalled. How could he explain one of the strangest days of his life?

Morgan continued with, "This sounds very mysterious. Why are you chasing them, and who's chasing you?"

She was, of course, as she remained pressed up against him so he couldn't flee with his running engine. And, he didn't want anyone else chasing after him, a big part of all this.

"Would you stop that," he chuckled. Only now did he realize how serious he sounded. Though this was serious. It concerned his retirement—possibly their retirement. Plus, he was now positioned to recover the retirement amount that had been ripped-off by a Waters in the first place. Since Laura's death these past three years, he'd been living with old issues that wouldn't go away. Infused with Morgan's energy, it was about time to move on. Money not only gave you options, but energy too.

293

With his mood lightened, Morgan continued her movie tryout. "Arrest me then." She showed him both wrists. "Slap on the cuffs, officer." Another anti-running strategy. It was harder to escape if you had to lug someone wearing cuffs. They'd watched an old American movie from the '60s about that.

"Okay. Okay. Maybe later," he stalled. She was being her usual sweet self, as she looked at him close-up with those magical eyes and lips, imploring him to tell her what the hell was going on.

When she started to ask something else he knew he didn't have a ready answer for, he preempted her with, "Would you let me talk, you nut?"

"I did it," she admitted. "I hid the missing newlyweds and I'm holding them for ransom. I took their valuables and secretly locked everything in our safe. I confess. Kiss me. My last kiss before prison." Morgan had been a communication major in college, with a minor in drama.

Talk about role reversals.

What else could Clarke do? He kissed her. As her hands drifted down his back, he removed them so she couldn't distract him any further, then led her over to the two wooden chairs next to that cluttered desk. "You're a nut, you know that?"

"Have you listened to yourself today?"

"Touché." He held her hands, in case he had to fend off another desirable but distracting attack. "I suspect the bride and groom were so interested in doing what you want to do, they forgot to leave the famed necklace behind before starting on their charm hunt. You know, the one I told you about." Months ago, Clarke had mentioned a little about the Divel and the upcoming wedding.

"Ohhhh. That devil-thing."

294

"Yep, that's the one." Feeling it had gotten safer in the room with some truth out, he released her hands. "And I don't blame them a bit, the handsome couple that they are."

Morgan picked up the old-fashioned receiver on the desk. "Selahe, anyone move anything in or out of our safe today?" She flicked her nice eyes at him, her dark lashes feminine and enticing on her square, handsome face. "Thanks."

"No. Our safe hasn't been opened today. But it could always be in the in-room safe."

"What are the odds of me seeing their room?"

"That would be highly unusual."

"Or seeing inside their safe?"

"Even more unusual," she said. Then a coy smile lit up her face "What do you have to barter with?"

Clarke leaned in, his mouth taut with urgency. "Do you realize how important this is to me? This thing is price—less. It was not supposed to travel all over the island today, unprotected. Me neither."

She said, "You're still priceless, though." But when Clarke's serious face didn't react to her good-natured joking, her smile melted away.

"Can you spell F-I-R-E-D?"

"Can you spell his and her prison cells?" she retorted.

"Could they be touching?" Clarke joked, though it was way too close to the truth. He colored.

"Oh, all right," she relented. "Stay here." She retrieved the master key for the tiny in-room safes. When returned, she offered, "Why don't we call them first?" It was clear she wasn't keen on visiting a honeymoon room, uninvited.

"There's this thing about their quest. They're not to be interrupted until they are finished. So, I haven't been able to call them all day."

"If they're here, aren't they finished treasure hunting?"

"I guess…you're right," whereby he kissed her for luck.

Morgan admitted, "Things seem a little mixed up, but I like the sound of calling them first. That would be much better than losing my job that I happen to like. Unless, of course," she smiled in place of the comma, "you're ready to sweep me away to Tahiti."

Clarke smiled an understanding smile, took out his cell, and called the number he'd gotten for them from their check-in data at the Princess. The call went directly to Sandy's mailbox.

"Her mailbox is full," he said.

"Okay, let's ring their room." They walked to the front desk to call. Again, no answer. She looked at Clarke with her face screwed up. "Okay, let's check the hotel first, then we'll go down to the room. They might be busy, you know." She smiled again, this one more devilish— seemingly having as many different smiles as Eskimos had words for snow. And this one definitely foretold of something different, if he'd had the decoder book: with them hidden from view behind the counter, she reached for an opportunistic body part.

Clarke intercepted her hand just a little too late. "This is a big complex," he said, not exactly keen on searching the entire grounds.

She looked down at his pants and nodded.

"Would you stop for a second?"

"Sorry," she said contritely, but in a way he knew she really wasn't.

"I meant the grounds, oh lady-of-quick-hands."

"We'll look, okay? If they're not about, we'll go interrupt them at their room. Okay, big fellow?"

Twenty minutes later, they hadn't found them.

When the rain let up, Morgan led Clarke toward the honeymoon suite. When they reached the outer door of the hotel, she whispered with the wind, "You're going to owe me big for this. I might even hold this over your head for the rest of your life, unless you make an honest woman of me."

When they reached those long flights of steps, Clarke led the way by holding her hand.

At the bottom, she added, "This is perfect symbolism with you leading me in the direction that no honest woman should ever be going."

"Very funny."

They came up on the newlyweds' room where Morgan froze, looking as if that door could actually be radioactive.

Clarke put his ear to the door. Nothing. "I should have brought a glass. I saw that in a movie."

She slapped his arm—now the serious one of the two.

He pointed at the doorknob, whispering, "There's no 'DO NOT DISTURB' sign."

Morgan wasn't moving. She was like a kid who knew she shouldn't do what she was about to do, and she was with some big, dumb galoot who didn't know any better.

Clarke expected Morgan to knock—it was her hotel—but when Morgan shook her head, when it became clear she wasn't going to do it, he did.

No answer.

He knocked louder.

"They're not in there," Clarke said as much to himself as to her.

Morgan gave Clarke her "that's obvious" look with those big dark eyes. When she began speaking again, her arms and hands had also begun to work again. "Well, either they're in there making love— making them

297

smart—or they're walking together somewhere private. Or, they're on their way back to the Princess."

That sounded like too many *ors* to Clarke, faced as he was with losing his elusive retirement account all over again.

"That all sounds reasonable," Clarke said. "So, let's check the room and see what we can see. Okay?"

No, she thought. They had gone from two people in the wrong place to a cat chasing its tail. She'd had a cat that had done that, and it had made her dizzy even then.

As they stood in the empty breezeway, the wind picked up. The gust blew Morgan sideways into Clarke. If Morgan had been really smart, she would have stayed right there and not moved. Under the press of Clarke's set jaw, Morgan slipped the card through the door reader, changing the dot from red to green. Cracking the door without walking in, Morgan announced in her most innocent voice, "Hello. Hello. Anyone in there?" Hoping like hell she wasn't interrupting two newly wedded newlyweds. Otherwise, she figured, that was precisely where she might be headed with a capital "H."

No screams, no cursing, no nudity. Along the floor, a trail of clothes led to the bathroom. No one was in there either. Along with those "breadcrumbs," there were empty sacks on the floor.

Morgan wanted to hurry, but watched as Clarke took in the room.

There was no necklace lying about.

With the closet door rattling from the storm, Morgan opened it, peered in, and then closed it tight.

The in-room safe was locked.

The key was missing.

Something had been put inside.

The bride's pocketbook was sitting on the bureau.

Morgan looked at Clarke. She was not comfortable with this, as he made his way toward the open pocketbook.

The bride's cell phone was sitting right up top. No necklace. Clarke turned and focused on the safe as if conjuring up x-ray vision.

They hadn't been inside a whole minute, and her skin was crawling.

Morgan began to hop up and down, trying to nonverbally encourage Clarke to hurry and finish. She chattered, "We keep a master for the in-room safes because the tourists are always losing their keys. But I've never used it without the guest present."

Clarke shrugged a *so*.

"Maybe we should wait for them to return? She might still be wearing it." Indicating the clothes on the floor with her left hand, she said, "Actually, it might be the only thing she's wearing. Women sometimes do that," she tacked on for good measure.

"Either she's wearing it or it's in there," Clarke said toward that dull metal-brown safe.

"Would you return to the reception without your pocketbook?" Ms. Detective continued, educating the male to female pocketbook protocol. They were still here somewhere.

"You're probably right, but the charms aren't in sight either. So maybe the storm encouraged them to hustle back. I need x-ray vision." Morgan remained silent next to her Superman.

Clarke said, "Well, it doesn't take a genius to figure out you don't want to open it. I guess I could leave a message on the door, if you're really not interested in ending up behind bars with me."

As their eyes met, Morgan didn't speak.

Clarke translated her look. "Then I need a paper and a pen."

"Over there," she said like a shot.

Clarke left his cell number on a hotel message pad, tore it free, and stuck it above the lock in the crack of the door.

When the door clicked shut, Morgan looked up at him. "You have your cell, so you won't miss them. How about checking another room for another naked lady?"

He stepped closer, slipped an arm around her back, and produced a little more romance in the honeymoon capital of the world.

Morgan then pulled him two doors down. She'd done her homework for the nearest vacant room when she'd fetched the safe key. Inside the dim room, she pinned him against the wall and kissed him a month's worth.

Impressionable Morgan then copied that line of clothes on the way to the warm shower.

Impressionable Clarke followed.

In no time flat, they'd put that forgotten month behind them. Unfortunately, from Morgan's perspective, Clarke climbed out of the shower before Round II got going.

As he began to dress, she wrapped herself in a towel. "Where in the devil are you running off to, hon? They haven't called yet."

"I'm not sure. I just feel like I should be doing something."

"We are doing something." She smiled that naughty smile of hers with her dark eyes taking him in from an angle.

He half-smiled back. "I'm too on edge. Sorry. I'll make it up to you. I promise. Really, I promise. This is just weighing on me."

She dressed to catch up.

300

On the way back toward her office, she said hello to another young couple coming down the stairs. They were not the Waters, unfortunately.

Alone again, Morgan said, "You're probably worrying about nothing. You know how you get."

"You're probably right. Except, the way this day's gone, nothing's been predictable. Nothing. Ever since that damned necklace has gotten loose, nothing's been easy."

"Nothing?" she demanded with her wicked smile.

No answer necessary. Holding her hand, he led her inside. Clarke said, "She was probably afraid to take the thing off."

"You may be right. Regardless, you need to come back soon."

"It was way too long," he admitted warmly.

She let that go. He had too much on his mind.

CHAPTER 30

GO WEST, YOUNG MEN

Frick stuffed the oversized necklace into his inside jacket pocket. It barely fit, and at an awkward angle at that.

Mrs. Waters had warned them about calling for a cab and creating more of a trail than they had to. The boys, thinking like a couple of pros for a change, remembered that part. Making their way to the front of the resort, hoping to spot a cab dropping someone else off, with the rain tapering off, they noticed a cab on the right with its lights off. Walking over, Frick rapped on the driver-side window. Inside, there was a man resting with his seat leaned back.

The man blinked his eyes clear, then lowered his window while remaining reclined.

Frick asked, "You available to take us to the Princess Hotel?"

"Sorry, mate. I've already got a fare I'm waiting on."

Frick the pro asked, "Do you know whether there might be buses running from here?" Otherwise, they would need to call a cab.

"Yes, buses stop out there on the street." The cabbie pointed toward the top of the lit Plexiglas enclosure standing near the main road. With the land curving down that way, they could only see that part of it. "But I'm not sure whether they're still running today or not."

"Thanks." The boys trudged down the drive to the tiny clear shelter next to the main road. Once inside, most of the wind coming from behind them was blocked. Only the one-meter wide gap at the bottom allowed any rain through.

Fifteen or so blustery minutes later, with the very bottom of their pants and shoes soaked, a cab came down the road and turned into Grotto's U-shaped drive.

They chased the tail-lights up the start of that small rise like two wolves trailing the scent of blood. With it raining more heavily, with the wind making a racket, Frick raised his voice while pointing, "You cut across the grass in case they pull away. We don't want to lose him."

Frack answered, "Why do I have to be the one to go through the mud?"

The pro responded in a quieter voice, "Because I have the Divel," as if that alone required no further explanation.

Nodding, Frack said a revelatory *oh* to himself, before trudging forward onto the soaked lawn.

After two rather inebriated and proper-looking gentlemen took their time exiting to find a wallet, the driver pulled away smartly. In his haste, the front bumper skidded to a halt just inches from the distracted Frack, who happened to be stomping his mud-caked shoes in the drive.

When Frick rapped on the driver-side window, the elderly driver jumped in his seat. After the window came down, the driver ventured, "What are you doing out in weather like this, mate?"

Still stomping his feet, now that he could see all the mud in the headlights, Frack used the front bumper to scrape off the worst of the mud.

Frick answered, "We've been waiting for a bus. Are you available to take us to the Princess Hotel?"

"You bet."

Frack tromped up at that moment heavy-footed and

offered, "The big pink one."

"Yes, I know it. One more fare won't hurt on a day like today." True, except for what was about to happen to his rear floor.

Clarke decided he should wait a few minutes at Grotto, just in case they hadn't left yet. If they didn't show soon, he knew it would be best for him to leave to prevent them from beating him back to the Princess. Because if that occurred, something really bad might happen. Tuttleberry could arrange to have the real necklace tucked back into the vault, where it would be out of Clarke's reach forever.

He climbed into his car, waiting a call from either Morgan or the bride.

When he woke, he realized he'd dozed off. The dome light made it clear it had only been five, ten minutes tops, but it felt far longer. Right or wrong, it was time to head for home.

The wet, windy trip back to Hamilton unfolded uneventfully. This was good, except for the lack of calls from Grotto. Morgan remained on his mind. The Divel remained on his mind; George remained in his face. It was raining harder the farther west he traveled.

Anyway, the Divel would turn up all right, that he was sure of. He'd just camp near the Princess's entrance and await its entrance. Then switcharoo, before coming upstairs.

Entering the outskirts of Hamilton, he drove past the Underwater Institute. In this slight downhill section, High Street running next to the Harbour looked anything but high. Somewhat dramatically, a small boat had come loose and was perched on the edge of the erosion wall. With continuous squalls coming ashore from the left, the street was inundated with water. He needed to get off this street to higher ground.

Making a right up the steep hill, he made his first left onto Reid. It was much better up here. He could see the street. Now he was running parallel to the Harbour, but safe, one street up. The city was gloomy and deserted. He took Reid as far west as it went, but then was forced to make a left onto Queen heading down the hill. Now the Princess was only blocks to his right. If he got really lucky, the ferry terminal at the end of Queen would protect this section from all that water coming ashore. Approaching Front Street, there were no waves coming out of the Harbour. Good!

Bad?! He made a right into Front Street. What had been a flat looking street splashed into a flat running stream. "No!" he wailed. The car plowed to a dead stop, like a boat running aground. Then the engine died, like a boat running out of gas. Water nudged the car sideways. This was far worse than the Edelson lake party.

Up river, closer to the Princess, another car had succumbed to the same fate.

Its rear lights were above the waterline and still on.

Someone was squeezing out through a driver's side window.

Clarke's own car-boat swayed again. He needed to get out before he was carried downstream.

His door wouldn't budge, but he was lucky he had old-fashioned, roll-down windows. Grunting at this definition of luck, he opened the window. Making sure he had his cell and the flashlight from under the seat, he stuffed the replicas from the glove box into his upper inside jacket pocket. With everything secure, he grabbed the top of the window facing up, and pulled himself through, all arms and legs. The dark, cold water swelled as high as his knees when he stepped down. It was undulating down the street with significant force.

He pushed his legs upstream toward the other car, believing it was too bad it wasn't deep enough to swim. He'd been a champion swimmer in school.

Ahead, three people were standing next to the upriver car.

Clarke heard raised voices.

They started splashing in the water with their hands. No, two of them were sifting the water with their fingers, like they were looking for gold. The closer he approached, the more they sounded American. A day for lost things, all right.

The agitated young man nearest him explained, "We've lost a wallet climbing out of the car," as if Clarke would stop to help them out in this maelstrom.

Clarke flashed his light on the man's face, then down into the flowing water. It was the boy from the wedding. He was sure of it. Their search seemed hopeless with all this water running down the street.

He didn't seem to recognize Clarke with Clarke's Australian rain getup. To Clarke, something didn't seem quite right about their search—the wallet would be floating, unless it did have gold in it. Coins. But guys didn't carry coins that way. Plus, why were they out in weather like this to begin with?

Clarke flashed the light toward the cabbie, recognized him, and waded over. "Hey, John."

"Oh, hi, Mr. Dearborne. Didn't recognize you in the pool." Given this mess, his good-natured self was still shining through.

"Helluva day, huh?"

"You can say that again, mate."

Careful to keep his voice just between the two of them, Clarke asked, "John, where'd this fare come from?"

Downriver, the boys had become more frantic with their searching.

"Grotto Bay, man. Grotto Bay."

According to Clarke's stomach, this was the right wrong answer or the wrong right answer. The Divel was involved in this somehow.

Now Clarke became upset that he hadn't checked that room safe. He would have kicked the water if he could raise his leg high enough. Not a second later, he guessed that no longer mattered. The safe, not the kicking. He still felt like kicking.

Given the storied history of the Divel, his intuition took a leap. Could the Divel be making one of its storied dashes toward deeper water?

Clarke scanned the dark vista. Could there really be anything to this curse-thing? Going home was the sentiment that struck him from a place he couldn't articulate any better than that. Clarke got an idea, turned away from John, turned away from the boys, and pushed his shins downstream through the thick water.

He took out his cell—careful not to drop it in the water—and called the bride.

On the third, slow ring, Clarke barely heard "hello" above the blowing wind. He widened his stance to stabilize himself against all the water going downstream.

"Mrs. Waters?" he asked. Careful to speak away from the boys so they couldn't overhear him in this tempest, that was most definitely not contained inside the Edelson's teapot.

"Yes. Who is this?"

"This is Mr. Dearborne. From the Princess Hotel."

"Oh, hi, Mr. Dearborne. I was going to call you in just a little bit. I got your note. We were getting ready to leave for your nice hotel."

Then Clarke barely heard, "It's Mr. Dearborne….from the Princess, sweetie."

"Mrs. Waters, we realized after you left your beautiful wedding that you forgot to return the necklace before leaving on the charm hunt." Then he took a breath.

"Oh, was I supposed to? I didn't know about that. I have definitely worn it all day."

"Naturally, I've been worried about its safety, but I couldn't call you due to the conditions of your Wedding Trust. I came out there to retrieve it but must have just missed you." A crackle of electricity surged through the phone before Clarke heard thunder all around him.

Clarke continued, "So I'm calling to check up on it now that the quest portion of the day has been completed. At least I'm assuming it's completed." The water was inching him downriver. He would have turned sideways to steady himself, but was afraid the boys might then be able to overhear.

"Oh. Yes, yes. We most definitely completed that part. I can assure you." Relief filled her voice when she said, "It is resting nice and cozy in our little safe, as we speak."

"Would you please check that it is in the safe, so I can be satisfied that it will be coming back safely."

"I assure you—"

"I've been very nervous all day worrying. Would you please do that to satisfy an old, careful man?" Turning his head, one of the boys was near the cab, but the other was coming closer, still searching.

"Well, okay. Hold on a sec." She retrieved the key from Greg, opened the safe, saw all the charms, but no necklace. She groped the small space, as if it might have a false back or bottom, like a magic-trick Halloween safe. "It's not here. It's not here, Mr. Stillborn!"

308

Greg bent down to help Sandy, who was now on the floor. From her phone, he heard a tinny, "Mrs. Waters? Mrs. Waters?" Greg brushed the wisps of blond hair off her face.

She stirred, came to, and spied the phone on the floor. "What happened?" she asked her kneeling husband.

"You fainted, honey."

Sandy raised herself on one elbow and reached for her phone.

"Are you still there Mr. Dearborne?"

"Yes, Mrs. Waters. What's wrong?"

"It's not here, Mr. Dearborne. It's not here."

"When was the last time you saw it?" His feet slipped, so he steadied himself against the constant flow. With one boy very close, he turned in the opposite direction. "When I put it in the safe."

Clarke shuffled farther downriver. "Did anyone else open the safe after you?"

"Not that I'm aware…of."

Clarke heard Sandy hitch. Either a bad connection due to the storm, or something was going on at that end.

Given her shock, given he was standing in the middle of a river in the middle of an electrical storm, amateur Clarke said the first professional thing that came to mind. Hotel professional, not crook professional. Habit. "Okay. Mrs. Waters. Call the police?" Lightning, then thunder interrupted, as if George was adding its own exclamation point. "Don't touch anything else until they arrive. And don't worry. For your information, if you don't know this, it is fully insured. So, everything will work out. Then I'll see you as soon as you reach the Princess. Okay?"

Clarke barely heard a meek, "Okay."

When Clarke disconnected, he couldn't believe what

he'd just done. He slapped the water, still unable to kick. He'd told her to call the police. What an idiot. He'd forgotten in the middle of this mess that he was in the middle of his own perfect crime. Amateur. He heard himself say it, all right, but it sure felt like it had been someone else speaking. Stupid.

Stupid amateur.

Stupid wet amateur.

Unlucky stupid wet amateur.

And now a dead amateur, if he didn't fix this. Was that even possible? Those stupid boys and all this stupid water all over the place. He was a dead duck. And tired. The easiest thing, would be to do nothing and let all this water just carry him away.

Off the phone, standing back up, recognition crawled across Sandy's face. There Greg was, seated on the bed, looking straight through the earth, which is what he did when something was wrong.

"Okay," he heard her say, compelling him to steal a glance her way.

Deliberately, Sandy rotated her body toward him. Dead on.

Here it comes. He was trapped like a dead duck.

"Did you open the safe?"

It was the only logical explanation—if there was to be a logical explanation, as opposed to a supernatural one.

Under pressure, Greg panicked and lied. "I, I haven't a clue what's going on. It's missing? Really?" Cokes were supposed to be an answer to anything that ails you, so he stuck to his Coke defense. "I was getting Cokes, remember?"

"Well, Mr. Dearborne was here, but I don't know if he came in the room or not."

310

Greg nodded and latched onto that, because how many alternative explanations could there be? He wasn't going to try to explain that there had been a semi-nude witch in the closet the whole time, and how neither one of them would have been happy if the witch had stolen it. But the witch had witnessed the whole thing. He could let Sandy try to ask her what had happened. That would be perfectly safe, because the witch probably would have said something already if she could speak. It sure wouldn't be his fault the witch couldn't say anything. How he knew that this coven of pointing witches was mute, he couldn't explain. But, why should he? It had been a very strange day. Day. Only a day. Electrified and all—with both the good and the bad kinds. Bewitched too. He didn't feel so good for it being his wedding day.

Yes, he would never forget his wedding day for as long as he lived. He wasn't sure whether that was good or bad, or, how long that would be, exactly.

Sandy, of course, had little clue why anyone who already owned it would want to steal it—and that there was an excess of that today, along with everything going on outside.

They got the number for the local police, at which point they waited. Sandy was not happy with any of this. At one point, she announced, "Maybe chivalry's not dead?"

When Greg didn't respond, Sandy ran off, "The Lightning Knight. Sir Night Light. Thor the Thunder Bolt King. I've always wondered how people got stupid nicknames, like Frick and Frack. And here it is happening right before my eyes. And my name is the one that should have changed this weekend. I'm feeling left out. I think I need a nickname too. Let's think of one, honey."

Greg realized he was hoping the police would get here

soon—which seemed worse and backward, all at the same time—like everything else this freakin' strange today.

Let the water carry him straight to where the Divel had gone, that's how he could track it. In the middle of this flooded road, Clarke stuffed his phone in the inside coat pocket opposite the one holding the replicas. The boys had to be in the middle of this somehow. What they didn't know was, the Divel was invisible in water. Well invisible or not, he had to try and find the thing. And quickly. He had to think like a necklace. Otherwise the perfect crime might transform itself into the perfect murder—Benny was just around the corner.

Far to the north, an incredibly loud rumble occurred right after the briefest flash of light.

Clarke held one tiny idea amongst the enormity of the elements whipping at his hat and coat. Slim was better than none. Downriver, he moved his shoes that felt like wet sponges. He'd walked this street a million times and knew where the pipes were that drained toward the Harbour. The problem was, he had to recall their location without the normal ground clues. Plus, with the water so high, who was to say the water wasn't running the wrong way. From the Harbour toward the street.

Heading for the riverbank, Clarke tried to imagine the size of those pipes. He was betting the Divel was too big to fit through them. There were two in this section, and they'd been put in when the Princess had flexed its sizable financial muscle to get rid of standing water. Standing?!—this water was definitely not standing, as he heard the unhappy boys coming up behind him.

He turned and looked back toward the commotion. Even the cab was being nudged by the swells. At that moment, one of the boys laid himself flat, as if he was planning to chase the Divel like Clarke.

Clarke stopped at the south side of the street, guessing that George would surely be known for its rain totals. He trudged to where he believed the first pipe should be. Bending over, he scrabbled with his fingers, found the opening and checked it. Nothing. But at least the pipe did seem too small for the Divel. Unfortunately, it was too difficult to tell which way the water was running.

Shuffling his feet downstream, he reached the intersection where his car was still beached, bent down, felt for the second pipe, leaned deeper, and when his chin touched water his fingers touched something. A chain!

He flattened his hand on the road, felt for its wedge shape and, yes! He pulled it up, but it slipped off his numb fingers and plopped back into the water like a fish coming off a hook.

He still had the chain.

He reached under again. This time, as he pulled the chain up, he wrapped it round and around. Then he raised his arm like a fishing pole. The two ends of the necklace appeared at the rolling surface.

He couldn't believe his stupid luck!

He was surrounded by angry water, angry wind, and possibly even an angry Divel, but he had it by the tail and wasn't letting go for anything short of lightning. He felt alive. He felt emboldened.

Bending down, placing both hands underneath it, he stuffed it on the inside of its cousins—just in case it had more thoughts of leaping toward freedom.

All secure, he sloshed his way toward the hotel. Wait a minute. Had he just managed the switch mid-river?! Ugh. No. the police were now involved. And Tuttleberry might or might not require an authenticity check now that it was known to be out. He was so close. This was getting ridiculous. Getting? Three amateurs had messed things up but good, and he was one of them. In the dim light, the one boy next to the cab who messed things up, checked him out as he waded past. Clarke said to the boy, "I thought I saw something, but it turned out to be nothing. You guys may want to go in and borrow some flashlights."

Disgusted and disgusting looking, Frick waded against the tide toward Frack. He'd hurt a couple of fingers when he'd tried to hang onto that car he banged into when the water carried him down a ways. When he came up on Frack, he kept right on pushing toward the hotel, mumbling out loud, really speaking to himself. "This is hopeless. Any idiot can see that. Maybe at first-light before anyone else gets out, we could get incredibly lucky— though I'm figuring that 'incredibly lucky' here would be if we'd brought a metal detector."

Adding insult to injury, they still had to pay the cabbie from the supposed one wallet they had between them.

Making their way to the hotel, they took showers, swapped into dry clothes, all the while refusing to speak to one another. Frick, for his part, kept repeating while undressing, while showering, and later while dressing, "We had it."

Frack, alone with his own thoughts, which was usually the case, kept repeating his monologue. "Stupid, stupid, stupid criminals." The worst part for him, the very worst part, was disappointing Mrs. Waters— afraid she'd never take him to bed now. With rounded shoulders, he slunk around the room refusing to look at Frick. He had been so eager to see her, to explain their success in the minutest detail, and now, empty-handed, Frack offered the uncharacteristically philosophical, "Nothing ventured nothing gained," toward butterfingers.

That word "ventured" caused Frick to recall the name of the prodigal ship that supposedly started all this. "Are you making a sick joke?" While venturing an eye toward his partner-in-crime, the prospect of long-term destitution penetrated him like the soaking they'd just suffered through. "Because if I hear you say something like 'Every cloud has a silver lining,' I'm going to hurl this very expensive lamp at you."

Frack noticed the potential energy furrowed in Frick's brow. "At least the alcohol's free tonight," saying, without saying, the cloud thing.

"Don't say another word to me."

Frack felt the effects of his future indentured servitude—lying far into his sadly seeable future—as it pressed down upon his discouraged shoulders. Visions of the leggy, experienced Mrs. Waters had been washed away as surely as they were surrounded by water on this spit of inhospitable land. If you could even call it land. He hadn't seen enough of that lately—except in the form of mud.

CHAPTER 31

AMERICANS

Clarke headed for the hotel's spare room, left the Divels in the coat, and the coat in the closet, showered, changed, and decided that Tuttleberry needed to be informed. The prospect, the threat of a high visibility third-party authentication process left him keyed up, despite, in addition to, having all three Divels.

And then it occurred to him: Maybe she never got through to the police because of the storm?

He rang the bride. No answer. He called Morgan.

"She asked me to call the police because you asked her to call the police."

Clarke heard Morgan's explanation home in on the idiot holding his phone. His teeth clenched down with the absurd circular nature of it all. His perfect plan had twisted around him like an eel—the electric kind.

"And the Chief showed up like greased lightning. He's never gotten here this quick in his life. He must be a mudder."

Clarke sat himself down in the straight-backed vinyl desk chair. He wasn't sure if the hefty Chief could exactly be categorized as a racehorse that preferred the rain. "I imagine she mentioned the Divel. That's all it would take. He's like an old hound dog. He's got a good sniffer for cases that can get him in the paper. Or, she reminded him about your food choices."

"That's probably it," she joked. "You need to know the

316

bride is very upset—poor kid. It's not every day you lose something like that." Clarke had the Divel, and it had him.

He made a snap decision. "All's good. I just recovered the Divel near the Princess. But don't say anything to anyone else yet. Okay?"

"Really?"

"Yes."

"But why shouldn't I tell her?" Compassionate.

"Trust me. This has gotten a little complicated because of where I found it. Do me a favor and put the Chief on, will you?"

He and the Chief and Morgan went back a ways, so he was hoping that would be worth something as he tried to safely handle this eel.

The Chief was a fixture on this part of the island. Over fishing, he and Clarke always spoke of retiring, but every year they ended up carrying on. Indeed, Chief Youngblood's blood wasn't young anymore. With a name like his, he'd wondered if he'd been raised by Native Americans, whether he would have come by all this detecting stuff more honestly. Tennessee, of the United States, would have worked out just fine if he'd been raised there as a country boy by his father's side of the family. But his mother's clan on the eastern side of Bermuda had won out, so here he was.

With his pony-tailed hair, fishing boots and suspenders, his fire plug image was so distinctive that more than a few locals mimicked him come Halloween.

Over the back of a chair near the newlyweds, dripping, the Chief threw his professional rain slicker and that hat with the crinkly plastic. This late in the afternoon, his pot belly was letting him know it was time to eat. He'd enjoyed the food the last time he'd visited Grotto. Well, he enjoyed his meals wherever, truth-be-told. Tonight, he was looking forward to his wife's rabbit stew. But with the rest of his staff out-and-about helping in this brutal storm, he'd been forced toward adorable Morgan.

The Chief slowly turned his low-set body toward Morgan, as Morgan told him Clarke Dearborne was on the line with urgent information. The Chief never moved quickly outside of a car. Never had, even as a tot.

The chief excused himself from Mrs. Waters, who was presently resting in her husband's lap, taking Morgan's tiny cell in his meaty hand. "Youngblood here."

"How're you, Chief?"

"Good, until I had to go out in this. Lucky my 4x4 did okay." Normally, he only used it to pull his boat around to the different fishing holes.

Clarke guessed he probably wasn't happy that he had to go to all the trouble to unhook his boat from it.

"I had a helluva time trying to unhook my boat in this rain, so the darn thing's still on like a tick."

"I figured as much."

"Might even need it before the day is through."

"You might. Well, I've got some good news for you. I need to talk to you before you speak any further to Mrs. Waters over there. It concerns a delicate matter that is critical to this…this whole thing." He almost said "case," which was the last word he wanted to speak. The last thing he needed was for the old bulldog to officially open this as a case.

"I see," the Chief said in his deep voice.

"You want to go somewhere private, so we can talk over the phone? Because it's too far for me to drive out there—even if I had a car— which I don't. It's conked out on Front Street. And I've already been involved in one

318

fender bender at the Edelson's."

"You too?"

"I could have used your boat."

"I reckon so. It's a good boat, she is. Remember that boat-car in the old James Bond movie. That would have been perfect today."

"That's for sure."

"Anyway, I'm putting two and two together. You've been on Divel high-alert all week. So, I am going to cut through our usual fishin' talk because my stomach is urgin' me on. I haven't gone too far wrong following it this sixty-odd years. This is about your necklace, right?"

"Your hunches have always served you well, Chief."

"You know what happened to it?"

"…Yes. Yes, I do," the directness of the Chief's interrogation had caught him a little off-guard.

The Chief's voice got a little lower. "You're not calling me from Tahiti—with the necklace— where they have all that great deep sea fishin' on Channel 35, are you?"

"No, of course not…the Bahamas…Ha, just kidding."

"Ha! Got me there, all right. Then seein' there's another storm here abrewin', why don't I mosey down to another room and we have ourselves a little chat, as Ma liked to say."

Clarke heard, "Where can I have a little privacy 'round these parts?"

Clarke heard Morgan's voice answer, "You can use the room right over here." Then he heard Morgan's lyrical voice get softer, "I'm sure lucky I have free weekends," as the Chief carried her phone away. Before the Chief closed the door, Morgan said, "You going to be ready for food."

"Yep."

Clarke heard the Chief grunt—probably settling his

bulk down.

"Okay, Clarke. What am I doing in your show today? Because it was today, right?"

"Right." Clarke stood up, went toward the door, and threw the inside lock over the hook on the door so no one could walk in on him. "You want the long or the short version?" As he asked, Clarke realized this was it. From here, things were going to go one way or another. Nothing in-between.

"Why don't you give me the short long one, or the long short one? That seems about right for getting enough details and giving Morgan enough time to have my food ready. Plus, I need to retire before the end of the year."

Clarke ignored the bait. "The bride forgot to take it off after the ceremony." Clarke bypassed how the general public believed the bride wore a replica for the wedding proper. That would be part of the long version. "For security purposes, it's supposed to stay locked up in my vault. Anyway, to make a long story short, it went all over the island with her today. And you can just imagine how Tuttleberry and I felt about that."

Clarke couldn't hear the Chief's stomach chime in at that point, as the Chief answered with his standard short, food-ready version, "Yep."

"Anyway, after they retrieved the required charms—at least I assume they got them—they stopped off at their honeymoon suite to await tonight's reception. I'm sure they were soaked and tired after being out in the storm all day, so I don't blame them for not coming straight back."

With his stomach behaving itself, the Chief chimed in. "Can't blame anyone for comin' in today."

"For sure. Tuttleberry gave me instructions to retrieve it as soon as possible. I drove all the way out there to do just that. When I got there, Morgan and I couldn't find them. That's when I left a note for them to call—" Clarke felt this was taking way too long. Had he heard someone in the hall? "You got me so far?"

"So far, so good. This is a comfy chair here. If you don't hurry, I'm takin' my afternoon nap. For all the hoopla surrounding this thing, this isn't exactly the most exciting case—" Clarke's skin prickled with that word. "—I've ever come across."

He heard the Chief yawn. Sitting back down, getting up, then sitting again, Clarke's legs began to hop up and down on the toes of his feet. "Of course, friends and relatives came with the bride and groom. They knew about the Divel. They knew about its value, and two of them saw fit to visit Grotto. It looks like they left with it, without the bride's knowledge. Between the time they showed up and the time they left, the Divel disappeared from the hotel. Then the strangest thing of all happened. While I was returning from Grotto, my car conked out in the flood on Front Street. When I climbed out, guess who conked out in front of me?"

"The visitors."

"Yep. And they lost the Divel right into the water. I ended up grabbing it without their knowledge. Fished it right out. Now, that is the biggest fish story we've ever told." He smiled at topping all their stories, and they had traded plenty.

"Well isn't that but the damnedest thing I've heard since Grandpa said he caught that twenty-five-foot tuna."

Clarke remembered that old story. "You don't believe me? Ask Morgan." That was his ace in the hole. "You've known Morgan your whole life. She'll tell you every word I've said is true." It was at this very moment that Clarke realized he'd miss Morgan if he went to prison.

"You been drinkin'?"

321

"No. No, Chief. Of course not…" Both legs were still bouncing up and down. "Here's the problem you and I face," drawing them together where he needed them to be. "I've got the Divel safe and sound now. I'm about to take it to Tuttleberry so it can go back into the vault until the next wedding. Thankfully neither you nor I will have to be troubled with it again from our fishing holes."

"Amen to that, brother. Amen to that."

"I know who took it. Those boys know who took it. I don't know how they got into the safe, but I have my suspicions, since only the couple had the key. And Morgan, of course. But I know Morgan didn't use her key. Lord knows, I wanted her to. But you know your Morgan. She wanted to do it proper—to wait for the couple to come back to the room and all."

Not hearing anything, Clarke asked, "You snoring over there?" He wished.

"Go on. Go on. I'm listenin'."

"Anyway, no one's going to admit to giving the key to those boys. Not the boys. Not the couple. It's going to turn out to be an embarrassment to the Princess, to me, to Grotto and to Morgan." Clarke was beginning to sweat in this tiny humid room in his dry clothes. "While those two reckless boys get to go back to Florida and go fishing in the sun. This will turn out to be a big black eye for Bermuda. And if the press really gets their teeth into this while the whole Waters group manages to escape back to Florida, USA with their double-talk, then you and I will get to retire over the biggest security breach since the Cross. How would that grab you?"

"We got ourselves quite a pickle."

"Quite a pickle."

"I like pickles, myself."

"On hamburgers. Not newspapers."

"Quite right. Hot dogs too."

"Yeah. That spicy relish was good your mum used to make with her peppers. You thought I'd forgotten about that. But my stomach hasn't."

"My stomach, neither. Thank goodness it's dinnertime."

"I know I'm going to eat better once this thing is back in the vault."

"Did they damage it? Are you sure they didn't pull a fast one and switch it, like in those James Bond movies?"

This was the line of questioning Clarke was sweating over. It wasn't helping that he knew how thorough the Chief could be when he latched onto something. "No, I checked it once I reached the hotel. It's got the authentic markings on the back. I have both. The only two. The original and the replica. Both will be back in the vault, like two peas-in-a-pod, as soon as I hang up. Naturally, I'm going to get Tuttleberry to check them first. I could have Mr. Tuttleberry call you as soon as that's finished." This was a good touch on the fly, until he realized that Tuttleberry might be suspicious of why Chief Youngblood was involved. More circles.

"Maybe so, maybe so."

Clarke stood and began pacing in the tiny space. "And we can tell my boss that because the Divel was loose out in your parish, you were called in just to make sure nothing fantastic happened before it came back. He'll appreciate your support."

"Let me speak to Morgan. Then I'll ring you right back. This number, right?"

"Sounds good." Clarke stopped moving. He liked the sound of that.

Less than three minutes later, Clarke's cell rang. The Chief had not dilly-dallied before his dinner. Clarke heard,

"It's me. Morgan's story jives with yours."

Clarke took a breath.

"In cases like this, big cases, usually the bigger picture is more important than how many small fish you catch. The wise thing to do is to make sure the Divel is safe and sound. Have Tuttleberry call me when your part is done. Then I'm havin' my dinner. Morgan has promised me a seafood stew. I digest my food better once a case is wrapped up. I'm like Pa in that respect. Always have been."

Clarke remembered that was true of the Chief, even though officially this case had never been "unwrapped." And he meant to keep it that way. "Sounds good. I'm hungry too. But you're one up on me, Chief. You've got Morgan for dinner company. I'm jealous."

"Then get over here, you young fart, and do something about it." On that side of the island, everyone knew how fond the two of them were of each other. "Oh. One more thing," the Chief tossed out.

Clarke's stomach dropped, like when he traveled in a plane. Now something else—all day long there had been something else. He forced out a tight, "Yes?"

"What about the happy couple here. What should I tell 'em?"

"Oh. That's easy. As soon as I place the Divel in the vault, I'm going to call them and read them their new bible. The Divel Bible. So, until Mr. Tuttleberry calls you back, you stay with the couple. Tell them everything is under control, and that I'll be calling them shortly to explain. I imagine they're way too embarrassed to have spoken to anyone yet. Let's keep it that way."

"New Bible?"

"Yes. Their new moral code: How for their own names, their parents' names, the family name, we will not discuss how the Divel got from around her neck to the streets of Hamilton in the middle of a hurricane. In fact, we don't really want to know. But the press will. And if that happens, some unidentified friends who visited their hotel in the middle of George will be facing jail time for the theft of a royal jewel. Do you think that would be laying it on too thick?"

"The gravy is as thick as you need it to be," the Chief said familiarly. "I loved your mum's gravy. I owe you a six-pack."

"Twelve-pack. I could have done with the short version, and the sun's been hotter than Hades up until all this rain."

Clarke's best chance had arrived. It involved a little risk, but with the Chief checking out Morgan's stew, and Tuttleberry preoccupied with his little butterflies, this was it. Time for the most lucrative bathroom break of all time.

He took the real Divel out of his coat and stashed it up in the closet. But as his arm reached out, it dawned on him he wasn't 100% sure this was the real McCoy out of the three. Before he made a five-million-dollar mistake, he placed all three on the desk. It wasn't easy to tell them apart, but after a moment's close comparison, the spread of the sparkle of the diamonds in the real one was more pronounced than what the low-grade diamonds of the other two were giving off. Yes, this had to be the real one. He turned it over to check the back. Satisfied, he placed it in a plain brown bag, opened the closet door, and stuck it way up high in the back of the closet.

Deed done, he wiped his hands together, put on his raincoat, looked around the room to make sure everything was in its place, grabbed the two replicas, and stuffed them back in his inner pocket to head for Tuttleberry's.

When he stepped into Winston's morgue, the room appeared to be in balance again, except for the two Divels on the same side of his coat. What had he been thinking? He leaned slightly to compensate.

Winston removed his nose from the middle of the latest Butterfly Digest.

Clarke started off his retirement program with, "The long and short of it is, I rescued the Divel from the water when I saw it drop in the street right in front of me." Then he took a needed breath.

After quickly relaying the details, Clarke reassured him, "And you needn't worry about any curses. The couple completed the charm quest." That was a good touch. Then he produced the two replicas— one in each hand—to close this case good and quickly, and to keep the room and his karma in balance. He handled the "real" one more carefully, as if such treatment guaranteed its authenticity.

Rimmed with red, Winston's eyes took in the two necklaces. The only two in existence. The one being handled more carefully, obviously, the real McCoy.

Winston didn't seem particularly interested in looking at or touching them. Clarke rode this sentiment with, "After today, neither one of us will have to have anything more to do with this pompous necklace."

With a sincere "Amen to that" and a "Congratulations," Winston said the magic words. "Then let's have the Devil's Necklace make its final journey back into our nice dry vault." Then he toasted the whole event with another quick nip.

Predictable, all right.

Clarke still had to tie up his loose end. "Winston, it would help close this whole thing up if you made a courtesy call to Chief Youngblood over in Hamilton Parish. He helped us by providing extra support, seeing as how the necklace made a pit-stop in his backyard today."

"That little thing has got the whole island spooked." Winston took another nip to prepare himself for the call. When his wincing eyes reopened, Clarke gave him Morgan's direct number.

Morgan answered, and again shared her weekend minutes with the hungry Chief. After the brief call, Winston commented on how excited the Chief sounded.

"He's getting Morgan's stew as soon as you hang up."

Winston then contacted Thompson to come down for another trip to the vault.

Clarke did his best to keep his balance and to keep the excitement from spreading across his too-easy-to-read face. He was almost home.

Minutes later, the tall Thompson lumbered in.

Winston rose from his chair, engaged a hidden catch in his floor-to-ceiling bookcase, unlocked a large metal box with a key from his chain, removed two keys, closed everything back up, and handed them to Clarke. Then off they went.

As Clarke walked down the hall in front of the towering Thompson—feeling more solidly balanced for some reason—he just didn't get any of that collecting stuff. To him, those beautiful and delicate creatures belonged out in the wild, beautifying the flowers. No matter how prized they were to a collector like Tuttleberry, dead, they couldn't compare with the live ones flitting about. Not to his amateur eye, anyway.

After completing the vault's outer security protocol, they entered the walk-in tomb. As they made small talk about the weather, Clarke knew that even though no one was watching from the monitor room at the moment— given that Thompson was here—everything they did and said was being recorded.

Like he'd done previously, Clarke reached for a nondescript square-faced lockbox in the wall of lockboxes before unlocking it with the two keys from Tuttleberry. Then he removed the two keys from this box and gave them all to Thompson. Tuttleberry's keys had small yellow tags—the color probably influenced by one of his favorites no doubt—while the vault keys were blue.

Clarke reminded Thompson how they had to try random combinations using one of each set, until they hit upon the combination that would unlock another nondescript square-faced lockbox. All this rigmarole made it next to impossible for a thief to do this quickly, never mind, do it at all.

Clarke wanted Thompson to be the one who actually placed everything back in the boxes. With Clarke becoming impatient, Thompson finally lucked into the correct combination, slid the box out, and placed it on the wooden shelfing before them.

Clarke removed the red velvet-lined case with its matching molded shape, then showed both replicas to the camera at the same time.

Thompson placed the supposedly genuine Divel back into its ornate case, and then returned it to the lockbox where it would wait to be joined with its new charms. Then the second replica followed suit. Sliding the cases back in, Thompson locked them all in place.

The vault keys went back in their box, and then Thompson handed the two butterfly keys to Clarke for Tuttleberry. Short enough and sweet. And best of all, it had all been captured on that jury-busting camera.

Clarke looked up at Thompson and reminded him, "We'll have to repeat all this a little later when the charms arrive. If one of us is busy, then Tammy Vee will fill in. Okay?"

328

"Okay by me. Thanks for including me in the big show today. I'm glad I could help."

"Your help has been most appreciated." Clarke expected to be the one who was busy later. Busy with Benny. In fact, now that he considered it, it might prove helpful if he wasn't here when the new charms joined the necklace. When they neared Tuttleberry's office with those keys, Clarke laid them in Thompson's paw. Clarke had had enough of that strangely balanced office, plus, he needed to call the newlyweds back before something else went wrong.

CHAPTER 32

TOPIC OF THE DAY

While waiting for the kids to return, Diane had quite naturally gravitated toward the small upscale bar. Pinned in by the weather, all the barstools were occupied, but one of the four tables next to wall was free. Ordering some fancy house drink that had gin in it, it came quickly. She needed it. She had held out hope for some secondhand smoke in here, but that sure wasn't going to happen by the looks of it. Alone with her thoughts, she hoped Sandy and Greg had come through the hunt unscathed by the storm. That they had fared better on the ferry than she and Mike had—if the ferries were even running today.

She wished, instead, that it could have been the type of "fairy" that had some fantastic ability to counteract the curse she somehow knew existed but couldn't prove. The other kind of ferry could easily sink on a day like today. Sink like the one that just sank off of India or Indonesia— one of those "Indie" countries over there. At least both kids were good swimmers—she'd never learned, herself. Something else she might tackle, now that that extra weight had been removed from around her neck.

Her hand was shaking when she placed the glass down on the table. All nerves, she spat to herself, *This damn storm.* Mike had said hurricanes weren't supposed to strike here. "I'll have another one of these, whatever you call 'em." The hell with it. Having given in to the urge to have another drink, she gave in to the urge to call the kids.

Reaching for her cell, she stopped short. What if the curse was true?

Mike was still up in the room communicating with the International Space Station or some such scientific thing-a-ma-jig. Downloading, uploading, or sideways loading all that hurricane data raining in. She pictured him in the room, happy as a clam, still dressed in his formal clothes with his long legs splayed out.

Diane recalled, relived really, the ill-fated ferry ride from her own wedding day. The last time she'd been on open water. The boat had pitched, and she'd gotten good and sick. She was sick again, but of the curse and all this worrying. Thank God it was over for her, but she felt awful about passing it on to Sandy. If only the boys could have come through. Frack's hound-dog face had told the whole story. Failed. He was so cute the way he wanted to please her, unlike some men around here.

She let go of her cell. An ill-defined disappointment was settling about her that went beyond the Divel. It included Mike. Included attention and affection and sex and caring. She felt like a woman who had prepared herself for the coming duty of this weekend—a duty where attraction and repulsion had become embroiled around each other to such an extent that they'd now lost their distinctiveness. Sort of like the Divel. She needed a cigarette.

She wasn't sorry she'd brought the boys into it. Not sorry at all. Even if they were bumblers. *Like fish out of water,* she quipped to herself. She swirled the ice around her glass, listening to it clink; waiting for the next one to arrive.

She was feeling sorry for herself. The next question followed as naturally as smoke from a cigarette: Exactly when had her marriage been sunk? She would have taken a good pull on a cigarette if she'd had one handy. She hadn't smoked in years. Mike hated cigarettes. She'd start smoking when she got home—if not sooner.

Sam was coming her way. He always looked so relaxed; she wished she felt that way more.

"Hi. Some weather we're having," Sam said. "Being cooped up is not the way I was hoping to spend our time here."

"I know what you mean. Maybe we'll be able to get out tomorrow before we leave?"

"That'd be nice. You want another of those?" She nodded *why not;* he ordered two drinks.

As Diane finished off another drink in preparation for the next, she was finding the young, sun-blond waiter cuter and cuter.

"Ready for the reception?" Sam asked with his natural casualness.

"More than ready. Famished. You?"

"Yes. It'll be nice to see the kids and hear about their little adventure."

She could only hope it had remained little. Rarely could she be accused of knowing too much before something happened—like Mike. But this was one of those times. She didn't like the feeling. It was far better not knowing stuff and just ad-libbing your way.

CHAPTER 33

TWO HEADS ARE BETTER THAN ONE

Sandy answered her cell with a tentative, "Hello, this is Sandy Waters speaking," as if she had really been expecting a call from the Queen herself after the Chief's Tucker Cross story. The Chief had given them two choices, that or food, and the decidedly unhungry newlyweds had opted to hear about the other famous gone-missing priceless gem.

"Mrs. Waters, it's Clarke Dearborne from the Princess. I hope you're feeling a little better."

"Well, Chief Youngblood here—who just left to get something to eat—tried to explain that everything is all right. That you'd be calling us shortly. But I don't understand that, since, well, since the Divel is missing."

"Are you sitting?"

"No. Should I be?" As soon as those words left her lips, the answer was obvious.

"Yes."

"Okay, I'm sitting."

She flipped opened her palm toward Greg in an I'm-waiting-to-find-out-what's-going-on signal.

Greg's face looked like how she felt—taut.

Sandy heard, "I'm happy to report to you everything is all right." Outside her building, it flashed bright.

Followed by a large boom.

Clarke heard what sounded like a bass drum through his phone. "Listen, Mrs. Waters, do you mind if we include your husband in this call? I think it is important that he hears what I'm about to say."

"Why of course. He's sitting right here."

Do the two of you have privacy where you are?"

"No. We're in an open sitting area where they have some magazines."

"I know where you are. Okay, please have one of the staff show you to one of the unoccupied offices right around the corner."

Sandy got a staff member's attention, and they were escorted to an empty office. When the door closed, and they were seated in the two chairs in front of a desk with neat, small stacks of paper, Sandy said, "Okay, we're alone."

"Okay, put your phone on speaker please…hello, Mr. Waters?

"Yes, I'm here, Mr. Dearborne." Sandy heard an edge to Greg's voice. He certainly hadn't been quite the same since Fort St. Catherine and its lightning. Except in more water, in the shower.

"Congratulations on your big day."

"Thank you."

"It's turned out to be a big day for all of us, of course. But I first want to assure the both of you the Divel is safe, and that it has been locked back up in our vault with the replica. The replica I might add, Mrs. Waters, you were supposed to wear on your journey today."

Sandy squirmed in her seat while answering with a defensive, "I know. I'm a little embarrassed by that mix up. I'm so sorry." She was being diplomatic. She couldn't really remember her mom mentioning that. "We must have forgotten." Sandy's blue eyes were blinking away. She glanced toward her new husband who looked older somehow from just this morning. Stiffer too. She was

334

fighting back tears.

"There is an old saying in sports, Mrs. Waters. It goes, No harm, no foul." Meaning, the Divel is safe. Mr. Tuttleberry, my boss, has already seen both the original and the replica, and authorized me and Mr. Thompson to secure them back in the vault. Once it is joined by the charms you've collected today, everything is done. You did get them all, I hope?"

Sandy looked at Greg and thought of that coin that had been rejected by the fort. How she had almost been blown from the top of the lighthouse—that should be renamed a "windhouse"—and because of it, they'd only gotten three out of the four pics. She wanted to come completely clean. They hadn't really finished it. Despite everything, they had broken the chain. Now look what was happening. It surely hadn't taken very long "Yes, yes, we have them all. They weren't touched." That much was true. Sandy took in a needed breath. She felt like she was harboring this big secret, and it was making her feel horrible. On the edge of sharing, she couldn't bring herself to snitch on her brand-new husband after what they'd been through. How these problems were probably all their fault. He looked to be in shock, actually.

"Good. When you arrive for your reception, please call security, so the charms can be rejoined with the Divel. Are we on the same page here?"

Greg hazarded, "Yes, but we still don't know what happened to the Divel. We had it locked up, you see."

"Well, Mr. and Mrs. Waters, that is a most interesting part of this story. Here it is, and then I'm going to ask for your cooperation to put this all behind us, for all of our sakes. Agreed?"

"Agreed," they answered in unison.

"Both of you have met Ms. James at Grotto, the

335

manager, who is a sweetheart. She was there when I was there, so if you have any further questions, you can ask her what happened. Suffice-it-to-say, Mr. Tuttleberry was very upset that the necklace was not immediately returned to the Princess this morning. It remains a great duty and privilege to look after the Divel for your family, Mrs. Waters. When we couldn't find you in the hotel, I traveled to Grotto Bay, per Mr. Tuttleberry's instructions, to retrieve it. Ms. James and I then searched the hotel, and ended up at your room, hoping of course that you'd be inside when you didn't answer your phone."

Sandy blushed. She'd almost been caught doing Thor the Thunderbolt King in the shower.

"Given Mr. Tuttleberry's directive, I even wanted Ms. James to check the safe, but she refused. She wanted to maintain your privacy as much as possible, even in the face of what the Princess Hotel deemed an emergency…" Clarke paused to let that sink in. "I hope you can appreciate that fact, Mrs. Waters, since we were forbidden to contact you until the quest was completed."

Sandy looked over at Greg, but his gaze was pinned to the floor. "I can see that, Mr. Dearborne." She was seeing, all right. Seeing her new husband in a new light.

"Then I left Grotto. When I got back to Front Street, it was completely flooded. I was forced to leave my car in the middle of a flooded street."

"Oh my god, Mr. Dearborne, I hope it's all right?"

"Nothing that a little insurance can't handle."

Greg flinched on that word "insurance," and his eyes came up from that spot on the carpet.

"When I got out, I noticed another car trapped by the flood. A cabbie and his two passengers had also been forced to abandon ship. When they did, they began searching for something in the water. Something dropped in the water, you see. They said it was a wallet, but the way they were searching, I became interested. Part of the job after all these years. You following me so far?"

"Yes." Sandy could hardly believe this fantastic story. The problem was, even though Mr. Dearborne hadn't told her the ending yet, she knew what was coming.

Flicking another look at her stone-still husband, Greg's face was flushed.

"They looked familiar, so I asked the cabbie where his fare was from. Take a guess where the cabbie picked them up from?"

"Not the Grotto Hotel, Mr. Dearborne?"

"Yes, and guess who they were?"

"Who," Sandy implored with her big blue eyes and that "o" with her lips.

"It was the two best men from your wedding. Your friends."

Sandy gasped, almost losing the phone for the third time today. And each time, it had been a smart thing to do.

Greg wasn't moving, wasn't breathing.

"I know this must be something of a shock. You see, all that water was flowing down the street toward the Harbour. And we have only two pipes in the area. I know where they are because I've walked that street a thousand times. When I checked the drains—it was the only chance you see—my hunch paid off. The Divel was stuck in the pipe. Isn't that just an amazing story?"

Greg looked like a sick stone.

"As good as any Divel story over the centuries. And every time it comes out of the vault, it creates another story. It's a story magnet. With curses and bad luck and everything."

That word "curses" came out of Clarke's mouth with

a peculiar twist in it. Making it sound to Sandy like he was one of these islanders who believed in them.

At that moment, the pitch of the wind grew higher at Grotto.

Greg used the small amount of air in his lungs to say, "Yes. Both of us were almost killed during the wit—" which was when he either ran out of air or changed what he was going to say. "I mean, not that kind of hunt, but the charm hunt today."

"I'm sorry to hear that, of course. Anyway, I don't know how your friends got it. I don't care how they got it. Unless someone wants to go to jail in Chief Youngblood's car, I suggest we all work together and let it go. Are you getting my drift here? And like this hurricane and all its water, this is a very strong drift."

Sandy looked at Greg. Her wedding day had turned into one those New Year's Eve *Twilight Zone* episodes they watched every year.

He looked guilty sitting like a stone over there. Sitting in the same room, he was far away somehow. He'd never been any good at bluffing in the poker games at school. His tell had always been trying to make himself look inconspicuous—like right now.

Sandy was struck by an impulse to ask Greg whether he'd slept with that damn dancer at his bachelor party. Before this moment, she'd been sure of the answer. But now, he seemed capable of far more than she would have ever imagined. Sitting as close as he was to her, he hadn't once tried to touch her or anything. *And those damn jerks,* she thought. She'd been right again. And it hadn't helped her wedding day one bit to be right. The more she thought about it, the angrier she was getting.

Clarke said, "That necklace seems to get people to do strange things and to take strange-risks."

Sandy heard Mr. Dearborne's words slow down at the end of that sentence.

Greg heard himself say from a supposed distance, "Anyone else have a key?"

Outside, the boom came immediately after the spike of light over the bay, causing both newlyweds to flinch.

"We are not going there, Mr. Waters," Clarke answered after the boom. "I'm not buying into any cockamamie theories. You got me? I saw what I saw. And I'm telling you straight away we need to be on the same side here. Or someone, or someone's, will get burned. Go to jail, with my buddy over there. *Comprende?*"

Silence. Uncomfortable silence. Even outside.

Greg appeared shorter to Sandy. She'd heard a lot of things about marriage, but that hadn't been one of them.

"I can't hear you. Either way, it's been a very stressful weekend because of the storm. If I could blame one thing for making your wedding less than perfect, an act of God would get my vote."

Dr. Waters, of course, had the evidence to disagree with Clarke's layman assessment.

Sandy was glaring at Greg now. She was all primed to end this call and have her first serious talk with her new husband—though she had to admit it felt like they'd been married thirty years, if they'd been married a day. A day.

Clarke asked into the silence, "Are we on the same page here, or do I need to invite Chief Youngblood back into the room? Who I can guarantee will not take kindly to having his dinner interrupted by American tourists. I have already told him of your situation, and he has agreed to look the other way if we never mention this again."

That clinched it for Sandy. No matter how angry she was at the moment, she couldn't let Greg get arrested. Dumb and Dumber were a bad influence on him. All this

339

commotion just confirmed her opinion of them, if she'd needed any confirming. Her parents hadn't sent her to college for nothing.

Sandy's blue eyes bore down on Greg's trapped brown ones. She said clearly and with conviction, "You've got our word, Mr. Dearborne. I, we, agree with you."

Clarke asked, "Mr. Waters?"

Greg cleared his dry throat, then managed to get out in spite of the insufficient air in his lungs, "Yes. What you propose is for the best. We will gladly, get back to our honeymoon, which unfortunately seems to have gotten lost in the storm."

Clarke added, "Right. Let's not forget the best part of all of this." Sandy wasn't so sure.

"I'll see you both when you bring in the charms." Then Sandy heard Mr. Dearborne say in a more relaxed voice, as if the big thing between them had been settled, "And the way I'm feeling right now, I think those charms are more important than any of us ever believed."

Another strange statement from this islander. Sandy ended the call, then raised her eyes slowly toward Greg. With his stooped posture, he had aged right in front of her eyes.

Greg noticed Sandy turn slowly toward him like actors did in those late-night horror movies. Directors chose slow movement like this because it heightened the suspense of the scene, while emphasizing that the innocent victim had no way to escape. He didn't feel innocent. Flush with guilt, he awaited his sentence.

"Well, what the hell was that all about?" Her blue eyes were boring into him like the mutinous pirate that he was.

It flashed bright in Greg's mind he could run outside, run fast and jump into all that water under all that lightning. No one in their right mind would follow him into the bay. Except, well, except that witch who appeared quite comfortable in the rain and electricity, semi-nude. She'd just wait him out—wait at the shore until he had to come out. As he stewed in his own juices, he decided the witch must have been pointing out the path toward Hell.

Trapped.

Cornered, like a rat.

All he'd done was cross the letter of some old "law" by throwing a sixpence, and then steal a priceless heirloom. His thoughts began to climb all over themselves again. Without him willing it, his numb lips moved. "I'm sorry." Actually, it was as good a place as any to start. Then he kicked at the carpet a few times, like it was a pile of dirt on a pitcher's mound.

Sandy's mouth opened, but nothing came out.

"It's all my fault," his electrified guilt prompted him to admit. Then it spilled out faster, "After it almost killed you, me, the boys talked me into getting rid of it because it was covered by insurance." He tried a furtive glance at her. "I mean, you hated the thing too and all." The pieces of rationale that had clung together before, no longer seemed relevant.

Sandy said, "This has been the wedding from Hell. Just like my mom warned. But, but, you." She waved the damaged phone at him. "Ugh…I love you, you big jerk, though I'm not quite sure why at the moment." With him not looking at her again, she slapped his arm. "Look at me. If my parents found out about this, they'd skin you alive. Well maybe not my mom, since she hates the thing too. Now I'm starting to see why. People do all sorts of crazy things around it. Maybe that's the real reason they keep it locked up?"

"I went a little crazy," he admitted, throwing up both

341

hands. "I'm not sure why." He wasn't going to tell her about the semi-nude witches running all over the place. He made his hand into a pistol and pulled the trigger toward his temple. "Can you forgive me, honey?" His eyes were moist around the outside. Just what they needed, more water.

"Maybe by the time our oldest daughter is ready to marry, if, you do exactly what I want later in bed."

"Forget it then. I'm jumping in the water. Taking my chances with the witches."

"You really are in a Halloween mood." She stood and hugged him.

They followed all those steps down to their room in a misting rain. Greg was convinced that it was true that good things happened to bad people—screwing up the adage in a way that would make Freud proud.

Greg was no longer in the mood for their party.

They placed the charms back in their bags and headed back up those steps.

Morgan caught up to them when they passed the front desk. "You two okay? Off to your reception?" They nodded.

"I hope you have a great time."

Sandy shared, "I feel like we've entered the Twilight Zone somewhere along the way."

"Well, I'm not familiar with that zone, but I think it's time to start enjoying your own honeymoon zone. And this is the perfect place to do it. We'll take good care of you when you get back."

Out front, the rain was still light. Greg knocked on Aarone's window. Reclined in his seat, he'd been fast asleep.

Aarone, rubbed his faced, smiled, and then gallantly stepped out and opened the door for Mrs. Waters. Then off they went. After the small-talk ended, it became comfortably quiet inside the small cab. Greg was wondering what he was going to say to the boys. He believed they needed to know that the local law was involved; that it all needed to go away and never be spoken of again.

PART VI

THE HANDOFF

CHAPTER 34

PREP WORK

With the wedding party waiting on the guests of honor, with the security staff waiting on the charms, and with Benny waiting on Clarke, the time had arrived for Clarke to hand-off the blasted thing. Though the weather was miserable and his car was beached down Front Street, he still needed to get to North Hamilton tonight. This area, known as the French Quarter, could be unfriendly to strangers after dark. But thanks to Clarke's new ally, George, it rated to be empty and safe, at least as far as uninvited humans were concerned.

Clarke decided it might be wise to check that Benny hadn't closed up shop and retreated upstairs to his apartment. Benny wouldn't want him ringing when his wife was there, given their loose-lips-sink-ships strategy. He needed to find a phone other than his cell, so a nondescript hotel phone was just going to have to do:

Yes, the man right over there, Clarke, Clarke Dearborne, left his fingerprints   on that phone that made the call to Benny's at.... you all know Clarke....

He also knew he needed another car. Ally or not, this was definitely not walking weather. He was simply tired of being rained on; the last thing he needed was to get wet again.

The question was, whose car? Well, that question would have to wait. He headed toward the bar on the main level to get a shot of liquor and a nondescript phone. With

347

everyone in the hotel pinned in by the weather, it was crowded for this time of day. Standing, as Clarke nursed the finger of scotch, his thoughts slid off Benny and back onto whether he should leave the island or not. And if he left, with whom?

He knew Morgan would go. What about Dee? Was there a way to get both of them to go? As unrealistic and as poorly teased out as this fantasy was, his mind kept fiddling with it. The problem in a nutshell wasn't that he really expected that to happen, but rather, that he seemed incapable of choosing between them.

Back to Benny. He downed the sliver at the bottom.

The other people at the bar were chattering about normal things. The storm, work, sports. He placed the empty glass back on the bar.

He was looking forward to returning to normal concerns after he tidied this up. He wasn't cut out for this criminal stuff. He'd spent a good part of his life protecting others—now look at him. Besides, nothing had been easy since the Divel escaped this morning. Well, except for Morgan.

CHAPTER 35

BENNY BADMAN

Benny Jimenez was an older man in a younger man's game. Where Clarke was a light-skinned Bermudian, Benny was dark. Conservative with his money, he'd socked it away, never quite sure when he'd get around to retiring. Even if the Divel had not emerged from the vault this weekend, Benny knew he was close to calling it quits. The Divel had accelerated matters, like a crescendo at the end of a symphony. There was nothing wrong with a little acceleration. The shifting landscape had encouraged Benny to consider what it would be like not to be doing deals every day. To go without the thrill of gaining the upper hand. It worried him a little that he might be bored without any action—without any fish.

Like today, with all this waiting. If the pawn business had taught him one thing, waiting was an invaluable part of any business deal. Even so, today had crawled by like one of those soccer games on the tube that always put him to sleep with the score tied zero-zero.

This was the biggest deal since Benny had engineered the disappearance of the Cross. He'd been a young man then. One big score in the beginning. One at the end. Bookend deals. Good stuff for a movie, he knew, but that would only happen if he got caught. And that wasn't happening.

The incessant buzzing of those dusty overhead lights was bugging him but good. Long delays like this usually meant trouble. Something was wrong at the hotel. Benny could feel it. His radar had always been good for such things. Clarke was to have delivered it around lunchtime, and here it was supper. The storm had made things difficult. But still.

He wasn't even hungry; he couldn't remember the last time that had happened.

Benny knew the more expensive something was, the more paranoia visited. He'd never forgotten that old Bogart movie, *The Treasure of Sierra Madre*. Instead of dust and the dessert and mules and Mexican bandits without any stinkin' badges, he had water and wind and lightning and thunder and darkness. Benny looked out at the storm through his wet front window that he alarmed and locked nightly by stretching that accordion metal frame across it. Like a caged animal, he began to pace the front of the shop over the dried white/black chessboard-patterned tiles. His gaze flitted off all the cheap junk he had for resale. Cheap, that is, compared to the Divel.

He plowed through the beaded curtain separating his small rectangular shop from his even smaller square office. The shop was made smaller by the overflowing knickknacks. But his office was small, period. The desk, two chairs, and two pull-string lamps filled it to the brim. The only thing smaller was the bathroom off of it—a sink and commode. There wasn't even room for a toilet paper dispenser on the wall. His tiny small-smaller-smallest three-roomed shoppe had served him well. He couldn't complain. When he'd first broken into the business, an old-timer had explained how the biggest deals tended to take place in the smallest spots. Benny had proven him correct, though he still hadn't a clue why that was so.

He'd spent his entire life in this jammed space, while living above it with Constance for thirty-six years. This arrangement made it easy to squirrel away money, though they had lived like they hadn't any. The plane he co-owned was in his brother's name. And he had an old boat like everyone else. But no one knew how much money he had in his off-shore accounts. Not even Constance.

This pitiful inner sanctum had a pitiful wooden chair wedged in behind his scarred desk. Squeezing into that seat that had always been cramped and hard—first due to space, then weight, and now age.

Clarke would come to him. Benny understood the different types of waiting. This was closing-the-deal waiting. He understood the art of negotiation. He understood the ways transactions began and ended. That they began long before you spoke. That you could kill a deal if you appeared anxious. He couldn't call Clarke, though every fiber of his wanting-to-retire being was compelling him to pick up that black phone. He knew it was still working in this storm because he'd picked it up several times to check for a dial tone.

Sometimes people with a fortune-in-hand believed their leverage had improved. He hadn't expected Clarke would get that way, but Benny had seen it happen.

In fact, he'd renegotiated things for himself many a time when conditions changed in his favor. And he'd be damned if Clarke was going to turn the tables on him like this. Clarke might be testing him right now. And he was going to have none of it. He had pulled off the Cross heist. And because of that and the reputation that followed, Clarke had sought him out. His connections were priceless. And one paid for such things in business. That's how the world worked. If Clarke didn't understand that, he soon would.

Over the decades, he had taped all those newspaper articles to the wall. Some concerned with missing or found gems from around the island, or more likely, from under the sea. And with all the shipwrecks, there had been no shortage of opportunities to decorate.

He'd been personally involved with many of those valuables. Often owners preferred liquid cash to the object itself. Some he'd bought. Some he'd sold. And some, he'd been only the middle-man for. All of it almost a hobby, if it hadn't been a living. One section on the wall was dedicated to the Cross—some two score years now. Though the articles were faded, the legacy of that heist had lived on, thrived even, within a culture built around a glamorized history of pirating. He was proud of that score. It had made him a part of Bermuda's history forever.

With this pleasant boost from the Cross's memories, Benny's fantasies and plans settled back upon his retirement: island hopping in his boat. Carefree. With just the wind and the elements and the coasts of inviting islands greeting him. And Constance.

Yes, the time had come. But a deal was not a deal until it was closed. Done.

Benny sucked in his gut for a brief moment, until he couldn't hold his breath any longer.

CHAPTER 36

YES, BENNY

Sidetracked by thoughts of Morgan and Dee, Clarke returned to the less pleasant but pressing matter of going another round with George—he was a biker and swimmer, not a boxer. He decided that if he managed to find a way to Benny's, that it would be simpler and safer to come back to the hotel to spend the night. There was no need to risk another trip all the way home. Plus, something might need attending to in the morning before he left the island. With everything going on, he couldn't remember if Dee was expecting him or not. But neither one of them could make it safely to the other's home.

Then his mind flicked back to Benny. The Benny whose dark eyes noticed everything. Even in dim light. Especially in dim light. Dark, beady eyes that would be on him shortly, if he was lucky to get there.

Clarke headed into the backroom behind the bar for its pink wall phone. Poking the buttons, waiting for the call to connect, he said quietly, "It's me."

"Everything okay over there? I hear people in the background."

"Sort of."

"Sort of?" Benny's grumble of dissatisfaction was clear.

"I'll be over as soon as I borrow a car. Mine's out of commission. It's floating down Front Street."

"That's all?"

"That's all, and that's enough."

"Who's with you?"

"No one. I'm near the bar area. See you soon."

Clarke hung up, blew a breath, and slumped against the wall. One down. He called Dee.

"Okay, luv." Dee understood, but wondered if that was all of it. He sounded distracted, the way he sounded when he'd been out Grotto way to see Morgan. Dee wanted to ask whether it was Benny he was really going fishing with. But she knew how jealous that would sound. She tried to disconnect her feelings from the more pleasant situation of hearing Clarke's voice. Trying to live in the moment and be practical—the way she ran her classroom. Some of that came through in her whitewashed, "You all right?"

"Exhausted from the day, that's all. Nothing's gone right and the mess is continuing through tomorrow morning. Oh, and remember, I'll be off the island for a few days if the airport clears."

"Yes, I remember. You've earned it. Goodnight, luv, see you when you get back." She figured as conscientious as Clarke was, that a high-profile weekend like this would be particularly taxing on him. That a few days away would do him wonders.

After the disconnect, Dee remained seated in her lonely chair with frightened Tiger shaking in her lap. Her little puff of white dog had pretty much planted herself there since the storm began raging outside. When Dee decided that Morgan had too much of a hold on him, she stood abruptly, dislodging Tiger, and headed to the kitchen to add something stronger to her next cuppa. With Tiger scampering around her heels, Dee poured a bit of coffee, a bit of whiskey and stirred in some brown sugar. Even with all those weddings taking place at his hotel every year, she remained without a ring.

Dee listened to the wet storm slap against her solid limestone house and its closed shutters, while another storm raged within. She made her way back and seated herself in her worn blue armchair with its tessellating leaf pattern. Tiger settled right back in her tight little spot. Continuously reaching for the comfort of her tepid but now bolstered coffee, she considered how people who hadn't had enough of something often stockpiled it later in life. Whether it be coffee, or money, or love, or possessions. She sipped her Irish coffee and stroked Tiger, drawing her much needed comfort from them both.

Clarke nodded toward Ami manning the front desk—though "manning" definitely didn't fit her statuesque form. All by itself, that little nod kicked-off their running joke that had a way of beginning whenever the front area became slow. Sidling up to the opposite side of her counter, he said, "Tough day, huh?"

"Never been so busy in my life," she played along with. Ami always looked sharp in her conservative navy blue Princess uniform.

"Well, since you're so busy, I need to see if I can wiggle a favor out of you."

"Anything. But the catch is, I might not have time to do it even if I want to, seeing as I'm so busy. You're going to have to be patient and wait your turn in that line there." She pointed toward the empty space next to him.

"Okay." After stepping into her line, he began his best whistle-waiting.

After a brief delay that gave the imaginary line time to dwindle, he said, "I need your car. I never thought I'd say this..." as his eyes betrayed just how wrong he'd been to join the rest of the staff in badmouthing her clunker. "I need Feisty."

Ami's smile grew and she held it for effect.

Clarke believed this was what it must look and feel like when the moon slid out from behind the clouds on a romantic night.

Ami said, "Thank you," to the imaginary customer in front of him. Then to Clarke, she milked this historic moment by spacing out, "Take her. She's yours. She's on hurricane special this weekend."

"I need her for a short trip. I wouldn't ask, except mine's afloat down Front Street."

She headed into the room behind the front desk. From back there she said loud enough for him to hear, "Who talks like that?" Then she followed up with, "It doesn't matter. You can speak Chinese for all I care. You want Feisty. You got Feisty."

She retrieved Feisty's keys which were distinct because of the tiny plastic koala bear. Everyone believed, knew, that her old Ford Fiesta was as quirky as she was—in the way that lots of people believed that cars and people or pets and people tend to take on similar personalities. Nice quirky. But all the same, after 203K miles, it had earned the right. The staff had suffered through its never-ending tales of woe. Given her salary, she'd been unable to keep up with every weird noise. The windows and accelerator had purportedly developed minds of their own. One of the staff had even used the word "possessed" after Feisty had hogged another recent lunch conversation with her creative symptoms. Ami just looked upon sweet Feisty as a family member who had developed into a hypochondriac. And everyone knew you didn't get rid of family members just because of a few aches and pains.

As she handed over her brown bear, she got right to the point. "If you wreck Feisty, you're replacing her with a car with less miles. Like the insurance commercial. Word-to-the-wise, if you try to do to her what you did to your Peugeot, she might survive. I've heard she knows how to float."

He laughed at that, thinking of the James Bond car. "Floats or not, every car has less miles than Feisty."

"Exactly. Then you'll have no problem finding her replacement." She looked at the wall in the direction of Feisty, who was sitting in the small front parking area. "Feisty, you didn't hear that, my love."

"That's a deal." He'd be able to afford it. Not the floating part, the buying part.

With Feisty's fate literally sold down the river, Clarke turned toward the front door just as another fate was delivered by the storm: Mr. and Mrs. Waters.

Stomping the water off themselves, they were surrounded by a bunch of small sacks. Clarke tried to hide the inconvenience from overtaking his face, but wasn't successful at first. The clouds had returned to block his moon.

One problem after another kept rotating front and center, and the day wasn't finished yet.

With Thompson back in the control room and Clara investigating a complaint, Clarke's sinking body knew a fraction of a second before his mind, that he was right back in the middle of the vault business again.

Clarke greeted them with an improving, "Congratulations, to the newest couple on the island."

Greg said a terse, "Thanks."

Sandy finished shaking out the water from her pink slicker, then looked his way. "Thank you. I'm glad to be back inside."

Clarke said, "At least you can look forward to enjoying your evening in peace." Unlike him. He accepted the bags containing the charms from the couple. Then turning his head and lifting his arm in the direction of the front counter, he raised his voice so Ami could overhear. "If you go wait in that short line right in front of Ami, she'll be able to direct you toward your high-and-dry reception."

Ami smiled his way, clearly in a good mood with Feisty being needed.

Now past the initial frustration, Clarke sensed this wasn't all bad. He was already later than late for Benny, so what difference could ten minutes make?

He soon realized it did make a difference. He was going to be walking the real Divel, the one presently snug in his coat, right back into the vault. Could this get any stranger? It had taken him an entire year and one day—a very long day—to get it out of there.

After summoning Thompson, after Tuttleberry and the keys again, Clarke's skin began to crawl as soon as he walked the real thing back into the vault. Plus, surrounded by the echoing quiet, a new humming sound began ringing his ears. Clarke decided he would say to a jury of his peers—if it became necessary in regards to his insanity defense:

That it could only be described as a silent humming sound.

That seemed right.

They began the intricate lockbox and trial-and-error routine again. Johnson finally opened the Divel's metal lockbox. When he lifted the lid, they could see the replica sitting in the form-fitting red satin indent, looking like the real thing. The perfect crime.

Thompson's huge hands placed the charms in a north, south, east, and west configuration around the necklace, like how the old ones had been placed. Once done, he slid the box back into place. Now everything was tucked in nightie night for a very long time.

As they exited into the hallway, Clarke chuckled some tension away. What a waste of time it had been for the newlyweds to track down all those charms. They were guarding a fake! Replica charms would have worked out just fine, whatever replica charms were. As he led Thompson from the vault, Clarke extended all this with as clear a thought as he'd had all day. With replica charms, he would have been able to take the real ones with him. Just in case, as if he was beginning to believe they might do some actual good. This realization, this insurance, this backup plan, unnerved him for the briefest moment, before he regained the smoothness of his walk.

He swept his hands down his jacket lapels, confirming that the damn thing was still in his inner pocket. That it hadn't managed to get away again. He decided, this flicking away of imaginary dust particles was another action perfectly suited to an insanity defense, as would have been tripping into the wall for no apparent reason.

Clarke looked up at the lumbering Thompson. "You realize, Thompson, you and I will never see the real Divel come out of there again." This play on words was absolutely true, not because they'd be too old, which could end up being true, but because the real Divel would already be gone.

Classic: Clarke had confessed to the perfect crime, after having returned to the scene of the crime, though technically, he hadn't left it yet with the whole island involved at this point.

Thompson answered, "You're probably right, though I have high hopes to see it again." Then he winked.

Looking up, Clarke said, "Keep your chin up, Thompson. One never knows."

CHAPTER 37

FEISTY

Clarke had lost track of how many times he'd been through this entrance today. He slapped the counter as he passed by Ami, "We're off. Wish us luck." If only half of the stories about Feisty held water, he'd need some luck. Too bad about those charms, he realized. He'd take anything that might help him at this point.

"Don't forget to pump the gas if Feisty has trouble breathing. I'd hate to hear my little darling had a coughing spell out in that bad storm."

"Great," he said over his shoulder.

The antique white car, or what should have been classified as an antique as opposed to a collector's edition, reminded Clarke that beggars couldn't be choosers. The entire island was filled with small, quirky cars. His car was quirky. Or had been. Now it was a boat. Up until today, he'd been one of the few islanders who'd never owned a boat.

It was raining again, though the wind had died down. Spotting the small white box out there in the bleak landscape, he had a sudden urge, a desire really, for Youngblood's small boat. Feisty might be a good swimmer, but she didn't come with paddles.

When he tried the door, Feisty was unlocked. He couldn't remember whether the locks no longer worked, or whether Ami might be leaving things to chance in the hopes that someone might borrow her. Closing the light, tinny door, the interior smelled musty, and the windows were fogged up. He noticed the gear shift. He hadn't driven a stick in years. He pressed the brake pedal with one foot and the clutch in with the other, then moved the stick through what he believed were four forward speeds and one reverse. After practicing, he wiggled the slick, black knob to confirm she was back in neutral. Ready, willing and able, he cranked her up. Defrosters on. The A/C could have helped to defog the windows, but it didn't engage when he finally found the tiny, dimly-lit button.

While waiting for the windows to clear, he listened to the rain pitter patter on the thin roof. In the grey light, he had for company an off-white religious figure on the dash and a cross hanging off the rearview mirror. When he discovered how the wipers worked, they streaked across the windshield in slow motion. Turning his attention back inside, he clicked closed the frayed seatbelt. With the windows still cloudy, he searched for and found a rag between the seats, cleared the front and side windows, and noticed that at least the rear defroster was working. It figured with the way his day had gone, that he'd be able to see better backward than forward. Nothing was going to be easy today. *Except for Morgan,* he reminded himself with a smirk.

Grinding the gears into reverse with that horrible metal-on-metal screech, the car lurched backward. He aimed her toward the high-ground street, put her in first, listened to the tiny engine whine up the incline, and lurched to a stop when Feisty ran out of breath. Recalling an old technique, he pulled up the emergency brake to hold Feisty at the edge of the running stream. At least it wasn't a river any longer. As he restarted her, he had to decide which way to go. Even though the rain had slackened, he wanted to go left, away from his beached car. But when he looked that way, there was something large lying across the middle of the street. He turned right.

Feisty's tires slipped onto the street, making beggar Clarke hope the tires had some tread. Leaning forward in the vinyl bucket seat to see better, as Feisty picked up speed, the sound of water became was very pronounced inside the thin wheel-wells. The car was so light, it was immediately obvious why Feisty would be an accomplished floater.

Regardless, Clarke's luck seemed to be changing. He was underway, the rain was feeling sorry for these pitiful wipers, and the taller buildings were sheltering him from the worst of the wind. Nearing Front Street with near-sighted Feisty, he slowed as he approached the intersection where his Peugeot was supposed to be. In this gloom he couldn't see it. It must have been pulled downstream along with everything else.

He tried Feisty's high-beams, and there was a reflection from an object off to the right. He hoped it was his car. He swiped the window with the tiny rag again. Yes, up on the right, close to the Harbour, his Peugeot was marooned.

Abruptly, the wind pushed Feisty from that side, leaning him left, and forcing him to compensate to keep himself from being blown from the left lane.

Benny, here I come, he said to himself. Warding off any bad karma, not to mention those gusts.

Lightning flashed far to the front.

Lightning flashed much closer in front.

Lightning flashed closer still through his fogged-up passenger-side window. *That was clos—*

With an earsplitting "crunch," Feisty was struck by bright lightning on her lee side. Clarke was pitched toward the bright light. When he rebounded, his right shoulder and head struck Feisty's hard inner frame.

It was fortunate for him the English had founded Bermuda—that he was sitting on the right side of the car after what had just happened to the left side of Feisty.

Feisty was still moving. Sliding right. Now his luck was continuing because the English drive on the left side of the road, giving him that extra lane before the Harbour.

Feisty slid across that extra lane. The sound of rain returned, but not the sound of Feisty's little motor.

He looked toward the crumbled left side of poor Feisty. Lightning hadn't done this!? There was a large bright-eyed animal out there. Probably a sea monster.

Then it came to him. *A bus. What in the hell is a bus doing out in this?* Someone else was crazy Two insanity pleas now.

Pressing the brake pedal did nothing. Feisty's four little tires continued to slide right.

The bus's brakes must have failed coming down the hill.

With two short bumps, Feisty was pushed atop the soaked patch of grass fronting the water. The strange part was—as he watched all this—the sliding part was happening in slow motion.

Out the front, his Peugeot slid across his field of vision. To the left. That wasn't good.

Suddenly, Feisty's achy joints jerked to a stop. *Thank Christ.* Still on solid ground.

Good.

Then the right side of the car rocked away from him.

Thinking quickly, he leaned toward the center.

Then with more creaking, Feisty came back to the left, level again.

Good.

Then it happened again.

He needed those gusts to keep blowing in. Another

foe switching sides.

Apparently, Feisty was sitting atop the wood-plank erosion wall like it was a balance beam. He sure hoped Ami's car continued to take after its gymnastic owner.

Clarke couldn't see anything out the sides. Then those two bright eyes went dark. With the passenger door mangled, he considered his door, but if he opened it, he guessed that would pitch him into the water below.

Feisty continued to teeter and creak, first in one direction, then back the other. He'd seen this in a kid's movie. Scenes like this were always shot in slow-mo. And slow-mo scenes rarely unfolded well for the characters because there was always a reason why the director chose to shoot such scenes in slow-mo.

The right side of his head and his right shoulder hurt.

Should he crawl out the window, in case Feisty was getting ready to go over?

Still leaning left, he grabbed the small window crank. It was stuck and slick. If he survived this, they'd never believe the latest Feisty story back at the Princess. Never. Scratch that, as he tried the crank with two hands. *They won't believe this whether I survive or not.*

The precarious position sharpened his thoughts to a point. Ami had gotten her wish. She was going to get her new old car out of this, come Hell or high water. Which might be the same for him in about three seconds. He undid his seatbelt. Just in case. Just in case he needed to get out quickly either above or below the water-line. With the crank beginning to make grudging progress, he remembered Ami saying something about the windows. The wind was gusting in through the crack. Now he wished he'd gone to the gym more or had a can of oil handy. He pulled for all he was worth.

The driver's window began to nudge open in fits.

Thank Christ. He hadn't included prayer in his perfect plan—an oversight.

The fog on the upper half of his window had now been replaced by wind and driving rain. More foes had become friends.

When the window was about three-quarters down, a man appeared to the front of the car. Clarke stopped yanking. They looked at one another.

Then the car leaned right, Clarke watching as the man tilted left. Feisty had begun her dismount.

As he dropped, Clarke had way too much time to consider how this couldn't be happening; how the water's chop appeared to be rising up to meet his open window. Feisty's right side smacked into the water's surface, reuniting Clarke's right side with Feisty's metal frame.

With her open window, Feisty resembled a large white mint being swallowed by a hungry Harbour. Clarke kept his left hand on the wheel while he transferred his right to the window frame. The water was cold as it began to gurgle in. Front heavy, the car listed forward and turned to the right as it sank, pointing Clarke away from the erosion wall.

When the front met the bottom with a soft jolt, the windshield popped loose, barely separating itself from the frame.

The Harbour was six meters deep here, so although it was over his head, it was not very deep for an accomplished swimmer—this by itself didn't bother him. But, being underwater in a car was being underwater in a car. Water continued to displace precious air. Then in more slo-mo, Feisty began to keel over toward her starboard side. The escaping side. Now he was bothered.

CHAPTER 38

SATURDAY NIGHT'S ALL RIGHT FOR FIGHTING, GET A LITTLE ACTION IN

Clarke grabbed the window frame with both hands, then maneuvered one knee and one foot onto the steering wheel. Filling his lungs with air, with the window sinking toward the grassy bottom, he launched himself from Feisty. The shock of the cold water washed over the protest coming from his right shoulder. Below him, Feisty settled on the bottom like she was lying down to take a needed rest. With no time to waste, up he went. When he broke the surface, the swells were continuously coming towards him before crashing into the balance beam wall. The lone man looking straight at him was getting drenched by the spray. The man from the windshield. Probably the bus driver.

Clarke maneuvered toward shore and grabbed onto the planking. Wearing a city slicker, the thick man bent down, offering his hand.

Clarke took hold, but when his shoulder spoke again, he slipped back into the water.

Something about falling back toward Feisty made him think of the Divel.

He patted his coat.

Gone!

No freaking way.

The next wave banged him into the wall.

This was a matter of principle, and competition, and

curses, never mind retirement and Benny.

Benny.

Then he heard over the storm, "You okay down there?" He wouldn't be able to face Benny without it.

Now, a matter of life and death, in addition to surviving a crash and escaping from a car on the Harbour floor.

Clarke gritted his teeth, filled his lungs with the confidence of being a competitive swimmer who used to be able to hold his breath beyond half a minute, and slipped under the surface. Heading toward the little-white-car-that-couldn't or shouldn't-have, his clothes felt heavy and kept snagging his stroke. With his right shoulder hurting, he compensated by pulling more with his left arm.

Even with the storm, even with the dimness, the water was surprisingly clear. His best bet was that the necklace was still in the car. It could have been jerked loose when the bus slammed into him, or possibly when he escaped through the window. It could be anywhere in-between, of course, and as he went deeper, he recalled that the damned thing was reportedly invisible in water.

The slumbering car looked more like a sleeping pet than an unwitting accomplice to the most messed up perfect crime there ever was. His window escape route sat flush on the grassy bottom, while topside, the mangled metal displayed the memory of Feisty's mishap with the bus. It hadn't been a fair fight. In fact, nothing seemed fair about the fight today.

There was a sparkle in the grass to Feisty's right.

He swam toward it, sifted the bottom with his fingers, but found nothing but sand. The Divel's invisibility, he decided, was almost like a defense when it was back in its natural habitat. He swam toward the front where the windshield had been jarred loose. If he couldn't get in, he'd have to come back with diving equipment. That was, if he could still swim after Benny got through with him. His lungs began their soft burning. Tugging on the loose windshield, he wedged it past vertical where gravity took over and hinged it toward the bottom. His lungs were reminding him he couldn't do this forever. He needed to find air.

Looking through the opening vacated by the windshield, he noticed a chain. He snatched at it, missed it, and grabbed for it again.

Without having the time to look, he headed up toward the rear of the car, found a small pocket of air, and gulped some in. Breathing with his nose and mouth jammed into this tiny space, he pulled the chain up. "Damn," he said, as he blew bubbles into the water. It was the cross from the mirror.

Resting a moment, shivering, filling his lungs with breaths, he climbed over the seat to reach the dash. He looked at the grassy bottom through the open window. Nothing. He looked in the small spaces near the seats. Ran both hands over the top of the dash. When he touched the statue, there was a chain hooked around its neck. The chain was taut, as if the current was pulling it out to sea.

With only so much air in his lungs, and afraid the roof-air in the car was shrinking, he ripped the statue and chain off the dash, pulled himself through the windshield-gap, and headed for the surface.

His right shoulder was still giving him trouble. With no time to check for the necklace, he felt the resistance of all his clothes, and what he believed was enough resistance on the end of that chain to be the Divel. When he broke through to the surface, there was lightning and rain. Over the wind, he heard on his right, something that sounded like a long, "You okay?"

Clarke looked toward shore. There were three men now, all wearing the same dark green city-ordinance rain slicker.

Clarke answered, "I think so," but this time, under the water, his cold fingers crawled along that chain. Yes! He had it.

Turning his back to shore, swimming backward, Clarke maneuvered the Divel into his jacket. It made his hand feel warmer. He secured himself to the planking with his left hand and then two arms hoisted him to safety. If being pulled by a sore shoulder into hurricane winds and closer to lightning qualified as safety.

"You okay?"

"I'm a little banged up." Even with Clarke seated on the grass, the wind was doing its best to blow him away like a tumbleweed.

"I'm Jimmy C., the bus driver. I lost my brakes coming down that hill."

Clarke nodded.

"Let's get out of this," one of the other men suggested.

When Clarke didn't get up right away, someone said, "Here, we'll give you a hand, mate." Two of them hoisted Clarke to his feet.

With his body feeling achy and unsteady in the wind, Clarke clutched his coat closed to keep the cold wind and rain out and the slippery Divel in. Leaning forward, leaving the balance beam portion of this competition behind him, he felt goose bumps hatch on his arms and a prickly feeling on the back of his neck. Was he getting ready to be struck by lightning? He followed the men toward the bus. Why was he frightened all of a sudden? Was there something to this curse business?

Like ducks following one another, they climbed into the bus.

In the light, Jimmy C. pointed toward Clark's temple. "Your head is bleeding."

Clarke raised his left hand to his head and touched the spot where he'd met Feisty up close and personal. "Just a scratch," he said, though it was sore.

Once seated, Jimmy C. commiserated. "That wasn't a fair fight between your little car and my bus," as he looked toward his two passengers before looking back at Clarke. "I'm terribly sorry about all this, Mack."

Clarke just nodded. Sitting there, sore, he felt triumphant in a beaten-up sort of way, and had the urge to confess that Feisty wasn't even his car, which almost made him laugh. He suspected if he laughed, that it would hurt, but, that it would also support his insanity defense.

He hurt in multiple places. At least the small checkered handkerchief offered by one of the passengers helped with the bleeding. With the rain slacking off and lightning far to the east, everyone agreed it was time to get out of here and return to the bus terminal.

And with that, the four men set off trudging up the hill away from the Harbour.

Clarke knew that as the crow flew in fair weather, he was not that far from Benny's. But this wasn't fair weather, and there weren't any crows flying about. They had more sense than he did.

As Clarke leaned into the hill, clutching his coat closed again, a feeling descended upon him, around him, maybe through him that was as resolute as these dismal elements. Worn down or worn out, he couldn't take any more of this. His cup had runneth over, along with everyone else's on this island.

And the strangest part was, that at this point, he was home-free— he had the Divel and he was close to Benny's —but he was a wreck.

And then it came to him: *It has me.*

Something about being in competition with the Divel, or opposed by the Divel? Yes, opposed by its curse, a curse he had scoffed at until this balance beam incident.

Clarke slowed his walk.

He was going to walk the damned thing home.

It's time to get rid of you came to him from a different place, a deeper, honest place.

The thought gave him the "jitters" in his stomach. The same thing that used to happen when the older kids frightened him on Halloween. That seemed fitting, in a memory-flashback kind of way.

It was time to finish this. It was better to be safe than sorry, unless it was too late to be safe. His aching arm reminded him what was no longer part of the correct answer. Swimming. No more swimming. No more cars. What could happen to him then? There wasn't any lightning close. He was wet. Pneumonia was likely the worst outcome now, but that would take a while. The three men were together and ahead of Clarke by two meters. Approaching the intersection of Queen and Church, Clarke cleared his throat. "Jimmy."

After the men stopped and turned, they huddled against the closest wall.

Clarke said, "I'm going to leave you guys here. I'm close to a friend's place," as he indicated to the right with his head up Church.

"You sure? In this?"

"Yep. I'll be fine," he heard himself predict. His coat was still clutched closed by his immobile right arm. "Our insurance stuff can wait till Monday, no problem."

"Okay. Fine by me." The bus driver dug out his card with those thick fingers and handed it to Clarke.

Clarke aimed himself east, into more wind and rain. Uphill too.

Now all alone in the deserted capital, fear stabbed him. He checked his inner pocket with his good arm. Still there.

Still time to retire, if he had enough energy left to retire. This didn't make any sense, because he was doing all this so he could retire. He hunched his shoulders, bowed his head forward, and forged on. He passed a window full of hats. There was humor in that because his hat had gone missing.

Benny was about a mile from here. With his arm hurt, exhausted, if someone robbed him, he didn't see how he'd be able to put up much of a fight; he wasn't sure he cared anymore.

Even though the streets were deserted, given the storm, given the day, given the neighborhood, he felt vulnerable. It began to rain harder. The horrible thought struck him that he really did need to get rid of the charmless thing if he hoped to make it out of this alive. He considered that he might be exaggerating, but didn't consider this train of thought for long because he lacked the energy for it.

Did that make sense this close to Benny's?

Yes. But he didn't know why.

Maybe reading all that true-crime stuff was to blame. All those bad ideas filling those pages. Real ideas. Facts. Facts could be stranger than fiction.

All the while, George kept reminding Clarke it didn't care about any of these fancy ideas. Rain was rain and wind was wind. At least Clarke could ignore that electricity that was far off.

Near the airport.

Lightning was streaking the sky there.

The convergence of all that produced, *It's unsafe*.

If I get on that plane with Benny, I'm going down.

He'd never been a superstitious man, but he knew it was true. Knew it. It certainly felt true. As true as Ami saying Feisty could swim and then Feisty went swimming. She had said that, right, or was he imagining that too?

He swiped water from his face with his left hand. He tried to keep his head down. Hadn't the newlyweds mentioned something about almost being killed today?

His clothes weighed a ton. The wind was howling through the downtown buildings. Lightning was coming closer. Or was he walking toward it? The distant thunder no longer sounded so distant. He would have picked up his pace if his legs had any strength left in them. What had he done? Maybe he needed to put the damned thing back. The lightning out there flashed in a "Y." Yes. A sign from George; he was a hurricane-talker now.

His legs felt like logs. They stopped moving, like logs.

They hadn't required much convincing.

He was standing in the middle of a deserted city, in the middle of a hurricane. *Yes, put it back.* That's what he needed to do.

But then he'd get caught.

He'd have to confess. He looked down at his shoes. What a ridiculous sight. He'd walked and swam in soaked shoes all day. Yes. Confess to Tuttleberry. He'd have to come up with some cock-and-bull story.

No, it wouldn't work. Would it? Either way, Tuttleberry would be afraid of the scandal and the curse and probably let him resign.

When Clarke regained his senses, he was standing at the end of a block. He was unsure which way to go.

Forward would take him to Benny's.

Backward, to Tuttleberry.

He teetered on the curb. Another balance episode.

Could he survive coming clean? Would he still be able to retire? Would either Dee or Morgan want him then?

Perched on this curb, there were real problems with both his present and his future. The wind switched directions, blowing him back, west, toward the Princess. Was this a sign? Then the wind caught him sideways from the cross-street. Losing his balance, he fell to his knees in the gutter.

A spike of pain shot through his right shoulder.

Sitting there, exhausted, in the gutter, it came to him what was wrong with all of this. *Benny.*

He dragged himself up and out from the streaming water running downhill.

Benny would kill him, if George didn't get him first.

The lightning was marching closer.

He couldn't go back. He was trapped by his own plan.

He had to give it to Benny. He stood and brushed his hands off in the middle of a deserted city, in the gutter, completely alone with echoes and thieves and ghosts, while a wet curse had infiltrated his shivering bones. Could he just hand it to Benny to get out of the whole thing? He knew how Benny's mind worked. Benny would suspect a set-up; might even kill him for that. Putting Clarke back inside Feisty as a message to everyone else. With the windshield out, that future was easily doable.

Clarke had to change the deal somehow. Not go to the Caymans. Not get his fifty percent. Maybe nothing? Benny hated last minute changes.

Clarke picked up one lead-foot and placed it in front of the other being overrun by water running downhill. He checked for the Divel. It hadn't made a run for it in the rushing gutter. Too bad, almost. That would have made things simpler.

This close to the end, Benny would never understand

why Clarke wanted out. Clarke couldn't say he fully understood it either. But he didn't care. He'd take whatever he could get just to get out; just a fraction would get his savings back, anyway. Greedy people paid the price all the time in the true-crime books.

For the first time in blocks, Clarke felt the pavement beneath his feet. Felt how each step was taking him closer to this new ending to his imperfect plan. Would he need to keep working? If he could keep working. First things first. Survival trumped everything. If he could survive the Divel, then he'd work on surviving Benny and Tuttleberry.

Clarke reached Benny's cross-street, where he leaned north into the wind that would have blown the legs out from under him if he wasn't so waterlogged. Up another hill. Now that he wanted it gone, the Divel seemed stuck to him like glue.

He had developed a weird respect for the thing. It's determination, something. He wasn't sure what to call it. It seemed to know where it belonged. Almost like an animal and its territory. The very opposite of him at the moment.

He spied the dim light escaping from Benny's front window. The metal accordion wasn't locked, so Benny was still there. The brick and wood three-story building seemed rundown and sad in the storm. Like him.

He couldn't believe he was getting ready to throw away five million dollars—if he could throw. He said, "Five-million-dollars," to make it more real. To snap himself out of this mood. To test his resolve, one way or the other. What force on this Earth was compelling him to do such a crazy thing? He didn't know. He was too exhausted to think straight. His brain seemed scrambled. No, waterlogged. And his head hurt. *Maybe this force isn't of this Earth.* He shook that strange thought away, clearing his head.

Approaching Benny's front door, he rehearsed, "Any retirement is better than no retirement," so George could witness the statement— as if George were alive, like the Divel.

He reached for the antique glass knob. With his fingers all around it, he hesitated, as if it would give him a shock, or something else unpleasant would happen. This was it. It was no easy thing to let go of so much money, cursed or not. Gritting his teeth, he said a little prayer, hoping he'd receive some type of answer. No answer, and time to get inside. His cold hand twisted that wet knob.

Overhead, that little bell announced his arrival, Benny's state-of-the-art security system.

When he shuffled in, the front room's overhead lights blinded him. Now even his eyes hurt.

CHAPTER 39

BENNY LATE THAN NEVER

Benny came out from his backroom carrying a water glass. "You look like hell. Like that creature from the Black Lagoon. Though I don't see my dream girl, Adrienne Barbeau, with you."

"Well, I feel like hell," Clarke growled. His shoulder and head were throbbing, and he was cold. At least he hadn't had to literally swim all the way here with a bad shoulder. Close enough, though.

"You brought the whole storm in with you."

"Most of the Harbour, actually." He was willing to have that confirmed by laboratory tests.

"You got it, right?"

"After what I've been through, you bet." As Clarke spoke, a pool of water had formed around him on Benny's scuffed black and white checkerboard linoleum floor.

Being careful not to slip, Benny made his way past Clarke, locked the door, extended and locked the metal mesh behind the window, turned out the bright lights, and led Clarke to the safety of the smallest backroom this side of the Princess. Fetching some old towels from his teeny bathroom, he handed Clarke one and tossed the others on the wet floor.

Even in Clarke's altered state, Benny's patience seemed impressive. Only after this housekeeping was completed, did he ask for and accept the necklace from Clarke.

Benny stuck a magnifying glass in his right eye.

"I could have brought you the fake any time," Clarke said in a subdued voice. Mopping his face dry, wet clothes and all, Clarke squished himself down atop the wooden chair that felt hard. With Benny still taking his time, it was only at this moment that the amateur second-guessed that he might have chosen the wrong one.

While still examining the diamonds through his looking-glass, Benny said, "This amount of money, you can't be too careful. Nothin' personal…It has a way of changin' a man."

"It's still me, Benny." Clarke admitted, while he continued to dab himself dry. "Though I'm afraid you're right. It has changed me."

Benny removed the looking-glass and wedged himself behind his desk. "You look like you've seen a ghost."

Clarke grunted. Had he done that too? He'd managed everything else out there. He'd even sat in a gutter for the first time his life. Three times, actually.

Given the presence of the Divel, Benny lightened the mood with, "You really do look like that creature-person from the Black Lagoon."

"Changed, yes. Fins, no." Terse was good. Terse required less energy.

"Old age can make men greedy to catch-up on money, women, drugs. You name it. You catchin' up on anythin', Clarke?"

"You know it's my retirement. But even so, it feels like something's been catching up on me all day." He eyed the Divel like an opponent. A possessed, charmless opponent.

With the disgusted look that Benny spied on Clarke's face, he asked, "You drivin' at somethin'?"

The last thing Clarke wanted to get into was the invisible curse that he was now convinced existed. And if he mentioned that curse word, he'd end up with even more problems given Benny's superstitious nature. Though, how more problems could fit into the day was incomprehensible. Lots of things seemed incomprehensible at the moment.

Even though its supposed curse was legendary, Benny might or might not have bothered researching its history. If he did know about it, he hadn't said anything yet. Possibly, Benny wasn't saying anything for the same reason—that he didn't want to spook Clarke, who could be superstitious. Well, that appeared to be true now, so Benny's silence had been smart. Right on the mark. The pro.

Clarke squinted at his opponent, still unconvinced he could give up on so much money. It didn't sound or feel like him at all. Despite this doubt, his desire to survive was prompting him to exorcise the Divel from his person.

Clarke bit down on his lip, stalling, and then said before he chickened out, "Here's the thing, Benny. I want out. Buy me out. That's all. I'm not cut out for this stuff." He raised the towel and swiped off his dry head and face, using it for needed cover from the consequences of these heart-felt, honest words in the midst of his first and last crime.

Benny's mouth dropped open, while his eyes narrowed down to dark beads. "Is this like reverse psychology stuff you learned in business school? Too much of a good thing is usually bad in my world."

Clarke wasn't sure what to say. It didn't make much sense to him either after he heard how those words sounded.

Benny said, "You know what you're sayin'?" appearing to maintain his composure over this last-minute change.

"Yeah. I'm throwing away a lot of money, is what I'm

saying."

"In this line of work that usually means guilt or the cops. Are the cops onto you? Because then we're both goin' down."

"No. No. Nothing like that. I wouldn't do that to you, Benny." Clarke pictured himself behind bars. "But I was struck by a bus. I can't take anymore. Lightning, thunder, two car accidents, and I almost drowned—" For a moment, he couldn't catch his breath, like he was back in the Harbour inside Feisty. "And, and gutters." Forgetting one accident, technically. Frankly, he considered himself lucky he still knew who he was—The Harbour Creature— the pro had been right again.

"I don't understand about the gutters but I do understand five mil. That much money will buy a lot of things. You're entitled to it. I don't welsh." Benny threw his hands atop his desk, emphasizing the point.

"I know. I know, Benny." Clarke's hands twisted the towel tightly. "I know it sounds crazy, really crazy, but I'd be no good to you in the Caymans." Clarke tried to read Benny's reaction. "Just buy me out." Under the towel, his hands began to shake, almost as if they were suffering withdrawal from the money they'd never touch. Clarke was listening to a complete stranger give his retirement away.

"Clarke, you understand this is like a backward negotiation." Benny began to rotate the prize with his thick, hairy fingers.

Only now did Clarke notice the half-empty bottle on the cluttered desk. "And if I was catching up on anything, I'd be taking the option of sharing the risk all the way down the line. Splitting everything fifty/fifty. But I found out today I'm not cut out for this."

Clarke wanted his old life back—to be able to collect

his normal $200 when he passed GO—without going directly to Jail.

"Some people are. Some aren't," Benny responded neutrally, like he'd had this same conversation before. "You know I've done some crazy things in the name of money, so you might be better off in the long run."

It sounded like Benny was going to share some specifics, but instead he remained silent.

Clarke admitted, "I hope so. My father used to say 'bird in the hand' and all that. I've already lost it twice today." Realizing he'd shared more than he had intended to, that towel became twisted tight again.
He eyed the bottle of spirits.

"Twice?" Benny grabbed another smudged glass and poured them shots. "I've forgotten my manners." Clarke's shaking left hand grasped the glass.

"Looks like you could use this." Down the hatches they went.

"Yep. I needed that," Clarke agreed.

"Well the offer is still open. I've told you from the start I'd go either way. It's a win/win, either way. It happens to be safer to have two at the other end. Not that anything will happen in the Caymans, mind you, but you never know how things have changed down there."

Clarke added, "You know I've been wanting to slow down from the hotel. Wasn't it that American actor Clint Eastwood who said, 'A man must know his limitations?' Well, I sure found mine today."

"Amen to that."

"I've had my fill of risk to last me two lifetimes."

"That's a lot of lifetimes."

It still remained tempting as hell, but Clarke felt marked by the Divel. And if he ever told anyone that, they'd lock him up in a rubber room surrounded by those charms that he'd be asking for.

Temptation was still temptation when he was looking at more money than he'd ever seen in his life. His one hand released its death-grip on that towel. "There's been too much of everything today," he said.

"Except for this." Benny poured himself another shot.

"Except for this." Clarke tilted his drained glass forward. After he sucked this generous shot down, the warmth spread calm that was appreciated after his swim/hike Divel Biathlon.

Benny nestled up to a familiar part of the negotiating process. The portion where he sometimes improved things for himself. "Well then, the next step awaits. Originally, we spoke of fifty/fifty, if we shared the risk down the line. And eighty/twenty, if not. But now this unplanned change, and you know how I feel about those."

It's what Clarke had expected. Exhausted, he said, "Yes. Yes, I know. Really, Benny, whatever you think is fair. I know I'm forcing you to shoulder all the risk at the eleventh hour."

"Well, eighty/twenty was the starting point. Now we're down to eighty-five/fifteen or maybe even ninety/ten."

Clarke wanted the quickest route out from this lousy day, but he refrained from admitting he'd take nothing. That would just make Benny impossibly suspicious. "I know how you like to split differences, so let's do that."

Benny's eyes lit up, like he was coming out far better than he had ever imagined. "Round it to one million, three."

"Done." Clarke was definitely done. Clarke raised his empty glass and clinked it against Benny's.

One million and change would sure improve things. That there was a balance in the universe, or not, he had just essentially recovered what he'd lost in his retirement account.

Confidence filled Benny's voice when he said, "I'll pull up my Cayman account and transfer the money into the one we set up for you. I pay on delivery. No sense making you wait for your portion just because I have to wait for mine. It's the least I can do."

Yes, Benny was making out far better than he'd ever imagined. For his end, Clarke hoped the internet was still up, given the storm. The sooner this part was completed, the better. As Clarke watched Benny concentrate on his small laptop, the prospect of this much money prompted him to start talking to fill the silence.

"I've had enough of Tuttleberry, too," he admitted. "Maybe I'll stay on for a while, maybe I'll resign? Maybe he'll fire me as soon as the Waters leave the island? You know, because of how the Divel got away from me today. He's probably waiting to do that as soon as the family leaves." He shook his head over all this. "Maybe I'll even take a lady or two with me? One point three mill still gives a person plenty of options." After the monologue stopped, he asked in a tiring voice, "What are you gonna do with yours, Benny?"

Benny pulled his hands away from the keyboard. "You know. I still want a big enough boat to take me and the missus island hopping. This ought to do it." He looked up at Clarke. "I almost called the whole thing off when you went off schedule."

"I can imagine."

"Imagination is a terrible thing 'round large sums of money."

"I'll try and remember that. After this weekend, boring is looking better and better. Boring, with a great woman thrown in, I mean." Benny returned his attention to the small screen.

Clarke was going to enjoy replacing Feisty for Ami.

Benny looked up at Clarke and asked graciously, "You sure?" Clarke nodded.

Benny hit the button to complete the transfer, and then leaned back in his seat that couldn't lean back. With the deal done, he offered the screen to Clarke and explained how Clarke could access his account to check on the deposited amount.

Afterward, they both leaned back into their non-leaning chairs. Deal done. Done deal. Clarke took in a deep breath. *Wow, what a day. Day.*

It dawned on him he didn't have a car. How was he going to get back to the hotel? He thought about borrowing one of Benny's. But that would violate trying to keep their involvement to a minimum. Maybe Benny had a canoe. Clarke's relief had put him in a much better mood, not to mention that one million plus. Clarke surprised himself when he asked, "You got an old raincoat and fishing hat, Benny?"

"Yep."

With the private-eye trench coat and a floppy hat, Benny unlocked the front door so that Clarke could plow back into the vicissitudes of George for the umpteenth time. As he headed down the rain-gray street toward the water, he let his mind wander in relief. Was it possible that all the energy from George and the energy of the Divel were related? There was a lot of energy here. Who could figure out mysterious things like this? Maybe a scientist. Or more to the point, maybe a gypsy fortune teller. And maybe he'd begin reading adventure novels, now that his own life had turned into a True Crime novel.

At the intersection, Clarke made a right toward the Princess. It was starting to sink in that he was free from handling the Divel again. It felt good. Really good.

He put his head down into the wind. Eventually, there'd be no more stuffy Tuttleberry. No more Princess. No more cars in Hamilton Harbour. Yes, he'd buy Ami a car. Get the settlement from the bus company. They'd be picking up most of it. But he'd add to it and get something much newer. With electric windows and A/C that worked. And a new statue, too.

He hoped Tuttleberry didn't fire him over this mess. Would it look better if he quit? Walking along, he had plenty of time to think about all this nonsense. To over-think it, really. Then he said the heartfelt, "Any retirement is a good retirement," to all the deserted buildings. Yes, he liked the ring of that.

Clarke soon discovered he was rather enjoying the freedom out here amongst the wild elements. Though his body was sore, there was a spring to his splashing steps. He let the light rain patter on his face. The money, even though it was a lot less than he'd planned, still gave him more options than he'd had yesterday. And the thing was, he'd recovered what he'd lost, so hopefully that would square it with his guilty conscience. If not, he could always donate it to charity. Some of it, anyway. If he ended up going completely nuts. If he hadn't already.

The first thing Benny did was hide the Divel. He had several good places—some here, some upstairs—most of them little cubbies in the walls. None of them as obvious as his safe, which a pro would easily defeat, naturally. His safe was for normal-valued items, making the Divel far too valuable for it. He chuckled, because that was the difference between the highfaluting world of business in downtown Hamilton versus the working-class French Quarter.

Grabbing a small Phillips-head screwdriver, he

removed the cover of an old switch, two black and white interlocked tiles behind it, thereby creating access to a square space in the wall. Securing the necklace in a drawstring gem bag, he positioned it carefully inside the opening before closing everything back up. When he wiped his hands together, it was a sign of how pleased he was with his choice.

When he'd been younger he would have jumped at the chance at not splitting the take with Clarke. But now, older, he had looked forward, expected really, that Clarke would see things through all the way to the end. Splitting the responsibility. Making it safer. Well, people changed. Situations changed. Even he had changed.

As he walked up the tight, creaky stairs to his apartment, it dawned on him that the so-called last heist was often the time when something went wrong. Well, it wasn't going to happen to him. He reached the top of those dark stairs, and pushed through the peeling wooden door, needing to give it a really good shove because of all this humidity.

Tonight, he'd have a quiet evening with Constance, enjoy his dinner as if nothing was different, and then follow his normal flight routine come tomorrow morning.

More or less, Benny expected to repeat the same steps he'd used to smuggle out the Cross so long ago.

Tomorrow, he'd kiss Constance good-bye for luck, and then head out in his motorboat just like he did so many Sundays—assuming of course the hurricane blew through the way the weather report was predicting. His water route would take him to a very private dock near the airport. There, he'd be met by a friend who would take him the final leg to the airport, just as he had done with the Cross. No hitches. No surprises.

The boat was perfect because it was less direct and

slower than a car. Using multiple modes of transportation made it more difficult for someone to tail him. And he'd definitely be checking for tails, since he was making the trip without any muscle. Bodyguards drew the wrong kind of attention. Again, another difference between the way movies portrayed crime and how it was really carried out day to day.

With dinner ready and waiting, they sat immediately at the old wooden kitchen table with the spices and napkins kept in the middle.

Constance clicked her tongue at him.

She had asked him about his day. "Sorry, hon. I was daydreaming," Benny responded. "The chicken is wonderful. I'm starved." He chewed, then added, "a wasted day." All days should be wasted like this.

He could not be too careful here, unless he tipped off a competitor by being too careful. *Amazin' how little time it takes to get paranoid,* Benny thought, as he chewed without tasting his food. That part the movies had gotten right.

Benny looked across the inlaid oval table at his wife. Innocent. Unsuspecting. He wouldn't share any of this with her. Not that she was a talker, but things like this often proved too difficult to keep secret. That was true, because it had happened even to him when he'd chosen to brag about some deal to his fishing buddies.

Finishing their dinner, Benny threw on the TV while Constance cleaned the few dishes. He sat in his comfy red plaid armchair, whose legs had been shortened so his feet would reach the floor. Before he fell asleep, Constance returned and found her corner in the sofa where her knitted pillow awaited her troublesome back. Many of the channels were snowy.

He imagined in his mind's eye how tomorrow's cautiousness would play out.

Constance picked up her knitting.

From the boat, it would prove to be easy to spot someone following either on the water or along the road. The only thing he hadn't worked out was a trailing plane. But he hadn't given that much concern because it was too fantastic to really consider—more movie stuff.

He trusted Clarke, though he would have trusted him a notch more if he hadn't bailed. But he knew, as he grew more settled in his deep cushion, that not everyone was cut-out for the handoff. Plain old fear
could easily boil over, unhinging the most confident person. Clarke had been unhinged, all right. Benny chuckled, drawing a look from Constance. Clarke had resembled that lagoon creature when he'd dripped water all over his front room. But where the hell was his Adrienne Barbeau?

DAS BOAT

Benny woke up and knew immediately he had a long trip ahead of him. Hitting the remote, the radar picture on the TV looked good. The hurricane had passed through during the night and pushed northward as predicted. The forecaster was busy commenting on how no one knew why its forward progress had slowed so much once it reached the north side of Bermuda. It wasn't like the island had any tall mountains that might have cramped the hurricane's style.

Bottom-line for Benny, which was the way he preferred to judge things, the airport would open after a delay. Bermuda's winds were presently breezy, no rain, with surf listed at a 5- to 10-foot chop. So, the worst place to be this morning would be in a boat on the ocean. That was fine by him, since he never got sick, and it would make any tailing more difficult.

As planned, Benny stuck to his normal routine, eating his normal breakfast of juice with wheat toast and a fruit preserve—strawberry this morning. Kissing Constance goodbye, he rechecked that the store was locked and the front lights off. With his housekeeping done, he unscrewed the Divel from its hiding place, admired it for a moment, covered his hidey-hole up, and placed the Divel in a hard-shelled attaché case. This eggshell-sponged case was used whenever he transported valuables off-site, and would be locked to his wrist or the car until he took off in the plane.

Picking up his small carryon, he entered the tight garage with a case in each hand. His gold, four-door Jag was crammed in here. He clicked the locks, loaded both cases on the passenger side, stepped in, then clicked the locks again. Pressing the door opener on the sun visor, the wide wooden door jerked upward in fits. He took his time backing through the tight opening, creating as much angle as he could manage in the tight alley. When he pulled forward, he clicked the door closed, and watched as the edge began its descent. Time to go. The alleyway was empty—of people, not trash. One of these days, he'd get around to painting that door, or, he thought, *maybe not,* if they took that boat and retired.

Arriving at the first stop sign, with no one about, he put the car in "Park," unhooked the chain with his palmed key, leaned over, and chained the case to the car's passenger-side door handle. No changes. Forty years ago, it had been Ford Fairlane—he'd come up in the world.

When he picked up North Road, a black car appeared behind him seemingly out of nowhere. Then it stayed with him a little too long for his liking. He cursed himself for not noticing where it had come from. He was getting old. Why did the villains always choose black cars? Repeatedly, he kept an eye on it in the rearview mirror. If he ever followed someone, he decided he'd do it in a less obvious white car.

Being cautious, he doubled back, relieved when the other car kept on toward the Flatts. Everyone went fishing Sunday morning, even after a hurricane.

A little past the Flatts, he made his way down a thin dirt road running between two strings of homes. The road was muddy and filled in spots with standing water. The road ended at a small turnaround that fronted a makeshift dock on the interior Harrington Sound. The locals called this place Skinny's Dock. It was home to his old white boat bobbing up and down in that agitated surf.

Braking to a stop, he eyed the weathered red top above its splotched white cabin. Its worn-out condition made it less appealing to anyone looking to borrow a boat. To be honest, to any landlubber walking by, it looked more like a flower pot than a boat. But looks could deceive. It was reliable and well maintained—like his Jag and his plane.

Benny checked in all directions. Even the sky. They weren't going to catch him napping again if he could help it.

That old flowerpot would take him through the Flatts to the open sea, then along the north coast, past Coney Island Park and eventually to Ferry Reach. And unless Benny called him off, Chauncey would wait right there for him. That was the best part of this inexpensive plan. No questions would be asked by Chauncey. In his world, business was business, money was money, especially drinking money.

With the coast clear, he leaned way over, unlocked the handcuff clasp, relocked the case to his left wrist, exited, and stood in the wet turnaround. Back down that muddy track at the main road turnoff, a dark car turned down the lane toward him. He rushed himself toward his boat, quick-stepping around and through puddles, and down the dirt path toward the broken-up dock.

How long had it been since he'd run anywhere?

On the old dock, with everything seemingly in motion, with the sound of the approaching car, there was no time to waste. He stuck a leg and an arm out to make contact with the bobbing boat, and as he did, the boat dipped.

Even with the rubber soles on his black shoes, he went down, though thankfully, enough of him remained on the dock to keep him from falling in the water.

As his arm and leg were getting wet, that car's engine grew louder behind him.

Pushing himself up on one leg, his foot slipped and came out from under him. Now he was stuck in the most ridiculous position, made worse by the boat pulling on its lines. He hated getting old.

Thank god he'd locked the case to his wrist, otherwise the Divel would be on its way to the bottom. He tried pulling the boat closer with his arm and a leg as the case dangled in-between, getting wet.

The boat inched closer, which should have been good, if his arm hadn't become pinched between boat and dock.

The engine and its tires pulled into that circle, though he couldn't see that way given his awkward position. This was ridiculous.

After all this, they were going to get him. He needed a gun. He hated guns.

Desperate, he leaned to get a knee under himself.

The car skidded to a stop.

On one knee, with the chain wedged in-between two boards, he yanked.

He heard two feet coming down the path.

He was acting like an old man. He was an old man.

He rolled on his side to give the chain some slack.

He got the idea that if he kept rolling, he'd pull the chain free as he fell into the water. Then at least he could swim away. He hadn't been swimming in years.

His heart was pounding in his chest.

Yes, he could just roll—

"Ben, dat you?"

Benny froze. "Carl? Carl? I could use some help here."

392

Carl fished from here too. He hustled over and freed Benny from the edge of the planking. When the chain came free, Carl tried to help Benny up by the arm, but instead, Benny collapsed on his back and lay panting.

"You a'right?"

Benny took a moment. "I scared myself—almost fell in."

"It's rough out der. Wouldn't be going out 'less you have to."

Benny sat up on his knees, still breathing shallow and quick. "Maybe you're right."

"You goin' out?" Carl was savvy enough not to mention the case that he was definitely not seeing. The same case he hadn't seen all those other times.

"Naw. Maybe not. Maybe I'll wait for it to settle awhile. Maybe tomorrow..." Benny checked the perimeter. "Thanks, Carl. I guess my boat had its way of warning me off." Benny reached into his pocket and pulled out a bill. Carl could always use liquor money. "Here, get yourself somethin'."

"Danks, maan. Don't mind if I do. Don't mind if I do." His white teeth were plenty happy this breezy Sunday morning.

Benny eyed his boat. If it was this rough inside the sound, it was probably a poor choice to head out to open water. He walked back to the Jag, got in, unlocked and relocked everything, and then headed toward the airport. No black cars in sight. Maybe his pursuers were waiting for him on the water at the Flats. It was the only way out. Maybe he'd faked them out. One thing was for sure, he'd scared himself into almost going swimming. And that was last thing he wanted to do after all these years—fully-clothed no-less—because the key to his retirement plan was remaining alive to enjoy it.

CHAPTER 41

SUNDAY BRUNCH

On this much drier morning, Diane was enjoying her brunch in the Princess's small café with Mike and Sam. The kids were still sleeping. When they had checked the airport's website prior to coming down, the current sentiment was that it would be opening to international traffic by early afternoon. And more specifically related to Diane's time table, their flight home was still scheduled to depart at 5 p.m. Plenty of time to fit something else in before leaving the island.

The airport was on the eastern side of the island near St. George, near where Sandy and Greg were staying. Diane was interested in visiting quaint St. George, was interested in saying goodbye to Sandy at Botto Bay, but remained most interested in demonstrating she was free from of all watery hexes while playing in the Divel's own backyard. Something that she knew might not make a whole lot of sense to someone else, but for personal reasons it felt quite compelling.

Riding a wave to do something forbidden, with Mike having no interest in taking to the water—uncharacteristically so, actually—she worked on Sam until he agreed to join her on a little ferry ride. Finishing her coffee and croissant—feeling like a cigarette, but no, she'd wait till she got home—Diane was delighted at the prospect of getting outside after yesterday's bluster.

Mike shut off his tablet when his eggs and bacon

arrived. "It looks like we need to gather more data before George keeps all its secrets from us. Fortunately, it isn't out of reach yet."

Sam said, "So you're really thinking of chasing it down again?"

Diane was thinking the same question, but not as politely, as she patted with her clean napkin her clean lips that were waiting for that future cigarette.

"I'm afraid so," Mike answered. "The first part wasn't exactly all fun and games, I can tell you that." He made eye contact with Diane. What was remaining unsaid between the them was far more important than what was being said.

Over his blueberry pancakes, Sam said, "Well, I'll be happy to keep Diane company. We've heard the north coast is beautiful." Then he returned to his tasty meal covered in imported maple syrup.

As Diane finished off her French toast with powdered sugar and strawberries, her quiet pride piled on that the water route to the airport might even aggravate Mike.

Not thirty seconds later, Mike's cell rang.

Diane glared across the small table-clothed table, suddenly wondering whether she might be clairvoyant. She found that funny, because it was her looney-tunes sister Donna that made such claims. Could this be genetic, and she just a late bloomer?

She heard him joke, "You know how expensive this call is on roaming?" Their three-year budget had apparently taken quite a hit with that first chase of theirs.

Diane waved one of the young waiters over. She asked him about the ferry that traveled east. He wasn't sure whether any of the ferries were running today, offering to check. He was being so efficient, that he turned away before she had a chance to ask him for a cigarette. Two minutes later, the waiter returned with the information and a brochure. Diane was in luck. The ferry's schedule would work.

Mike ended his call.

With Mike ready to speak to her, Diane continued to peruse the two-sided brochure by maturely reading the fine-print on the back. Long ago, sister Donna had explained to her the history behind a Pyrrhic victory—was this what she'd meant?

Mike interrupted Diane's reading. "They've arranged to come pick me up. You okay with that?"

Diane stopped not-reading, cocked her head, and said, "You're not interested in the slow boat to China tour, and I have Sam for company. So, I'll see you back at the ranch."

"I should make it home late tonight." He returned his focus to his cell and repeated what someone was saying to him. "Four hours, with four good engines. Roger that."

Then it was Diane's turn for her cell to sing out. Fearing some unknown calamity, it was her sister checking on her. Diane assured Donna, "Everything has gone wonderfully well. No end of the world stuff here. Really…" She looked at Sam who had heard a few of the stories about Donna. Then Diane shared excitedly, "And I'm even getting on a boat after all these years. Can you believe it?!"

"Why do you think I just called you, you nincompoop? Don't do it," Diane heard from the amateur clairvoyant back in Virginia.

"It's fine." She looked at Sam again and smiled. "I have big, strong Sam here to protect me from any roving bands of pirates." Her phone went quiet.

After hanging up, Donna, from all the way in Virginia

had known it. Felt it. That's why she'd called, for Pete's sake. It was just like her fanciful sister to go and do something foolish. Out in the ocean, after a hurricane, no less. Near the Divel, no less. Jeez Louise. How many languages could you say "stupid" in? She felt she should go check her Tarot cards. It was Sunday, and the impulse to read some spreads hadn't felt this strong in a month of Sundays, literally.

Not surprisingly, the kids had little interest in taking a moving boat anywhere. With that detail settled, Diane took two Dramamine and headed out with Sam to catch their cab to the dock. The patchy sun and high swirling clouds were a most welcome sight after yesterday's dismal day that had had more similarity with night than day.

Ten minutes after the two gung-ho Americans arrived at the water, the nearly empty ferry left port. Onboard were two couples, two local men who loved to ride storms, one loyal dog, and two crew members comprised of one rusty Irish-descent old-salt captain and a string bean newbie.

The solid wooden boat had looked plenty large from shore, but once they were surrounded by that immense undulating sea, it seemingly shrank right up. The farther from shore they traveled, the smaller it seemed given the waves and the wind. With the shrinking boat pitching this way and that, everyone ended up clutching the thick wood rail to keep themselves from slipping to the deck.

Contrasted against the dark storm-churned waters out here, the color of the water closer to shore was a stunning turquoise—almost inviting Diane to go back. But the new Diane was not going to shrink from this freedom, this challenge, sort of rekindling how she'd felt when crossing those wrong-side-of-the-town railroad tracks. Sprinkled inside that pastel color-pool close to shore were dollops of coral. Wherever coral broke the surface, white-capped foam scenically marked the spot so the captain knew where the shallows were located. Such beautiful water confirmed she'd made the right choice by coming out here. She wondered if any of the crew had a cigarette she could bum. The crusty sea captain looked like a good candidate—unless he preferred a pipe.

Sam began snapping pictures of the scenery on his cell. Shoreward, blues and greens and whites were everywhere. The sea was alive with movement and energy and color. It was cooler out here than back on land, so the sun's warmth was appreciated whenever it slid free from those broken clouds. With everyone mumbling how cool the wind was, zippers were zipped up and caps put on.

The more the slow-moving boat bobbed, the more Diane added to those colors—mostly green. With her dizzy head, warm ears, and queasy stomach anticipating trouble, she leaned over the thick, hand-smoothed railing. Too soon, her breakfast added more color over the side. Why had she eaten breakfast? Stupid.

With Diane hacking into the sea, Sam came over. Transferring his cell to his left hand, he placed a comforting hand on her back. Leaning in so he could be heard, he asked, "Can I do anything?"

Feeling embarrassed, Diane bent lower and waved him off. She was not pleased the meds had failed to work again, just like they did thirty years ago. This made her think of Mike, *how some things never ch*—.

The boat pitched sideways down a deep swell, sending Diane chasing all that color. With her left hand behind the gunwale, she managed to check herself from going straight in the water. Sam's hand reached for her wrist, but with everything slick with moisture, it was too little too late.

She punctured the surface of that shocking-cold water feet first. And with all those clothes weighing her down, surprisingly quickly, the only thing left was her short blond hair. If you hadn't witnessed her drop—which meant everyone except Sam—the temporary bright spot could have just as easily been a shallow of coral being swallowed up by the rough tide.

CHAPTER 42

BENNY AND THE JETS

Benny approached the airfield and was happy to see a fuel truck pulling away. That was a good sign, and he was all for good signs. Yesterday he'd heard gas might be in short supply because of the storm. Pulling up to his hangar, sure enough, another dark car was coming along the outer fence. A bad sign.

Normally, he would have stopped and shot-the-shit with the workers—having always believed it was bad luck not to do so—but not today, for the obvious reason of that other bad sign that kept reoccurring this morning.

Stepping through the side door, when his eyes adjusted to the dim interior of the hangar, he noticed water scattered on the floor around the three planes. Benny turned and pressed the large red button for the main hangar door. As it whined upward, he thought it rather fortunate that the aluminum structure hadn't been blown away by all that wind. Another good sign.

With the huge door open, he poked his head out. No cars in sight. Hustling to his Jag, he pulled in next to his plane, left the Divel locked in the car, jumped out, and pressed that red button, sending that wide, grey-aluminum door rattling downward.

After completing his pre-flight check, he filed his flight plan, and then arranged for the maintenance crew to pull the sleek white plane outside.

Benny hadn't flown in a while. A trip over one

thousand miles was no problem for this long-range beauty, but it certainly wasn't a short hop. The worst part was that he was being forced, of course, to traverse the Devil's Triangle. The Caymans were directly on the other side of that huge triangle of cursed waters. He lacked the range to fly around the damned thing, otherwise he'd be doing just that. This realization shot a chill through him.

While they towed his plane out, it occurred to him that this could be the very reason that Clarke had backed out.

His last long trip with the Cross hadn't gone particularly well, he remembered now. Low on fuel, they hadn't been sure they were even going to make it till the very end. But he'd been young, hopeful, and importantly, not alone. He reminded himself that he was older and wiser now.

As he watched his plane head into the sun, being lost for a moment in his past connected him to his little research about the necklace's storied history. It had been called the Devil's Necklace. Whether there was any connection between the big triangle and its little cousin flitted through his mind. There were certainly enough curses flying about this tiny island, that one of them could have drawn it here so long ago. The curses he was familiar with didn't have time limits on them. Because of this, it made it difficult for him to downplay another well-known fact: That the per capita curse rate in Bermuda was quite high—like many islands situated within the Bermuda Triangle—making it evermore-likely that a curse could be involved here if one was going to be involved anywhere. Alone, beginning a risky trek, he wished he didn't know all this.

As the two men left the plane in the ready for him, he knew all too well that the world provided plenty of places where curses could hide from the uninformed. Bermuda possibly as much or more than most, though who knew such things? He hated curses with a passion. Just like his dad. Maybe Clarke hated them too. Or worse, had Clarke been touched by the fingers of one last night? Clarke had come in with "crazy eyes" from the storm, that was for sure. Could that explain what was happening here?

Benny headed for the spartan restroom and heard the hangar door coming down. Finished, ready, he took a final look at himself in the cracked mirror. "You can do this." Yes, he was older. But he needed that wiser part to pull its weight. He said a quick prayer and crossed himself for luck.

Walking back through the wet hangar, he made his way outside into the sun. As he had asked, the plane was waiting with the door facing him. He stopped, checked his perimeter, and was glad there were no dark cars in sight. Another good sign.

Time to go.

Retreating inside, he unlocked the briefcase from the car door, locked it to his right wrist, and hurried back into the sun and up those squat steps with both cases. After closing and locking the door, his heart was pounding in his chest. Making his way to the cockpit just with the jewelry case, he peered out for any dark cars lurking about. The coast was still clear.

Unlocking the chain from his wrist, he sat the case atop the other seat, as if it, not God, would be his co-pilot today. He'd take all the help he could get: It was a long trip.

After hastily completing his internal pre-flight check, he started up the sleek looking *Jeweled Cross*, nicknamed after the last gem that had changed his life. Upon his return, he was looking forward to changing the plane's name to the *Devil's Cross*—his way of perpetually returning to the scene of his bookend crimes.

He started the plane. Both engines coughed and ran roughly— something that happened all too frequently after the plane had sat for long stretches. Neither he nor his brother had taken it out recently. Regardless, Benny didn't need to have this problem today of all days. He checked the pilot's logbook and noticed, yes, it had been three weeks since she'd been out.

Even so, the possibility of bad fuel—given the storm—given that both tanks had just been topped off for this trip, occurred to him. Benny knew that cheap gas was used more frequently than most pilots realized, shortages or not. The pragmatic businessman knew how the world worked. If you paid, you got the best. Dammit, with so much on his mind, he'd forgotten to refuel with the high-quality stuff.

Sitting motionless, he gave the engines a chance to burn themselves clean. While they did, he reminded himself he was a pro, and a pro would roll with this. Maybe the plane just needed to flex its muscles a little, like him. To take some deep breaths, like him. When he checked outside again, black smoke was coming from each engine. Black was bad, but he'd take this over any black cars approaching.

He felt one engine smooth out. When he looked at it, there was less smoke, but—speak-of-the-devil—a dark car was approaching along the outer fence.

Innocent or not, he wasn't taking any chances.

Benny pushed her forward, taxied to the runway, received his clearance, stood on the brakes, revved the one clean running engine and the complainer, saw the smoke that he sure hoped would blow clean at altitude like it often did, and pushed the twin throttles forward. Letting off the brake, the *Jeweled Cross* sped northward toward the end of the runway and that endless sea, leaving all dark cars in the dust.

As the landscape rolled by while he was pushed back with the rush, the plane vibrated with the cacophony pouring from those engines. Benny mused he would have made a good chess player, if he knew how to play. No one was going to checkmate him today. And someday soon, when he had the time, maybe he'd learn—something he had fantasized about given that the floor in the shop had been a giant chessboard. Another sign.

Just before clearing the ground, the roll smoothed out over the runway. He was looking forward to viewing the scenic north coast. The jagged coast and fluctuating depths produced some of the best color variations for photographers. Because of this, Benny and his fishing buddies had always agreed that a bad day near the water was always a good day.

Gaining altitude, he flew right over Ferry Reach where he would have tied up his old boat. There were no boats down there, but a dark car was parked near the wharf. "I knew it!" he announced to his copilot, slapping the half-wheel with the palm of his hand.

With the plane now high enough and gaining altitude normally, Benny made a snap decision to reach for his passenger. Like so many before him, Benny had wanted to admire its workmanship that had been so obvious when Clarke produced it last night. Plus, right at this moment, something historic was happening here. Ala the Cross. Without understanding the "why," he felt that it would be fitting for the little Devil to witness its own beautiful coastline for the last time. After all, this had been home for over four hundred years. He'd gotten attached to his own home, and he hadn't lived in it for nearly that long.

With his prize sitting atop the case on the co-pilots seat, he was looking forward to admiring it during their trip together. Having forgotten, he now recalled that he'd taken the Cross out, too, to admire it; it pleased him that he was continuing his strategy of making as few changes as possible between the first and second bookends.

Just like the Cross, it was beautiful and unique. Truth-be-told, he hated to part with it. Checking his altitude, checking the smoke, he cut his eyes back to the exquisite workmanship that was at a level rarely approached by the newer stuff. It was a shame to sell it. Truly a shame. But a necessary shame. No one really appreciated how much he'd admired many of the pieces he'd moved over the years. It had been his admiration for them that had drawn him to the business to begin with. He was a romantic at heart, really, so it seemed fitting that Bermuda's crown jewel should take a more visible part in leaving its home after so long—the same as Benny would be doing when he retired from these shores.

He had disciplined himself over the years not to let this side of things affect his business decisions, though he'd been tested on occasion. Really tested. No matter how much he'd wanted to keep some of those incredible pieces for his lovely Constance—and he remembered each of them like it was yesterday—he'd moved them. So, he wasn't going to start now, regardless of the glistening thing's almost hypnotic pull from over there. Maybe he'd even have to put sunglasses on before the day was through, seeing how brightly the light caressed those diamonds. Yes, he had felt the same about the Cross, though in that transaction he hadn't been in complete control of the sale like he was here. In another life, Benny would have been a collector. But no, that had not been his lot. And he had done a decent job of accepting that.

This trip had just begun and it already was turning nostalgic, like a band's farewell tour.

Mesmerized by its beauty, hypnotized by the light playing within the stones and the sameness of the light and sea ahead of him—enveloped so quickly by nostalgia or déjà vu or whatever this was—it hadn't registered that he was clear of land. Not that that was a big deal or anything this morning. Few planes normally came in and out of this airport, and this morning, the air was positively deserted.

When he checked the troublesome engine again, it surprised him that smoke was still pouring out of it with the flight proceeding so smoothly.

Regardless, he had a long flight to the southwest over hazardous territory, so there was no point in making the flight any longer by daydreaming and travelling north.

Compensating, he banked her hard to the west, back toward the coast, proud of how she responded—showing off for the Divel and for anyone who happened to be watching helplessly from those dark cars. Now the Divel would have no problem seeing the coast through his window.

With him leaning into the turn, his copilot leaned into it too as it vibrated right off the seat.

At that moment, the outside engine that had hung onto its smoke, coughed, sending a vibration through Benny's seat and thicker black smoke out the back.

That was a bad sign.

Worse, it then quit with another cough.

As if this event needed to be broadcast further, an unpleasant beeping began while a lit yellow triangle appeared on his center console.

What are the odds of that? he asked calmly. He still had another perfectly good engine which would keep him aloft. Well, he could make the flight on one engine, but he'd have to travel at a lower altitude and lesser speed. It was rare for one to quit. But at least he'd have time to restart her.

As he muted the beeping and located the restart, he felt a vibration on his left. When he looked toward the inside engine, he saw another puff of black smoke, another yellow triangle, and heard more beeping. "At least the freakin' lights are working," he yelled to the plane and his co-pilot. Too busy, Benny hadn't noticed that his copilot was trying to abandon ship.

He left the annoying beeping alone to busy himself with those restarts.

Meantime, the Divel was busy vibrating down the center aisle. When it reached the base of Benny's seat, the chain snagged itself, causing the necklace to lean in toward the turn.

"Bad gas," he harrumphed. "Bad gas," he mumbled. His thick fingers worked quickly to restart either of the smoking engines. Both engines whined but refused to catch.

Thank God for the auxiliary tank! He flipped a switch, tried that gas, and received the same whining sound. *Damn!?*

Now he was gliding. Or diving.

Now he was looking at water.

A lot of water.

And those two flashing, yellow triangles.

He had too much time to watch as he headed straight for that huge field of water covered with those windblown whitecaps.

Desperate, he retried both engines.

It had been said that people can think strange thoughts when they stared down death. For Benny, this appeared: *What would James Bond do?*

Just before slicing into all those white tips that looked like puffs of icing, he yanked the yoke up.

The plane skipped off the surface and skipped again.

Abruptly, Benny was snapped against his 4-point harness. When he could pick his head back up, water covered the windshield.

Behind him, he couldn't hear, of course, as his copilot had been thrown into the back of his seat.

He'd survived! Unreal.

Lucky that he hadn't gotten really high or really fast yet. At least the plane was staying afloat. Bobbing up and down. But it was tilted slightly to the left. The portside wing must have taken the hit on impact.

Within the rush of surviving the dive, Benny couldn't believe what had just happened. Technically, he wasn't even in the freakin' Devil's Triangle yet. Dumbly, reflexively, he hit the switch for the windshield wipers so he could look out. Nothing but water and blue sky, but they were in the positions expected from a boat, not a plane.

That was when he looked over to check on his co-pilot.

DOUBLE-CHECK

Thinking he'd heard something, Clarke startled awake. He was in the spare room at the hotel, not home. The room where he'd hidden the Divel the day before. His body reminded him of the bad part of yesterday. He angled himself out of bed and limped toward the shower. His head was not great, but his shoulder seemed the worst of it after tightening up on him. He took as hot a shower as he could stand. Out of the shower, he took a look at what hadn't been washed away. He had a good scrape on his right temple and his shoulder was black and blue.

Tuttleberry had been mysteriously quiet last night— more quiet than usual, which was really saying something—so it was possible that something was up. With this scheduled as an off-day, he believed it best to escape the hotel and its foreboding air as soon as possible. Without a car, he changed into his biking clothes, grabbed his bike downstairs, and pedaled toward home. As sore as he was, and with all the slick debris strewn everywhere, the trip had to be made carefully so as not to run over something in the road. At least the sun was out and the breeze felt warm.

At home, Easy and Hard seemed fine. He fed them, cleaned their litter, and got the bright idea to check his new Cayman account. It couldn't be a dream with all his aches as proof, could it? On the third try he typed the password correctly and got through. The funds were really

409

there!

He checked the clock on his side-table. Benny had left by now. That meant the Divel was off the island. Good.

Feeling more confident than just minutes before, he made his way to the kitchen and made himself a comforting cup of black coffee. What was conservative Tuttleberry going to do about this weekend's mess? After playing over the possible scenarios, after sipping some coffee from his mug, after being unable to concentrate on the Sunday paper out on the front porch, Clarke decided that Tuttleberry

wouldn't get the chance to fire him come Monday.

Taking out his cell, Clarke called Winston from the front porch. To his surprised boss, he explained how things had gone less than perfectly this weekend—which of course Winston already knew—that it all had been his responsibility, how the last thing he ever wanted was for the Princess to suffer embarrassment because of his actions, and that the best thing for all parties concerned might be for him to resign.

Feeling that the porch was too public a place to have such a private conversation, Clarke rose and walked inside to sit in his living room.

He explained how he didn't want to leave Winston high-and-dry; that either Tammy Vee or Thompson could make a suitable replacement from within. Well, at least Tammy Vee.

There was no time like the present to distance himself from the two tattletale replicas that were set to go off like time-bombs in thirty years.

For the most part, Winston remained silent, like he probably did while waiting to trap one of his beauties out in the wild.

At the end of his monologue, Clarke added, "I'll have

410

it on your desk in writing in the morning." Though, at the finish, Clarke's own voice sounded less than sure of what he was trying to convince Winston of.

Winston offered in his usual stoic manner, "Clarke, I want to thank you for your years of service to the Princess and to me, but before you do this, before I accept your resignation, I hope you might reconsider. I know it has been a very stressful weekend for everyone—especially for you. But, I won't stand in your way if you feel enough is enough. I understand that sentiment. Between you and me, I'm getting a little long in the tooth, too. In a couple more years, I expect to retire, so I can spend more time with my beloved butterflies—"

Clarke pictured Winston decked out in his butterfly gear, leaping through the trees with that long net held high.

"So I'm sympathetic. But I'm sure the staff would like to see you stay. I would like to see you stay."

Winston's response caught Clarke by surprise. After the tiniest of delays, he said graciously, "Well, thank you, Winston. I, I will consider it. Maybe I've overreacted to the weekend?" Whatever fingers of fear had reached out and grabbed him this morning were already beginning to loosen their grip. "I guess I'll see you tomorrow, then."

Winston offered, "Clarke, why don't you not only take off those couple of days you planned but extend them. I know you have to deal with your car. Ami's car. And I heard about your arm. It might do you some good to take some time to get things straight. Okay?"

"Winston, that is very generous of you. I appreciate that."

Clarke disconnected and turned around to find a speechless Dee behind him. She had come in to see to the cats and read his Sunday paper, with her not expecting him

411

to still be on the island.

"What was that all about?" she asked.

The word "retirement" flew out of his mouth.

CHAPTER 44

COSMIC BALANCE

"Man overboard!" Sam yelled. Snatching up a weathered, orange vest that had enough cracks in it to qualify as a roadmap from afar, he flung it like a Frisbee toward the spot where he'd last seen her blonde hair. Sam didn't know whether Diane could swim, but he knew he sure couldn't.

As he ran toward the back of the ferry, he gawked at the receding rectangular float.

Reaching the stern, he called out, "Diane! Diane!" He was sorely tempted to jump over the high wooden rail. But who would save him? People and crew appeared next to him, while behind them, that muscular dog kept barking with all the excitement. Was it a rescue dog?

The cold water chilled Diane quickly as she sank tangled in clothes. Shedding her windbreaker and flats, she pulled herself toward the brighter water above.

Breaking the surface, she moaned, "Damn, I love those shoes." Present tense, as if she still had them. She loved her shoes.

Amongst the slapping of water and the sucking of air, she heard what sounded like, "Get the live perservon!" She was the live person. She spat out water and worked at keeping her head above the rolling surface.

That slow-moving ferry didn't look so slow from this angle.

Sam was leaning over the back, yelling and pointing, "Get the life preserver!"

There was a small orange patch going up and down with the water. The water that no longer looked so picturesque from this angle. Swimming over, she hooked one arm and then the other around the orange fabric.

The ferry was very quiet. The engines were off. Another preserver was tossed into the swells, this one with a line attached. Before she could kick over to it, the boat's momentum straightened the line and dragged it away from her.

Above the ferry and far in the distance, something trailing black smoke fell silently from the sky. Diane wondered if the water was playing tricks with her eyes, because Mike hadn't mentioned anything about a meteor shower today. Could it have been Mike in a plane? "Fitting," she breathed, because that's exactly what it would be if the two of them ended up in the drink at the same time on Divel Weekend.

The ferry's engines fired up with a rumble, churning the water behind it. Diane guessed it was going to circle back, rather than risk reversing. Though she wasn't sure ferries could reverse. One thought strange thoughts when one fell into deep water with their clothes on.

While Diane clung to her small orange patch, more thoughts came to her that had never occurred to her on land. What else might be swimming out here with her?

A Portuguese Man-of-War?

Sharks?

In the calm, she thought of the Divel, of curses, and of past boat rides avoided. That train of thought connected her to Donna and what a lucky guesser she was, unless she could really foresee things as she claimed. Well, wet or dry, she wouldn't be challenging Donna for the family's clairvoyance crown anytime soon.

It became rather peaceful out here after the stressful weekend. The water wasn't really that cold. The sky was a beautiful sunny blue with those high clouds up there. The ferry was coming around, albeit slowly, and, she was no longer nauseated. She had discovered a cure for sea-sickness: Panic. Pure panic.

CHAPTER 45

BUOYANCY IS UNDERRATED

The Divel was gone!?

When Benny checked the floor near the passenger seat, the case was floating, but the Divel was missing. It wasn't in the aisle either. Only water. Rising water.

He went to undo his harness. It was jammed. This only happened in those old WWII movies.

Benny recalled something about the necklace being invisible in water. Leaning against the armrest, he checked extra careful for any signs of it. Well the good thing was, invisible or not, it couldn't have gone far.

Money wasn't going to do him much good where this plane was headed, unless he could buy a life preserver real fast.

Thinking of Constance, thinking of fishing—and he'd swear to her that was the order in which they came to him—he reached for his buckle and pulled harder. No dice.

Pooling water reached his shoes.

He was not a young man anymore, but at least he knew how to swim. But in order to swim, he had to get out. There was no time to "dilly-dally" as his dad liked to say. He would soon be joining him, if he didn't "snap to" like his army days. Funny, the memories that popped into your head at a time like this.

As his hands struggled against the harness release, he noticed the shoreline through the left corner of the windshield. He fished out here all the time, so he knew exactly where he was. The problem was, out this far, he wasn't sure he could make it to shore.

Sure as hell, this plane was going to sink once it filled up like a big white water-heater—he'd just replaced the one in the house. So, at least Constance was good for hot water if he went under.

Two more quick tugs with his short, thick fingers finally freed the stubborn buckle.

Now it was time to find the Divel. Not trusting just his eyes in the seemingly empty aisle, he walked it two-handed with his fingers.

Nothing.

He went back and checked around the passenger seat.

Nothing.

Then he checked all around his own seat.

Nothing.

He looked down the aisle again. Already, three inches of water had accumulated. How much would it take to sink her? He didn't know. But what did seem clear was as more water seeped in, the more the plane was rotating to the left—toward the side that had apparently absorbed most of the impact. Surrounded by water, his carryon was still in the back where he'd left it. He wished he'd put the Divel in there instead of up on the sear.

Four inches.

Unseen, in the water behind Benny's seat, the Divel continued to lean left, along with everything else in the plane.

Swishing his feet through the water as he moved—searching—Benny opened an auxiliary storage bin, hoping he or his brother had thought to put in life preservers. There were plenty of supplies: flares, an extra blanket, a medicine box—but nothing that would float. He'd been amazingly calm up to this point—except for the crash that is—and was sensing that time was no longer on his side. He wanted to fish again. He wanted to see Constance. But he'd deny that order of thoughts, if he lived to tell her to her face.

He wished Clarke was here. Clarke had been a champion swimmer back in the day.

Benny damn well hoped swimming was like riding a bike. Then old information came to him, not from a biking article, but from an aviation magazine. Seats were often made to double as life preservers. But how did they come apart? He'd never been one to read the manuals to things.

Leaning against his seat, there was a lever on the back of the passenger seat that he'd never used before. Maybe that small yellow symbol meant something? When he pulled the lever down, the seat rotated all the way back. He yanked on it, and the top slipped off. Well, he had the seat apart, but would it float? He dropped it on what he guessed was five inches of water now.

Yes!

As the plane continued to lean left, he guessed he had only a minute or two more before the door would be below the waterline. He shuffled downhill toward the door. Reaching into the deeper water with both hands, the Divel was still eluding him. Pulling himself back toward the aisle, only the floating case was visible up front. To the rear, he tried searching first with his feet, and then his hands.

This was ridiculous. It had to be right here.

Regardless, it was time to go. Leaning starboard to counterbalance the tilt of the plane, he shuffled aft toward his floating seat and the exit door on that port wall.

At least he knew the necklace was in the plane.

He'd come back with divers. Inexpensive divers.

418

Maybe only one diver—Clarke. Clarke's percentage would go back up for being so smart.

Clutching the white leather seatback, he readied himself for the rush of water when he unlocked the door. Rotating the lever upward, water surged in through the crack around the bottom half.

Water churned around his feet, kicking something against his ankle.

Leaning against the door with his shoulder, he searched one-handed under the froth.

Something slid against the back of his hand.

Along with everything else—except the Divel—his carryon had slid to this side. He didn't thin k it would float, but who knew. He hated wasting things.

The water was rising much faster now, as the plane shifted, bringing in more water and causing more tilting.

He stuck his butt against the door, bent at the waist, and plunged both arms beneath the water.

Nothing.

Abruptly, the plane shifted to port.

He grabbed the carryon, grabbed the white seat, used the deeper angle to secure his feet, and released the door.

Water flooded in with such force that the plane shifted suddenly left, knocking his legs out from under him and sending his head under. Water went up his nose.

He coughed and spit, while his feet sought purchase on the slick bottom.

When he righted himself with his hands on the wall, the carryon was next to his legs and the preserver was floating.

He pushed the carryon through—nothing to lose—if it floated he'd have two things to support him. Then he grabbed the upper edge of the door opening and used his thick arms to pull himself through the upper half above

419

the waterline. Twisting onto his back, he pulled his life preserver through, then placed his feet against the plane. With a grunt, he pushed off the side for all he was worth— now, ten million dollars less, give or take.

The carryon must have sunk—it made him feel enterprising that he had tried to save it. Positioning the seat under his chest, he kicked with his legs. Afraid if he didn't get away from the plane, that it might suck him under to join that carryon.

Away from all that rushing water and commotion, his heart was thumping away in his chest. With the seat staying up, it wasn't so bad out here, though he was wet, which made it cold when the wind blew. He looked back at the sinking plane, congratulating himself on his ingenuity and survival.

Yes, he'd just come back and retrieve it before anyone was the wiser. He triangulated his position by looking first left, then right. The McBanes' home was lined up with the flagpole on that side, and the rocks on the shore were fronting that small stand of trees. He could remember that.

How Clarke had known when to get out of this, he hadn't a clue. Well that could wait. He needed to keep kicking. Occasionally, Benny checked behind him to confirm where the plane was filling up relative to his new position. It had been a good plane, but he wasn't attached to it like his boat.

The water seemed cold compared to what it normally was. Maybe the storm had something to do with that. Too soon, Benny's legs were burning. When they did, he had to rest them a bit and float. He could see the distant shoreline grow larger on the ups. Then back down he'd go, before coming back up. Down and up. Down and up.

He knew the current well here. If he just floated

without kicking, he'd be carried east to the point at Fort St. Catherine's. The north waters were famous for pushing everything toward the northeast tip of Bermuda; toward those coral reefs that had grounded many a boat. Even with his kicking, he was still being carried as much in that direction as straight.

If he really got lucky, one of his fishing buddies would spot him. He scanned the horizon above the choppy water for any boats. The weather report had said it would be rough out here today, and for once they'd been right. His friends had probably heard the same report and stayed in the Sound. Smart choice.

When he rose to the top of the next swell, he looked west partly to check his bearings and partly because he thought he heard an engine start up. He saw a glint of a boat. Then smoke. The smoke reminded him of the ferry. But when he reacquired it on the next crest, it appeared to be...turning away. No! He felt in his wet and tired bones that if Adrienne Barbeau could come rescue him, it would make all this okay. Better than okay. That seemed fair, given the number of times he'd rescued her from that creature in the lagoon.

He was gradually getting closer to shore.

At least it was October and not February.

With his legs cold and drained, he occasionally kicked his way south. The current was definitely carrying him east, ever east, away from the boat on his right.

"I can do this," he huffed and puffed, taking solace from the fact that at least the plane's insurance was up to date.

Checking back again, he watched the last of the plane slip under the surface. It went quietly, like it was better at accepting its fate than he was. Whatever his fate happened to be. He turned and checked its final position against the shoreline's landmarks. Off to his right, he spotted smoke again, and this time it was closer than before.

When the ferry came around for Diane, she was pulled aboard, where a coarse navy blanket and Sam's arm were wrapped around her. She was led into a tiny captain's cabin, where she shivered under that heavy wrap. A cup of steaming black coffee appeared from a stainless-steel thermos, but she was shaking too violently to hold it steady. Sam took the coffee and provided her with sips. It was bitter and strong and hot, and Diane accepted it like it was medicine.

She considered what else could happen during this crazy weekend. She was ready to get her tired ass home. Sandy's wedding had filled the Waters clan to the brim with another generation of priceless Divel stories—and too much water. Again.

Fifteen minutes later, Benny heard and saw that ferry approach him from the west. After all these years, Adrienne Barbeau had missed her chance. But he'd been fortunate indeed the ferry had sailed this frisky morn. When a blanket was wrapped around him, he discovered they had lost one passenger and found one passenger today, so they were back to even in some sort of weird balance with the sea. The woman gave up her seat for him. He couldn't stop shivering. She was blond rather than a brunette, but she was good looking like Adrienne. That was something.

The old grizzly captain said to Benny "Say what ya will, a life spent on water always has stories worth tellin'."

Benny accepted a mug of hot coffee from the young crew member who came up from his other side. As Benny tried to manage a sip while shaking, he knew it was a far better story than anyone would ever know. Except for Clarke.

WORK AS (UN)USUAL

Mike reached the deserted airport about two o'clock. There certainly was no shortage of data to work with, but for their purposes, it was contaminated because of the other plane's chemical rolls. Possibly chasing northward after George would net them valuable data for comparison purposes. This, a nothing ventured, nothing gained, type of thing, though it was hitting their budget hard.

After sitting a quarter of an hour, he overheard that a small plane had gone down to the north—the way the Busters would be coming in and heading out. What would be the odds of it happening again? Infinitesimal, he knew.

About three-quarters of an hour later, the Busters landed their big white plane that needed every bit of that runway. As Mike walked to greet them, he decided not to share anything about the downed plane after the earlier tragedy in the eye.

After the initial greetings minus their team uniforms, everyone seemed on edge with the elephant in the room: What had happened with George, exactly?

Mike preempted any discussion with, "I want to get in the air as quickly as possible. We can discuss all of that later once we've got fresh data."

Klink said, "Well, at least we've got Miss Piggy this time." Meaning, they had a battle-tested plane with four well-tested engines this go-round.

Mike asked, "How'd you get it on such short notice?"

Stacy answered for him. "Braxton cashed in a favor."

With the plane needing to be refueled, they took bathroom breaks. Not ten minutes later, Klink's two boys showed up. "I called them," he admitted, "since we'd have to refuel." Everyone said hi, before they walked away to get something to drink.

Waiting, the ladies wanted to be caught up on the fun wedding details that hadn't been shared over the internet yet.

Eventually an airport employee dressed in light blue shirt and dark blue pants informed them their plane was refueled and ready. Stacy went to fetch Klink.

Carla looked tired to Mike. They smiled a tired smile at one another, before he asked, "You okay?"

"I guess. I'm just hoping we can get some useable data out of this. But as you know, we may have to wait till the next trial to actually accomplish that."

Mike nodded.

When Klink and Stacy appeared, they all made their way out to the long, white plane. Climbing aboard, the two pilots turned toward the cockpit, and the ladies went to the radar station. Without the aerosol system to contend with, both ladies would be involved with data gathering this go-round.

With Klink resting this leg, Mike taxied the plane and faced it north.

Klink announced optimistically, "All four engines are a go."

Mike whispered to himself, "Here we go."

The big Orion needed most of that runway to reach its minimum airspeed. As Mike pulled heavily on his wheel to coax the plane into the air, he gritted his teeth and thought, *infinitesimal*—but he knew that the connotation of infinitesimal was some amount greater than zero. The last thing they needed was to be the second plane going down from this airport today—like they'd been the second plane in George's eye. The only other thing they could have in common with that plane, besides this runway, was contaminated gas. But the gas seemed fine so far. Once clear of land, there was nothing ahead except for the brilliant choppy ocean as far as the eye could see.

Gaining altitude slowly, Waters turned back toward the girls and tried to sound more cheerful. "Well, we're off. Work ahead." Work would be good for everyone, he knew, as long as no one else was lost to the sea.

There was a puff of smoke on the port side.

A bump.

Then a puff of smoke on the starboard side.

Another bump.

CHAPTER 47

TIME TO GET OUT OF DODGE

After showering, dressing, and catching a quick bite, the younger portion of the Waters party dragged themselves out of the hotel. Given Mrs. Waters' message concerning all the luggage left behind, they made sure they had both Mrs. Waters' and Mr. Bliley's before leaving for the airport. With the plane's original departure time still accurate, they arrived at the airport at 3:40, just about two hours prior to takeoff.

Not ten minutes later, a cab pulled up depositing Sam and the drying out Diane to the terminal. Not bad considering, but they'd lost their chance to see the newlyweds.

They all said hi. Diane explained she'd gotten a little wet, dug into her suitcase, took out a change of clothes, and went off to change.

Everyone settled down in the small, very clean, very deserted seating area, where they surfed on their phones or sat content to rest.

When Diane returned, and sat next to Sam, they commiserated over how they could do without any more water. But they were still on a tiny island, so they'd have to deal with it for a little longer. That, or walk on water. But as far as Diane knew, no one in the family had ever been able to do that. Clairvoyant maybe, cursed maybe, but not the walking thing.

Diane opened up a *People* magazine she'd just bought.

Though she was uninterested in the gossip, it gave her something to look at. She took some comfort from knowing that the Divel was packed away back in the vault with its new set of counteracting charms. That was something. And as long as Sandy didn't tempt things too much with large bodies of water, her daughter would be fine. Diane had made it through, so her resourceful daughter would too.

CHAPTER 48

LESS IS MORE

After spending their honeymoon night at the Princess, Greg and Sandy left the hotel along with the best men and maids of honor. With all that drama involving that endless cab ride yesterday, here they were right back in another one. Though today's sun and lack of rain were a definite lift to Greg's mood. No more death-defying hunts. No more Divel. No more scantily clad witches. He even could see the north coast and its scenic ocean, though there weren't any pink beaches up here. The southern pink ones were on his honeymooning to-do list. And as far as he was concerned, he planned to just forget the bad half of yesterday. Sitting right next to him was the reason why he'd traipsed from one end of Bermuda to the other in a hurricane. Sandy was what mattered. And it had nothing to do with pointing nude or semi-nude witches, thank-you-very-much. Without the cover of darkness or thunder or rain or closets, they were conspicuously absent today.

Sitting next to her quiet husband, Sandy was looking forward to getting to their resort and staying put. She was married, but it had sure been a strange wedding all the way around. Looking out the window, feeling the nice breeze, she realized she'd seen so few animals since being here. And they'd been mostly strutting chickens and roosters, at that, rather than her usual dose of dogs and cats. For sure, she was missing Bran and Muffin a ton.

She'd feel better when they finally stopped moving and were able to just sit in those long lounge chairs looking out at the bay behind their room.

No driving.

No questing.

No tryouts for TV shows.

No Divel.

Drinks in their hands with those little umbrellas.

No rain.

With a nice warm breeze.

And sun. Definitely this sun.

Greg found her hand with his. She looked toward him and heard him ask, "So, how does it feel to be married?" On that, he raised their hands together in a triumphant expression of unity.

Sandy looked into his brown eyes that still looked a little dazed. In a tired, somber tone, she quipped, "Same, except wetter. A lot wetter."

"Well, maybe your father will help with that someday?"

Sandy sighed, "Honey, one can always hope." The topic made Sandy feel like they'd gone in circles all weekend. She had learned a lot in just two days. The first was that sometimes less was more in a good partnership. Way less. So, she didn't share that part of her reaction included the hope, the resolution really, that she, they, were going to have less to do with those two numbskulls moving forward.

As the pleasant countryside slipped by, Sandy's less-is-more perspective brought forth another question connected to "Dumb and Dumber." It touched her in a way or touched her in a place that remained vulnerable after yesterday's escapade with the two idiots. Sandy closed her eyes to it. She was willing her mind to shift to something more pleasant. It was their honeymoon and all.

Not anyone else's.

Regardless, someone else kept intruding. Yes, she found herself wondering anew what really happened with that so-called "dancer" who had popped out of Greg's cake.

She felt his right hand in hers.

She wasn't sure she should ask, wasn't sure she could deal with another confession.

She was a bride, not a priest.

Her eyes popped open.

She looked out the window to distract herself. Just above the trees, the faint moon was rising. Well, she'd missed the sun yesterday, but was catching a beautiful moon today. It was looking down on her and following them.

Watching the moon stick with them reminded her that today was different than yesterday. That pleased her, because today needed to be different from yesterday, though there was sadness here because it had been her wedding day.

Like her mom, Sandy was glad the Divel was on the other side of the island. This side of the island was for chilling out.

Sandy looked down at the little good-luck bracelet Marcia had given her before the wedding. She wasn't sure it had accomplished anything the way their luck had run yesterday, but maybe it could help with today.

She thanked the moon, the bracelet, squeezed Thor's hand, and closed her eyes to it all, as the breeze cleansed her face. She realized that a consistent wind was good, unless it was bad. Someone had sure been right when they'd said that one day can sure make a difference.

431

SMOKE

The Busters looked out their windows as the puffs of smoke cleared. It looked to Waters like compromised gas. Starting out this leg a little bit rough, Waters suggested that everyone take meds if they hadn't already. After this initial drama, it became very quiet in the plane. Maybe, too quiet—except for the constant hum. Tainted gas or not, those four well-used engines were running beautifully now.

CHAPTER 50

SMOKELESS

Several hours later, the wedding party said goodbye to the island that was drying out quickly due to the sun and that prevailing wind.

On the plane, given an undisclosed delay before take-off, the stewardess began her safety spiel while they were still on the ground. Diane wasn't really listening, but when the woman mentioned life preservers, Diane's attention perked up. As the stewardess carried on, Diane was touched by how a stranger seemed so concerned for keeping others safe. She could have used a little more TLC like this the last couple of days. Especially from Mike.

She closed her eyes and was thankful that at least something good had happened this weekend—besides the marriage that is. They had saved some animal-like man from a plane crash after plucking him out of the ocean right after her own rescue.

When the engines wound up, Diane's eyes popped open. It wasn't long after she tightened her grip on her armrests, that the plane accelerated quickly and rose above all that north shore water she'd gone swimming in.

She was on the way home. Away from the Divel. Probably forever, she reminded herself. When the pilot began a sweeping turn to the west, Diane's eyes closed and her hands relaxed. She'd let the vibration put her to sleep.

Flying smoothly for several minutes, the plane lurched down, popping Diane's eyes open like a puppet's. This

433

time, her hands were not so willing to let go of her armrest/wooden railing combination. Fittingly, or otherwise, they passed right over the spot where Benny's plane would make the newest fish sanctuary.

Diane was sure looking forward to having dry, solid land underneath her once they reached home. And a cigarette.

As Sam looked at the north coast below, he said to her, "That coast looks beautiful from up here, too. I sure hope the kids have good weather the rest of the week."

Diane leaned towards him. "Let's hope the island just forgets about them."

Sam nodded agreement with that sentiment, before turning back toward his window and remaining silent.

Diane felt like a drink. She didn't think they served that type on this short flight. When that same caring stewardess came down the aisle, Diane asked, "May I have a drink please?"

The plane dropped a bit before stabilizing quickly. The air was unsettled around Bermuda, similar to the day they'd flown in.

Sam said, "Just an air pocket, nothing to worry about."

The stewardess straightened herself up, smiled, and said to Diane, "As soon as we gain altitude and level off, we will be serving drinks."

After this stewardess's earlier spiel about the life preserver, Diane felt a closeness to her. She looked at the lean woman who looked like a smoker, and asked, "Do they allow smoking on planes anymore?" She sort of already knew the answer, but there was nothing wrong with making friendly conversation. Especially if she could bum a cigarette for later. She had to start somewhere.

"I'm sorry ma'am. There's smoking only at the terminals in those designated areas." Then she added,

"But this is a short flight."

Such a kind face, Diane thought. "Thank you." A smoker, all right. She could tell. She could tell things. Never mind Donna.

THE DIRECTION OF THINGS

As Dee and Clarke sat on the front porch sharing tea and the Sunday paper, Clarke had offered snippets of how badly the weekend had gone for him. Because of all that, he explained, he hadn't left the island as planned.

Eventually he got around to mentioning that he had enough money stashed away. More than enough. "I might even leave the island. Who knows? Travel." He straightened the paper, then admired the nice dry, blue sky out there. "How would you feel about doing something like that?" he said with in an almost casual tone that downplayed the importance of the answer. After almost being killed yesterday, there was no time like the present to discuss the future.

Dee's eyes went wide. Stone still, not breathing, she managed, "Let's freshen our tea, shall we?" After doing just that while the conversation remained in their heads, they came back outside.

Then taking a long sip of her temporizing tea, Dee ventured, "Okay, what's this all about?"

"Just that I might take some time off for real. Maybe even retire?" There it was. Part of it. The safer part. The question of the hour was, with whom?

"What about my career? I just can't leave in the middle of the school year, now can I? But come next summer, who knows?" She paused for a moment. "And to go anywhere after that, I'd need a teaching license." Dee was very pragmatic. To survive the milieu, teachers had to be. She was not fortunate enough to have one million stashed in a Cayman account, which would qualify her as the wealthiest, single, secondary-school teacher in Bermuda, if not the world.

Clarke said, "You think I should stay on? Take my time given it's October?"

"Why not? What's the rush?"

Her controlled reaction made sense once he realized that teachers were used to planning their schedules out a year at a time. "Maybe you're right." Just like that, the reason for all his urgency had escaped him. Though to be honest, he wasn't sure how he was going to feel when he walked back inside the Princess to return to work. In his head, he knew the issue was more psychological than real, though he'd latched onto the imagery of a silver, metallic, thirty-year digital clock counting backward on the vault—just like the timer on a bomb.

They headed inside, cleaned up the dishes, after which Dee embraced him while being careful not to squeeze his hurt arm. "I care about you, you big lug."

"I know."

"Don't go doing something crazy on me."

Clarke smirked at that. That horse had already escaped the barn. "I'm just in a weird mood. I've never been pushed in the Harbour before."

"I've got papers to grade. Stuff to do for tomorrow. I'll call you later. Okay?"

"Okay." He kissed her goodbye, thinking how teachers never received enough credit for all the work they did. He'd found out what he needed to find out. The question was: How did he feel about the answer? How did he feel about her willingness to go, but her unwillingness to run? What was this, practical love? Fondly, he thought back to Laura. How their life together had been part practical and part romantic— like the combination he'd created with these two great women.

Clarke went and sat in the living room, giving Easy and Hard some company after the tough couple of days. He tried to take his mind off everything by going back to Sunday's crossword. But really, the thoughts of retirement and Dee and Morgan wouldn't go away, like the memories of this dusty room. He petted both cats as they brushed up against his hands. Then at some point, silently, both settled on either side of him like a little family.

Without any progress on the crossword, without any progress on anything besides the family unit, after a leisurely hour, he was bored and achy. He decided that the sun and wind would probably do him some good, as long as he avoided walking or swimming.

He took two aspirin to ease the dull throb of his shoulder, told his cats to hold down the dusty fort, and headed to his messy garage. Clearing off the scooter, he stuck a paperback under the seat, and ventured out onto the no-longer-innocent street that was full of debris. All he needed was another accident. With his shoulder protesting, the scooter that was normally easy to manage felt ungainly.

Once out, with the warm air doing its best to take his aches away, the scooter carried him to the corner store. He did need bread and soup, come to think of it. Instead of a crime of opportunity, this would be a shopping of opportunity. When he came out with the silent sack in his hand, that payphone he hadn't noticed on the way in was now speaking to him. He reversed course, went to get change, which set off the familiar courtroom scene in his head:

You all know Clarke sitting right over there...pointing.

Outside, he dropped in those not so innocent coins, before punching in the well-known number.

"Hi, it's me."

"Hi, me."

"I almost quit. I mean I did quit, but Tuttleberry talked me out of it. Or is trying to talk me out of it. This whole weekend turned into quite a mess. I was afraid of that, you know?" He hadn't even told Morgan about Feisty yet, never mind the Divel.

He was talking fast, too.

"Yep. Poor baby. Sounds like your engine is still running from yesterday? Want me to make it all better?"

"Isn't that why I'm calling you?"

"I don't know, but I sure hope so."

He was unsure about returning to the way things used to be—back to the Princess with that new timer counting down—back to enjoying the company of these two great women he cared about. This weekend had sure stirred things up with stuck triangles and dizzying circles.

And the strange thing was, as he considered answering Morgan's last question more fully, he was feeling the way he'd felt atop that balance beam. And he well knew down to his sore whatevers, how all that had worked out.

He swallowed. His slight smile grew larger, which was possibly a sign if he believed in signs. Maybe he did now. With the sun warming him and the breeze cleansing him, today certainly felt a whole lot different from yesterday.

"How do you feel about moving somewhere?"

"Anywhere. When? That's one of the advantages of my profession. Free rooms in lots of places."

He heard the smile on her ace.

Big changes weren't easy for islanders to make. He started with, "Would it matter—" but stopped himself from saying anything else along his worn chain of thought.

439

Stopping the fantasy that the Divel had fueled for a year.

"Would it matter what, hon?" she asked.

He shook his head. "Oh, I'm not sure. My brain is behaving like I was hit by lightning yesterday." He felt the weight of the sack in his hand. But today it was only holding innocent bread and soup. Even though the tug of gravity was similar, the difference was significant.

He placed the weight down on the ground so it wouldn't keep distracting him from facing a less innocent truth.

He said, "You always pick me up, you know?"

"I'm strong. Even one-handed."

"Would you stop that? I'm trying to be serious here." Really serious, as he considered giving her what she'd always wanted. Serious, as he pictured their line of clothes on the floor worthy of a honeymoon suite.

He loved both these women. But loved them in different ways. That was the crux of it. Did he need to give up one in order to get the love he thought he'd never find again after Laura? Had the act of giving up the Divel shown him the way—of how letting go of one thing makes something else possible? It was all beginning to spin around and around itself again, like a hurricane.

With his silence, she added, "Then why don't you come be serious over here, seeing as I'm busy keeping all these hurricane survivors entertained."

"Okay, okay," he said, as he recalled yesterday's one-armed swim and today's one-armed scooter ride. It was Sunday. He had the time, which fit, because it was time to look for answers. "I'm riding out there right now. Let's have something to eat and talk."

"Talk!"

"Would you stop that?"

"Oh, I forgot," she moaned. "I'm having lunch with the Chief."

He didn't know what to say to that. It figured the Chief would return to the scene of the crime and want more of her delicious food. It figured after yesterday's endless ordeal, that today it would take only a normal, short lunch to put his whole future on hold. Why that figured exactly, he couldn't say exactly, but it did.

Before he could figure out how to say just how important this was to the two of them, Morgan rescued him with, "Just kidding."

"You."

Up until this week, he had pretty much known what to do every day of his life.

But not this week, not yesterday, and certainly not today. George and the Divel had double-teamed him but good.

THE ELEPHANT IN THE PLANE

While Clarke was mopeding west, the Busters were barreling north. With Stacy not busy with flying the plane nor with those radars, surrounded by the silence and the humming of those four engines and her emotions from inside George's eye, she touched Carla on the arm before nodding for them to go toward the cockpit. Once there, she positioned herself behind Klink, while Carla found Mike's high-back seat with her hands.

There was concern in Stacy's voice when she said, "Mike, I think along with Klink and Carla that we need to talk about what happened out there. Of course, we're getting ready to gather even more data, but you know we had the opportunity to analyze and discuss what we already had."

Mike said, "Okay. Klink, take the plane for a bit, will you?" Mike wanted his full attention on the discussion if they were going to do this now. He stretched his arms out, as he turned his head toward them to listen.

"This is preliminary, mind you. But still." Stacy placed her hands on Klinky's shoulders. "It appears that our chemical concoction did succeed in reducing the evaporation rate of the saltwater—"

Mike watched Klink nod along with Stacy's words. At the end of Stacy's sentence, Mike's eyebrows went up.

"However, we all know the storm did not weaken as expected. Two things here. Maybe three?" Then she added another, almost as if she hadn't wanted to stop on the number three. "Four really. Either the excessive amount of all that chemical produced some sort of paradoxical effect that we as yet don't understand. Or, there was an "x" factor in the other team's mixture we don't know about yet—and may never. Which sucks. Barring those explanations, there could be some unseen dynamic-at-scale that are SimTank trials didn't and won't illuminate?"

"That's three," Mike counted. He turned back to face the blue sky ahead of them.

"Or lastly, that it was just a matter of coincidence that George strengthened and turned after we intervened—even with the lack of competing fronts or land masses. But, as we know, that would be highly unusual."

Carla added, "And in the process, it made itself the most unlikely wedding guest on the planet."

Mike harrumphed at that.

Stacy continued. "The last two particularly scare us, because further SimTank trials won't help us moving forward."

Mike grunted again. The breath of the possibilities remained impressive, even given all the data they'd amassed. As a researcher, he knew that data tended to lead toward one conclusion when there was an underlying truth, or, point in unexplained directions when unseen forces were at work. Welcome to the scientific method. *How on this green Earth am I going to be able to explain this to Braxton?* Looking for some clarification, Mike asked, "What about the Chinese angle?"

Klink said, "You might be a little surprised by this one, boss. You remember that Braxton went to Beijing last winter, right?"

"Sure. For the International Symposium," Mike recalled easily. It was the trip that Carla had wanted the two of them to go on. But with Braxton already attending, he'd chosen to save the money.

"Well, Braxton remembered that at night over dinner and drinks, hypothetical pieces of ours and their projects were often shared in the name of goodwill. Whether it was just small talk or deliberate prying, apparently, she mentioned our chemical mix. She recalled staying away from any chemical specifics, but whatever she shared, she had believed it to be risk-free because we had already decided not to use the roll-protocol delivery system given the unsolved challenges.

Mike chewed his lip. "As advanced as they are, that's all the Chinese would need to reverse-engineer the whole thing. It's not surprising they managed it. But the speed with which they accomplished it is a little scary."

Klink said, "Yes, that all seems obvious now. But it still leaves us with our chemical mixing with their unknown chemical. We may never be able to untangle some of this until we're able to execute a clean trial."

They all knew what that meant. Next season. Plus, if they published anything involving this trial, they might unwittingly provide the Chinese with enough information to ensure that the Busters finished second all over again.

CHAPTER 53

PAST-IMPERFECT TENSE

As Clarke's scooter hummed along, the stirred-up air seemed to fit his stirred-up thoughts involving the ladies. Would Morgan go? Would she really go? She was like that. Dee could be like that as well, but had more ties to the calendar, a teacher and all. But teachers could teach anywhere in the world. So theoretically, both could still go.

That was his fantasy playing in the wind, again.

He had wished to return to his old life. But now, he wanted a different old life. Not that there was anything wrong with dating two women—as long as it was open and none of the parties wanted more. But both women wanted more—more commitment—and maybe he was ready for that too, now that his affair with the Divel was *fini.*

As the landscape zipped by and the warm air met him head-on, he didn't fancy hurting Dee. But he loved her in a different way than he loved Morgan. He couldn't put it into words. But something as formidable as the struggle against the team of the Divel and George— life and death—darkness and light—the stakes—had forced some contrast out from the shadows. That as important as he and Laura's life had been—all his cherished memories— he needed to stop denying that she was gone. It hadn't been fair to either woman, never mind to him either.

With the loud hum of the scooter driving away all the birds near the road, he was utterly convinced this crime

445

stuff was for the birds. That it should be left to the pros like Benny. He wondered how far Benny had gotten in the plane already. The Divel was trouble, so he was happy it was gone from the island.

Slowly, he came around to the point of it all for him. He had risked everything in the name of this or that for a better life, when his life had been just fine, really. So, he'd talk to Morgan when he was opposite her eager face and see what was what.

The freedom of the scooter was a great time to be thinking about all this, and not to be thinking about it, all at the same time. He reveled in the warmth of the sun and the warmth of the air pummeling him. *Wind Therapy*. But then he thought of George's harsh winds, so he renamed it Scooter Therapy.

With his focus turning from the past toward the future, with the new Clarke all about change, he would toss out that X'ed-out calendar that had dominated his kitchen for a year, clean the living room, and go find a new genre at the library. Maybe even sci-fi. Yes, the future and some fantasy, escapist adventures, rather than crimes and detectives and reality. He'd lived it, so he didn't want to read about it any longer.

It was time to return to reading for enjoyment, like the old Clarke used to, only different.

ACKNOWLEDGEMENTS

The story seems to have been "done" forever, but its structure has seen major revisions. These were driven first by Bob Pustilnik, who took on both large and small challenges alike, the most persistent being my creative English.

Later on, Robin Elvove weighed in with insightful input that helped build the first solid version. At that point, Cindy Rivercomb and Teresa Horgan gave critical input, enhancing the believability of key subplots. I cannot overstate the value these readers had in helping to identify what elements needed to be cut from this final version.

An agent in New York, who I have sadly lost track of, and Agent Chris Frank in Florida, both gave me the advice of losing the preface at that point. It, of course, only represented what might have been some of the best writing in the book. I loved that preface, but finally came around to agree with them. It only took years. Chris was also particularly supportive, sensing the potential in the story, even if it wasn't ready yet in the version she read.

The hospitality and sheer beauty of Bermuda is awesome; thank you, Grotto Bay Resort.

I would be remiss if I didn't thank the people who make up the professional writers' community in Richmond, VA, spearheaded by the James River Writers group, for all their support and expertise they have given and shown over the years.

And lastly, Cate, and all the professionals at Kwill Books, who helped to take the first book of each of my 3 series to the start line together!

Of course, all errors remain mine. Thank you, all, really...

Richmond, VA, 2018

BY THE SAME AUTHOR

1. P.O.VEE ;

2. Re:VengeFul/

This series tracks the creation of the first android (VEE) on the planet, circa 2040, and the colorful characters that become involved in this historic effort. Efforts both good and bad, team and individual, both in the U.S and China. The R&D climate in the world has become so competitive by this decade, that new products are rushed into production to prevent them from being stolen by snooping companies or their governments. That can turn out to be very, very tidy process, if it goes well, or, in terms of VEE, most untidy indeed. Think Isaac Asimov, with a dash of sex and a twist of humor—but, not yet in space...

1. SPACE VACATIONS R US (SVRUS) – YA

   [Study Guide included with paperback]

Twelve going on thirteen, Timmy Mayan is dreading the imminent annual adventure odyssey (he refuses to call them vacations any longer) his family forces him to go on. Sometimes traumatized, if not hurt, artistic Timmy will soon be dragged by daredevil Dad, astronaut-bound 17-year-old sister, and novelist Mom on "The best family vacation on the planet--that is literally off of it!" Naturally, they are slated to be one of the first families to fly up to the new space hotel orbiting the earth--leaving Timmy speechless--which makes sense--because everyone who's completed 8th-grade science knows there's no air up there...

Proof

Made in the USA
Columbia, SC
16 July 2018